The cold barrel of the gun was shoved into her spine between her shoulder blades.

"Type what I tell you. Type this: THERE WILL BE NO HEMINGWAY RESORT."

She attempted to shift in the chair, but an iron hand in a rubber glove encircled her throat.

"Type it."

"But there's no paper in the machine," she whispered, the iron fingers on her throat.

"I don't care. Type it. If you make a mistake, I'll kill you."

She typed, dazed and terrified, her fingers stiff. She was slow, the entire message taking almost forty-five seconds on the antique Royal.

"Now take the ribbon out."

She leaned forward in the chair, lifted off the top of the typewriter, and worked the spools loose from their setting.

"Put it on the table."

She deposited the ribbon to her right, her thoughts racing, her limbs trembling. She tried to picture the studio lighted, tried to picture objects behind the gloom, tried to remember if anything like a weapon was within reach, and she did not notice that a thin hand had slid onto the table to take the ribbon.

Without warning, the black cotton typewriter ribbon was jerked across her throat. . . .

DELL BOOKS BY HIALEAH JACKSON

The Alligator's Farewell
Farewell, Conch Republic

Farewell, Conch Republic

HIALEAH JACKSON

A DELL BOOK

Published by
Dell Publishing
a division of
Random House, Inc.
1540 Broadway
New York, New York 10036

ISBN: 0-440-22663-5

Printed in the United States of America

Published simultaneously in Canada

September 1999

10 9 8 7 6 5 4 3 2 1

OPM

This one is for Terry.

I would like to express my deep gratitude
to all the volunteers at the
Ernest Hemingway Estate and Museum
in Key West, Florida.
These people who give their time are living proof
that not everyone in Paradise is chillin'.
And those six-toed cats are fly, mon.

THE WEEK

Maybe it is like the dreams you have when some one you have seen in the cinema comes to your bed at night and is so kind and lovely. He'd slept with them all that way when he was asleep in bed. He could remember Garbo still, and Harlow. Yes, Harlow many times. Maybe it was like those dreams.

ERNEST HEMINGWAY
For Whom the Bell Tolls

MONDAY

It would be a pretty night to cross, he thought, a pretty night. Soon as the last of that afterglow is gone . . .

ERNEST HEMINGWAY
To Have and Have Not

ONE

THE MUSEUM SECURITY GUARD NEVER NOTICED THE
rosary. It was old and almost grossly sensual, a relic
of an austere Spanish faith that had sustained itself on transfer-
ring the excesses of the flesh to the spirit, the fervent consecra-
tion of the vital principle to sadistic appetites, to grave
indulgence in sensuous cruelty, to obsessive physical degrada-
tion—an intemperate distortion of another consummation: *el
abuso Pentecostal*.

Now the rosary lay against the smoothly sanded white
wood of a parabolic hollow, open to the steady, dying radiance
of the sun. The alternating beads of ruddy garnet and vibrant
Sicilian-red coral glowed against the wood in the deep warm
light of sundown. Their bloody color was endowed with a
vitreous luster by the departing fires in the west, beyond the
long windows; the chain glinted with dull gold insistence. And
on the heavy crucifix itself, in grotesquely ornate detail, the
golden tortured form of the Christ writhed in a deliberately
savage, bared-teeth, and nearly obscene carnal excess. The
warm metal collected the sanguine fire of both the beads and
the sunset, crimson streaks of reflected light dripping down
the arms and legs, a twisted concentration of the Passion. The
tiny, delicate countenance of the figure was an intricate study

in the solid geometry of agony, the planes of the cheeks buckled and wrenched with a miniature, anguished craftsmanship—and with a faith that had fed on the contemplation of pain.

Milady de Vargas sifted the ring of beads through her long white fingers and drew the red rosary from the concealed compartment at the foot of the staircase in the Ernest Hemingway Museum. In Hemingway's day the compartment had been called the children's cellar; a true cellar was a rarity in Key West, a city built on solid coral rock, and the word had come to mean "peculiar place."

As Millie lifted the coral sacramental above the newel's grooved wooden depository, its brass cover in her left hand, the last sunlight of the day touched the crucifix in her right hand, and a bright burst of color shot from the small torment forged in a smithy of Spanish pietism, striking across the entrance foyer and brushing intense red-gold pinpricks—concentrated splinters of fire—on the slim glass window panels in the vast double door and on the passing shadow of the guard.

With quiet firmness she replaced the brass cover and screwed it onto the top of the painted wooden post, listening for the metallic click of the secret lock against the silence of the mansion. She had begun hiding the rosary in the post's bowl-like hollow two months earlier, but the time had come to relinquish the red beads—the Madonna's Crown of Roses—to their final owner.

Millie's stewardship had been tense and clandestine and careful, exacting a devastating toll on her emotions. She faced the double door and elevated the chain of scarlet beads in the sunset's bloody light and kissed the feet of the tortured golden Christ, not with pious humility and patient reverence but with an aching greed.

The rosary was priceless, a seventeenth-century Spanish religious artifact that had lain at the bottom of the Gulf of Mexico for almost four hundred years, caressed by the shifting gray sands—a red and gold masterpiece of piety and material wealth—while its stern original owner was incrementally and surely obliterated by the indifferent, hungry procession of time and carrion fish.

Salvage teams had labored sporadically over the centuries, and divers had dreamed of locating the sunken riches of the *Nuestra Señora de Antorcha,* and had been teased by occasional silver pieces and muskets scattered widely over the ocean floor, but the mother lode of the Spanish treasure galleon had kept her resting-place and her sacred opulence from the grasping scrutinies of those who would ravish her out of the sleeping centuries.

Until Millie had found it.

And Millie, a modern daughter of the faith and the greed that had ravaged the Americas for Spain, had brought the rosary to this house as proof of the modern reality of this nearly incalculable sunken ecclesiastical wealth. The bulk of the treasure still lay on the gray, sandy floor of the Gulf, but she had brought this one coral-and-garnet rosary ashore, hiding it in the Hemingway Museum to have it nearby: a token to touch, to fondle; to absorb and to inhale the permanent spiritual value that must still cling to its beads—like a fragrance of sanctity—blessed and indulgenced so many centuries ago; and finally to offer to its rightful owner as a costly inducement to intercede for her trespasses.

But her time of secret enjoyment, her private communion with the intangible wisps of antique, austere virtue, a holiness from a more faithful age, must now end. She had been careful about wearing the rosary, touching it, holding it, but it must not become a liability, a threat to her, a temptation to others.

This evening Millie pulled the rosary over her head for the last time, her white linen business suit bathed in the dying glow of the departing day, her short, silky black hair taking on a vague red outline, her feet spread slightly apart in spike heels on the thinly carpeted floor, her breath exhaling slowly. The

17 and ⅝ inches of gold chain allowed the antique cross to fall just between her breasts.

The mansion seemed to breathe around her. Soft murmuring breezes from the Gulf swept across the island city and through the screened windows of the narrow formal dining room to the right of the foyer. She could hear the whisper of the chalice vines swaying outside against the veranda that encircled the house, their heavy shadows falling through the dining room windows and over the six leather chairs chained to the long Spanish walnut table.

She smoothed the rosary against the collar of her white silk blouse, stepped to the tall, central double door with its half-oval transom, and twisted the small brass knobs. They were reassuringly unresponsive. She had remembered to lock the doors.

She turned left, into the dark and spacious living room, her heels echoing briefly on the luminous wooden floor that framed the scarlet oriental rugs. She glanced distastefully at a small white china figure of a naked woodland girl in a window nook—a gift to Hemingway from Marlene Dietrich—that seemed to absorb the fading colors of the sunset, and pulled the two sets of French doors together firmly and locked them. A blue-shirted security guard passed quietly by on the veranda, saluted her with a casual wave, and nodded when she returned his greeting with a perfunctory stiffening of her hand.

The security guard was not especially fond of Millie de Vargas; none of them were, she reflected. They thought her cold, and distant, but she knew her regular habits made their jobs simpler as they made their rounds, securing the estate after the tourists had gone for the night. This one, after a quick glance around the veranda, headed for the front gate, which he would close and lock.

When he had gone, Millie surveyed the living room, with its statuary and its paperback biographies of the Nobel laureate, its Spanish antiques, its crystal cats, its fringed cardinal's chair from the set of Hemingway's play *The Fifth Column*, its statue of a triumphant horse and rider trampling the fallen bloody corpse of a bull. With this room closed, the mansion had grown still, the earlier illusion of breathing ended. She listened to the slight but familiar sounds of the mansion with a fresh interest.

Millie had grown tired of and cynical about the house, with its daily pandering to hundreds of literary fans and sightseers and amateur photographers, but the hour after closing time still retained some of the spiritual mystique that had first drawn her to Hemingway's Spanish Colonial home in Key West. The shadows today, and the sunset, and the approaching climax of her caretaking of the rosary—these gave the handsome old rooms a special luster that Millie accepted as her due, her rightful reward for the volunteer hours she had spent away from her law practice to oversee the staff of this secular shrine she was beginning to despise because she no longer understood or shared the devotion of the women who slavishly maintained it. She could not respect the earthy claims on veneration made by such works as Hemingway's. But Millie knew all his mansion's secrets, and she still respected them, and used them. She had discovered the secret of the staircase's compartment from documents in her care, and that, too, she had accepted as her due, a small payment from the mansion just when she had needed a place to hide the rosary. But that need had come to an end. She had served the mansion faithfully, and now that she had made her final visit to the children's cellar, the mansion had served her.

Returning to the foyer, she checked the ground-floor lights and started up the stairs. She thought she heard a noise, a fluid smoothness of sound, perhaps behind the stairs, from the kitchen at the rear of the house, beyond the dining room. She stopped, one hand on the railing, the other involuntarily covering the priceless rosary resting against the warm flesh over her collarbone.

No, it was just the wind, the soft sighing breezes, rustling the hand-blown Venetian chandelier in the hall, the whispering of the glass teardrops against each other.

She continued up the eighteen narrow, carpeted stairs. At the top she glanced around the cramped bedroom hallway lined with framed photographs of Hemingway. It was quiet up here, and stuffy, and she could tell that the windows were all shut by the stillness of the air. Nothing disturbed the faintly musty closeness.

She descended the stairs. The sun must have sunk below the gingerbread cityscape of Key West, for the foyer was now dark, and she turned toward the pale light streaming into the hall from the kitchen. That room was roped off from the public, and she reached inside the doorway for the light switch, her white skirt brushing the plush purple velvet cord across the open door.

Again Millie thought she heard some fugitive noise, some unfamiliar sound that did not belong to the ordinary settling of the house after its dense crowds of guests had been locked out into the night. Her palm touched the light switch and she hesitated, listening, straining to identify that alien note, that vague tremor somewhere in the air of this mansion, a swishing sibilance behind her. Maybe it was one of the cats.

She stood without moving, her hand once again shielding the rosary; she listened. She turned her head quickly. The sound was not repeated, but she withdrew her hand from the light switch. The light would stay on tonight.

The back veranda showed mistily through the screen door, awash in the gentle lime greens of lush foliage shading the yellow exterior lights, the trailing leaves suffocatingly close to the house. She walked outside, pulling the door closed behind her, took a turn on the veranda, and stepped down onto the cool lawn. She crossed the brick patio to the mansard-roofed cottage directly behind the mansion, her spike heels ringing dully on the bricks. A double staircase in wrought iron climbed against the stucco walls in a tall inverted V, up to the low edge of the gently sloping shingled roof that covered the entire second floor, to the writing studio that was the centerpiece of the estate.

A cardboard box blocked the left stairway, filled with replacement metal straps for the security cage upstairs in the studio. She struggled to lift the heavy box, noticed with annoyance the gray smudge it left on her white skirt, and looked around for the guard.

Pacing beside the brick wall to the south, the blue-shirted guard was patrolling the acre and a half of the estate's grounds. She waved imperiously to him through the banyan leaves, and he acknowledged her summons, walking quickly from the perimeter of the grounds to the studio cottage, his flashlight creating large swinging arcs on the ground.

He lifted the box onto his shoulder. She nodded and went before him up the iron stairs, rapidly, her heels clicking on the steps, took a ring of keys from her jacket pocket, entered the open studio foyer, and unlocked the iron-barred cage that allowed tourists to see, but not penetrate, Hemingway's inner sanctum.

The yellow lights from the grounds filtered unevenly here through the tropical vegetation surrounding the cottage and in through the many studio windows, only dimly illuminating the books and spartan furniture. Millie had never tired of this room, and she usually took a moment to savor the emptiness, the freedom from people, in the place Hemingway must have valued most, for it was here that he had written his best novels. But the guard was close behind her, and she gestured abruptly toward a corner. He slid the box under a wooden table and backed out of the dark room, discouraged from curiosity by her unfriendly expression. He had never before been allowed in this room, and his eyes moved furtively about as she followed him to the studio door. She watched him until he was off the stairs and headed once again for the perimeter walls, his flashlight swinging in white, blurred circles among the dense ferns.

She turned on the light, another crystal chandelier like the one in the foyer of the mansion, casting an indistinct warmth in the center of the room over the round wooden gateleg table Hemingway had used as a desk and over the naked Cuban tiles of the floor. Opposite the door and the cage, the horned head and massive neck of the stuffed elk on the far wall assumed menacing shadows, and Millie looked away from it.

Crossing the room, her heels tapping on the tile, Millie briefly surveyed the studio, its books, its hunting and fishing trophies. She pulled out the cigarmaker's chair and sat at the writing table, her right elbow resting on the smooth wood, her left hand idly running over the keyboard of Hemingway's battered Royal typewriter, her bare legs stretched out under the table.

Among the soft whisperings of the palm fronds against the low cottage roof, there had crept in that foreign sound, that barely discernible false note in the familiar chorus of the estate's night atmosphere. She cocked her head and listened.

The noise stopped.

Perhaps the mansard roof had acquired termites, the invisible scourge of Key West. Perhaps wearing the rosary had made her especially nervous, especially attuned to subtleties of sound, for now the air carried to her ears only the comforting normality of the studio cottage and its grounds. To be imagining things now would be absurd, counterproductive, distracting.

She drew her feet under her, preparing to stand. She would leave a note that the table needed dusting tomorrow. The boxed replacement straps for the cage door would wait until the end of the week, when the estate's carpenter could get that work under way, when she might mention a termite inspection. The typewriter could use some attention, too, but that would have to wait indefinitely, because she allowed no one but herself to touch the machine.

Again she heard the ghostly caress of the palm fronds on the roof.

The light went out, and her hand flew to her throat, brushing the warm coral beads. She blinked into the gloom at the cage door, sorting out the usual shadows from the darkness now superimposed over the cage's partially open iron bars.

"Who's there?" she said softly.

The veranda lights across the patio from the cottage framed the dark shape at the door with a spectral, pale-yellow glow.

"Who's there?" she repeated, her knees suddenly weak, her elbows curiously weightless at her sides.

The darkness loomed closer against the bars, and the silhouette of an arm and a pistol divided from the obscurity.

A velvety voice spoke, but it carried a crackling sound, as if cellophane tape had been applied across an open mouth.

"Stay where you are," it said. "I can see you quite clearly, and I'll blow your head off if you move or speak."

Her lungs seemed heavy, and her heart thudded so sharply that she could feel its lurch in the vibrations set up in the beads under her hand. She did not move.

The dark shape advanced into the room. She could just make out a glimmer of white in the center of the darkness.

The voice spoke again. Again with that horrid crackling articulation. "Turn the chair around and face the antelope."

She complied, trembling, her joints feeling detached and fluid, but she managed to make the boxy cigarmaker's chair slide silently on the floor.

Behind her she heard a slow, deliberate advance of feet on the Cuban tiles, so similar to the cold sureness of the voice. Closer to her now, the voice spoke.

"Put your hands on the typewriter keys."

Stunned, unable to reason, she sat still.

"Do it."

She blindly pulled the typewriter to her on the table and put her left hand on the keyboard.

The crooning voice issued from behind the crackling barrier. A vague yellow light picked out the shadows on the typewriter.

"You're a touch typist. Put your fingers where they belong."

Her fingers automatically obeyed, but they were trembling on the old keys. An irregular and strong beat of her heart seemed to travel into her shoulder, and it twitched spastically.

She swallowed. Unable to control the trembling of her hands, unable to think clearly, she turned, an involuntary motion, and in the faint yellow light she saw the pink outline of a pale rubbery cheek framed in blackness.

"Who are you?" she whispered, her mouth dry.

"Shut up," the voice cracked and floated behind her. The cold barrel of the gun was shoved into her spine between her shoulder blades. She could feel the icy bite of steel through her thin linen jacket and silk blouse. "Type what I tell you. Type this: THERE WILL BE NO HEMINGWAY RESORT."

She attempted to shift in the chair, but an iron hand in a rubber glove encircled her throat and she at once remembered the rosary. It must not be damaged.

"Type it."

"But there's no paper in the machine," she whispered, the iron fingers on her throat impeding her attempt to swallow.

"I don't care. Type it. If you make a mistake, I'll kill you." To the crackling was now added a wet sound, like spittle collected under the tongue.

She typed, dazed and terrified, her fingers stiff. The typewriter keys responded sluggishly, the spools of the old ribbon turning with a low-pitched squeak. She was slow, the entire message taking almost forty-five seconds on the antique Royal.

She had typed what the voice demanded, her imagination blocked by fear, her fingers seeming to belong to the voice behind her that iterated the letters of the sentence one by one as she picked them out on the keys.

"Now take the ribbon out."

In a reflex her hand reached toward the rosary.

"Get your hand away from your flat chest."

Abruptly her head turned, her jaw caught from behind in the gloved hand. The vertebrae in her neck cracked audibly and she stared into the blank rubber features of a Halloween mask.

"There will be no Hemingway Resort"—the words came hollowly from behind the bulging rubber mask. Despite the crackling and the wetness, and the heavy velvet of the tones, the words were distinctly uttered. And her fear burgeoned with a ferocity and a focused clarity that had been absent when it had been directed against the earlier nightmare of the anonymous shape of darkness, now transmuted into these rubber human features that hovered close to her face, only darkness visible behind the eye holes.

She leaned forward in the chair, lifted off the top of the typewriter, and worked the spools loose from their setting, jerking at their rusty, stubborn resistance.

"Put it on the table."

She deposited the ribbon to her right, her thoughts racing, her limbs trembling. She tried to picture the studio lighted, tried to picture objects behind the gloom, tried to remember if anything like a weapon was within reach, and she did not notice that a thin hand had slid onto the table to take the ribbon. Nor did she notice the drop of saliva that fell over her shoulder to her lap.

She could not remember or imagine a weapon in the room. The typewriter was the only object within reach. She placed her left hand back on the keyboard, ready to make a grab.

Without warning, the black cotton typewriter ribbon was jerked across her throat from behind with such force that her trachea snapped. In a lightning instant of superb physical clarity, she could feel the bubbling rush of her own breath under the skin of her neck. The ribbon curled in on itself around her throat, acquiring a strength like wire. The spools were twisted around each other against the bones in her neck and the ribbon lashed around in front a second time and tightened behind on the spools. The whip force of the second pass of the ribbon burst through the rosary's chain, and the beads cascaded down her chest and spilled, bouncing, onto the floor.

The pressure of the ribbon remained steady. Her lungs were bursting. Her neck was liquid fire. Millie knew that she was dying. With her last desperate thought and a spasm of energy she clawed at the keys.

Her struggles quickly subsided, and her left hand closed and slipped off the table, across her lap.

The ribbon was kept tight for many minutes. A hissing, wet breath was expelled in the room finally, and the ribbon was dropped, the metal spools clicking against each other behind the chair.

The dark shape shrugged and flexed. It left Millie's body slumped on the cigarmaker's chair and dropped to the floor, squatting and crawling among the coral beads, dribbling a fleck of spittle on the Cuban tiles. One by one, or in still-linked groups, the beads were collected and counted in a slow, wet, blind search on the cold surface of the tiles, conducted with the handicap of latex surgical gloves. The search encompassed the entire studio floor, for, in the darkness, only fifty-seven beads were found. And the terror was now shifted to the dark shape.

How many beads should there be? Surely a rosary would have an even number? The gloved hands moved over the floor rapidly, feeling its uninterrupted smoothness. The cross, the beads—most of them still on large pieces of the chain—they were all gathered; they had to be. There was simply nothing on the floor.

The dark shape stood and moved to Millie's body. A quick patting down showed that no bead had settled on her clothing. A hand shot into her jacket pocket and closed over the studio keys.

Shuffling across the room and melting into the outer gloom, breathing wetly, the shape closed the cage door quietly, locked it, and threw the keys in a long, low silent toss along the floor. They came to rest at Millie's feet.

And the noise that Millie had heard earlier returned briefly as the dark shape whirled, expanded enormously, and then dropped suddenly to the floor outside the cage and lay still and flat.

TUESDAY

*and he held her to him once hard, hard, but he did not look at
her, and then he slapped her and said, "Mount. Mount. Get on
that saddle, guapa."*

ERNEST HEMINGWAY
For Whom the Bell Tolls

TWO

THE TWO-TON SLAB OF PINK GLASS SWUNG EIGHTEEN stories over South Bayshore Drive, suspended from a cable attached to the steel boom of a mammoth crane. Traffic across from Miami's city hall and Dinner Key Marina had been detoured away from the street and around through Coconut Grove, but despite the fact that it was only nine in the morning, pedestrians and bicyclists and Rollerbladers and even a pair of bikini-clad equestriennes had gathered to contort their necks and witness the restoration of a Miami landmark, only a few weeks past its scheduled New Year's Day target completion. Television news crews were in place, one team in a helicopter, one on a crane of their own. A video archivist from the University of Miami was sharing space on the crane.

After the October bombing in the penthouse suite, the Pink Building had become a sightseeing Mecca in a city with few genuine architectural marvels; the jagged remains of the southeast corner of the building's top floor had rained splinters of glass and fragments of the blueprints of Miami's most expensive homes, and savvy street pirates had quickly capitalized on this windfall by gathering the debris and selling the bits from makeshift stalls in City Hall Plaza and on the docks of the marina.

A local artist, inspired by the spectacle, had purchased the entire stock of one such pirate and had assembled pink glass and blueprint patches into a collage that now, framed in raspberry-pink acrylic, hung over the bar at Señor Frog's—a popular Coconut Grove nightclub that was quick to spot and encourage freaky trends. The owner had paid four thousand dollars for the collage, titled *Terrorism in Miami-Nightmare Pink, the Aftermath of Anxiety—Anticipating the Urban Millennium*.

Dave the Monkeyman had another name for it: "Shit on a Raspberry Shingle."

The debris that became *Terrorism in Pink* had come from the offices where Dave worked. On public documents and on the cornerstone, the building was officially called the Dorothy R. Krutulis Commerce and Technology Tower—a tribute to a woman nobody remembered—but Miamians had never called the daring rosy edifice anything but the Pink Building. Hardy Security and Electronics owned the Pink Building and occupied its top two floors, and the blueprints scattered by the bomb had included the layout of state-of-the-art electronic alarm systems, codes for microwave generators, and the location of private vaults and priceless art collections—"real art," according to Dave, who so classified pieces not having three-part titles, not preying on the gullible, not made out of materials found on the street, and not milking a profit from a bomb meant for him and his boss.

Dave now stood on a catwalk on the eighteenth floor of the Pink Building with his employer, the president of Hardy Security. She, like the crowds below on the street, was mesmerized by the ascent of the first sixteen-foot square plate of sheer pink glass—tremendously heavy for such a fairylike apparition, and capturing the reflection of the bright January subtropical sun like a slim wall of pink fire.

"How many people do you think will report UFO sightings today?" Dave asked with a cynical twist of his lips and the rapid, fluent gestures of an expert signer. Not only was his vocabulary in American Sign Language extensive but Dave the Monkeyman also had a flair for drama that gave eloquence and colorful immediacy to his signs.

"The usual number," Annabelle Hardy-Maratos replied, her green eyes reflecting the vision of fiery glass swinging in space about fifteen feet from where she stood with Dave, her hands in the back pockets of a faded pair of blue jeans, her denim workshirt billowing out behind her in the gusts of wind whipping in from the Atlantic across Biscayne Bay. Her mane of almost-black hair was confined in a ponytail and protected from the heavy flying dust of construction by a white hard hat. The dust swirled on the buffeting blasts of air as the Action News helicopter brushed past the catwalk and top story, and a struggling seagull vanished into the shell of a corridor leading out to the scaffolded corner of the Pink Building from the still-intact offices on the eighteenth floor.

"Plus one," she amended.

Dave brandished a long cigar in a friendly wave at the small yellow and orange helicopter and stuffed the cigar in his mouth. The lit end promptly blew off, leaving a ragged stub behind, looking like a corroded flashlight battery between his even white teeth. Dave brushed tobacco from his satin lapel, eyeing with dignified accusation both the helicopter and the video cameras trained on him.

Dave had chosen to grace this auspicious occasion by showing up fully accoutered in a maroon smoking jacket, gold-lamé bow tie and matching cummerbund, electric-blue polo shirt, baggy black Bermuda shorts, and the well-shined and expensive women's black flats he nearly always wore. A clear plastic wire about the width of a piece of yarn ran from the gold tie, across his thin chest, and into his shirt pocket. In the commodious pocket of his jacket he carried a bottle of Veuve Clicquot Ponsardin champagne, and tucked under his arm he cradled a box of Cuban cigars—illegal, he said, but "the fine smoke of the discriminating marginal criminal."

"We'll go in as soon as the first glass is in place, and you can start working the phones," Annabelle said. "I really wanted to see this." She gestured expressively toward the slab of glass. "Of all the days for the Key West cops to arrest one of our guards. It has to be some jackass mistake."

"Yeah. They should have considered our convenience."

"And our construction schedule," Annabelle said, but she smiled slightly, her eyes narrowed as the slab of glass was swung in toward the scaffolding.

Annabelle leaned closer to Dave and fingered his shiny bow tie, the loose waves of her ponytail blowing around his chin.

"How come it feels bumpy?" she asked in her soft voice, running the tips of her fingers over the gold fabric. "Like gooseflesh."

"That's the bulbs," he said. "Be careful, you might crush them."

"Bulbs?"

"Lightbulbs, hundreds of tiny bulbs. You'll see. It's a fashion statement, my dear, but you must be patient." Dave waved his free hand airily, a gesture he had borrowed from old David Niven movies. "The time is not yet ripe. The fashion blossom unfurling its fragile petals cannot be hurried."

"I'll just bet," she said, her eyes shining with sparkling skepticism. "You ought to consider changing your name to Petunia."

"Don't be a sap. 'Petunia the Monkeyman' would sound ridiculous."

He gazed critically at the helicopter as it came in for another pass at the building.

"Seriously, Dave, what does the tie say when it lights up?"

"I'll show you at lunch. I'm taking you to Señor Frog's."

The catwalk swayed unevenly under their feet, and Annabelle turned to see the round form of Arantxa, her secretary, advancing uncertainly on the narrow, swinging platform. Everything about Arantxa was round: her dark eyes, her face, her shape, her lips pushed together in a frightened moue, her plump little hands curling like biscuit dough around the steel cable of the catwalk's rails. She was terrified of heights, but she was also afraid that such fear was part of the female stereotyping dropped on her like a suffocating cloak by the benignly patriarchal culture of her macho Cuban relatives; so she braved the catwalk.

"Dr. Annabelle, there's another phone call for you from Key West," she reported breathlessly, closing her eyes and taking small shuffling steps but speaking clearly so that Annabelle could see the shapes of her words. "It's urgent."

"Christ on a carousel, woman," Dave said disgustedly. "Go back and try that again. You absolutely threw away a great entrance."

Arantxa opened her eyes and shot a look of deep reproach at Dave.

"Mr. Dave, you shouldn't swear this high off the ground. God's wrath is not a thing to tempt."

"Come on, Arantxa," Dave said in brightly coaxing tones. "Surely you've been in this country long enough to know that an essential part of the Cuban-American experience is learning that God supports free speech."

An arrested look crossed Arantxa's round face. She tried to spot some trick in his statement, but Dave had invoked, and linked, the two most powerful of the only three forces she believed in fiercely: God and the United States of America.

The third force was women. While she did not believe in women less fiercely, she did recognize that they were not yet as powerful as they one day would be, especially now that there was this popular backlash against women's liberation, and she drew herself up to her full height of four feet ten inches and addressed the woman who had inspired her to become a feminist, against the dangerous current philosophical backsliding, against all the iron tenets of her Latin background, and to study part-time toward a bachelor's degree in Political Science.

"Dr. Annabelle, it's about the Hemingway murder in Key West, and the guy on the phone is waiting," she said in a rush, facing her employer and waving a small blue memo sheet. Dave, of course, would be the one to take the call, on account of Annabelle's deafness, but Arantxa made a point of seizing every opportunity to remind him that even he, chief financial officer of the corporation, had to go through proper channels, in this case herself. She folded the memo in half, slipped it into the pocket of her yellow blouse, pursed her lips, and turned to leave the catwalk, wobbling a little but with a straight spine.

"Who's on the phone?" Dave shouted at her back. "Is it the cops again?"

Arantxa turned slightly and gestured at the circling helicopter.

"You want me to tell Action News?" she demanded, and she wobbled off the catwalk into the building.

"Looks like she had the last word," Annabelle said, grinning at Dave.

"Yeah, free speech is a wonderful thing. You'll be happy to know that I support it too."

Dave's ragged cigar stump waggled as he spoke, and plucking it out of his mouth between thumb and forefinger, he eyed it ferociously and stuffed it into the buttonhole of his jacket as he followed Annabelle into the building.

They were using his small office temporarily while the Pink Building underwent restoration, a crowded but homey solution to the problem of her elegant suite having been blown into oblivion. The arrival today of the elements of the outer glass walls meant that soon they could resume business as usual. In the meantime Arantxa's freshly painted office was their communications headquarters. The telephone line to Dave's office was still out.

While Dave picked up the receiver, Annabelle glanced around at the dust drifting into Arantxa's office from the windy corridor. On the tidy desk lay a blue file folder that the secretary had already labeled *Hemingway Murder*. Annabelle smiled at her efficiency and wiped dust off the folder with her hand, flipped it open, and saw that it contained only one item: the report faxed to the Pink Building from the Hardy Security guards at the Hemingway Museum at 8:48 this morning, which Annabelle and Dave had read before going out on the catwalk to see the arrival of the pink glass.

Dave was now signing rapidly while he conversed on the phone, and Annabelle closed the folder and read his hands:

"More stuff on the guard. This guy on the phone is attorney N. S. Green. He says his partner Millie de Vargas was murdered yesterday at sundown. Body found this morning by a Hardy guard at the Hemingway Museum, where the deed was done. Other Hardy guard, last to see her alive apparently, has been arrested. Name of Gabriel Perez. Green says Perez used his one phone call to call him, and he's passing on the call to us. Says he can't help Perez, not a criminal attorney. Also says he doesn't usually practice law for the fun of being a good Samaritan, so he reversed the charge on this call."

Annabelle allowed her mouth to fall open.

Dave shrugged. "I'm only relaying what he says."

Annabelle passed a hand along her sleeve and gazed blankly out Arantxa's small, dusty window; just last week Annabelle had seen a photo of Millie de Vargas in *The Miami Herald,* accompanying yet another of the increasingly frequent stories about that controversial new resort hotel down in Key West. Here, in Arantxa's crowded office, the fact of death was reduced to a series of fluent gestures, themselves a secondhand relay from the dead woman's partner, a partner who had called collect.

Dave reached over Arantxa's shoulder and hung up the phone.

"The charge is 'material witness,' for now," he said. "I got the impression from Green that the cops'll be happy to make it 'murder' when they're through torturing Perez." He poked a finger at the secretary's shoulder. "Why did you accept the charge?"

"I thought Dr. Annabelle would want to know the latest information. He didn't ask to talk to you, Mr. Dave," she said, her voice matter-of-fact, even slightly singsong in its elevated unconcern.

"It was person-to-person?" Dave squawked.

Annabelle opened the folder to reread the report faxed from her guards. Almost as tersely as Green, they had reported that Millie de Vargas had been found at 7:05 that morning, by another guard, not Perez—a new Hardy employee named Fernando Boswell. The body had been discovered in Ernest Hemingway's studio, cause of death not known but definitely not natural causes. The Key West police had been called, had arrived and taken charge, were holding Perez for questioning. Museum staff were also notified. Guards were urgently requesting instructions.

"Let's go to your office," Annabelle said, removing the hard hat and taking the folder with her as she went down the hall.

Annabelle put the blue folder on Dave's desk and sank onto the Black Watch tartan love seat, smoothing her hand over the soft wool of a black and white throw covering the blue plaid. The throw was a map of the earth, polar projection—the South Pole. Her hand came to rest over Byrd Station as she tried to remember the little she knew of Millie de Vargas.

Only two months ago, when de Vargas had called out of the blue demanding an appointment with "Ms. Hardy-Maratos herself," Dave had urged the unusual personal meeting on Annabelle, thinking she would enjoy a literary diversion, since, after all, she had a Ph.D. in English from Yale, even if she didn't use it for anything that he could see, never dreaming that Annabelle despised Hemingway. So de Vargas had come to Miami, to arrange for the guards who now patrolled the museum. Annabelle had been surprised that the museum had employed no security personnel in the past, but de Vargas had been silent about her reasons for changing long-standing policy and hiring guards now, after almost thirty years of uneventful operation by the museum, and Annabelle had been silent about her own condemnation of Hemingway's works as flagrant but simpleminded exercises in excessive testosterone combined with an inability to punctuate compound sentences.

De Vargas had wanted guards, Annabelle had agreed to supply them, and that was that. Hardy Security's subsequent contact with de Vargas had been minimal, merely a low level of paperwork involving the guards and their time sheets. The museum had wanted no security more sophisticated than around-the-clock guards; de Vargas had been inflexible on that point, refusing other suggestions from Annabelle regarding interior electronic surveillance of the mansion. Inflexible and uninformative—those were her only clear memories of the dead woman, and they might not have represented typical behavior.

Annabelle watched Dave absently as he stepped behind his cherry-wood desk, his maroon smoking jacket tossed over his shoulder, the bottle of champagne in his hand, the cigar box still under his arm, and a heavy frown on his face.

"God, I hate talking to lawyers," he said, placing champagne and cigars in the dust covering the high polish on the cherry-wood desk and glancing at the blue folder. "Especially when I have to pay for the privilege." He picked up the folder. "You have dust all over your face," he said. "Makes you look like a shelf."

She nodded. "What else did Green say?"

"His partner—our client—Milady de Vargas, is dead all right, mainly because someone got carried away while showing her how stylish a typewriter ribbon would look around her neck. Apparently this fashion demonstration took place in Ernest Hemingway's writing studio, in a little two-story cottage behind the mansion. The ribbon, incidentally, seems to have come from the typewriter used by the Nobel Prize–winning author himself."

"My goodness. The choice of weapon is certainly unusual. I wonder if it would be in *excessively* poor taste for me to suggest that killing a woman with such a weapon might be a comment on Hemingway's well-known male posturing?"

"Probably just the right amount of excessive poor taste, but I doubt this murder is a piece of literary criticism. It's just too bad Hemingway himself is dead, because he was my first suspect. Now I'm stuck with our own employee, this Gabriel Perez. I hope his little problem with the law won't screw up our lunch date. Wanna hear the good part?"

"Can you top what you've already told me?" Annabelle asked, rubbing her face with the sleeve of her workshirt.

"I guess that depends on your point of view. The police are holding Perez because he apparently is the stupidest clown ever to take a pratfall onto the scene of a murder. Listen to this: Perez and his partner were on duty at the mansion at the time of the murder—now estimated by the medical examiner at a little past sundown yesterday. Which sundown, I can now reveal to a nicety, was at five fifty-six P.M. in Miami; I looked it up on the weather page of the *Herald*. Key West's version would be two minutes later. I may share this priceless piece of detection with the Key West constables. Anyway, the guards are prepared to swear—in fact they are swearing—that nobody but de Vargas entered or left the estate from five o'clock yesterday afternoon until this morning at seven, which leaves only themselves with means and opportunity. Perez's fingerprints are on a cardboard box and a table in the studio—a room never open to the guards and which was locked when the police arrived, the dead woman's keys inside on the studio floor, out of reach of the door. The police can't find any other key that will unlock that door. That may mean nothing—just because the local gendarmes can't find a key doesn't mean there is no such key. The box with Perez's fingerprints was delivered to the estate by UPS yesterday at four forty-five P.M. Perez must be the only guy in America who doesn't watch enough TV to know he's supposed to wear gloves when he enters a room to commit murder. I recommend we wash our hands of him and buy him cable in prison."

"He may not have much time to watch it," Annabelle said, expelling a long breath and frowning. "The state of Florida may use its electric chair to teach him a sharp lesson so that he won't be that dimwitted again."

"You don't have to give me sharp looks," Dave said. "I happen to agree with you about frying people in tasteless copper-embossed furniture."

Annabelle smiled slightly and shrugged her shoulders. "This attorney, this N. S. Green, seems unusually well informed, doesn't he? How many guards total were on duty? How big is the estate? How sure are they?"

"Just the two guards already named, an acre and a half, they cross their hearts and hope to die."

"That's not such a big estate, little more than a large suburban yard. If the two guards had their eyes open, they should have seen something to spell out this murder for us." Annabelle accompanied her words with the sign for "murder," sliding her right index finger under the left hand and out the other side toward the left with a sharp twisting motion, an imitation of inserting and twisting a knife.

"It's an especially rancid murder, Annabelle. One with a nasty flair, even a sickly imaginative twist."

Dave pulled his purple velvet high-backed chair from the desk and perched on the edge of its uncomfortable seat.

"Why do you say that?" she asked.

Dave crossed his legs and opened the box of cigars, silently offering her one with a raised eyebrow. She shook her head.

"Well, our murderous guard is quite a little prankster—in a burst of intelligent creativity, perhaps to offset his doltish lapse about the fingerprints, he left a couple of unusual calling cards. Calling-card number one: This morning the other guard found a cape on the stairs leading up to the cottage studio."

"A cape? Did you say 'a cape'?"

"Yeah, like a Dracula cape," Dave signed. "Black velvet, with black satin lining. Green said it was lying like a black puddle outside the cottage door. Perhaps we should just conclude that Dracula himself paid the de Vargas woman a visit, arriving as a bat, and departed at sunrise, in an indecent state of undress. Our guard Perez is probably just a minion, an advance man of sorts for the man-of-fangs."

"What was the other calling card?"

Dave ducked his head over his desk, willing the smile away from his lips. When he looked up, Annabelle was watching him closely, waiting to see what was making him hesitate.

"It was a rubber mask," he blurted, signing the words as well. "Ernest Hemingway's face."

Annabelle burst into gales of loud laughter.

"And the cape," she giggled, after collapsing back on the love seat. "A cape doesn't have sleeves—it's a sort of *Farewell to Arms*."

Dave gazed at her, uncertain amusement on his lean face.

Annabelle's laughter subsided into a distant smile. She stood and walked to Dave's window. She could see no swinging slab of pink glass and thought it must have been placed on the building by now. She turned to face Dave.

"Any other indications at all as to the identity of our Hemingway Dracula?"

"Again, that depends on your point of view. The medical

examiner pried open de Vargas's cold little hand and found a typewriter key—and there's a key missing from the Hemingway machine—a battered old Royal, if you're picky about such details."

"Which key?"

Dave closed his eyes and put his hands into space before him over the desk, moving his fingers on the empty air. He opened his eyes.

"Left hand, little finger, second row from the bottom."

"The letter A," she said.

Annabelle put her hands in the pockets of her jeans and crossed to the desk, leaning against the dusty edge of the cherry wood and smiling to herself.

"I'm glad you're finding this all so amusing," Dave said caustically. "How would you feel if it had been a mask of some woman writer you happen to like, say Elizabeth Barrett Browning?"

Annabelle's lips quivered, and a flash of playfulness gleamed in her green eyes. "Then it would be her famous poem 'How Do I Love Thee? Let Me Count the A's.'" She grinned.

Dave shook his head, eyeing her with disapproval. "I hate it when you make puns." He thought a moment. "Was that a pun?"

"I'll stop," she promised over a lingering smile. "Dave, we need to go down there quickly and look at the place, before anyone starts cleaning up. I've been there once, years ago, but I can't remember the layout all that well." She glanced over her shoulder at the window, catching a glimpse of pink glass. "Drat the luck."

"I knew lunch was off," he said sadly. "Oh, well. I'll get other chances to hobnob with Señor Frog. Annabelle, I wish we at least had a blueprint of the museum, but de Vargas didn't want any electronics." He wagged his eyebrows. "I'll bet she's sorry now. Think that typewriter key means anything?"

"Who knows? If Perez is not the murderer, and I hope he's not, then if that typewriter key is supposed to stand for something, a name perhaps—if it's the final message from the murdered woman—then we only have to go through the town and see if anybody has a first or last name beginning with the letter A. That should be a snap. What's the population of Key West?"

"About thirty thousand, but don't let that stop you, fathead. They can't all have names beginning with A," he said with a sour smile.

A shadow fell across the deep red carpet, and Annabelle looked up. Standing in the doorway was a tall, broad-shouldered, entirely bald man, a man with sparkling green eyes remarkably like her own.

"Dad!"

Annabelle rose quickly and crossed to hug her father. Then she stood away from him to gaze at his beaming face.

"I've come to see how the building looks," Jacob Hardy said, facing her and once again regretting his inability to master any but the most rudimentary building blocks of sign language. She was an excellent lip-reader, but he felt handicapped in his ardent desire to share with his only child what he thought must be a lonely, silent world.

"Well, Dad, we're about to cut out on you, to take care of a little problem that's come up in Key West."

A sheepish look spread over Hardy's face. "Actually I already heard. Captain Tony called me this morning out on the boat. I'll go down there with you, if you want, and straighten out this crap about our guard. We can stay with Tony."

Annabelle turned her head and rolled her eyes at Dave, a look of frantic supplication on her face. Captain Tony, the colorful ex-mayor of the southernmost city in the continental United States, was an old fishing buddy of Jacob Hardy's—and he was also the ubiquitous ex-mayor whose bearded face and colorful political philosophy were emblazoned on posters throughout the island city: "All You Need in This Life Is a

Tremendous Sex Drive and a Great Ego—Brains Don't Mean a Shit."

Dave had no difficulty interpreting Annabelle's expression. She had taught him to sign, and in their two and a half years together he had also learned to read what he thought was a mesmerizingly beautiful face, with its subtle and not-so-subtle displays of the complicated and deeply emotional person she was. Dave had not known Annabelle before her gradual hearing loss had become total and all hope of surgical help had been abandoned, back in 1992, but unlike Jacob, Dave did not think her silent world was lonely. If anything, that world was too liberally populated with personal demons, and one of those demons was Jacob, the powerful loving father who would stifle her with his protective urges, attempting to shield her from experience and cushion any blow he could.

And Dave the Monkeyman rose nobly to the occasion:

"Jacob, you're a sight for sore eyes. Annabelle and I were just wondering how the hell this building is going to survive the trickiest part of the repairs with us out of town. Why, they might put the glass in upside down or install it in the men's toilets—and here you are like the Royal Canadian Mounted Police, arriving just in the nick of time."

Annabelle threw him a grateful look.

A keen, assessing light had entered Jacob Hardy's green eyes, and Dave was immediately certain that his strategy had been too blatant.

"I've had a few ideas about how the old building should be nursed along," Hardy said, fully aware he was being detoured by Dave. "But I didn't want you two to think I was butting in."

"Dad, we wouldn't think that," Annabelle said reassuringly, patting his thickly muscled arm.

Hardy had turned over his giant security company to his daughter nearly two and a half years earlier, and he had allowed her to run it as she saw fit without overt interference, watching proudly as she increased its high profile not only in Miami but also in six other cities around the country. She was expanding now into foreign countries, supplying security staffs to embassies, and she had even purchased the Pink Building in a financial coup that had shocked Jacob, taking him as much by surprise as it had other potential investors. He had always been content with the top two floors. He was disturbed that some of her tidy little profits were being plowed into women's crisis centers and pro-choice rallies and even that raving lesbian organization up in Washington, that brawny bunch of dikes called NOW. Still, Jacob counseled himself philosophically, it was Annabelle's company now, and he had tried to stay away, and he thought he had done a good job of doing just that, but wondered what a good-looking girl like Annabelle found to interest her in a left-wing hag club like NOW.

Occasionally, however, there had been times when Jacob's twenty-five-year tenure at the helm of the company had overshadowed Annabelle's innovations and her politics. Jacob could pull more strings in Miami than anyone else Dave knew of, and Annabelle often found herself crossing her father's trail or that of his cronies, to Dave's frustration, and to her own dismay. And now even the Hemingway Museum murder—155 miles and several states of mind away from Miami—apparently already had Captain Tony's dire footsteps approaching, threatening to muddle the terrain.

"We'd love to have you with us, Jacob," Dave lied, "but if you can stay and oversee the Pink Building's new wardrobe, we can be on our way to Key West with a clear conscience. Well actually that would be two clear consciences, one apiece."

"You sure you don't want me to come along?" Hardy asked. "Want me at least to call Tony back and tell him to put you up?"

Annabelle shook her head hastily. "We'll be fine. Dad, Arantxa has all the specifications, and everything else you'll need," she said.

She considered her father's tanned face carefully. He seemed, if not openly pleased, at least not hurt by their refusal.

Dave opened the middle drawer of his desk and dropped the blue folder inside, locking the drawer. He popped open the champagne, took a long, gurgling swig, grabbed the lapel of his smoking jacket, stuck the battered end of his cigar into the throat of the bottle, and pushed a button on his intercom.

Arantxa appeared at the door.

"Get a messenger and see that this champagne is delivered to Señor Frog's," Dave said. "Annabelle and I will be in Key West."

Arantxa eyed the sloppy cigar in the bottle's neck with loathing.

"Just the champagne, Mr. Dave? And that filthy cigar?" she asked. "No message?"

"My dear, the champagne *is* the message. The filthy cigar, now *that's* fine Cuban craftsmanship."

Dave flicked a forefinger on the bottle, producing a thick *ping,* grabbed his box of cigars, patted Arantxa on her round shoulder, shook hands vigorously with Hardy, and he and Annabelle left the office and headed for the service elevator.

The older man stepped into the windy hall.

"I'll charter a plane for you," he bellowed. "Be at Watson Island in an hour."

Dave waved his hand over his head in acknowledgment, without slowing or turning around.

"That was pretty smooth, Dave," Annabelle whispered as she summoned the elevator. "But the Canadian Mounties don't arrive in the nick of time."

Dave smiled woodenly at Jacob and almost pushed Annabelle into the waiting elevator car.

"They don't?" he signed, leaning against the wall of the car and tugging at his shiny bow tie as the door closed. He reached over and rubbed dirt from Annabelle's chin with his thumb. "What do the Mounties do? I know they do something."

"They always get their man."

THREE

"LOOK, ANNABELLE, YOU CAN SEE A NURSE SHARK AND A big mother of a barracuda, down there by that boat with the red and yellow sails. From up here they look like Vienna sausages."

The G-73T Mallard seaplane dipped and coasted onto the powder-blue waters off Key West, America's self-styled Caribbean island, after a fifty-minute flight from downtown Miami, its wings catching the midday sun. The flight had taken them in over Old Town, a crowded and largely two-story Victorian-Bahamian mélange of wooden gables, gingerbread trim, raised foundations, and overhanging balconies that shared the town with tin-roofed Caribbean clapboard houses. The island was trimmed with coral beaches, all of them dotted with sun-and-water worshippers and the expensive toys they used in pursuit of the quintessential signs of spiritual progress in that religion: Jetskis, parasailing platforms, windsurfing boards.

Annabelle sat in the front of the seventeen-passenger cabin of the flagship of Chalk's Seaplane fleet, a hardbound copy of Elaine Showalter's *Sexual Anarchy* open on her lap, her long legs stretched across the aisle as the plane's pontoons bounced over the lively wakes forged in the busy waters by Jetskis and powerboats and Coast Guard cutters and crowded glass-bottom boats, and the more gentle, stately masted vessels with crisp white sails straining in the vigorous wind.

She missed the nurse shark and the barracuda; she was gazing instead down the aisle toward the rear of the Mallard. The plane was otherwise empty, except for Dave, who was seated at the back of the craft—at least, he was kneeling on the cushions of the last seat, his arms draped over the chair in front of him, in defiance of the FASTEN SEAT BELT warning. Since they had been charged the full regular fare of $1,500 per hour, not catching a corporate break from Chalk's even with Jacob Hardy's intervention, Dave was in no mood to accede to any demands the airline might make, including highly arbitrary electronic demands regarding his seat belt—"fascist wearing apparel," he called it.

He had been edgy during the flight, disgusted by the arrest of Gabriel Perez, dogged by ugly visions of pink glass shattering on South Bayshore Drive, and nagged by riddles and literary references and, indeed, everything he'd ever heard about the letter *A*, from Nathaniel Hawthorne to Dr. Seuss.

Dave had moved from seat to seat, especially the window seats, ruminating as he tracked the shadow of the seaplane over the lush green archipelago—which he cataloged as beginning with *A*—of the Florida Keys and playing alphabet games in his mind. The sight of the big hunter fish off Key West had recalled to his bilingual thought processes that the Spanish word for "water" was *agua*. He gazed abstractedly at the pastel-blue water, musing on the ninety miles of it that separated this artsy, baroque capital of American high camp from Cuba, that other almost mystical island he could scarcely remember from his boyhood.

"Annabelle, maybe the letter on the typewriter key stands for something in Spanish; de Vargas is certainly a Spanish name," he signed, taking advantage of the power of sign language to communicate over both distance and noise—the plane's noisy engines, combined with the myriad sounds of the hyperactive harbor, would have made it impossible for them to converse in the ordinary way across the length of the plane.

"And maybe it doesn't stand for anything at all," she suggested. "Maybe she just grabbed and it came off. It was an old typewriter. Or maybe she had it in her hand before she was murdered. I'm just grateful the guard's name does not begin with the letter *A*."

Dave shook his head impatiently. "Not Gabriel Perez, but in the Bible, Gabriel was an *arch*angel. Think about it."

"You think about it."

From the window seat beside Annabelle, an eruption of green feathers shot into the aisle, whizzing past her shoulder, grazing her loose and luxuriant cloud of dark hair, and streaking toward the rear of the cabin—and making Annabelle flinch.

"Damn," she said. "I wish he wouldn't startle me like that."

Dave's miniature green parrot Marcel swooped across the blue upholstery, halting in the air above the last seat and alighting on his owner's shoulder.

"Did you see that, Annabelle?" Dave signed, momentarily diverted from his chaotic thoughts. "Sometimes I'd swear he has hummingbird blood. That was a three-point turn."

Marcel waddled along the shoulder of the electric-blue polo shirt, stopping at the collar and turning to lean against Dave's neck.

Through the window Dave caught a quick glimpse of downtown Key West, all antique-pastel nineteenth-century wood and modern white stucco, as they passed the Truman Annex on their way to the naval docks near the foot of Trumbo Street. A ship from the Carnival Cruise Line was docked near the heart of Old Town at Mallory Square, its looming white hull briefly obscuring the island from Dave's moving vantage point low on the water.

Dave strolled down the aisle toward Annabelle, stepped

lightly across her bare knees, and plumped himself down in the window seat beside her. Marcel hopped onto her shoulder, spreading his tiny green wings and squawking an effusive but random greeting. She absently stroked the bird's head and glanced at Dave's profile as he stared at the cabin wall in front of them, once again in a brown study, oblivious to the sights and sounds of the port.

His thick dark brows were drawn together in profound concentration, and already a dull shadow grazed his jaw—he must have shaved in a hurry, she thought, before heading for the Pink Building at eight in the morning for their date with its new glass. Beyond his regular and deeply tanned but peculiarly delicate features, the outlines of the Pier House took their putty-colored shape, its second-floor al fresco Sunset Bar crowded with seagulls whose hungry mouths, even at this distance, could clearly be seen gaping open, ever on the alert for scraps to scavenge.

Annabelle liked Dave's face, partly for its outrageous mobility, partly for its chameleonlike ability to reflect his unabashedly eccentric thoughts. She was glad he had stopped wearing foundation makeup. That fashion spasm had lasted only a few days, but it had made him look prematurely old. Shifting her regard to his gold tie, she wondered what statement lay dormant in the tiny bulbs so ingeniously concealed in its shimmering folds.

Dave became aware of her scrutiny and shook off his reverie. Over the noises of the port and through the thick Plexiglas window, he was surprised he could hear the oddly sweet, faraway song of the gulls. He struggled with his pity that Annabelle would never again hear that haunting, mournful melody so at odds with the ravenous—often vicious—behavior of the gulls, but the struggle was strictly interior: He never showed those feelings to Annabelle. By unspoken agreement they treated her deafness as a purely logistical matter, not an emotional one.

The seaplane's engines stopped. Dave suddenly reached over and took Annabelle's hand in his, giving it an avuncular squeeze.

"I like that dress," he said, delivering his opinion as a fashion oracle. "That particular color of red almost does you justice."

Much moved, Annabelle thanked him, and they leaned together toward the window, gazing up at the dock. On the smooth concrete platform they could see the sharply creased white trousers of a contingent of naval personnel, the highly starched white fabric snapping lightly in the wind.

"Looks like we have a welcoming committee," Dave signed. "God bless our fresh-faced boys and girls in uniform."

"Dad must have started burning up the phone lines as soon as we left," she replied, shaking her head. "We'll have to ditch this posse before we do anything else."

"I wish I had a sailor suit," Dave signed, and Annabelle was amused at how much sarcasm her talented interpreter could put into his histrionic version of sign language. Ample evidence, she thought, that hands could have a tone of voice.

The plane rocked against a portable aluminum ramp that had been extended into the water from the pier. The pilot stepped from the small open cockpit and smiled at Annabelle.

"Welcome to Key West, Dr. Hardy-Maratos," he said.

She returned his smile and stood.

Keating Jones, their usual pilot, had just returned from a trip to Nassau before being snagged by Jacob Hardy, and he still wore his long blond hair in the cornrows plaited for him down there by the women in the Bahamian Straw Market. He pushed open the door of the plane and offered her his hand as she stepped out, wearing bright red heels, onto the steep ramp, which was slippery from the water lapping around the plane's pontoons. At the top of the ramp another hand was stretched down to her.

She looked up into the crisply sparkling blue eyes and

serious, handsome face of a tall young lieutenant, his dark-brown hair close-cropped under his visored cap and his smooth skin showing the deep tan tinged with red that was the hallmark of someone new to the sunny islands but not to the sea—both in stark contrast to the immaculate white of his dress uniform.

As she reached the lieutenant's level on the dock, still grasping his hand, the brisk, warm wind caught the full skirt of her short cherry-red dress, swirling it smartly around that serious officer's hips and bringing spontaneous and appreciative grins to the faces of the male sailors standing in the group behind him, while the women sailors preserved professionally blank countenances.

She fought the folds of her skirt, laughing; the lieutenant himself struggled to suppress a grin and the quick response in his blue eyes; and Dave, alertly and with nimble energy, hopped onto the dock at her side, a puritanical gleam in his eyes and a prim, disapproving tightness about his mouth.

Really, he thought, if it weren't already bad enough that a blue-shirt had been arrested, now Annabelle would need his services as clucking duenna to stave off these lecherous sons of Sinbad. That was the funny thing about Annabelle: She just couldn't keep men at a proper distance, even with her firm feminist principles. Although, he had to admit, she never dated them, never went any farther than innocently letting them worship her, while they, like a pack of slave idiots, took her to long lunches and allowed her to boss them around, an allowance that he privately considered bad for her budding executive genius.

Annabelle, in her turn, almost as if she had heard his thoughts, bent her green-eyed gaze on Dave, perhaps alerted by the change in his demeanor, the rigidity of his bearing, the fierce angle of his jaw. He was going to be difficult. It was one of the funny things about Dave, she thought: He would be the first to scoff at the fanatical machismo sexism of his Cuban forebears when it came to professional advancement, but he was also the first to invoke the fanatical creed of puritanical sexual safeguarding of women.

Dave faced the lieutenant squarely and—for once, using his real name, giving it a full Spanish lilt, rolling the rs and generously pronouncing all the vowels—said, "Jorge Enamorado, reporting for duty. Remember the *Maine*, Popeye."

The lieutenant's composure was unshaken, for he was not surprised by Annabelle's sidekick. Dave's reputation for casual rudeness and studied attire was well known to Commander Ivan Rzadkowolsky, and the old man had passed the word to his junior officer: "The little Cuban snot who travels with Dr. Hardy-Maratos will probably be wearing plaid knickers and a top hat. Just ignore the weird edges and humor him. I hear he's pretty sharp." The old man's words now reverberated for the lieutenant as he took in both the magnificence of Dave's gold accessories and the quick attack of his apparently ready store of unpredictable language.

The lieutenant *was* surprised by Dr. Hardy-Maratos. This tall, gorgeous, laughing woman in a red designer dress was not at all what he had pictured when the old man had ordered him to "take Jacob Hardy's little deaf girl in tow. She's sort of a latter-day feminist, one of those women with dry intellectual causes. Probably doesn't have enough to do with her time. You know how it is. Show her the old charm."

Turning now to Annabelle, the lieutenant said, "Commander Rzadkowolsky asked me to meet you and make sure your needs are anticipated."

"She doesn't have any needs, Popeye," Dave piped in. "Why don't you just direct us to a cab and we'll be on our merry way."

Annabelle frowned, and eyed Dave narrowly. "I hope the lieutenant isn't armed. You are clearly asking for it from both barrels."

But the lieutenant, determined to follow the spirit and letter of his orders, bestowed a lazy smile on Dave and said, with a slight southern accent, "I'll be happy to arrange for a cab. Do you folks have luggage?"

Balked by this exercise of unruffled good manners, Dave turned his head to one side and scanned the officer's classical features and serious expression skeptically, as if he expected to see a yellowtail snapper swim out of those suspiciously dark-blue eyes. *Could be contact lenses,* Dave thought, briefly considering buying some for himself.

"Forgive us, Lieutenant," Annabelle said, offering her hand again, this time with great formality. "I'm Annabelle, and this is Dave."

The lieutenant looked puzzled. "I thought he said—"

"Never mind what I said," Dave interrupted hastily. "You just pipe us ashore and tend to your spinach farm. We haven't got time for naval exercises."

"Dave's his nickname," Annabelle attempted to explain, suddenly suppressing an undignified smirk, her green eyes shining. "The Monkeyman."

These were deep linguistic waters for the lieutenant, but he responded generously by taking Annabelle's hand, shaking it with professional heartiness, and saying, "I'm Lieutenant Roy Ricou, but I'm hoping you'll call me Roy." He extended his hand to Dave with an open gaze and the best of goodwill, and said, "If you like, you can call me R.R.; I sometimes go by my initials. That way there will be enough names to go around whatever comes up."

"Are you trying to be funny?" Dave said, taking the offered hand reluctantly. "If you say it fast—R.R.—it sounds like a laugh."

Annabelle wanted to kick Dave.

"Give it a rest, *amigo,*" she said, pinching his arm surreptitiously but with unmistakably authoritative fingers.

"I was told that you read lips, Annabelle," Ricou said with

simple friendliness. "I hope you don't mind my directness, but I've found that it saves time when communication is the goal. What's your efficiency rate?"

"Ninety-three percent, sometimes higher, depending on the speaker. I get the rest from context. Are you a communications officer, Lieutenant Ricou?" she asked, raising her eyebrows, surprised at such candor about her deafness.

"No, ma'am, weapons. But I read up on it this morning."

So the lieutenant had done some research, Dave thought. A stubborn light shone in his brown eyes. "What kind of weapons do you need here in paradise, Captain Ahab?" he asked. "Harpoons?"

"There are some of those in the Naval Museum, sir," Ricou answered, with what Dave thought was maddening politeness. Perhaps the lieutenant suffered from simplemindedness.

Keating Jones arrived behind them on the dock, carrying a large tan leather suitcase and a gleaming copper birdcage. He set them down on the concrete, draped a necklace of pink shells around Annabelle's neck, planted a shy kiss on her cheek, and returned to the seaplane. Its engines roared into life.

Dave shook his head, disgusted by the pilot's performance.

"I hope you weren't asked to dance attendance on us at the expense of some real job," Annabelle said, clearly considering Ricou's perspective with more than a twinge of guilt. "I feel like such an unpardonable interruption."

Ricou gave her a glance that was filled with gentle kindness and mild humor. "I'm honored by the detail; this is much more fun than scuba diving."

Marcel, spotting the luggage from Dave's shoulder, let out a squawk and hopped to the copper-barred dome of his cage, giving it an exploratory peck.

Ricou elevated his brows. The cage was crammed with clothing, books, a black leather traveling case, and a wooden cigar box. Through the bars was stuffed an elegant, silver-tipped lavender parasol.

Dave saw the direction of Ricou's glance and hastily explained: "I packed in a hurry."

Ricou signaled to a couple of the sailors standing beside him in the 82-degree sunshine, and they picked up the luggage, Marcel casting a cautious glance at them, sidestepping away from a well-manicured feminine hand on the copper handle, as they bore him off toward Trumbo Street. He looked back at Dave with a bright eye.

"Where are you folks staying?" Ricou asked as they followed the sailors and the luggage toward the street.

"At Ocean Key House," Annabelle said, "but we won't be checking in right away. We need to get to the Hemingway Museum first."

"Oh, yes. You're here about the strangling." Ricou gave her a searching look.

She nodded. "Does everyone here already know about it? Or was my father blabbing?"

"Seems to be a lot of gossip around this morning," Ricou said noncommitally. He quickly grasped Annabelle's arm as a bright-green moped brushed past her in the street, its horn beeping raucously. They crossed to the other curb, where a taxi was waiting, hastily summoned by the two sailors with Marcel and the luggage.

The taxi was a 1988 Chevrolet Caprice painted a bubble-gum pink, a Five Sixes cab. Stenciled in black on the side were their phone number, 296–6666, and their slogan, "We Give Good Cab."

Dave sneered at the taxi.

"I'll see that your luggage gets to your hotel," Ricou said. He handed Annabelle a typewritten note. "That's a list of places where you can reach me if you need anything else. The navy's system for messages is pretty efficient, even though I tend to be fairly peripatetic."

Dave raised an eyebrow at Ricou's last word.

Annabelle smiled, and put the note in her red handbag. "I'm sorry about your scuba diving, Lieutenant."

Dave placed his hand on Marcel's cage, and the little bird waddled up his arm. They got in the cab.

Annabelle shook hands again with Ricou, and he handed her in beside Dave with old-world courtesy.

"The Hemingway Museum," Annabelle told the driver.

Ricou leaned in the window, his cap now under his arm, and aimed a steady look at Dave.

"Submarine-launched ballistic missiles—rockets, Fidel," he drawled, his sleepy grin spreading across his lips but not reaching his deep-blue eyes.

"So you're human after all," Dave murmured.

"No, sir; don't count on it. I'm just off duty now."

Ricou touched his fingers to his forehead, spoke to the sailors briefly, and strolled away down Trumbo Street.

The taxi pulled out into the traffic, scattering bicyclists and pedestrians. Dave sat quietly for a few moments, absorbed in his thoughts.

"I thought for sure he'd say his weapons specialty was typewriter ribbons," he announced abruptly. "But his name does not begin with A, so he's all wrong."

"Dave, what is your problem with him? He seemed perfectly normal and nice. You're so strange sometimes."

"Normal? Nice? He's a professional killer, in the pay of the biggest war machine in the world. You're not going to allow that kid to follow you around, are you?"

"Kid? He's probably in his late twenties—about your age."

"You think so? Well, he's got a New Orleans accent. That's probably what misled me. Southerners always seem younger." Dave slewed around toward her on the cracked leather seat. "They're so delightfully peripatetic."

Annabelle threw up her hands in exasperation.

They rode west to Duval Street, the heart of Old Town, a

palm-lined carnival of souvenir shops, bars, artist's studios, small ad hoc museums, head shops, bike-rental booths, jewelry boards, craft stalls, restaurants, and people, people of all nationalities, lifestyles, races, genders, people in shorts, or biker leathers, or hippie beads, or cowboy boots, or formal wear, or uniforms.

They made a right turn toward the west, and the taxi took them around another corner to Whitehead Street. The driver pulled the pink car up to the gate of the Hemingway Museum, at number 907 Whitehead, and Dave hopped out onto the street. A few tourists, some curious about the rumors of a sensational murder and some merely disappointed that the museum was closed, milled around the entrance. Two empty white police cars were parked about twenty paces up the street.

Annabelle paid the driver and stepped onto the sidewalk. Dave circled around and through the tourists, and together he and Annabelle read the hand-lettered sign on the gate: CLOSED BECAUSE OF A BEREAVEMENT IN OUR FAMILY. OPEN TOMORROW 9 TO 5.

They stepped to the intricately wrought, painted iron gate. Annabelle opened her handbag, took out her sky-blue ID card, and thrust it through the iron bars. A uniformed policeman took the card, examined it, and handed it to a blue-shirted guard, who stared back and forth from her face to her ID with his mouth gaping open before fumbling with the lock and pulling back on the ironwork to admit her.

He nearly shut the gate on Dave, who looked to him like the worst sort of tourist, with that hideous tie and that bird on his shoulder, but Dave, with surprising strength, leaned on the gate and walked through.

"Who do you think you are? Saint Peter?" Dave demanded. "Do you know who I am?"

The guard shook his head mutely.

"I'm Oprah Winfrey," Dave said aggressively. "This month we've chosen a famous dead author who kills from the grave."

Suddenly the guard realized who this character must be. He'd heard of Dave the Monkeyman from his cousin in Miami. But the policeman held out his hand for Dave's ID.

Dave quickly followed Annabelle up the cement walkway, detouring around a small, dry fountain to the veranda that encircled the mansion on the ground floor. A matching balcony wrapped around the second floor.

The place was alive with cats. They were everywhere. There were at least a hundred of them. Dave picked his way among them as he stepped onto the veranda.

"Annabelle," he said, grabbing her hand. "Look at their feet," he signed, pointing down twice for "feet" and spreading his hands apart for "big."

The cats, at first glance, seemed to have swollen paws, but Annabelle had been here before and remembered these unusual animals. She stooped down and pointed out that they were all endowed with extra toes. In fact, six toes per paw.

Dave studied the estate's layout while he took in the enormity of the incest he was witnessing if these cats had all received their six-toed DNA from a single source, as seemed likely. Stately frangipani and royal poinciana trees and Indian banyans with spreading root-trunks, chalice vines, bougainvillea and hibiscus, and coconut palms cast a dappled and dreamy green shade over the grounds and the mansion. A brick wall about Dave's height surrounded the estate; the only opening he could see was the gate they had used on arrival. The mansion was white, with lime-green shutters flanking the many floor-to-ceiling windows. The floor of the veranda was shiny and green, obviously recently painted, and cushioned wicker chairs, variously draped with cats and cat hair, were placed at frequent intervals against the walls of the mansion. Insects droned in the grass and dense fern cover.

Dave squatted beside Annabelle and watched her face as she stroked the white, patchy fur of an extremely old cat.

"It looks like the moths have been at that cat," he signed, crossing his open hands at the wrists, palms against his chest, and locking the thumbs; he wiggled his fingers to make them "fly," the sign for butterflies and moths. "And the cat's apparently conducting a séance, because you've both gone into a trance."

Annabelle smiled and stood. She stretched.

"Let's see who's home," she said.

They went to the tall double doors under a glass half-oval transom in the center of the veranda and knocked. Dave bent down and peered closely at the tiny brass knobs on the doors.

There was no answer to their knock.

Annabelle knocked again and waited.

After a few minutes Dave signaled to the blue-shirted guard, who was standing ill at ease by the gate, beside the policeman, who had snapped open a newspaper and was leaning against the ironwork, reading. The guard trotted to the veranda, eager to change the impression he had made on the man who signed his paychecks.

"Do you have a key to this door?" Dave asked.

"Not anymore, sir. The cops took our keys and sealed the house."

"Then how come there's no police tape or anything?"

"There is around back, at the studio. The other cops are still there."

"Where's the other guard?" Annabelle asked. "Aren't there supposed to be two on duty?"

"The cops sent him for coffee and sandwiches. But there's the other two guards from last night—Boswell and that Perez, the one who strangled Miss de Vargas. They're all in the back at the studio."

Dave glared at the guard. "Did you witness this fascinating strangling with your own two beady little eyes?" he demanded.

"No, sir." The guard flushed.

"Then be more careful what you say."

Annabelle walked to the end of the veranda and gazed up a dark-green outer staircase leading to the second floor of the mansion. She stepped down off the veranda and took a few paces across the lawn, just able to see the corner of the studio cottage and its mansard roof from where she stood. She studied the mansion from this angle and returned to the front door.

"Did the police confiscate all the security keys?" she asked.

"Oh, yes, ma'am," the guard replied eagerly, avoiding Dave's eyes. "There's only two."

"Who else has keys?"

"Just Miss Ashleen. She's the oldest volunteer. Been here since the sixties."

A tortoiseshell cat wound itself around Dave's bare legs, openly eyeing the bird on his shoulder.

"Dave, take a good look at that lock," Annabelle said. "We need to know how vulnerable this old mansion is."

"I already did. I could open it with a credit card. A mildly intelligent eel could open this door. Do you happen to have an eel?"

The door suddenly squeaked open, and they faced a tall, gray-haired woman who was glowering at Dave from arctic eyes and an Olympian height.

"You won't be needing an eel, young man," she said, her voice a soft southern drawl, her blue eyes icily fierce. "What do you want?"

Dave cleared his throat.

Annabelle stepped forward quickly.

"I'm Annabelle Hardy-Maratos, from Hardy Security." She gestured toward the blue-shirted guard in explanation. "We'd like to speak to the person in charge of the mansion and studio now that Millie de Vargas is dead."

"I'm in charge now," the woman said.

"Who are you, if I may ask?" Annabelle said, directing a clear look of inquiry at those glacial eyes.

"I'm Ashleen Ricou."

FOUR

DETECTIVE LIEUTENANT BARBARA RUGGIERRIO STOOD AT the door of the studio cottage, looking out over the grounds of the Hemingway estate toward Key West's inland lighthouse, just across Whitehead Street. This was one of the island's best days, the kind of day in January that made for unfettered, rum-soaked picnics for nearly naked tourists and wide profit margins for the residents of paradise: clear blue sky, petaled breezes, softly murmuring palm fronds.

The studio behind her, by contrast, felt chilled, shadowy, unpleasant, and opaque, resistant: a bad day for a cop in paradise.

Ruggierrio reached out her hand and touched the cold metal straps of the cage that had been installed by the museum to separate the studio from the public areas of the estate. The cage door was folded back and standing open now, opened with the keys she had fished from the floor of the studio this morning, from beside the body of Millie de Vargas.

The blue-shirted guards had also called the Hemingway Museum staff by the time Ruggierrio arrived. And the head of that volunteer staff—since the murder—was a blue-eyed old tartar who had immediately insisted that the dead body was no concern of the museum staff. It was up to the police to get it off the property. Those had been the words she used: "Get it off the property." Ruggierrio had shaken her head philosophically; every islander knew about this old lady's bad temper.

Miss Ashleen Ricou had claimed she had no key to the Hemingway studio, that de Vargas's key had been the only one. Ruggierrio was having trouble believing that. The old lady probably had a key taped to her chest. The Hardy Security guards said they didn't know anything about Ashleen Ricou's keys; they only knew that their keys did not open the studio cage. They were never allowed in Ernest Hemingway's studio, any more than tourists were. As far as they knew, the only one who ever went in there was Millie de Vargas, and the cleaning staff when she took them in herself. Miss de Vargas had been very protective of the studio.

When Detective Lieutenant Ruggierrio had arrived this morning, to confront Miss Ricou's official and belligerent indifference to the overnight strangling on museum premises of the museum's attorney-director, Ruggierrio had been overjoyed to learn that there had been two reliable witnesses on the grounds at the time of the murder, and that those two witnesses were impartial, not answering to crusty old Miss Ricou. Now it looked like one of those witnesses was a murderer.

Ruggierrio frowned deeply and ran her fingers through her short, thick blond hair until it stood on end. This case had almost solved itself, and she was having trouble believing that. Ruggierrio was not a deep thinker, but she had certainly been around long enough to regard the easy gift of the guard's fingerprints in the studio as a potential Trojan Horse.

She walked back inside, her new tennis shoes squeaking on the clean Cuban tiles, and studied the two blue-shirted guards standing against the wall under a stuffed animal she thought was an elk. Ruggierrio's partner, Frank Ho, was sitting quietly on Hemingway's battered brown trunk beside the guards, the black cape folded on his lap, the Hemingway mask at his side, a study in quiet patience.

Ruggierrio had asked these guards at least twenty different ways about who had dropped that cape, who had worn that mask, who had been on the premises, and she had kept at them even after handcuffing the guard Perez and charging him as a material witness, reluctant to believe the guard was dumb enough to stick to a story that was damning him, hoping he'd add some detail or remember some circumstance that would take the air out of this tale of a perfectly guarded and closed estate.

No, Ruggierrio didn't like their story: Perez and Boswell had been on the estate during the night, all night; Boswell had discovered the body—and they were unmoving about the rest: nobody had dropped that cape because nobody had been here but them and the dead woman. Nobody had worn the mask, because nobody had been here but them and the dead woman.

"Do you at least admit that she was killed?" Ruggierrio had demanded in frustration. They had nodded, together, together like the rest of their story. It was a simple story, to be sure, one they had not needed much time to work on. The answer to every question was, "Nobody."

"Look, guys," she said, her voice turning reasonable and slow, "if you stick to your story that no one came in or went out of this estate last night, do you see where that leaves me?"

The short guard with the broken nose, the handcuffed, dark Hispanic named Gabriel Perez, the one with his prints all over that box and that little table, had apparently appointed himself spokesman, with silent agreement from his nervous partner. Perez lifted his hands to gesture, the metal cuffs clanking against each other as he tried to express himself the way all these Cubans did. Ruggierrio was really tired of Cubans. They thought they owned Key West, thought they were some kind of old blood—island royalty.

"Lieutenant, I was here. I saw no one. No one was on this estate but us and Miss de Vargas. I carried that box up for her and left. That's not a story. That's what happened. Nobody else was here." Perez rubbed his thumb across the bridge of his distinctive nose. A fighter, Ruggierrio thought, and probably not a very good one or a very wise one, not with that nose, a nose that had been on the collecting end of the punches too many times, a nose that had imparted a nasal hollowness to Perez's voice.

"And we're not going to change what we say, no matter what you say," Perez continued.

Ruggierrio nodded.

"Well, if that's the case," she said, "Perez, you're on your way to jail and maybe a charge of murder. Your material-witness status can change just like that." She snapped her fingers to illustrate. "In the four hours we've been going over this, I still haven't figured out a way de Vargas could have strangled herself. That leaves you."

Involuntarily the tall guard, the redheaded kid dubiously named Fernando Leroy Boswell, glanced toward the now-empty cigarmaker's chair where the body had been found—by him.

Two lines in white chalk marked the position of the body when he had found it. Boswell shuddered. De Vargas had just been sitting there, her head down, her hand in her lap. Boswell had thought she was asleep.

Perez snorted—a squeaking puff of air wheezing through the twisted corridors of that mangled nose.

"Yeah?" Perez snickered, squaring his shoulders. "I don't have no motive. My lawyer will make meat out of you."

"Don't give me that tough shit, Perez. You don't have a lawyer. Green turned you down. And if he was the only lawyer you know, you'd better start thinking up a better way to tell your story."

The tall guard silently separated himself from Perez. He did not like to hear that laugh and that bragging about the lawyer. He stepped into the sunlight pouring into the room through the south window of the tiny bathroom abutting the studio, his skinny arm swinging out from his side in a long twitch that brushed the wood of the bathroom door. He jerked his arm back, as if the door were hot.

Ruggierrio glanced at the visibly jumpy Boswell. That was South Florida all over, a scared security guard with a name like Fernando Leroy Boswell—a special ethnic mix was standing there quaking by Ernest Hemingway's bathroom door. This guard was badly frightened, even though he had done everything properly this morning when he had found the body of Millie de Vargas at the end of his shift. He, like Perez, said that nobody and nothing had entered the estate—during the hours when the murderer *must* have acted. If she believed them, then the murderer must have been invisible, entering the grounds and making his way up the stairs, into the studio, and somehow off the estate, all without being seen by these two professional eyeballs now standing in the studio. Nobody would believe that. Perez would be convicted by his own story, and the other guard's.

"Boswell, do you think you could have missed seeing someone, someone maybe who came over the wall?" Ruggierrio asked. She badly wanted to smoke a cigarette, but this was a National Historic Property, and she didn't dare.

"No." He cleared his throat. "The estate's not that big, and we never even sat down or anything." Boswell's voice was barely a whisper. "You'd have to see anyone who came in. Especially if they came near the buildings—they've all got lights. And we're always careful about watching the walls. I'm really sorry."

Ruggierrio was sorry too. And she was tempted to let Boswell go. Hours of walking the guards over the estate and then standing around the studio had not shaken this simple but impossible story the guards were telling. She was going to have to let Perez stew until he found a lawyer to bail him out or she found a way to make a murder charge stick.

"You can go home now, Boswell, but don't go anywhere

else. Stay on the island. Make sure we can find you when we need you." Ruggierrio felt her pocket automatically for her Salems, then, remembering she couldn't smoke, ran her hand through her hair again.

Boswell almost loped out of the studio, ducking as he went through the open cage door onto the sunny iron landing of the double staircase and colliding with Dave, who had just stepped onto the landing with the toe of his polished black flat.

"Whoa, Secretariat," Dave said. "Stud farm on fire?"

Boswell swept Dave with huge, uncomprehending, frightened eyes and pushed past him down the stairs, brushing by Annabelle without a glance, vaulting the yellow police tape at the bottom of the stairs, and loping across the brick patio to the mansion's lower veranda, his blue shirt stuck to his back with a thick streak of perspiration, and on around to the front of the mansion.

Ruggierrio stood in the studio doorway, looking at the newcomers, wondering why Mittman and the guard stationed at the gate had passed them through. Mittman was a good cop, and Hardy Security had a reputation for better-than-average guards, which could add to her problem of trying to prove Perez and the other bozo were lying—or blind, or incapacitated, or something else.

Dave turned back to the studio's doorway and assessed the fortyish, slightly beer-bellied woman in a T-shirt and jeans, her blond hair a wild thatch, but with a police-issue shoulder holster over the shirt and with the unmistakably pugnacious attitude of a harrassed cop.

"Who are you?" Ruggierrio demanded.

Dave liked most cops, but he saw no reason for instant cooperation with them. They were, after all, in his view, merely fellow citizens, crossing his path as he proceeded toward their common goal of democratic living and peace on earth.

"Guess," Dave said brightly, an encouraging smile on his face.

The mellow green shade of swaying coconut palms fell across the deep eaves of the cottage's low mansard roof, the fronds stroking the weathered Cape Cod shingles. Dave trailed his hand across the shingles languidly but kept his eyes on the cop.

"If I was any good at guessing, I'd buy a crystal ball and go off to join a *real* circus, instead of enforcing the law in Key West," Ruggierrio said evenly, but through clenched teeth, her sense of frustration mounting. "Why don't you be a good little boy and tell the kind officer your name so she doesn't have to take your fingerprints at the scene of a capital crime and run them through the computer prior to a charge of obstructing justice."

"I'm Jorge Enamorado," Dave said, bowing to the inevitable and recognizing that note of frustration. He took his wallet from the back pocket of his baggy black shorts and offered his ID card to Ruggierrio, who examined it and handed it back to Dave.

Annabelle reached up the stairs past Dave and handed her card to Ruggierrio.

"So, these guards belong to you," Ruggierrio said, returning Annabelle's card. It was a long moment before she shook her gaze away from Annabelle's green eyes. "I'm Barbara Ruggierrio. You can come on up and see if you get the same tidy little story Perez has told me."

Dave was disgusted by his first glimpse of Hemingway's lair. The stuffed elk's head immediately accosted his eye and offended him. Dave was a permanent member of the South Beach Rescue Team, a volunteer outfit that refloated and nourished whales that had beached themselves on South Florida shores, and he could not imagine the taste that led a man to decorate his walls with the partial remains of his kills, much less engage in the sport of killing. For Dave, there was no moral ambiguity in this room—it was a shrine to killing and, Dave thought, a cold, nasty place, despite the warm breezes circulating from the graceful and open windows. Another antlered head adorned the adjacent wall, and the mounted body of a large fish stared blindly from above a bookcase stuffed with old volumes. This display in the cottage was the tangible reality of the faded photographs he had just seen in the mansion—the pictures of the big, healthy, and handsome young author posed, his mustached mouth open and grinning, with animals from safari hunts and from deep-sea hunts. Dave was appalled, and he turned to see how Annabelle was reacting to the studio's decor.

She seemed to be studying her foot in its cherry-red heel, rubbing it over the Cuban tile where she stood next to the cigarmaker's chair. She caught his glance and signed, "It's sticky; I thought I stepped in some gum."

Ruggierrio stiffened. One of these two visitors was deaf; she couldn't tell which one. But she'd seen sign language before, and it made her nervous, like all foreign languages.

Annabelle glanced around and sat on the end of a rattan chaise longue, her cherry-red dress an incongruous note of vibrant life in this place of both the old and the newly dead. Her gaze was concentrated on the guard, whose nose was badly off-center.

"I'm Annabelle Hardy-Maratos," she said. The guard shifted his weight, but she did not ask him to sit down. "I understand you're being held for questioning about this murder—"

Ruggierrio interrupted. "I've booked him on a material-witness warrant."

"Have you ascertained what his motive is?" Annabelle asked softly. "Does he have a history of vital disagreement with Milady de Vargas? Or are you simply avoiding that issue?"

A deep flush blossomed up Ruggierrio's neck. "No, I don't have no motive for him. But can you explain the fingerprints?"

Annabelle exchanged a glance with Dave, who was sign-ing, and then continued, her eyes moving to the guard. "I know very little about the details of this tragedy, but I think you said that it was impossible for anyone to get in here last night without your seeing them?"

For the first time, Ruggierrio noted, Perez seemed less than sure of himself.

"I didn't exactly say that," Perez said. "I said I didn't see anyone get in here."

"Oh." Annabelle continued to gaze at him. "Someone did get in here last night, isn't that so? Unless you killed her."

"I didn't touch her. I only carried her box. That box over there." He pointed, indicating the partially open box of metal straps under a small table.

"But you saw no one, no one at all?"

"I only saw Miss de Vargas. And my partner Fernando."

"Where was Miss de Vargas when you saw her?"

"She was, well, lots of places."

"Tell me," Annabelle said in her soft voice. "Tell me ex-actly and everywhere you saw Miss de Vargas."

The guard looked into the middle distance, seeming to replay a videotape of the evening in his mind's eye, his oddly focused gaze shifting along a narrow window of space before him.

"First I saw her come in the gate and go up the walk into the mansion, like she always does before closing time. There was a lot of people around, tourists and stuff. I saw her petting Frank Sinatra—that's one of the cats. I saw her inside, in the hall by the door for a few minutes. I saw her standing in the dining room door, by that nigger statue from Africa for a while. I think I heard her check the front door to see if it was locked. Then I saw her later by the living-room window, when I was on the veranda. She closed the living-room windows and waved to me. Then I went to the front gate and talked to some people, and then I went to the side of the house. I saw her again on the front veranda when I was fooling around with Greta Garbo and Jean Harlow. Then I saw Miss de Vargas again when she went out the back door and across the patio to the studio stairs. That's when she made me come help her with the box—"

"Wait a minute," Annabelle interrupted. "Do you mean she was on the veranda in front after you heard her check the lock on the front door?"

Perez thought a moment.

"Yeah. After."

"You said she came out of the mansion through the back door to go to the studio?"

"Yeah."

"But you also said you saw her on the front veranda."

Perez looked confused.

"I guess she went back in the house and then went out the back door," he said, frowning, replaying the picture in his mind's eye suddenly out of its first, sharp, certain focus.

"Go on," Annabelle suggested gently. "Where else did you see her?"

Perez shut his eyes, opened them, and again looked into that private window he seemed to see in the air.

"I saw her when I took the box upstairs to the studio. It was dark in here, and she didn't seem to want company, so I left—you know, she gave me one of those looks. She put the light on, and I saw her shadow on the window. And then she turned off the light, and I couldn't see her anymore. It was getting pretty dark."

"Where were you?"

"I was walking on the south lawn. It was a little while after sunset."

"Is that the last time you saw her? Alive?"

"No. I saw her again later."

Ruggierrio's face registered surprise. She looked curiously at Annabelle.

"Where did you see Miss de Vargas later?" Annabelle asked.

"In the mansion kitchen." Perez seemed to consider this detail. "I saw her. By the window."

"Are you sure it was Millie de Vargas?"

"Positive." Perez nodded to himself. "Yeah, it was her all right—"

Ruggierrio interrupted, her angry flush angrier, her eyes glaring at Perez. "Why the hell didn't you say anything about seeing her in the kitchen before?"

"You didn't ask me about Miss de Vargas." Perez hunched his shoulder, frustrated by the cuffs around his wrists. "You just asked about who else was here. Nobody. I repeat: nobody. You want me to spell it?"

Ruggierrio took a step toward him. "Since when can you spell, you snotty little—" She stopped suddenly, aware of Dave's frank scrutiny of her face as he continued to produce signs.

Annabelle's eyes flickered over Perez.

"What time was that," she asked, "when you saw Millie de Vargas in the kitchen?"

"It must have been about seven-thirty, because I remember that her being in the kitchen made me hungry, and I could hear the calypso band still playing from the docks by the restaurant."

Now Annabelle looked at Ruggierrio, an eyebrow lifted in inquiry.

"The medical examiner says she was dead by six-thirty P.M., at the latest," Ruggierrio said, her voice low.

Annabelle shifted in the chair, her green eyes wide and focused on the guard's troubled gaze.

"Are you still positive that it was de Vargas you saw in the kitchen?" she asked.

An obvious struggle was taking place in Perez.

His chest heaved on a deep breath.

"I see what you're saying," he muttered. "But I know what I saw. It was her."

"Could you be wrong about the time?"

"I don't think so. They always play the same songs at the same times. It's like a clock. It's like I told myself, 'Seven-thirty.'"

"Did you see Millie de Vargas anywhere else after you saw her in the kitchen?"

A profound silence filled the studio, except for the palms stroking the roof's shingles and the drone of insects from the dense ferns below on the grounds.

"I guess not." Perez hesitated, and Dave looked at him searchingly. "It's just that, you know, it sounds so stupid now when I tell it, but it's true."

"Are you sure it was Millie de Vargas you saw, each time you say you saw her?" Annabelle asked.

"Yeah. Positive. Same as we saw her this morning after Fernando found her in here. It was her. It was nobody but her."

"How well did you know Miss de Vargas?"

"I saw her every day. She was the queen of this place. She made sure you saw her. She was like that."

Annabelle looked at Dave, her brows raised. He shook his head. She looked at Ruggierrio.

"Perez was the last to see her alive," Ruggierrio said. "He admits it. His prints are on that box." She pointed to a cardboard box on the floor by a table. "And on that table. He was here. And the cage door was locked. And now he's going down to a holding cell."

"May I remind you that you cannot even suggest a motive for this man?" Annabelle asked, a hard look in her eyes. "Most Florida juries are curious about such things."

"Motives can wait. It was probably a fight. Or some job thing." Ruggierrio's gruff voice took on a threatening edge. "And the charge is going to be murder."

Perez sputtered, phlegm accompanying his words. "You're wrong," he snarled. "I had no quarrel with Miss de Vargas."

Ruggierrio took a step forward.

"Get him out of here, Frank," she said. The quiet detective by the window stood, placed the folded cape carefully on the trunk, and approached Perez, taking his arm.

The guard glanced at Annabelle. Her face was expression-less.

"I had no quarrel with her," he repeated. He left the room with the detective, and Dave could hear him taking the stairs angrily, two or three at a time despite his manacled hands, followed by the lighter steps of the detective.

Annabelle stood and crossed to the gateleg table. The typewriter was placed at an angle to the edge of the table, and there was a key missing from the second row. The key lay on the table beside the machine, still attached to the metal prong that had connected it to the striking mechanism. An uppercase A was inscribed in white on the black surface of the round key. The spools and ribbon were gone.

"Fingerprints?" she asked.

"Only hers, the dead woman's," Ruggierrio answered.

"Where's the ribbon?"

"It was still around her neck when I saw it last, but by now it's probably on its way to the lab."

"And the body?"

"In the morgue at Lower Florida Keys Health System on Stock Island—autopsy."

"Is there any doubt what killed her?"

"No."

"May I see the cape?"

Ruggierrio nodded.

Annabelle crossed to the trunk and lifted the heavy cape. She unfolded it, its black velvet and satin folds swishing softly to her feet. She pointed to the rubber face of Hemingway on the trunk. "Have you taken prints already?" When Ruggierrio nodded, Annabelle took the mask in her other hand.

"Are you going to try tracing these?" she asked, carrying the cape and mask toward the bathroom and its bright sunlight. Dave came to stand by her side as she inspected the costume.

"We already have," Ruggierrio said. "The cape came from the Margaret Truman Costume, Tuxedo, and Piano Shop on Duval. It was stolen last Friday."

Annabelle took a deep breath, frowning over the cape.

Dave gestured into the bathroom, and signed, "Pretend we're consulting secretly, but look. A Nobel laureate's powder room."

"I expect that's where he did his best work," Annabelle signed, suddenly smiling brightly.

Annabelle turned to Ruggierrio, who was watching Dave lean into the bathroom.

"What about the mask?" Annabelle asked. "Can you trace it?"

"Not likely. They sell 'em all over Duval Street. I own one myself."

Dave spun around and stared at the detective, the look in his eye suggesting that she might have depths—or bad habits—he would previously have considered impossible.

Annabelle spread the cape and swirled its folds open fully. It was a long cape, almost as tall as she was at five feet ten inches, and made from at least six yards of the heavy fabric. The cape fell from her shoulder height to the floor of the studio.

"What a terrific cape," Dave signed. "It's just like the one I wore to the Miami Heart Association Costume Ball last April. The theme was movie titles."

"Oh, yeah," she said. "Who did you go as?"

"Mighty Mouse."

"With a cape?"

"It was very original," Dave said smugly. "I won second prize."

"You won a prize for a mouse in a cape?" Annabelle's skepticism showed in her widened eyes.

"I was *A Might at the Opera*."

FIVE

 "OH, DAVE. SHE'S BEWITCHINGLY LOVELY—FLAWLESS."

Annabelle pointed to a life-size doll, its painted mahogany face made in the image of Katarina Witt, clothed in the same scarlet and black colors Witt had worn during her gold-medal performance at the 1988 Winter Olympics. The authenticity of the details extended to the white skates on the pretty doll's dainty feet: The blades were shiny steel and honed to sharp precision, the laces tied in perfect bows. The doll sat on an expanse of aluminum foil in a shop window, her smooth legs positioned as though she had done a split on the ice, her short skirt placed in folds around her hips, her arms gracefully spread at her sides. The doll adorned the cramped window of a woodcarver's studio and was surrounded by wood etchings of Key West scenes and mahogany statues of other women athletes. The woodcarver, an elderly man in denim overalls without a shirt, nodded at his visitors through the window and continued to whittle a slim block in his stained, gnarled hands.

This was a poignant moment for Dave. The same hand that had set the bomb that had shattered the top floor of the Pink Building had mysteriously destroyed his "Ethel," a six-foot Radio City Rockette doll with a painted-china face. He had thought Ethel irreplaceable but now looked with longing at the skater doll.

Annabelle and Dave had walked when they left the museum, having tried in vain to find a cab on Whitehead Street, and had hurried up Duval on their way to the law offices of de Vargas and Green, stopping at a pay phone where Dave called Arantxa to arrange legal representation for Perez, and stopping to buy coconut-mango ice cream at a sidewalk wagon, eating the rapidly melting confection as they dodged around strolling tourists bent on contributing as quickly as possible to the island's economy. Many already had, wearing new T-shirts that said "Save the Sunset" or "Sink Tank Island" or "Earth First/ Resort Never."

"Local business sentiment seems to be running against that new harbor resort," Dave said. "Too bad the shirts are so ugly, or I'd buy you one." They had also visited six stores that sold the rubber Hemingway masks, and Dave bought one finally for $29.95 at Dizzy Izzy's, a skateboard boutique that also operated the annual Half-Mile Ernest Hemingway Look-alike Contest and Skateboard Derby down the center of Duval; the boutique sold the masks under a large sign offering "Papa Pusses," apparently for those tourists unable to compete naturally with their own physiognomies but who nonetheless wanted to race or march in the parade of bearded faces. A salesclerk said that the boutique sold most of their masks to women.

"It's another men's club," Annabelle said disgustedly. "I'll bet nobody wearing a mask ever won."

"Well, all I can say, Annabelle, is, like it or not, Hemingway *was* a man, and you'd expect a look-alike contest to reflect a certain amount of testosterone."

"And what an excellent use to put it to!" she retorted with tart emphasis.

Dave's rubber Hemingway mask was now stuffed into his hip pocket; they stood before the woodcarver's shop, which was called Mahogany Maid. Dave was stunned by the sight of the lovely doll and transformed into an island of immobile emotion in a rushing stream of pedestrian humanity on Key West's busiest street.

"She's beautiful, Annabelle," Dave signed, oblivious to the reflection in the window of his dramatic and heartfelt gestures, and of Marcel pacing on his shoulder.

Annabelle stood patiently on the sidewalk, touched by Dave's open rapture, but soon she reluctantly grasped his wrist and consulted his watch. It was nearly two o'clock, the time Dave had appointed to meet N. S. Green in the offices he had shared with Millie de Vargas.

Dave dragged his eyes away from the doll in Mahogany Maid and walked beside Annabelle, his head turning occasionally to glance back at the woodcarver's window. At Number 202 Duval, Annabelle stopped, and Dave nearly bumped into her.

"This is it," she said.

A modest sign, simply saying DE VARGAS AND GREEN, swung over the dirty sidewalk, which was cluttered with remnants of goods for sale along the street—beer cans, ice-cream wrappers, maps, film canisters, pizza crusts. From the doorway at street level the smell of stale beer, lemon rinds, and musty dough floated on the warm air. A dark, narrow staircase rose beside the faded white shingles of Conch Out, the twenty-four-hour tavern at 202 Duval.

They climbed the stairs to a pristine white door, fitted with shiny brass and bearing, in small gold lettering, another simple legend: LAW OFFICES. From the top stair Dave twisted the brass knob and stepped up onto a luxurious and velvety deep-piled burgundy carpet into a small anteroom decorated with three chairs, covered in a white and ivy-green forest print, in a row against the wall, and a long mahogany coffee table across from two vacant desks. A tall, gracefully fluted brass urn holding five silk palm fronds was reflected in the relentless shine on the tabletop. In a brass-lined niche on the far wall of the small room, there stood a fifteen-inch, hand-carved and painted mahogany Madonna. Dave felt an urge to genuflect, which he suppressed.

"This doll's not as beautiful as the one in the woodcarver's window," he signed, indicating the Madonna.

"That's not a doll," Annabelle said scornfully.

"Well, what's the difference?" Dave's expression clearly suggested that he saw no difference. "If you're going to say that the difference is one of function, then I'll point out that an ice skate is an ice skate, no matter what I use it for, and a doll is a doll, whether I use it for religious purposes or not. My logic is impeccable."

"You're comparing apples and oranges. A doll has moving parts. A Madonna does not and never will. Therefore a Madonna is not a doll, just as an ice skate is not, say, a vacuum cleaner."

"You're separating religion and recreation, which is a false and artificial distinction, as well as a common mistake. You've been spending too much time with that Ruggierrio woman, whose mind works like a glued toothpaste tube."

Dave's gestures were growing larger, demonstrating his mounting irritation, and before the argument could escalate, the door opposite the chairs opened and framed a small, slender man in a dapper blue pinstriped business suit. His thinning dark hair was combed from a prominent part that showed the healthy pink of his scalp. He twirled a pair of gold half-glasses in his right hand and rubbed his moist eyes with his left, the different but diminutive circular motions of both hands reminding Annabelle of a squirrel.

"Are you Ms. Hardy-Maratos? You're right on time." He stepped forward, placing the glasses on his nose and offering his hand mechanically. "I'm Noah Green." He gestured to the vacant mahogany desks in the room. "I've had to give my girls the day off. When they heard about Millie, it was the perfect excuse for a little office hysteria."

Annabelle introduced Dave, who had winced at Green's use of *my girls* to describe his paralegal staff. Green also probably wasn't winning points with Annabelle, Dave thought, with his overflowing absence of grief.

"Why don't we go into my office where we can talk more privately?" Green said.

Dave glanced around at the empty room, cocked an eye at the Madonna, and shrugged.

Green turned back to the door and led the way across a narrow hallway, through another doorway, and into a large sunny office decorated like the anteroom but without any religious statuary. The top of the mahogany desk was covered with neat stacks of papers, folders, and legal pads. All the mahogany on display, Annabelle thought, manifested a pronounced affection for the common native wood of Key West.

Marcel, always at home in office environments, leaped spontaneously onto the mahogany desk, landed on a loose sheet of paper, which immediately shot out from under him, and took flight again, circling the room several times while Green held his arms protectively over his head. Marcel finally came to rest atop a polished mahogany file cabinet, squawking with apparently unabated cheer.

Green shuddered. "I'll have to ask you to take your bird into the waiting room," he said. "I'm allergic."

Dave opened his mouth to protest, encountered a fastidious grimace from the attorney and a mild smile from Annabelle, and gathered the bird onto his shoulder. Dave left the office, punctuating his exit by closing the door behind him with a snap.

"Now, then," Green began, facing Annabelle, his little hands making the busy circular motions, "have you already begun to add to your mess at the Hemingway Museum? I understand you've been nosing around there without so much as a thought for anyone's authority."

Annabelle considered the man, her gaze unwavering, her brow clear. He certainly kept his information current, she thought. She wondered if he had sent Dave out of the room to try a minor intimidation tactic on her. She would try a tactic of her own.

"The only mess that involves Hardy Security," she said quietly, "is the wrongful detention of Gabriel Perez. Any other untidiness almost certainly involves the personal affairs of Millie de Vargas, of which you are a part. My call here today is a simple courtesy, since our client is the museum, not your law firm."

"A mess is a mess," Green said, twirling his glasses and frowning at her. "If you want to split hairs, go right ahead."

An impatient expression flitted over Annabelle's usually composed features. "Mr. Green, why did you agree to see me when my associate asked for this appointment?"

Green sat wearily in the swivel chair behind the desk. He put his glasses on a stack of legal pads and then picked them up again immediately, waving them at a leather chair beside the desk, and Annabelle sat down in the deep luxury of its thick green cushions, crossing her long legs.

"Ms. Hardy-Maratos, I find myself in the reluctant position of delivery boy. Millie left something for you." He opened a desk drawer, reached inside, and stood slightly to offer Annabelle a sealed envelope. When she stretched to take it from his hand, he retained a corner of the envelope, scrutinizing her face. "Millie said you'd be expecting this," he said.

Annabelle preserved a noncommittal expression, hiding her surprise. He released the envelope and sat back in his chair, regarding her silently.

Her name was written on the envelope in neat black characters, but there was no address. She turned it over, noting that the elaborate wax seal was unbroken.

"Where did you get this?" she asked.

"Millie gave it to me about two months ago. She said that if anything happened to her, she wanted me to see that you received it. I did not know that your acquaintance was that intimate."

"It wasn't."

Annabelle slid a finger under the seal and opened the envelope, which contained one piece of paper, a brief letter on the firm's letterhead:

November 18, 1998

Dear Ms. Hardy-Maratos:

This is to inform you that you will find, hidden under the brass cover of the newel post at the foot of the main staircase in the Ernest Hemingway Museum, here in Key West, my last will and testament. The document is executed as a holographic will, quite legal in the state of Florida, and represents my final intentions regarding the property of which I die possessed. The hidden will supersedes any other made previous to the date of this letter to you, including the one now in the keeping of my law partner, Noah Green.

I have judged you to be a woman of some discretion, and I have made inquiries that confirm my opinion. It is my hope that you will act as executor of my will or designate a person whom you trust and who is as much an outsider in Key West affairs as I take you to be.

This is also to terminate the contract between the Hemingway Museum in Key West, Florida, and Hardy Security and Electronics of Miami, Florida. The terms of that contract specify that the Museum may cancel at any time during the first year the contract is in effect. Please send any outstanding bills to Miss Ashleen Ricou, who is now acting for the Museum in all financial matters.

Thank you.

Millie de Vargas, Esq.

Annabelle finished reading the letter but kept her eyes on the paper for an additional moment, thinking rapidly about its startling contents, then refolded it and returned it to the envelope. She looked at Green.

"She terminated the Hardy Security contract at the museum."

"I'm surprised," he said, but he nodded to himself, long, slow, deliberate, thoughtful nods.

"So am I."

"But I did assume that Millie's letter somehow concerned your company's involvement in museum affairs. I'd like to know," Green said, after pausing to rub his fingers along the rims of his eyes, pulling down the bottom lids to reveal the especially bloodshot corners, "whether she discussed with you her reason for putting on guards at the museum in the first place."

"No." Annabelle longed to look decently away from the rubbing operation, but the need, in Dave's absence, to concentrate on reading the attorney's lips prevented her.

"She never even hinted why all of a sudden she had to have guards there?"

"No."

Green frowned at his desk. "Are you aware that the museum has been in operation for almost thirty years, perfectly uneventful years, and it's never had guards before?"

"Yes."

Green sniffed and transferred his frown to Annabelle, changing the subject abruptly. "Are you satisfied that your guard killed Millie?"

"No."

Green rubbed his eyes with the heels of his hands, his glasses swinging where they were lodged between his fingers. He spoke while holding his palms steady against his eyebrows, the glasses dangling below his lips, causing Annabelle to have to squint and sit forward in her chair. "Neither am I. The police have no motive for him, from what I understand. I imagine that situation will spur you to make an outcry and send you plunging around the back doors of Key West, looking for all kinds of dirt. Why, you've already done that much at the museum, and it's only two o'clock. I hope, in your zeal to free your employee, you won't clutter up the city with amateurish and misguided attempts to involve me or this law firm any further. No doubt Millie knew what she was doing when she fired you." He removed his hands from his eyes and regarded her dryly.

Annabelle kept her feelings from showing on her face, the earlier display of impatience gone, replaced with an absence of expression that Dave knew well, and disliked, knowing that it represented not lack of emotion but strong emotion, powerfully suppressed.

"I'm sorry my interest in this matter has worried you, or that it makes you feel threatened, counselor."

"Let's get something straight. I have no reason to be worried, except for the incompetence of other people—yours, perhaps." He stopped talking and bent a cautious gaze on her. "Why are you staring at me like that?"

"I'm quite deaf, Mr. Green," she answered, her outward poise undisturbed. "I'm having some difficulty reading your lips because of those glasses."

Green fixed his watery eyes on Annabelle's still-stony face.

"Well, isn't that interesting?" He pursed his lips. "I take it you mean to investigate this murder anyway? You came hurrying down to Key West on some personal mission to save your guard, and you're deaf?"

"I'm deaf, Mr. Green, not dead. I'm also in full possession of my faculties."

"Shit. You're a total outsider, that's what you are. That's two handicaps. Let me make it clear to you what an outsider can hope to accomplish in Key West—nothing. Consider this: Plenty of people had reason to fear or dislike Millie, and I think she hired your company because she was afraid for herself, apparently with some reason, but going to Miami was a mistake. Hiring Miami rent-a-cops obviously did her no good. That's why she's firing you now." He held up a hand. "Don't interrupt me. Millie was a frightened woman. And I think I know what was frightening her. Can you understand what I'm saying?"

"I don't have a problem at all now."

"Of course not. I'm making a concerted effort to be clear in what I say, but that won't be the case with everyone in this town. Key West is a very complex place, and Millie's life involved complexities you may never get straight. You'll be hearing—excuse me, *learning*—about Millie's unpopular involvement in something very important. How much do you know about the Hemingway Resort? This much you must understand."

The door to the office opened inward. Dave strolled in and dropped into an ivy-green leather chair opposite the attorney, without waiting to be invited to sit. He crossed his legs and shifted some in the commodious chair. He quickly signed, "Did I miss anything?" and Annabelle sighed with relief, reached over and handed him the letter from de Vargas, and, when he had taken the envelope from her, signed "Be careful," making a V with two fingers of each hand and striking her left wrist with her right.

Dave met her eyes, cracked his knuckles, and began to sign Green's part of the conversation for Annabelle, starting from "Hemingway Resort," as he simultaneously read the letter. Green watched Dave with guarded interest for a moment while he continued to direct his words to Annabelle, enunciating consonants and broadening vowels.

"Do you know all the ramifications of the proposed resort? I want you to hear this from my point of view before you hear—learn—the stories from every rumhead in Key West about Millie's alleged rape of the environment. Anything that involves this firm involves me, and I want you to get it straight, if you can."

Dave looked at Annabelle in shock. He signed, "What the hell set him off?"

Annabelle ignored Dave, and she tried to ignore Green's provocative jibes about her deafness.

"Key West is still in Florida, Mr. Green," she said, "and that resort is hardly a private little local dispute among this city's attorneys. I certainly know what's been printed in *The Miami Herald:* that it's going to be the largest resort in Key West, and that it's supposed to go up on Tank Island directly across the harbor from Mallory Square, and that Millie de Vargas was representing the developers and owned a considerable share in the property herself. That she was the target of strong local resentment because the hotel will effectively block the island's view of the sunset. The *Herald* even published a photo of the plans, but it looked like every other big resort I've ever seen, nothing special architecturally, not particularly imaginative, nothing going for it but its absolutely unthinkable location. Just another tasteless, big, Las Vegas/Bahamas-style hotel, but one that's going to gobble up an entire sunset for itself. I completely understand the outrage among large segments of Key West's voluble population concerning that location." She could not resist adding, "You don't have to be able to hear to enjoy the sunset."

"You won't find any sympathy for that viewpoint here," Green said baldly, linking his little hands over the vest of his suit, his glasses dangling over his belt buckle. "You, or anybody else. All that balderdash about Key West's only God."

"What's this?" Dave straightened in the chair, handing the envelope and letter back to Annabelle.

"The sunset. When that hotel goes up on Tank Island, old Key West's daily and admission-free ritual down at Mallory Square will be finished, and it's about time, thanks to Millie de Vargas. Are you getting all this in sign language, young man?"

Green snorted, producing a wet noise that caused Dave to examine the desktop furtively before he nodded. "All the island gathers every day to witness the miracle of the best sunset in the world—on that tourists and conchs agree—and nobody pays a penny. That's hardly the way of the world, even for conchs." He pronounced the word "conks," the local lingo for Key West natives. "Since the wrecking industry died, this town has always depended on getting its full tourist dollar, and liking it—that is, until this hysteria about the Hemingway Resort. The resort will only be doing, but doing better, what Key West has always done—charging tourists money for our natural wonders."

Green paused to wipe his glasses on his tie.

"Photographers and artists come from all over to capture Key West's incomparable sunsets. The town sells more liquor at sunset than at any other time. We have sunsets on every tourist brochure we've ever produced, on every T-shirt we've ever sold for more than ten dollars. The chamber of commerce has a collective heart attack if it rains at sundown, which it rarely does. Everything in Key West happens because of the sunset, and around the sunset, and with the sunset in mind. An eight-story resort on that naked island out in the middle of the harbor will mean that Key West has finally given away its last free sunset. If you want to see the sunset, you'll have to check into the hotel. In some bleeding-heart circles that's a crime, Ms. Hardy-Maratos, and Millie made some enemies. She was the *force majeur* behind the project. Nobody else could have weathered such resistance, for such a long time, with such solid results. She was a brilliant woman."

Dave rubbed his ear. "Now that she's dead, what's going to happen to the resort? If she was such a powerhouse, if Millie de Vargas was holding the reins, what now? Is the resort doomed? Her murder might just scare people enough to alter the destiny of that harbor monstrosity."

Green almost jumped out of his chair. He stood, shaking with anger.

"That's just the kind of irresponsible speculation I was afraid of from you outsiders. You see? You don't understand. Just because Millie de Vargas made a few enemies doesn't mean her death was connected to the resort. And if anyone thinks I'm running scared because of Millie's death, they can just check my record in this town. The firm of de Vargas and Green had been in the forefront in Key West when it comes to development, and I've been proud of the ground we've broken, literally and figuratively. There's absolutely no indication that Millie's death had anything to do with the resort. Sure, she was targeted. Sure, there's been noise. Sure, she was even afraid, enough to hire guards. Conchs can be stubbornly backward about real progress in development, unwilling to see when they're cutting off their noses to spite their faces, but they always come together when it's best for Key West. They're not killers." He stared at Dave. "Don't go running away with dangerous ideas." Green took a deep breath and adjusted his vest over his waist. "I hope I answered your question responsibly. De Vargas and Green has led the way for twelve years in enlightened, forward-looking, rational growth. A few enemies won't stop us."

"Apparently"—Dave was adding a sentence of his own to the signs he was producing for Annabelle, a thoughtful look on his face—"a few enemies was only enough to stop one of them."

"But where does the resort project stand now?" Annabelle asked, pursuing Dave's line of thought and following Green's progress as he took small, almost fitful steps beside his desk.

"I think you can say it's a done deal. Millie was negotiating the last hurdle when she . . . when she was murdered. It will be impossible, I suppose, to replace Millie, her energy, her ability to bully the town planners into doing what's good for Key West. But I'm going to try."

"What was that last hurdle?" Dave asked.

"The navy."

SIX

ANNABELLE AND DAVE EXCHANGED GLANCES.

Green continued, savoring their apparent mystification. "The navy retains some of the rights to Tank Island, which used to be a fuel station out there in the harbor. Nothing's going up on that island until those outstanding rights are secured."

Dave faced Annabelle again and signed, "I hope against hope that our warriors in white turn out to be good guys, instead of the Pentagon puppets I take them for. Frankly, my dear, this resort is going to suck." That it was rude to use sign privately in front of Green, Dave knew and was glad. Annabelle opened her handbag to insert the letter from de Vargas and glanced at the typewritten note Lieutenant Ricou had given her. She closed the handbag and sat quietly for a moment, her eyes focused on the middle distance.

The attorney paced across the thick carpet, his glasses once again twirling from an earpiece in his hand. He stopped behind Annabelle's chair, considering the back of her head with an air of bland superiority, nodding to himself. Dave watched him alertly, ready to interpret for Annabelle, disliking that look.

Green seemed to reflect for a moment, measuring his

words, delivering them in his soft, polished voice, which struck Dave as oddly in emotional opposition to the attorney's edgy, fidgeting physical self.

"Those rights to Tank Island are a side issue. Everything will fall into place in time. For now I can't think of anything more wasteful than a pack of Miami detectives stumbling around in what they don't understand. The Key West police are slow, but they'll get the right thing done. Your man Perez will get off, you'll see, without your help. I hope you'll heed my advice. People who live in Key West don't like outsiders. And I was born here."

Annabelle rose while Dave was signing what to her were Green's thoroughly disgusting xenophobic views, his smug placement of the island city at the center of the universe, the omphalos of time and tide, and she turned to see for herself the adamant light in the attorney's tired eyes. She was several inches taller than he and found herself looking down at him, wondering at such local ego.

"If there's no link between the resort and Millie's murder," she said, "and I'm not insisting on one, there must be some other powerful motive, and I think you'd be the one to know that motive. Tell me, Mr. Green, are you executor for Millie de Vargas?"

A spasm of annoyance showed on his face, but he nodded his head, a quick but deliberate movement. The glasses slipped out of his fingers, and Dave picked them up off the carpet and placed them at the far end of the arm of his leather chair, repelled by the smudged fingerprints on the lenses, the ugly pink discoloration of the earpieces, their generally dilapidated hardware. Green glanced down and snatched them impatiently.

"Yes, I'm her executor, and I'm also one of the principal legatees—the firm is now mine. We had an agreement that endows either partner with absolute ownership on the death of the other. Plus there's a considerable personal legacy of two million dollars—out of gratitude for our partnership in the firm. I'll profit by Millie's death, but it will be nothing compared to the loss of her drive."

"Who are the other heirs?"

He hesitated, gauging her with a steady gaze. "There's the Hemingway Museum, with a sizable maintenance fund, entrusted to the administration of Ashleen Ricou, the oldest and most devoted of the volunteers at the mansion on Whitehead—Millie was also born in Key West, and she felt a duty toward the city's second biggest tourist attraction—after the sunset. And there's Millie's brother. She was unmarried and had no children. The brother will get her house and her other real estate interests, which are sizable."

"How sizable?"

Green looked up at Annabelle.

"She was worth close to three million dollars in property, irrespective of her extensive holdings in the Hemingway Resort. Those are her brother's now—"

Dave interrupted. "Who else owns shares in the resort?"

"That's a matter of public record. Go look it up." Green rubbed his eyes again. "Your bird should never have entered this room."

Dave cast an intrigued look at Annabelle and signed, "I thought he was exaggerating about the allergy."

"Did you do something?" she signed.

"Maybe." Dave's sign was unenthusiastic, lacking his usual histrionic force, but his accompanying smile was saintly.

Whatever Dave had done could not be serious, Annabelle knew, for he was the soul of kindness, despite his often aggressive sense of humor, so she dropped the matter and turned back to Green.

He sneezed violently. The effect of the sneeze on his eyes was pronounced; they seemed to bulge, to glaze, and he rubbed them furiously. "It's the cat. Millie kept a blasted cat, and its enzymes are always all over the place, no matter how hard I try to keep it out of this office."

Annabelle rapidly passed under review her feelings regarding the man's obvious suffering, but she shook her head frowningly at Dave, who was signing, "Good for Millie. I like her partnership style." It would do them no good to add open hostility to Green's already well-primed and overflowing nervous antipathy.

"What's the brother's name?" she asked. "Does he live here in Key West?"

"Francisco. Yes, he lives on Margaret Street. Millie had no business leaving him a nickel. He'll piss his inheritance away on his eccentricities."

Annabelle felt her interest in Millie's brother leap.

"What kind of eccentricities?" she asked.

"Look, about Francisco. We really don't travel in the same circles. Some aspects of Millie's brother's life are, well, let's just say interesting." He smiled the first smile they'd seen from him, a twisted effort. "He runs the Waterfront Playhouse, or tries to. That outfit is more or less always outrunning its creditors. I hope you'll leave little Fransy Pansy alone. He's got enough to worry about. I wish you'd leave us all alone."

Annabelle contemplated the attorney's busy hands. The phone on his desk rang, and he picked it up, his eyes on Annabelle.

"You'll have to excuse me now," he said, dismissing them suddenly and taking little steps around his desk, his progress impeded by the partially blinding motion of his fingers in his eyes and the phone that covered his face at an angle.

"A moment, counselor," Annabelle said.

Green cradled the phone in his hand against his vest and looked at her impatiently.

"Where were you at sundown yesterday?" she asked.

"At Mallory Square," he replied dryly. "With about a thousand other people. You got that?" He started to raise the receiver to his ear, but suspended the action, pausing to look over the instrument at Dave. "Make sure she got that straight."

"She got it straight," Annabelle said. "Thanks for your time." The irony in her voice was lost on him as he pressed the phone against his ear intently, sank into his desk chair, swiveled away from them, and twirled his glasses.

Dave opened the door into the narrow hallway that ran behind the anteroom, stood aside as Annabelle joined him, and closed Green's office door quietly. There was a door next to Green's, and Dave touched the brass doorknob, his shoulders lifting in silent inquiry at Annabelle.

"Let's lose our bearings on the way out," she signed.

Stepping back and putting his ear against Green's office door, Dave listened and then signed, "I hope his law school did not teach the mechanics of dialing Nine-one-one. Strictly speaking, Green might object to our sense of direction."

"Oh, I don't know," she whispered, a whimsical smile playing on her lips. "I got the feeling he sort of liked us. But let's use sign so we don't interrupt his important phone call."

They entered the other office, done like the rest of the suite in mahogany and green, with another Madonna in a brass niche, and with law books in a floor-to-ceiling case behind the desk, the shelves displaying several smaller statues of the Virgin, several rosaries, and other religious objects, including votive candles and holy cards. Dave closed the door softly behind them.

"I guess she was one of the stauncher Catholics," he signed. "Gives me the heebie-jeebies."

Annabelle patted her handbag. "Speaking of heebie-jeebies, this letter about the new will feels like a ticking bomb. I don't think Green has any idea. Where did you leave Marcel?"

"In the anteroom," he signed airily.

"Let's take a look at the dead woman's tabernacle of real estate delights. Maybe de Vargas had more surprises Green doesn't know about." Annabelle stood by Millie de Vargas's desk. "You look in that file cabinet. I'll take the desk."

While Dave opened drawers, which were unlocked, and leafed through files, Annabelle sat and rapidly sorted papers on the desk. They consisted mostly of recent correspondence, most dealing with the proposed Hemingway Resort. She ran her hands over the cotton weave of the slim blotter under the stacks of correspondence, encountering a slight ridge. She slid her hand under the blotter curiously and pulled out two short letters, both unsigned and childishly printed on cheap lined paper. Cheap white envelopes were taped to the letters at the corners. The addresses had been executed crudely on the envelopes, evidently from a block printing set and an ink pad, the ink a garish purple. The wording of the letters was in the same block printing, and was assaultive, frightening, terribly personal.

"Dave, have a look at these," she whispered.

He stepped to the desk, saw what she was holding, and studied the envelopes. He took the top letter from her hand and read,

WE'LL GET YOU BEFORE YOU GET THE SUNSET, YOU UGLY BITCH. BE CAREFUL WHERE YOU URINATE YOU MAY FIND A GUN UP YOUR CUNT.

Dave shivered eloquently but handed the letter back without a word and took the other one:

STOP FUCKING WITH THE SUNSET OR WE'LL TORCH YOUR SKINNY UGLY SPIC GREASY BODY.

"Got 'em?" she asked, wrinkling her nose.

He nodded, made washing motions with his hands, and went back to the files. He had a photographic memory, and anything he processed with his eyes would now be available to them again on demand, but something about those letters stirred a fresh visual memory. He scratched his head for a moment.

Annabelle slid her hand again under the blotter, farther under the pile of papers. She almost missed a finely textured sheet of paper stuck to the underside of the cotton-weave fabric, but caught her nail on its slim edge. She lifted the blotter gently, pushed the chair back and leaned sideways, peering under the blotter, and pulled out a distinctive piece of stationery. It was the silver and white letterhead of the Catholic Archdiocese of New York.

"Dave, here's one you should see," she whispered.

Again he came to the desk, and read over her shoulder as she examined the letter's contents:

January 14, 1999

Dear Millie:

I am intrigued.

The old house has certainly seen some interesting uses, but none, I expect, so worthy of heaven. Your letter exaggerates, I feel sure, but I am eager to see what you have found and appreciate your thinking of me first.

I can't get away until next Tuesday or Wednesday; the Cardinal's conference on AIDS is set for this week. It's terribly controversial, and I can't be spared. I shall get the first plane I can and be with you soonest to help you celebrate, if not gloat, which would partake of the excesses of the Tenth Commandment.

Really, I hardly know what to say. I wish I could be there today. You must be in alt.

Until next week, I remain, on the edge of my seat,

Yours in Christ,

Tim

Annabelle looked up at Dave, saw that he had finished, and replaced the three letters under the blotter. She sat for a moment in thought, finally putting her hand under the blotter again and taking out the papers. She held them in her hand, undecided, looking around the office.

"This is a problem," she whispered.

"Yeah. What to do? Leave 'em or take 'em? If we take them, they're not evidence. My memory is not admissible in court like primary evidence. All that nasty stuff and a religious friend too. She covered the gamut in her office correspondence. Arriving today or tomorrow. 'Not to gloat.' I wonder what was up?"

"I wonder who Tim is."

"I can call the archdiocese if you like. I've got the number up here," he signed, tapping his temple and reaching for the yellow phone on the desk.

"Maybe later. Green may have his ear pressed to some other phone by now. If he's not on his way in here with a can of Mace."

"Or Key West Kops, with a K. Where'd you find that trash?"

"Under the blotter."

They finished searching the desk and files quickly, nothing else appearing to be anything but routine paperwork for a real estate attorney. Annabelle did find a copy of the plans for the resort, which she spread open on the desk for Dave, along with photographs of an architect's model and a dredging study of the harbor on the west side of Tank Island.

"The resort-plot thickens," she signed. She pointed a finger at the harbor study. "The dredging operation for the resort would, no doubt, disturb some animal-rights activists. The *Herald* stories missed this angle. It looks like they were planning to deepen the harbor to provide anchorage and steerage for cruise ships. God knows what living beings would be losing their underwater homes."

"And their underwater lives. Annabelle, let's go get Marcel and get out of here. I'd hate to give Green the satisfaction of calling the cops on us. Besides, I've got to wash my hands after touching that purple filth. And I'd like to get our hands on that will hidden in the staircase," Dave signed. "Unless you'd like to take up the carpet and see if there's a postcard from the pope?"

"Wait." She had caught a flash of movement at the window. She crossed the room and pulled back the ivy-green curtain.

There on the narrow window ledge, trapped, with nowhere to go but down a full story onto a small concrete lot covered with broken glass, huddled a large ginger cat, too hoarse from what must have been a night and day of howling to do more than emit an open-mouthed, silent cry.

Annabelle quickly but silently yanked the window up, gently pulling the cat inside. "Poor kitty," she murmured, stroking its head and nestling it in her arms.

"There's your hiding place," Dave signed, his lips compressed in a thin line of checked emotion, taking the cat from her.

She put the three letters out on the window ledge, anchored them with a heavy votive candle from the bookshelves, glanced toward the harbor over the low, sunny rooftops flanking Mallory Square, shut the window, and pulled the curtains together.

Dumping the cat back into Annabelle's arms, Dave stepped quickly to the bookshelves. He had spotted the distinctive blue and white dust jacket of *The Gender Contract: Common Law, Sexual Difference, and the Battle for the Pen*, Annabelle's highly successful study of the historical legal basis for excluding women from the project of writing. Dave had read his autographed copy twice. He pulled the book out partially, gesturing to Annabelle.

"She's got your book," he signed.

"I've always been surprised how many lawyers have read it," she returned. "Not just the usual ivory-tower crowd."

They left the office, Annabelle carrying the cat, which was still silently crying, and Dave following them into the ante-room.

Green, the skin around his eyes now a frightening red band across the upper portion of his face, stood transfixed in the center of the room, staring at the brass niche. Marcel, from his perch on the mahogany Madonna, spotted Dave and flew to his shoulder, alternately eyeing the attorney and the open mouth of the large cat in Annabelle's arms.

"We had to go to the bathroom," Dave said with dry insouciance. "This your cat?"

Green shook his head vehemently, apparently struck dumb in the center of the room.

Annabelle, deciding that the only discrete course open to her was to pretend that she was not there, ignored the attorney and stalked toward the outer door. Dave followed her.

But when she turned at the door, contemplating a parting glance at the attorney's face, she was stopped by a vision in the niche.

A yellow light emanated from it, flashing on and off at regular intervals. Dave's huge gold bow tie, the tie he had meant to wear to lunch in Miami, had been fastened around the smooth wooden neck of the Madonna, and a plastic squeeze-bulb was encircled neatly with a tight rubber band and stuck to the base of the statue with clear tape. On and off, on and off, the tiny bulbs in the tie flashed. Against the golden background of the bow tie, a miniature and exceedingly bright-green electric frog wearing an inane grin pumped his underside with happy vigor against the rear of a smaller raspberry-colored frog and discharged a cheerful electric-green stream, under the flashing lighted words: *Now THIS is art*.

Dave studied the effect, his head tilted to one side.

"Words to live by, Green," he said urbanely, and followed Annabelle down the dark stairs.

SEVEN

MARCEL REFUSED TO ENTER THE PINK CAB WITH Annabelle and the cat, leaping nervously onto the car's roof whenever Dave ducked his head to get in.

"Get another cab and follow us," Annabelle finally said, her patience worn out. She pulled the door shut and spoke to her driver.

Presently two cabs drew up in front of 907 Whitehead.

Annabelle and Dave stepped out of their respective pink cars, left their respective animals as hostages, and walked through the gate held wide open by the blue-shirted guard.

This time Annabelle's knock was answered almost immediately, Ashleen Ricou's unsmiling face taking stock of them once again.

Before the older woman could say anything, Annabelle launched into speech, at the same time opening her handbag and taking out the letter from de Vargas. "You can read this if you like. I have instructions to open a secret compartment and get something belonging to Millie de Vargas."

"Who gave you those instructions?"

"Millie de Vargas."

Grudgingly, Ashleen Ricou opened the screen door and held out her hand for the letter. She stepped back under the foyer's Venetian-glass chandelier to read the letter. Then she returned to the door, gave the letter back to Annabelle, and stood aside for them to enter. Her face evinced no emotion beyond what seemed to be her customary freeze, showing no special reaction to the existence of a new will, or of a secret hiding place.

Annabelle went quickly to the staircase. The white newel was topped by a shiny brass dome. She examined the dome, saw nothing to indicate how to open the device, and, throwing caution to the wind, gave it a firm twist.

Nothing happened.

"I wonder if you have to utter special words," Dave put in. "You know, something like 'Open Sesame.' Or 'God Save the Queen.' Do you have your gun? We could blast its ugly head off."

Annabelle frowned. "If we have to get a hacksaw, we can. But it would be a pity to disfigure this beautiful post." Her frown deepened.

"You'll touch nothing in *this* house with a hacksaw, you godless hoods from Miami, with your violence and your drugs," Ashleen Ricou declared icily through gritted teeth. "Unless you kill me first. And from what I've seen today, killing is now a done thing even in Key West. Gun indeed. Hacksaw indeed. I've got a good mind to call the police."

"Stand back," Dave said, giving Annabelle's arm a gentle nudge. He ran his fingers lightly over the metal surface of the dome, scanning the metal tactilely for its secret. Under the ridged bottom of the piece, facing the ascending railing, he felt a tiny imperfection in the smooth surface, like an enlarged pore.

"If you can open that thing with an eel, you smug varmint," Ashleen Ricou said, a nasty gleam in her cold blue eyes, "you're a better man than you appear."

"Oh, I'm definitely a better man than I appear," Dave said,

a hint of surprise on his mobile features as he contemplated the snide curl of her papery lips.

He bent toward the dome, having extracted a needle-thin slice of metal from a black plastic case he had caused to materialize, as if by magic, from the pocket of his baggy shorts. He inserted the needle's tip into the pore and heard a faint click, almost like the first note of a cricket's chirp, suspended in mid-utterance. He twisted the dome lightly, and it rotated easily.

Lifting it off the post, he turned the piece over in his hand. Packed inside the roof of the dome was a document, wrinkled tightly along the curve of the metal; he had to pry the paper loose with considerable strength and the help of his pick before it showed any sign of being capable of removal.

Annabelle stuck her hand into the bowllike white depression now revealed in the post itself. It was empty.

"Good place to hide trinkets," she said. She gazed at Ashleen Ricou. "Did you know about this secret compartment?"

"What I know and don't know is none of your business, as I told you before. The only thing I have to say to you—to the police, to the press, to anybody—is, 'This is the Hemingway Museum. It will open tomorrow on its regular schedule. Get out.'"

"We'll get out," Annabelle said. "But I hope you remember where we just found this document." She took a pen from her handbag. "Will you please just initial it on the back?"

Ashleen Ricou considered the document skeptically. "You initial it," she said after a long moment. "I'll remember your initials."

Dave held the paper. Annabelle wrote, *Found in the presence of Ashleen Ricou and Jorge Enamorado, January 21, 1999. AH-M.*

Dave replaced the brass dome, stuck the document in his back pocket, and walked out of the foyer onto the veranda, replacing the black kit in his pocket. Annabelle exchanged cold looks with Ashleen Ricou.

Feeling oddly bold, like a novice actress secretly experimenting backstage with the costume of a streetwalker, complete with tall boots, Annabelle decided to tempt her fate and studied the older woman's wrinkled, aloof face. "Miss Ricou, where were you at sundown yesterday?"

Annabelle did not know what she was expecting from the older woman, but she was surprised to notice the glimmer of a grim smile on those old lips; it was gone as quickly as it had appeared, and the answer came succinctly. "At home, eating dinner like a Christian. Alone. Now, get out."

And then Annabelle, too, left the house, unable to think of another single question the woman was likely to answer, and bemused by her own fantasy.

"I'll meet you at the hotel," Dave signed. "What a cold fish she is, brrrr."

The cabs departed the museum, to rendezvous at Zero Duval Street, the address of Ocean Key House.

Annabelle's cab was slightly behind Dave's, but they arrived at the hotel during a rush of tourists checking in, so both cabs discharged their passengers half a block down the street, and they walked to the hotel. Fortunately the manager had alerted the front desk about "Dr. Annabelle Hardy-Maratos and her party," and they were escorted across an underground parking lot to an elevator, bypassing the long lines. After an initial flurry of protests from Marcel, it was decided that two cars would again be necessary, and they took separate elevators.

Dave inserted the flat plastic key in the door of Suite 409 and pushed. The wind was blowing in from the huge balcony at the other end of the suite of rooms, and Marcel dug his claws into Dave's shirt to brace himself. Dave yelped, the bird squawked, the cat in Annabelle's arms lunged forward, and the door slammed shut again, leaving the cat inside and the others outside in the hall.

"*Cristo en el cuarto de aseo,*" Dave growled. "Annabelle, I'm getting really tired of these pests. I'm beginning to sympathize with Noah Green, the allergy king." He opened the door again, this time with force, forewarned about the wind. The management had apparently been busy, demonstrating their thoughtfulness by opening the balcony doors for a favorite guest.

Suite 409 at Ocean Key House, the room they always gave her, was Annabelle's favorite place to stay in Key West, for it commanded a spectacular view of the harbor, poised—four floors above Mallory Square and Key West's largest sunset dock—on an imaginary line dividing the Gulf of Mexico from the Atlantic, facing the long, slim, low bump that was the now-controversial undeveloped Tank Island, bare except for a few scrubby bushes, an almost negligible interruption in the line of sight between the waterfront and the western horizon.

She had spent her honeymoon here in this suite with Nikki Maratos, nine years earlier, and even his death, two years later, had not cast a pall over her attachment to the place. Her brief marriage to Nikki, when they were both fresh with large ideas—fostered for Nikki by the Yale Law School and for her by the graduate school—had been perhaps the largest idea of her life, an idea founded on zealous ideals and nurtured on common altruistic goals. Now, at age thirty-four, an acclaimed book on the legal basis of sexist writing and a practically unused Ph.D. in English Literature behind her, her hearing loss total, the active presidency of her father's security company the focus of her life, Annabelle wondered what Nikki, beloved Nikki, would think of what she had become.

Dave, who had never been in Suite 409, wandered around with ostentatious nonchalance, ostensibly looking for the cat but, she knew, actually snooping for ghosts. Dave knew her story, knew that this was the honeymoon suite, probably expected to trip over memories. But the memories were not in this suite of rooms; they were locked away in some dark and forbidding library of the mind, a library not even she bothered to visit anymore, a dusty room—ruthlessly cataloged and systematically comprehensive of her romantic and sexual self, but closed forever, she thought, to the foundation of new memories of the kind she had built with Nikki. Despite Dave's essentially prudish belief that men had base and basic designs on what he imagined to be her widowed virtue, Annabelle had not, except for one brief temptation that had only confirmed her celibacy, looked twice seriously at another man since Nikki.

She swallowed, dropped her handbag on the glass dining table, which had chairs for eight people, and walked into the living room. From there, standing beside the L-shaped couch, she could see Dave exploring the enormous balcony, which spanned the width of the living room and the bedroom next door to the left, a total width of approximately twenty-five feet. Both rooms opened onto the balcony, and she stepped out from the living room to survey the harbor view, framed by the fronds of a coconut palm that reached almost to the fourth floor and by the weathered two-hundred-foot dock below that contained tables, chairs, space and electrical wiring for a band, and a thatched Tiki bar and grill. Dave, temporarily uninterested in the outer scene, stepped into the bedroom, disappearing from sight.

He emerged again almost immediately, wearing the Hemingway mask he had purchased at Dizzy Izzy's on Duval Street.

Annabelle gasped and put out her hand to touch the balcony's railing.

"Ho, low-life scum woman," he signed, "wanna see the hair on my chest and other manly goodies?"

"Jesus, Dave, you scared me."

"Frankly, *I* scare me. Being a posturing male like Hemingway is not easy for me. I may have to work up to the part. The Jacuzzi, by the way, is the end of bourgeois attempts to return to the days of the Roman Empire. In fact it's downright vulgar—comes up to my chest."

"Take that ugly thing off."

"Silence, woman! I'm feeling an urge to demand my dinner or a rousing brawl in a dockside bar, before I fight a bull." Dave shook his masked head violently. "Christ on a carillon, my voice echoes around inside this thing." He shook his head again. "Let's get back to that Jacuzzi."

"There's one like it in your room too," she said, thumping the rubber mask with the flat of her hand. She pointed to the balcony over her head. When they had been escorted past the line at the desk, an oddly assorted foursome with the addition of the cat, she had been told by the apparently romantic concierge that Dave would be in 509, told that he would be *very* comfortable in a room close to hers, told that other rooms on the fourth floor would not give him the same sense of nearness. The balconies were what mattered here on the harbor, she was told unnecessarily, because of the awesome sunsets over Tank Island, and Dave's balcony would be directly above hers.

"Do you think they had to kick some poor sucker out to give us these rooms?" Dave asked. "It's the high season in Key West."

"I don't like to think about that. It makes me feel like such a bloodsucking capitalist."

Dave leaned far over the balcony and leered through the mask at people strolling on the bright sunset dock, four stories below him, and lounging in swimming suits on boats crossing rolling wakes into the marina. He waved his hand in what he imagined was the ruthless manner of a bloodsucking capitalist. When he righted himself, he obligingly changed the subject, casting a long glance at Tank Island.

"Sure is gonna be a shame when that hotel goes up," he signed. "Sure is gonna be ugly. Sure is gonna be stupid to sit out on this nice balcony, or down on that dock, or over there at Mallory Square, and stare at the backside of eight floors of modern stucco at sunset time."

"It makes me sick," Annabelle said. "Makes you wonder about the navy's role in this farce."

"Speaking of naval farces, young Popeye Ricou was as good as his word," he signed. "Your suitcase is in the bedroom. And so is the cat. It's really shy, so it's hiding on the center of the bed, lying there on its back in an attitude of great reserve and modesty. It's a boy, by the way, a cat Hemingway would have been proud of—*cajones* the size of key limes. I couldn't help noticing. Shall we open the will?"

Annabelle kicked off her shoes and walked barefoot on the warm balcony into the bedroom. She smiled at the cat, who was indeed asleep on the king-size bed, and flopped down beside him. He opened one yellow eye and regarded her as she propped herself on her elbow, then closed his eye partially, truly asleep but presenting an odd air of casual scrutiny to her sideways vista. Dave sat on the edge of the bed, plucking impatiently at the floral coverlet. Marcel waddled down Dave's arm and, giving the cat as wide a berth as possible without falling off the bed, made his way up to the pillows and squatted, his head cocked alertly, apparently willing to share space with the cat as long as that space was not enclosed.

Dave took the wrinkled document from his pocket and dropped it on the bed. "I wonder what's behind door number three," he signed, before rotating his wrists, picking up the will, and snapping the thick paper in the air.

"You haven't already peeked?"

He shook his head. "I'm the soul of discretion." The paper crinkled as he unfolded it. "Besides, my cab driver was trying to date me." He started reading.

"I wish you'd take that hideous mask off."

Dave continued to peruse the document through the eye holes of the mask, turned his head from side to side. "It's sure short." He handed Annabelle the wrinkled document:

I, Milady Maria de Vargas, being of sound mind and body, hereby leave all the worldly goods of which I die possessed, with the exception of my share of the law firm of de Vargas and Green, to the use of Monsignor Timothy Cullen, Archdiocese of New York, on the hopeful assumption that his good judgment will tell him how to use any part of those goods in support of the Hemingway Museum or the Waterfront Playhouse, both in Key West, Florida. My share in the law firm of de Vargas and Green I leave to my partner, Noah S. Green, and I hope that he will continue its proud tradition of making Key West grow. It is my wish that Annabelle Hardy-Maratos, of Miami, Florida, will see to the probation and proper execution of my last wishes.

Annabelle finished reading, and looked at Dave searchingly, but could discern nothing of his reaction because of the mask. She returned to the will.

It was executed in black ink, entirely written by hand, including the date at the end, which was November 18, 1998, and the flowing signature. Two different signatures followed that of Millie de Vargas, and the document bore the raised seal of a Key West notary, as well as his signature.

"Holy sweeping change of mind," Annabelle said, fanning herself slowly with the paper. "But it sure looks legal."

"I'll just make a little call to our legal department," Dave signed.

He dialed a number on the phone beside the bed, flipped the mask up over his forehead, waited, spoke, waited again, spoke, waited again, and finally spoke at some length, reciting the will from memory and describing its execution entirely by the signer, and then listened briefly, but with concentration. He hung up the phone.

"Joel Schockett says it's legal if it's her handwriting. He says it's an unusual thing, but probably quite legitimate."

Annabelle raised her eyebrows.

"Did he tell us what to do with it?"

"He said not to let it out of our sight. He'll be here tomorrow morning, with a handwriting expert." Dave pursed his lips and reached for the paper in Annabelle's hand. "I wonder who Damien Balsamo and Elaine Dudley are." He rubbed his thumb carefully over the witnessing signatures.

"Isn't there a phone book in that nightstand?"

Dave opened the single drawer in the table and pulled out the slim Key West phone book. He flipped pages. "Here's a D. Balsamo on Truman Avenue." He flipped more pages. "And here's an Elaine Dudley." He dropped the phone book on the carpeted floor, reached for the phone, and dialed the first number, tossing the will onto the pillow beside him.

Annabelle rose and opened her suitcase, extracting a hairbrush and studying her reflection in the large mirror over the dresser opposite the bed. When Dave hung up the phone, she watched his face in the mirror, but she became disoriented by the reversed image of his lips and turned around. He started over, using sign.

"They both work at Danny's Fish Market, a restaurant on Duval next to the notary, who operates out of a photo shop. Balsamo says they never saw the words of the will, just witnessed the signature. Says Millie paid them each twenty bucks to come watch her write her name."

"Think Noah Green will have a fit?"

"I'd love to be the one to tell him he's not getting his two-million-dollar bonus. Nothing personal; I just think it would be interesting."

"Yeah." She returned to the bed and slid the will under a pillow. "Green." She plumped the pillow. "I imagine his ego's made out of steel and horsehair. No, he'd be allergic to that. Steel and galvanized rubber."

"And maybe a little typewriter ribbon. I think he killed Millie de Vargas."

"You sound so definite. Why? The two million?"

"That, and the fact that he's a consummate donkey. But, just consider his name."

"Green?"

"Noah, dummy." Dave pulled the mask down over his face.

"What's so significant about Noah? Because of Noah's ark? *Ark* begins with *A*?"

"Use your brains, woman, or whatever you have in that pretty little head. No . . . ah. No *A*. When Millie pulled that letter off, she left a typewriter with *no A*."

Annabelle considered for a moment, then waved her hand dismissively. "That's hideously clever. Nobody but you would ever think of it."

"Ah, I see you're suffering a mild case of penis envy." He stroked the brown rubber mustache on his mask. "My dear, that's a piece of classic deduction, pure genius on my part, something a mere woman could not understand. Now I shall indulge in what we shall call speculation, which is at least twenty percent of the lifeblood of the male detective, the other eighty percent being raw and savage muscle. Listen carefully and learn something from a man. Green may have been in a hurry to inherit. Or maybe he was getting hate mail as well, two reeking samples of which you have hidden on Millie's windowsill. I hope it doesn't rain, but it never does in Key West. So, anyway, he threw Millie to the environmental wolves as a human sacrifice. And he now inherits the whole partnership and, he thinks, two million. I call that a fair day's work for a strangler. Too bad for him about the new will, but you can't plan for everything. Green has a grade-A motive, if you'll pardon the alphabetic expression. Unlike Perez." Dave stroked the cat's white belly.

"What shall we call him?" Annabelle asked, idly glancing at the sleeping animal.

"Let's call him Millie's Cat."

"Why didn't I think of that?"

"Because you're only a miserable, feeble-minded wench. Where's my dinner? Let's make a baby—a boy baby that you can smother with your unhealthy desires and I can teach to kill things."

Annabelle giggled and lay still on the bed, her green eyes staring at the ceiling fan turning slowly above their heads. She stifled a yawn. "I'm falling asleep. Let's get out of this bower and go find the brother."

"The *poor* brother."

EIGHT

THEY TOOK MARCEL AND STROLLED IN THE SOPORIFIC
heat toward Mallory Square and the Waterfront Playhouse. Annabelle had once seen a depressing production of
Elmer Rice's *The Adding Machine* at the playhouse, and she
remembered its almost hidden location behind the livelier
shops and museums of the square.

"This is really pig city," Dave said, gazing up at the mold-
and-mildew-stained white stucco walls of the little theater.
"Real squalor, compared to the rest of Old Town."

"It's not so bad inside," Annabelle said. "I'm told it enjoys
especially good acoustics"—she gave him a rueful smile—"because the interior walls are made of coral rock. And you can't
beat the location. One of the best views of the sunset in Key
West. That must be quite a draw."

They tried the doors at the front of the theater but found
them securely locked. Annabelle studied a sun-faded playbill
posted inside a glass-fronted case mounted beside the steps.

"They just finished *Cinderella*. I didn't know they did children's plays." She gestured toward the side of the building.
"Let's try around back."

But the stage door, too, was locked.

"Okay," Annabelle said, frustrated. "Why don't we go find

those public records on the resort? There must be a chamber of commerce or something. Aren't you hot in that mask?"

"Of course I'm hot. What red-blooded man wouldn't be?"

They walked through the open-air Sponge Market, signing to each other and picking over the sponges, shells, and jewelry in crates along the walls.

"I wonder if we can see the votive candle and the letters from here," Dave signed. "The cat window overlooks the square. If I had binoculars, I could see if Noah Green is in there strangling someone with his glasses."

"I wouldn't be too quick to settle for Noah Green as the strangler." She yawned. "It seems much hotter here than in Miami." She covered another yawn and stroked a shell necklace. "But Green did give us a great deal to think about. Including why Millie chose me to find the new will. And why she came to Miami that day two months ago to hire us for the museum. Do you think she was looking me over? Dave, why do you think Millie really hired us? And why have us guard the mansion, instead of her home or office? Was she scared, as Green says? She only hired us two months ago, and the resort project is much older than that, if that's what frightened her." She stopped suddenly and dropped the necklace back into a wooden bin. "That hate mail. I never noticed the dates on the postmarks."

She turned her eyes to Dave's masked face, aware that several shoppers had stopped to take in the spectacle of a slim man wearing an Ernest Hemingway mask and communicating in sign language in the middle of the Sponge Market.

Dave flipped the mask out of his way. "Both last month, December fourth and December sixteenth. Both after she hired us."

"Then it wasn't fear inspired by those disgusting letters that made her hire us."

"Maybe she hired us two months ago for another reason. Maybe Green's speculating through his hat. He should get a mask like this one; it really clarifies my thinking." He patted the rubber face on the top of his head fondly and beamed at Annabelle.

They left the Sponge Market and strolled in front of the Key West Aquarium, which was between shows and deserted.

"Maybe Millie hired us for the same reason most people hire a security firm," Annabelle signed. "Maybe she had something really valuable at the mansion. Something that showed up two months ago, or something that she brought there two months ago. Perhaps something that made her alter her will in favor of that priest. Of course I have no clue what it could be that Millie found—perhaps a rare book? A manuscript she uncovered? A previously unpublished Hemingway novel?"

"We should ask Ashleen Ricou," Dave said, pointing and pulling his mask in place. "See the sign? She's over there by the chamber of commerce office, with an armload of brochures. She doesn't like me, so you'll have to ask her. She's probably waiting impatiently for us to run over and ask her a few probing questions."

"She doesn't like me either. I wonder what makes her so sour."

"Maybe the fact that she killed Millie de Vargas, after waiting in line behind Green, the varmint."

"Why? Because her name begins with *A*? That's stretching things."

"No, my dear. That's a piece of deduction. She killed de Vargas to gain control of the museum's finances. And, according to the first will, the museum does inherit money. Maybe old Ashleen wanted to buy a new dead animal head for the studio. She struck me as a strong woman, quite capable of threading that ribbon around Millie's silken throat. Ashleen now reigns supreme over the Hemingway legend, untroubled by outside interference."

When Ashleen Ricou had left the two-story frame building

housing the chamber of commerce, Annabelle and Dave went in. Dave approached one of the women staffing the desk.

"I'd like to see the public documents for the new resort out on Tank Island," Dave said.

"Planning and Zoning is upstairs, to your right," the clerk said. "Is that a miniature Brazil parrot?"

"Yeah. You want him?"

The clerk narrowed her eyes. "How much?"

"Two thousand."

"That's not bad," she said.

"Let me know."

"Where can I find you?"

"Two-oh-two Duval Street. Just ask for Noah Green."

Dave and Annabelle climbed the winding stairs to the stifling second floor.

"I guess they haven't heard of air-conditioning," he signed.

Inside a cramped little office filled with buzzing flies, they were shown a thick folder, almost a foot thick, containing what appeared to be randomly organized papers—requests for variances, commission minutes, expense chits.

"Are they kidding?" Dave demanded. "This is a jungle."

"Nikki used to say that all planning-and-zoning offices are like this. They're always the most powerful group in a town, and he said that keeping their papers legally available by the Freedom of Information laws, as well as impossibly filed— well, that helps them protect their butts. The average citizen can't tell what they're up to, but they're well within the law."

"Jeez." But Dave started going through the stack of papers, one by one, shaking his head and sighing.

"Here, give me a stack," Annabelle said.

They stood side by side at a counter in the hot office, taking the papers one by one, eliminating them quickly if they could, reading a few paragraphs if necessary.

Dave was heaving sighs every few minutes, perspiration

having soaked his shirt. He pinched the fabric away from his skin and went back to his stack. He swatted flies futilely, but at last achieved a victory of sorts when he landed the flat of his hand on a particularly sluggish fly that had taken a position on the chin of the Hemingway mask.

"Got him," he exclaimed proudly, but drew his hand away hastily when he saw the mess he had made. He wiped his hand on his shorts and went back to the stack.

Annabelle glanced at the mess on the mask, made a face, and looked up at the clock. It was already 4:10.

She returned to her stack, now also heaving sighs.

"I think this is it," Dave said at last, holding out a slim sheaf of papers stapled together. "It's dated December fourth. The most recent list I can find."

Annabelle looked it over quickly. Investors in Hemingway Resort and Marina, Inc., were indeed listed on the third sheet, following what seemed to her to be many useless pages of real estate junk. It looked like Millie de Vargas was the chief private investor, holding 40 percent of the shares.

"Memorize it," she said. "And let's get out of this inferno." Her red dress was sticking to her back, and she was heartily sick of the flies buzzing around her hair.

They practically ran down the stairs into the relative coolness of the chamber of commerce office and out onto Mallory Square.

They threaded their way through a crowd in front of Dirty Don's Deep Sea Dive and stood at an outdoor counter, where they ordered and ate cold she-crab soup and consumed a pitcher of iced tea between them. They walked back to Ocean Key House, stopping first at the Waterfront Playhouse, which was still closed.

The elevator was hot, and Annabelle drooped against the wall. "We should go for a swim," she said. "I haven't done laps today."

They entered Suite 409, walked languidly toward the balcony, where Annabelle at once again kicked off her shoes, and almost immediately Dave heard a knock on the outer door. He signed "door," pulling the mask in place again over his face. Annabelle went into the bedroom and dropped onto the bed.

Dave returned with a towering arrangement of orchids and bird-of-paradise in full bloom and the mask still on his face. He dumped the flowers on the dresser in their heavy vase and ripped the small white envelope off the plastic support tied to one of the stems.

"I'll bet I can guess who sent you this little posy," he signed, the envelope still in his hand. He sniffed the envelope through the mask. "Yes, yes, the aroma of canned spinach."

She stood hastily, crossed to the dresser, touched the orange and blue flowers, and snatched the card from Dave's outstretched hand.

"This seems to be my day to receive unexpected messages," she said, smiling.

"Is it too much to hope that this one is also from the grave?"

She opened the card. It said, simply, *Welcome to paradise. Roy.*

"Well?" Dave prodded.

"It's from Lieutenant Ricou."

"I knew it!" Dave slapped his thigh explosively. "I can't take you anywhere. You must have hormones nobody ever heard of." He massaged his thigh and yanked up the billowing leg of his black shorts. There was an angry red splotch above his knee. "Ouch." He went out and took a turn on the balcony, tripped on one of her red shoes, and picked it up angrily, carrying it back into the bedroom and flipping up his mask.

"Annabelle, you must never leave your shoes lying about. Do you have any idea how big they are? I know you're a tall woman, but really. This looks like it was made for Larry Bird." He held the offending shoe at arm's length. "What were you doing with your shoe in Hemingway's truly annoying studio cottage, that museum of dead heads? What was that stuff on the floor by the chair?" He tossed the shoe and it bounced behind her suitcase.

"I don't know, just something a little sticky," she said. "It probably wasn't anything."

Annabelle sat on the bed, gazed at the flowers from Ricou, and exercised control of her facial muscles, preventing a smile from arriving on her lips.

"Don't screw your face into a dried apricot like that," Dave signed. "Makes you look like an empty light socket. Besides, Ensign Ricou is no different from all the other little boys who like to dangle on your tree."

Annabelle threw a pillow at him, which he caught before sinking onto the bed. He felt Marcel leave his shoulder, and glanced around the room, finding the little green bird at last tucked into a compact ball between the pillows and the mattress, perfectly content, his eyes closed.

Dave, too, had arisen early that morning—it seemed an eternity, or a different universe, their building renovation in Miami—and it had been a long day. It was also an unusually warm day for Key West in January, and the balmy breezes had exerted a soporific influence on his customarily energetic system. The opiate of floral scents was draped over the town like a stuffy blanket and was considerably augmented by the positively sedative orchids from Ricou. The planning-and-zoning office had been hell. And the bed was very inviting. But he hesitated when the idea of lying down occurred to him. He had no wish to insult Annabelle by falling asleep while conversing with her; indeed his only wish on that score was to insult her *while* conversing with her. And though it was true that they were extremely close friends, such callous behavior would no doubt border on being rude. He tried to picture himself as Spencer Tracy falling asleep while Katherine Hepburn was speaking, and the picture was fuzzy. He then tried

Fred Astaire and Ginger Rogers, and found his eyelids closing as he sat on the side of the bed.

Annabelle gazed at him. "The only question the Ricou dragon lady answered on our first visit to the Hemingway Museum was about her naval relative. Lieutenant Ricou should have mentioned that his aunt sort of runs that place. Are you awake?"

Dave's eyes flew open. He was disconcerted, his wandering thoughts still running toward a two-step, and he stumbled back mentally to their conversation. "Ricou? Why? Maybe he's only a busybody when he's sending flowers to beautiful women he barely knows. It was probably because of his aunt that he got the call from Commander Whats-his-Polish-name to come chaperone us. I see nothing sinister there."

"I thought you didn't like Lieutenant Ricou. How come you're defending him now when you've been accusing everyone else of murder?"

"Oh, I was only defending him about the aunt. Great-aunt actually. But when it comes to Millie's murder, he's as guilty as everyone else on this island."

"Why? All of his names begin with R. You're being silly."

He pulled the mask over his face to shade his eyes from the sun before cracking his knuckles and bringing his hands together in front of his chest. "No, you dumb broad." Dave stroked the rubber mustache between signs. "I'm being hideously logical, if you can understand such a thing. The letter R itself begins with A. Say it aloud to yourself in your mind." He thought she had a perfect memory for sounds, given the devotion she still lavished on poetry.

She laughed.

"You're right."

"Of course I'm right. Besides, Popeye Ricou must have killed her, after Noah and Ashleen had expressed themselves sartorially by fashioning new neckwear for the victim. Ricou got his aunt to give him the inside scoop on Millie's movements, put on his cape, flew into the estate, lightly tossed his makeshift garotte around her neck, and flitted away again into the night, having satiated his blood lust. He killed her to get you down here so he could lure you into some naval seduction, speaking of lust." Dave's sign for "lust" was followed by another sign, an extremely vulgar gesture he had been proud to include in his visual-gestural vocabulary long before he had met Annabelle and learned American Sign Language.

She grunted sleepily.

"Try this," Dave continued. "He killed her because that was easier than negotiating her out of the rights to Tank Island. Those rights include an Uncle Sam thing about eminent domain, which in this case could only mean weapons or tactical stuff like that. Maybe those rights to Tank Island included his job, and he was worried he'd have to leave paradise and go manage weapons at some outpost in Alaska, where he'd have to make all of his own sailor suits by hand out of whale blubber." Dave watched enviously as the cat stretched in his sleep. "Or maybe he killed her because she was scuba diving in his space. It's a small ocean, the Gulf of Mexico, hardly more than a respectable lake."

Annabelle yawned audibly and lay back on the pillows. "Dave, whoever killed Millie de Vargas, for whatever reason, we've still got a guard in deep shit. Perez needs legal help. Was that Arantxa who put you through to Legal when you were asking about the will?"

"Yes. She's found Perez a Key West lawyer named Goodman, Bob Goodman. Very appropriate name. But he'd better be good, because I definitely think Gabriel Perez is our strangler. I can't imagine what his motive was, but let's face it, the guards were the only ones with opportunity and means, and Perez thoughtfully left his fingerprints where they have no business being. Forget Green, Ricou, and the other Ricou. What a mess. We have people with possible motives who could not possibly have done the murder, and we have our own guards who could have done it but had no reason to do so. Nobody but the guards was there last night. Unless Millie strangled herself, leaving us that clue of the letter A, which in her case would stand for *attorney*. I don't know what her motive would be." Dave yawned behind the mask, pushing the rubber chin out with his jaw.

"That's the silliest of all. Much worse than 'Noah/no A.'"

"Oh no, it's not, Annabelle. Now that I think of it, it had to be her. She planted the cape on the stairs to the studio to implicate supernatural forces. We know how interested she was in religion. Women are prey to that sort of nonsense, you know."

"And what about Tim, you male-chauvinist piece of pork on a skewer?"

"Isn't that a phallic image? You women really give yourselves away every time. Let's see. Tim? Oh, the Archdiocese-of-New-York-Tim, the new heir to the de Vargas fortune. Well, I think he killed her. Jesus, that studio must have been crowded."

"Why Tim? He wasn't even in Key West. Oh. Because of *archdiocese* beginning with *A*?"

"Don't be silly, woman. Even with your powder-puff brain, you can use some powers of deduction. Archdiocese Tim killed her because of what she found and because he really wanted to gloat and thought she would tell on him to the pope. And maybe she told him she was changing her will. That's it, of course it was him. Archdiocese Tim inherits the whole fortune. As for his not being here in Key West, perhaps he had some long-distance help." He gestured lugubriously toward the ceiling. "And I don't mean MCI."

Annabelle sat up suddenly.

"Dave. That's it. That puts it all together."

"What? MCI?"

"Listen. She found something, as Tim said in that letter. Something valuable. About two months ago, when she hired us. And she wrote to Tim about it. I wonder what she would write to an archdiocesan about? I don't think the Catholic church would care about an unpublished Hemingway manuscript." She paused for a moment, her brow wrinkled in thought. "Anyway, it was something so valuable that she wanted to hire guards to protect it. And somebody killed her to get the valuable thing she found. This scenario has the principal virtue of being simple and direct."

Dave rubbed his sleepy eyes through the mask, sticking his fingers in through the eye holes.

"Pardon me," he said, "I'm developing an allergy. Little woman, you may have stumbled onto something with your intuition, or whatever you call that PMS stuff. And, convenient for this little script you're writing, where Archdiocese Tim knows about what she found, he also inherits control of her fortune by the new will. Then, in this scenario, what does the A stand for? I bet you can't answer that one."

She smiled seraphically.

"It stands for me, Annabelle."

"Don't be so conceited."

"Dave, she also called attention to me with that letter about her new will."

Dave raised his legs onto the bed and tentatively rested his head on the pillows. Marcel squawked suddenly, and Dave tugged the pillow forward to give the bird room. "These pillows are vulgarly soft," he said. "This is a den of decadence, Annabelle. I never sleep in the afternoon, you know. You must be doing one of those vaginal things to emasculate me. What do you call it? It's in your book."

Annabelle sighed. "I've told you a thousand times. *Vagina dentata*. Latin for 'toothed vagina.' A medieval medical construct formulated by sleazy monks as the rational basis for their irrational fear of castration by women, and thus the rational, medical basis for restricting the participation of women in society. Men are so hideously rational."

Dave was holding his eyes open by an effort of will. "Yeah, that's what I meant. Very sound theory." He patted the mask. "Speaking of hatred of women, maybe the cops will find those frightfully purple hate letters we hid out on the window, and something will turn up that way. Maybe Green was Millie's pen pal, getting even with her for the C-A-T. Maybe we'll learn something when the autopsy's finished," he signed sluggishly. His right arm dropped across the pillow toward her side of the bed.

"Maybe," she said, yawning. "What about the brother? He inherits quite a bit by the first will. But his name, alas, begins with F. I wish the playhouse had been open."

She lay back on the pillows, absently stroking the cat.

The breeze had died down, softly blowing warm sea air in now through the open door to the balcony. The ceiling fan turned slowly overhead. The mattress moved rhythmically, a radiation of the gentle snores emanating from Dave the Monkeyman via the mask of Ernest Hemingway.

The sun seemed to inch across the sky during the next forty-five minutes, its rays gradually invading Suite 409, casting yellow warmth across the sleepers as it approached its assignation with the horizon and its date with the crowds gathering on the two-hundred-foot dock below and at Mallory Square beside the hotel's waterfront.

As the yellow rays paled, fading into whiteness, the shadows in the room grew sharper, and Dave startled himself out of a dream. Annabelle's luxuriant hair tickled his chin under the mask, and he glanced in confusion at the sight of her nestled in his arms. In his sleep he had apparently wrapped himself around her rather liberally, like a watermelon tendril around the parent plant, or as if they were engaged in an energetic dance, and his right arm was asleep.

A homey sound reached his ears, and at first he thought the cat had developed an interesting variation on purring, but he soon realized, with the kind of sensational insight that had stunned Archimedes, that his best friend—a respectable female—was snoring like a drunk on a Bayfront Park bench.

Inch by slow inch, the increments of his progress as imperceptible as the sun's on its westering course, Dave withdrew his arms and legs from Annabelle's cozy warmth. She was deeply asleep, and Dave finally made it off the bed onto the pale-green carpet without waking her. He tiptoed around the bed toward the living room, Marcel following behind in a kind of uncertain wobble on the thick carpet. When Dave reached the bedroom door, he tiptoed across to the dining table. There he found Annabelle's handbag, which he opened. He was surprised to see that she had been carrying her .32-caliber Walther TPH—he had been kidding about her gun back in the Hemingway Museum when they had opened the concealed compartment; they had not discussed guns before they had hastily packed for the trip to Key West, and his own Colt was in his office in the Pink Building.

He extracted Ricou's typewritten list of phone numbers, spread it open, turned it over, took a pen from the pocket of his baggy black shorts, and, on a sudden happy inspiration, removed the mask from his sweating face. He placed the mask on the table, propped up against a cardboard in-room movie schedule, and scrawled a hasty pair of messily executed sentences on the back of Ricou's note: *Anna, meet me on the sunset dock when you spot me from your balcony. I'll be the one wearing a Fred Astaire suit and will be taking you to dinner. Dave.*

He patted his note appreciatively, folded it, and stuffed it into Hemingway's rubber mouth. Dave stood back to study the result. Not bad, he thought, and the note was just right too. He would surprise her with an idea that had occurred to him in his sleep, an idea combining investigative skill with social razzle-dazzle.

He departed the room, Marcel ensconced on his shoulder as they went quietly down the breezeway toward the elevator. When the few puffy clouds over the harbor were themselves beginning to show soft gray shadows, the sun's long rays imperfectly penetrating their mists, Annabelle awoke. She stretched, saw that Dave had gone, and stripped off her badly wrinkled cherry-red dress, heading for the shower with the comfortable motions of someone at home in her surroundings.

Aware of the acute need felt in all the Florida Keys to conserve fresh water, she took a quick, very hot shower, emerging once again into the bedroom wrapped in a large white towel, steam rising from her arms.

"Well, Millie's Cat," she said, "we'll have to find you something to eat. I hope they still stock anchovies in the servi-bar."

She stepped into the living room to turn on lights and saw, through the frosted-glass panel, the shadow of a tall man standing beside the door of 409. She recognized the strong profile of Lieutenant Roy Ricou. Padding on still-soapy feet down the hall, she put the chain on the door and opened it a crack.

"I'm not decent," she said. "I met your aunt today. Twice."

"I thought you would. But only once, if you were lucky. If you're expecting me to apologize for failing to give you advance warning, I won't. Ashleen Ricou casts a long shadow on this island, and I don't brag about the connection. I wish you'd invite me in. Your steaming shoulder has given me an idea I'd like to explain to you."

She smiled crookedly.

"Is that why you're here? To explain things to me?"

"I've come to take you for a cocktail and a Key West sunset."

"On orders?"

"Certainly. And my career will be in shreds if you turn me down. What kind of soap did you use? I smell roses. I should have sent you roses. Red roses."

"Go away and let me get dressed. I'll meet you on the dock."

"Well, hurry. If you look behind you, you'll see the sky is already streaked with pink."

"Five minutes," she promised, closing the door.

Millie's Cat watched her from the bed as she flung clothing out of her suitcase and grabbed a pair of white slacks and a violet halter embroidered with one tiny white egret above the left breast. She found, to her annoyance, that she had failed to pack any but the red heels she had worn to Key West.

Ten minutes later, conscious of having indulged the cat in a rare treat of anchovy paste and sardines marinara from the bar in the kitchen and of having dressed in record time, she strolled barefoot onto the crowded dock, where hundreds of sunset worshipers—with pretty yellow and green paper umbrellas in their tropical drinks and many camera attachments around their necks—faced west, their faces bathed in pinks and oranges, their eyes variously reflecting an otherworldly fire. She shaded her eyes with her hand, finally spotting Ricou at the far end of the dock seated at a weathered table. He stood and waved to her.

She made her way slowly through the crowd, past the calypso band whose rhythms were visible to her in the swaying of the sunset party, to Ricou's side. He pulled out the other chair for her and gestured to the table.

"Thanks for the flowers, Lieutenant. They're lovely."

"They should have been red roses. I couldn't think of a drink that reminded me of red roses, so I ordered you a strawberry daiquiri," he said. "It was either that or wine, and you don't seem the type."

"I'm not usually the type at all. I almost never consume alcohol, but I'll make an exception to celebrate this glorious sunset with you."

He lifted a Corona beer bottle with a lime wedge in its clear neck. The serious expression she had noticed earlier still dominated the lieutenant's features, but his tanned face was touched now by a warm smile. "To pink skies."

She brushed the Corona bottle with her drink and said, "To explanations."

NINE

TALL BLACK SAILS AND RIGGING SLID BETWEEN THE SUNSET dock and the fiery pink ball so close to the edge of the Gulf it seemed that the water must soon sizzle and extinguish the great blazing sphere. The thirty people on board the black ship—in that light also turned into black silhouettes, their champagne glasses tiny black appendages—called out to those on the dock, laughing and waving, one frolicsome passenger going so far in his party spirit as to moon the revelers on the dock. The *Wolf*, an evocation of early nineteenth-century pirate vessels, complete with flying Jolly Roger and swashbuckling, sword-toting deckhands, was putting out into the Gulf for a sunset cruise, providing a visual story in thousands of photos of this breathtaking meeting of night and day.

Ricou saw the shadow of the *Wolf* cross Annabelle's face, winking out the hot blush on her smooth skin. When the shadow slid away, the jade depths of her eyes sparkled with fires from across the water, and with something else, he thought.

"You're staring at me, Lieutenant Ricou," she said, sipping her daiquiri and regarding him quizzically over the rim of the plastic glass. "You're supposed to be watching the sunset."

"I have strict orders to watch you," he returned, moving

his chair closer to hers. "I'm a very competent officer, and I always obey reasonable orders to the hilt." He tilted his head to one side. "Besides, I'd rather watch you, orders or no."

"What would you be doing if you had no orders to baby-sit me?"

"I'd be minding the sunset, probably. This is Key West."

"Do you watch it every day, Lieutenant?"

"So far. I've only been here three weeks. This is a temporary assignment. I wish you'd call me Roy. Don't you like the name?"

A waitress in tight yellow shorts and shirt, carrying at least fifteen bottles of Corona on a huge tray, dumped a heavy platter of conch fritters on the table next to them, along with three bottles of beer. Ricou reached into the pocket of his white trousers and stuffed several crisp bills into a cup on the tray. He took one of the bottles.

"Do you want another daiquiri?" he asked. "Something else?"

She shook her head, stirring her straw around the pink froth in her glass. "Roy's an anomalous name for an American sailor, I think," she said, watching hungrily as her laughing neighbors dipped fritters in lime sauce. The she-crab soup and iced tea at Mallory Square had not been filling. "It's French for 'king.' Dave says you're from New Orleans."

"That's right, so this carnival atmosphere makes me feel right at home. On the 'Dave' topic, where, precisely, does he hail from? Andromeda? Somewhere in this galaxy?"

"It's difficult to explain Dave to the casual observer," Annabelle said, treating herself to an inward and fond smile. "He's from Cuba, came over in 1970, but he's completely assimilated into American culture, mostly through his experience of the American cinema. I think that because Dave had so few friends as a child—the language barrier when he arrived in Miami was extremely strong—he sort of found his peers in movies. A mutual friend once described Dave as a cross between Peter Pan and James Bond. I thought that was good, but it did leave out pertinent elements of a large personality."

"What a bizarre way to grow up."

"I'm just glad he didn't watch much television."

The hot disk of the sun slipped under the Gulf like the edge of a dinner plate into a sink.

The dock grew quiet, even the calypso band muting its island melody; lilacs and pinks and golden reds smeared the thin clouds, spreading out from the west, across and up the cobalt sky, across and over the turquoise sea, the smoldering colors suffusing the vaulted dome and sparkling floor of the cathedral of night, the gilded tones fading even as they swelled and diffused through the clouded stained glass of the western firmament.

Another boat running under canvas, this one sporting a lofty midnight-blue sail, glided across the lavender-rose splash left now on the canopy of sky by the departed sun. As the boat slipped gracefully by the dock, a small figure scooped in the sail with efficient grace and economy of motion.

"Look, Roy," Annabelle gasped, pointing at the figure.

In the dying light from the west it seemed that a hundred lavender-rose butterflies surrounded the figure, now seen to be a woman as she turned to face the course of the boat. The boat rounded the end of the long dock, close to where Annabelle sat staring, and the woman's pale-blond hair streamed behind her tattooed shoulders in the wind.

"Isn't she wonderful?" Ricou waited to speak until Annabelle had finished gaping at the woman and faced him once again. "She's part of the show. I see her every evening. The butterfly tattoos change color with the color of the sunset. She's absolutely covered with them."

"Who is she?"

"She's called Butterfly Sue. She's the crew on that charter dive boat. I think it also does junk salvage."

"She's beautiful," Annabelle breathed, lost in admiration

for the tattooed vision that had sailed past the faded shell of the sunset into the dull, grayish waters of the marina behind the long dock.

"Yes, she is," Ricou said seriously, gazing into the depths of Annabelle's green eyes as though he were in a museum, considering a much-discussed painting. "But her beauty lies in some cold extreme, at some remote and artificial distance. She's almost intangible. Your beauty, however, is warm and palpable. It's almost hot. I can feel it from where I'm sitting now."

His blue eyes were steady as he watched her, and while tiny laugh lines crinkled at their corners, there was no sign of a smile on his lips.

"Are you adding your own interpretation to your reasonable orders, Lieutenant Ricou?"

"A good officer always does." He smiled suddenly, withdrawing his gaze and taking a long draft of his beer. "And I'm happy to say that my orders concerning you are long and detailed."

"How did you get assigned to the Annabelle detail, anyway? Surely a weapons officer has better things to do with his time, or at least more dangerous things to do with his time."

"I suppose it was the Aunt Ashleen connection. Commander Rzadkowolsky heard from your father that you were coming to look at the scene of Key West's most colorful crime, knew I had a connection at the museum, and, putting two and two together, thrust me into your orbit. I'm glad he did. As to what I could be doing with my time, let me just say that I've never been gladder about Ashleen Ricou than I am right now." He tipped his chair back on its legs and regarded her from under his lashes.

"Your aunt is not very friendly to strangers. She snarled at Dave and me this afternoon, actual fire pouring forth from her thin aristocratic nostrils. A formidable woman. I tried to ask her a few questions, and she just glared at me from her frosty blue eyes, which, incidentally, strongly reminded me of yours."

"You think my eyes are frosty?" he demanded, righting his chair and suddenly grinning. "I feel they must be shouting out the condition of my naked soul, which is hardly frosty. You must be thinking of someone else."

"I just meant that your eyes are that same dark blue. Not frosty at all."

"That's better. Now let's talk about your eyes. I've never seen such an intense green."

"Let's talk about your aunt instead," she suggested. "Is she gruff with everyone?"

"Everyone she can find. That's why I have yet to call her attention to the fact that I'm in residence, however temporary, on her little coral island. You didn't mention me, did you?"

"Of course I did, you coward, although I don't think I let the cat out of the bag that you are in Key West. I did ask her immediately if she was related to a dashing young rocket lieutenant. Do I have your title correct?"

He nodded, a lazy smile on his lips.

"Dave's afraid of your Aunt Ashleen. Or so he says." She pushed her unfinished drink away from her across the rough wooden table.

"Many people are. You know, she probably already knows I'm here, despite my precautions. She knows everyone who matters in Key West, and I must have left some trail. I'll get hell when she catches up to me. Either that or she'll just freeze me by offering a cold cheek to be kissed and saying, 'Well, Roy, it's about time.' "

Annabelle pursed her lips and regarded him steadily. "I don't imagine for one minute that you're afraid of her," she said. "Any more than Dave is."

"No. But the fact is she'd try to pump me about my assignment here, and I'm not supposed . . ." Ricou seemed to reconsider his sentence, a subtle shift in his expression showing that he was amending his words in midthought: ". . . to be thinking of anything but you."

"That's not what you were going to say."

"You're right. That was awkward of me."

"We could talk about the weather. It's unusually fine for this time of year."

"I didn't mean to stiff you that way. You're not offended, are you? My assignment here really is classified."

"Of course not. That's why I suggested the weather." She smiled to indicate her sincerity.

"You're a nice woman, Annabelle."

"Oh, my. A few moments ago I was 'hot.' Next thing I know you'll be punching me on the arm and saying I'm just like a sister to you."

"Not a chance," he said. "I'm much more likely to drag you off screaming to my lair, like a trophy from the hunt. I'm feeling tremendously hunterlike tonight."

"The atmosphere here in Key West seems to bring out that brutish element in men. Even Dave has been doing a pretty good impression of a latter-day caveman. Did they teach you lair-dragging and other fossilized dances at Anapolis?"

"No. I was fortunate to be born with fully developed brutish instincts. What kind of instincts do you have?"

"Oh, the usual female stuff—tender, ministering, docile, completely submissive, that sort of delightful thing. The Angel in the House, as Coventry Patmore expressed it in a poem that Victorian men loved for its ruthless idealization of women."

"Where'd you go to school? It's only fair to tell me, now that you ferreted out Anapolis so slyly."

"Yale."

"And you studied angelness there?"

"It's called angelosity, stupid. I happen to know, because I studied English. I wonder what your ultrasecret assignment in Key West is."

He lifted his bottle, drained it, the chunk of lime touching his lips, and stood, his tall frame stark in his dress uniform.

"Let's go for a walk. The show's over anyway."

The sky, without their noticing, had lost its pale-lavender fire and was now a gray and purplish blue, rather flat and unremarkable, a vacancy where there had been full being and presence.

"Darkness made visible," Annabelle said, standing up.

"What's that?" Ricou asked, bending closer, his face so close to hers that she could smell the lime on his breath.

"It's from *Paradise Lost*. Describing the special nature of hell."

"Then it's a thoroughly inappropriate choice, because this is a night in paradise," he said decisively. "You must now pay the forfeit for stupid quotation."

He extended his hand commandingly, she placed hers in it, and he noticed her wedding band for the first time. They started to walk back along the dock, which was now only sparsely populated with a few sunset worshipers finishing drinks, the others having moved their party to the bars and restaurants of Duval Street. He stopped suddenly, thereby tugging her back to where he stood.

"You're barefoot," he said.

"Don't your reasonable orders cover this situation?"

"Certainly not. I'll have to interpret."

And she thought, *Oh, no, this is where he picks me up and carries me. I'll be so disappointed. It'll be as if he received the same memo all men receive when they're about sixteen, just at the age when they also learn to thump their chests.*

Ricou withdrew his hand from hers and sat on a wooden chair. He took off his socks and shoes, tossed them over the railing into the water, and stood up, taking her hand again.

"I can see that I, too, have much to learn about correct conduct in paradise," he said. "How else can we dance after dinner in the moonlight, our naked feet caressed by the sand, if we're wearing shoes?"

"That's twice you've used the word *naked* in this conversation, Lieutenant. Are you trying to tell me something? And are we having dinner together?"

"Those are my orders. Followed perhaps by a midnight swim. Of course I'm trying to tell you something. Don't be dim-witted."

"You're not going to tell me what your assignment in Key West is, are you?"

He gave her a serious smile. "The navy is not called the Silent Service for nothing."

They turned toward the lights of the hotel and almost immediately collided with Dave, who was standing with his arms crossed, tapping his foot on the end of the dock near the bar. He was attired in a magnificent full black tuxedo and for the first time in Annabelle's memory wearing a pair of regulation dress shoes. His black tie was arranged with both correctness and decorum against the starched and snowy backdrop of his dress shirt, the pearly black studs in the shirt were sparkling, his brown hair was combed precisely, and a faint wafting fragrance of Nino Cerruti cologne perfumed the air. He carried a single long-stemmed white rose, a white ribbon streaming along the stem and over his hand.

"Be warned, Lieutenant Ricou, about your midnight plans," he said, a sardonic gleam in his brown eyes and his tones acid. "She snores like a basset hound."

He pivoted and stalked off the wooden dock, his shoes echoing smartly on the pavement as he hurried across the parking garage under the hotel, headed for the multicolored lights and raucous music of Duval Street.

Annabelle felt as though she had been hit in the chest.

Ricou arched an eyebrow, looking slightly saturnine as he studied her face.

"Which movie was that from?" he drawled. *"The Exorcist?"*

Annabelle drew a long, shuddering sigh, getting her wind back.

"God, I don't know. I've never seen him like that."

Now Ricou hesitated. He dropped her hand and walked back toward the railing. He stood for a moment, looking out to sea, his experienced eye locating Rigel and Betelgeuse in the Orion cluster, thinking. He turned back and stopped beside Annabelle, who had not moved. He tilted her face to his with his cool hand.

"I said I liked directness, so I'll be direct. Are you lovers? Are you married?"

"Dave? And me? No." She was clearly aghast, and he almost laughed at the ludicrously shocked expression on her face.

"I wondered about your ring."

"I'm single now." She hurried past the reference to her ring. "God, what an idea. Dave offers me cigars. He makes fun of me. He doctors my scrapes. He advises me on what to wear. He does Ernest Hemingway impressions. He's practically my brother."

"I wonder if he thought that when he put on that tuxedo? He looked to me like a man with a heavy date. I wonder why he thought a white rose made any sense for you?"

"You know," she said, her eyes blank with dismay, "you're right. If I didn't know better, I'd say he was jealous."

"Let's not waste all that jealousy on innocence." Ricou acted quickly, taking her in his arms and kissing her, not in a brotherly fashion, nor in the fashion of a hunter dragging her off to his lair, nor in the manner of a man bestowing her due on the Angel in the House, nor in the chaste and shy style he had observed in that awkward puppy who had flown her plane.

It was a kiss of great variety, and Annabelle found that her response was also varied, including an unusual absence of resistance, and wondered at herself. She felt giddy. Was it Key

West? she wondered. Some form of sunset madness? The dai-quiri?

He felt her response.

"How are your instincts now?" he asked, standing slightly away from her and gazing into her green eyes.

And in the midst of her awakening and passionate desire to thwart her customary reserve, to annihilate the self-imposed strictures of safe reticence, the specter of a satanic Dave in full tuxedo rose before her, and she lost impetus, pulling away from Ricou.

"How could he do that?" she demanded, flinging up her hands. "I'll kill him. What a jealous-husband thing to do." A light dawned in her flashing green eyes. "I've got it," she announced, snapping her fingers. "Rhett Butler, thinking Scarlett's been, uh, processing lumber at the mill with Ashley."

Ricou was unsteady, but he knew that the moment had turned, and he observed her passionate concentration with fascination and appreciation.

"I'll tear him limb from limb." She laughed and sputtered angrily at the same time, thrusting her hands into the pockets of her white slacks. "I'll pull his nose off. God! How could he tell you I snore, just like that? He knew what you would think. Besides, I don't snore."

Ricou reached for her right hand and pulled it out of her pocket.

"How does he know you snore?" he asked gently.

"Yeah, how does he know I snore?" she demanded, contradicting herself blithely. "I'll tie his ears in knots. I'll boil him in oil. I'll feed him to iguanas." Her breast heaved.

"I can see that you're going to be an extremely dangerous assignment," he said, grinning.

"I'm starving," she said in a soft voice.

"Me too." He put his hands on her waist and kissed her deeply, slowly, and this time with some tenderness, some element of patient exploration, something she could not quite label. Then he took her hand again, and they walked onto the cool sidewalk, passing beside boats rocking at their slips in the marina, slapping water up against the concrete. They passed the *Reef Cowboy*, with its salvage tackle neatly stowed on the deck, and the much larger glass-bottomed *Miss Key West*, its red-and-white canvas roof dimpled by the breeze, and the *Flying Witch*, its deep-sea-fishing winch gleaming in the lights from the hotel. They walked on toward Duval Street, and when they came to the jostling crowds and blinking lights of that carnival strip in the full force of its nightly revels, Ricou put his arm across Annabelle's shoulder, walking silently with her into the dense center of the swirling maelstrom of partymaking.

They crossed Duval a couple of blocks past the hotel, toward the open doors and country cadences of Sloppy Joe's Bar, the island's most famous nightery, and Ernest Hemingway's favorite watering hole, according to the legend cultivated by the bar itself. The sidewalk was cluttered with motorcycles, most of them big Harleys, most of them heavily accessorized.

They entered the bar, assailed by the huge blowups of the famous face and by the sea of tourists drinking the strong tropical rum drinks that the Hemingway legend dictated they should drink. The mustached face also grinned at them from T-shirts on every other torso and from cocktail napkins around their drinks.

Ricou waded into the crowd, edging a path for them with his wide shoulders.

American bikers and Japanese tourists and extended German families with guidebooks and men looking for women and women dressed in tropical prints stood at the bar, several bodies deep, waiting to be served at this fountain of literary booze. Hemingway stared down at them all, posed with lions and antelope, the Great White Hunter, from his blown-up photographs on the walls. A baseball bat Hemingway had used once was in one glass case bolted to the wall, his birth certificate on display in another. A lighted neon menu above the bar offered drinks that interlaced the writer's name and works with tropical fruits—the Hemingway Hibiscus Colada, the Papa Pineapple Hurricane, the Ernest Lime Rum Runner, the Farewell to Amaretto Mango Margarita, the Old Man and the Stinger, the For Whom the Banana Fizz, the Short Happy Life—and with prices starting at four dollars.

Annabelle and the lieutenant found a tiny round metal table against a wall near the band platform, almost within reach of the drummer, who was pounding away on a pair of cymbals crashing beside their heads.

"What'll you have?" Ricou mouthed.

"I don't know. Those Hemingway drinks look lethal."

"I'll be back." He left the table and pushed his way again through the crowd, back to the door to read the food menu, a tall board on wooden legs standing free on the cracked linoleum floor in a circle of bikers.

He returned quickly, surprising Annabelle with the efficiency of his progress through the swirling, dancing, shouting, drinking mass of humanity.

"I ordered the High-Roller Joe," he mouthed at her, the cymbals flashing neon lights at them from behind the country band, Jake Balls and the Hell Raisers.

"What's that?"

"I have no idea."

With the crashing strains of a song called "Come Get Shuck-faced" pounding around them, Ricou put his hand under the table and grasped hers.

"It's cold," he said, holding her hand and placing it against his chest.

"You're a very nice man," she said, and beamed a smile at him, the neon lights reflected on her face.

"I can't hear you," Ricou mouthed, pointing to his ear. "The band."

"In that case let's get naked, scream our heads off, and

make love on the table," she said, smiling at him with wide eyes and an innocent face.

He gave her a perfunctory smile and patted her hand.

A big-boned blond waitress wearing tight white leather and scuffed spike heels deposited two paper plates on the tiny table, the reddish-orange juice from two sloppy joes running in little rivers on the white paper and standing in pools on the table, a spill of neon lights blinking in the grease. Between the plates she thumped down a cold bottle of Dom Perignon, causing the table to rock on its wobbly legs.

"That'll be one hundred and thirty-five dollars," she yelled.

Ricou, who had seen the price list on the menu board, peeled some bills from the roll he drew from his pocket and handed them to the waitress.

Annabelle was speechless. As she turned to follow the waitress's leathered form with her eyes, a protest forming on her lips, she caught a glimpse of Detective Lieutenant Barbara Ruggierrio at a table about twenty feet on the other side of the Hell Raisers.

She forgot the price of the High-Roller Joe, taking in the words she read on Ruggierrio's lips, as the police detective addressed her companion across several beer bottles and a large manila envelope on their table.

"I'm telling you, on the typewriter ribbon, clean as can be, it said 'There will be no Hemingway Resort.' Want me to bury the report?"

A pair of gold half-glasses lay atop the manila envelope. Ruggierrio's companion was Noah Green.

TEN

 RICOU GENTLY TOUCHED ANNABELLE'S ARM, AND SHE
turned to him.

"What's the matter?"

"Those two people," she said.

"What?"

The cymbals flashed, and she reminded herself that he
could not hear her.

She had so cultivated a low voice, working with a thera-
pist, that now she could not estimate how to modulate her
voice to make herself heard over the noise. She reached for her
handbag and searched for something to write on, puzzled
when she could not find the typewritten list of phone numbers
Ricou had given her earlier. She had last seen it in Green's
office. She grabbed the letter from Millie de Vargas and a pencil, waved them at Ricou, and scribbled a note. He squinted
over her hand and read as she wrote, *See those two by the
window? Guy with half-glasses. There's something awful going on.*

"Who are they?" Ricou mouthed.

She wrote, *Dead woman's law partner and head murder cop.
Don't let them know we see them.*

Ricou glanced casually at the pair by the window and

back at Annabelle's face. "I wonder what they're doing here. Together. They seem friendly."

"Exactly."

She thought for a moment, put down the pencil, and took a bite of her sloppy joe.

"Good," she said, pointing to the sandwich and chewing.

He, too, ate, watching Annabelle eating as she watched the couple by the window.

She saw that Ruggierrio was opening the manila envelope. The detective extracted some eight-by-ten glossy black-and-white photographs, showing them one by one to the attorney. Annabelle read her lips as she talked to Green about the photos.

"The autopsy said strangulation . . . sure," Annabelle read. "Not that there was any doubt." Ruggierrio drank from a bottle of Corona and wiped her lips on the back of her hand. "Something funny, though. There's a little round bruise"— here she pointed to a photo—"right here. See the dark circle? Right on the line . . . ribbon made." She put that photo at the back of the slim stack in her hand and returned the entire group to the envelope.

Annabelle could not see Green's face, but he obviously responded, saying something brief. Ruggierrio drank again and put her bottle on the table. Annabelle read the detective's lips: "There's no other marks on the body . . . just that little circle and the ribbon mark. Those typed words . . . a fairly even impression on the ribbon, which was old but never used, but . . . are two Ws and one A in the words 'There Will Be No Hemingway Resort,' and they're lighter than the other letters . . . . think means touch typing, the little fingers being weaker than the others. Millie . . . a touch typist?"

Again, by the motions of Green's head, Annabelle knew that he had responded.

Ruggierrio continued. "It was just her fingerprints on the machine, so she typed . . . sentence on the ribbon. I don't know how, but the killer must've made her do it, or . . . her to agree to do it. It's somebody hating that resort, all right. That makes Perez a doubly bad bet. He's not a Duval shopkeeper, he's not a rumhead artist . . . his living from painting or shooting the sunset, and he's not a member of the old guard. He's not even a philosopher or poet or dock bum." Ruggierrio picked up her beer and held it in the air as she went on, blocking Annabelle's view.

"Damn," she said, craning her neck.

Ricou felt helpless, stranded in a loud but essentially voiceless place, his ears useless to help Annabelle, even his newly prescribed reading glasses left uselessly back at the base in a fit of vanity. The couple by the open window obviously had a strategic advantage, the quality of sound apparently much better by the window and away from the band.

Ruggierrio drank from the bottle and lowered it to the table. "I bet they're already back in Miami," she said. "Big-city smart-asses."

Annabelle frowned.

Green picked up his half-glasses, twirling them in his characteristic way. He said something to Ruggierrio, who responded, "Not yet. I expect tomorrow, though. He's got a lawyer now." Ruggierrio's eyebrows rose as Green said something. Then she said, "You going to—" Here Green interrupted with a gesture of his glasses. Ruggierrio turned away, and Annabelle made a small, impatient gesture.

When she was able to read Ruggierrio's lips again, the detective was saying, "a thing in her shoe. I don't see how she could walk with it . . . especially in heels. The M.E. says there's not a bruise or blister on her foot. Some sort of bead. Red coral . . . only one."

Ruggierrio reached her arm into the envelope and took something out, holding it up between her thumb and forefinger against the bright lights from the street. Whatever she was holding was something small, but Annabelle could not see it.

Annabelle hastily wrote on the letter, *can you see?*

Ricou took the paper and pencil and wrote, *something red, round, little.*

Green reached for the thing, but Ruggierrio shook her head and dropped whatever it was into the envelope. "Probably some good-luck token. Lot of good it did her." Ruggierrio put the envelope on the table and reached into her pocket. She squinted at her watch and seemed about to rise. She patted her pocket again, took out a cigarette, and lit it, blowing smoke across the table.

Annabelle grabbed Ricou's sleeve and indicated she wanted to leave. He stood and watched her as she scribbled again and stuffed the letter into his hand, pointing urgently to it. It said, *knock envelope off table.* She reclaimed the letter, jammed the pencil into her handbag, and plucked a five-dollar bill from a fold as she stood, and Ricou followed her as she walked in front of the band. She stopped at Ruggierrio's table and tapped Green on the shoulder.

"Let me buy the next round, counselor," she said, bending close to Green. She dropped the five over the bottles. It floated to the greasy table. The gold half-glasses paused in midtwirl as Green reached for the five in a jerked reflex of his arm.

The attorney opened his mouth to speak, but Ricou clumsily jostled his shoulder, causing Green to knock over a beer bottle and send the envelope sliding off the greasy table to the floor.

Green jumped out of his chair, wiping beer off his slacks; Ruggierrio pushed her own chair away from the table, and Annabelle stooped quickly to the floor. When she arose, Green had his glasses on his face, eyeing the mess on the table. She tossed the envelope onto the table and smiled.

Ruggierrio exhaled a cloud of smoke through her lips and sneered through it at Annabelle, who smiled.

"See you later, counselor," she said. She took Ricou's

hand, he mumbled an apology, and they worked their way into the dancing, gyrating, rum-scented crowd.

Out on the sidewalk, surrounded by crowds of bikers that had overflowed from the bar and were now drinking on the sidewalk and singing, Ricou took Annabelle's arm and steered her toward the street. They crossed Duval and stopped in the relative calm of the lights spilling from Conch Out, the bar downstairs from Green's office.

"Roy, you were perfect. You looked like a clumsy drunk in there."

"What did you do?" Ricou asked her. "With the envelope."

"I felt inside. There was a small bead, like something from a necklace. I wish I had seen it. But I know its size and texture."

"I only saw it from a distance."

"Describe the color."

"I'll show you." He turned and walked down Duval, peering in at windows and finally stopping at one, waiting for her to catch up with him.

"There," he said, pointing to a display in the window of Island Baubles and Bare Bodies. She peered through the thin glass at a bikini he indicated near the front of the display. It was a daring suit with a deeply scalloped outline, the shade a dull garnet. "That's almost the color." A slow smile touched his lips. "I've seen this window display many times, but the bikini is now powerfully evocative. It's your shade of red."

She tugged at his wrist, and he followed her past a few more stores. She pointed. "Like that?"

He gazed into Mahogany Maid, the woodcarver's studio, at the ice-skating costume of the Katarina Witt doll. "Exactly," he said. "That's the color I saw in the cop's hand."

"It's like the color of red ink in a bottle—very dark, a sort of deep red with black undertones. A color that won't be seen outside the arteries of an archangel."

"That's very poetic."

"It's also Mark Twain's."

"Is that bead thing important?"

She raised her shoulders. "I don't know."

"Annabelle, look at your feet."

She did, noting in horror that they were filthy, black and a muted orange, no doubt from the sloppy-joe sandwiches that over the years had stained the linoleum in the bar. She saw that Ricou's feet were in the same condition.

"Do you know that you have perfect toes?" she asked abruptly.

"What?"

"Perfect toes. See how the lengths are all graduated precisely toward the little toe?"

"Do you have a fetish? If so, I'll have to start studying up." He smiled at her again in his lazy way. "I like other parts of the body better myself." He leaned against the shop window, crossing his arms and scrutinizing her face as she ignored his remark.

"Seriously, Roy, you have perfect feet. And I don't have a fetish. Dave does. He says my feet are too big. But yours are like statue feet—perfect."

He curled his toes self-consciously. "Since you're disregarding all of my allusions to sex, let's go find a handy swimming pool and dunk my perfect feet—and your big ones."

She hesitated, glancing up and down the street, half expecting to catch sight of Dave's tuxedoed and willowy form, but she soon realized that he could be anywhere on Key West, in any of the countless nightspots, or on any of the beaches or docks, or even back in his room. "Let's do that, Lieutenant Ricou. But chlorine may not be enough. We may need to be sandblasted."

"We'll try a pool first. Not that I'm a coward, but even the Iron Duke of Wellington advised before Waterloo that a good officer should try to get over rough ground as lightly as possible."

They strolled back toward Ocean Key House along Duval Street, passing other strolling, or lurching or stumbling, night people. One such person—a big man reeking of rum and wearing a T-shirt that still bore its price tag and announced, "I Saw the Lower Keys on My Hands and Knees" in bold letters—made a grab for Annabelle's wrist. "Wanna get lucky, sweetheart?" he breathed on her.

Ricou tensed.

She slipped nimbly out of the man's grasp, his slurred words lost on her but their import clear from the direction of his eyes and the style of his touch, and kept walking.

Ricou glanced at her face and saw that she was not at all disturbed by the contact, almost as if the man no longer existed, perhaps had never existed. Her serenity was perfectly unaffected, and he walked on beside her, wondering at such calm or such abnormal detachment. And he knew, without asking, that she *would* have been disturbed if he had intervened needlessly. Maybe her inability to hear the man took the sting out of the encounter. But, he thought, immediately changing his mind, that should have made it more frightening. Maybe she had more than her share of physical courage.

They walked through the parking garage toward the waterfront, under the hotel, and emerged into the cool and subtle darkness of the sunset dock, where the bar was open, but with only one die-hard drinker sitting on a stool and listening to the tired calypso band still playing from the dock. Annabelle and Ricou walked together up a small flight of wooden stairs to the weathered pool deck abutting but separated from Mallory Square by a high stucco wall. This place was deserted, and they rolled up their pants legs to their knees and sat on the edge of the pool, dangling their feet in the warm water, bathed in the glow from the underwater lights. Wisps of steam rose around their legs as the water made contact with the night air.

He wanted to put his arm around her, but he also wanted to talk to her, and he couldn't do both and still allow her to read his lips. He opted for talking, feeling some diffidence for the first time since meeting Annabelle.

"Annabelle, why the hyphenated name?"

She smiled. "When I got married, I thought it was the thing to do, the liberated thing to do. I'm not so sure I'd feel that way now."

"What happened? A divorce?"

"No. Nikki died seven years ago. A stupid car accident. I was devastated—out of my mind a little, I think—and the hyphenated name actually may have helped me through the long nightmare. I guess I felt I still had a part of Nikki."

He took her hand, saw the gold band, and cleared his throat. "Seven years is a long time. Your name is still hyphenated."

"Now it would be too much of a hassle to change. You wouldn't believe the amount of paperwork that has my very long name printed on it. Plus, everybody knows me by the name. Miami's the biggest small town in America, and everybody knows everybody else's business. Sometimes I hate that about Miami, but sometimes it's rather nice."

"What would you do if you changed your name?"

"I'd just use Hardy. I don't know why I thought adding Nikki's name to mine was such a statement. It was still a case of the bride taking the man's name. After all, he didn't hyphenate his name."

"Think you'll ever remarry?"

"I've never even thought about it," she said, a surprised look on her face, the surprise obviously directed inward.

"You shock me," he said, smoothing a dark, curling strand of hair away from her forehead with his fingers. The breezes from the harbor were strengthening, and her hair waved over the back of his hand. "You are so incredibly beautiful, I'd think men would have made you think of marriage."

"You're very gallant, Lieutenant Ricou. But I've avoided situations where the subject could come up."

"Let's not avoid things."

Ricou placed the palm of his hand on her cheek and kissed her, softly at first, then with increasing ardor. Their feet touched under the water, and he encircled her ankles with his.

Her reserve had slipped away, her usually rigid scruples were oddly silent, and she was breathless, bewildered. She wanted, for once, to fling away the antiseptic denial of seven years, and she gazed at him as he withdrew his arms from her and clasped his hands together unsteadily on her knees. She covered his hands with hers.

"Don't avoid things, you say? How's this for direct: I may be woefully out of practice, but I see that I still know when I want a man." She spoke on a deep breath, watching his serious eyes with curiosity. She thought he was surprised that she would express her desire so simply. "See how flagrantly unconfined, how far off the marble pedestal, this Angel in the House is, after all? But I don't know how these things are done gracefully anymore in the world ruled by the couple-ocracy."

"Graceful? I don't think there is a graceful way. We're now supposed to have an absurdly clinical chat about condoms and sexual history, according to at least one depressing journal in my locker aboard the *Ohio*."

She smiled wanly.

"I've been thinking about this moment," the lieutenant said on a deep sigh, "ever since I met you on the dock this morning and Dave called me Popeye." He grinned. "Among other names." He shook his head and squeezed her hands. "I've thought about you all day—all day, Annabelle—and I think I know how I'd like to handle the awkward moment."

She raised an eyebrow, a little stir of alarm at the back of her mind.

"We could forget the chat and the histories, throw the journals out the portholes, and get blood tests," he explained, a light of hesitation in his blue eyes. "Start with a clean slate, like a new American Adam and Eve in this tainted paradise." Suddenly he grinned at her. "Of course, the hard part is waiting to express my lust. Lair-dragging was not meant to be like this."

She was relieved, and expelled a puff of breath through her mouth. For that one alarmed moment she had been afraid that he was on the verge of proposing marriage.

"Oh, *that* kind of blood test," she said. "It only takes ten days or so, doesn't it, for HIV? And who knows what can happen in that time? Maybe we'll discover we don't even like each other. I can wait."

"Well, it would take more waiting than that. I'm shipping out in three days."

Ricou withdrew his hands, plunged them into the water up to his elbows, and began to scrub his feet, the black and orange dirt floating to the top of the water. He turned his head toward Annabelle and, still scrubbing, said, "I didn't know how to tell you, other than springing it like that."

Annabelle stared at him while internally examining her first reaction, which was to slap him, but he continued before she had time to consider options.

"When I got the word to meet the deaf Dr. Annabelle Hardy-Maratos at the wharf this morning, I went naively to my doom, picturing you as a drab social duty, probably a little boring but certainly nothing worse than a trifle unpleasant."

Annabelle made a face at him, but again he went on.

"I was so gauche, asking you about your efficiency rate, just as though you were a robot. I could have kicked myself. If I were living a normal civilian life, I would beg your pardon instead of propositioning you like this. But you took me by storm, and now my defenses are all down, and I can't think logically. It's shocking to me, but I can't think." The smile that accompanied his words was crooked, self-mocking. "But I don't have a normal life. I'm leaving Friday night. I know the timing is brutal, but it's really not my time; it's the navy's. On the other hand, I did warn you about my brutish instincts." His smile was gone. "Annabelle, it's never taken me long to know exactly what I want. When I was only six years old, I decided I would go to school at Annapolis or nowhere. And, in precisely that bull-headed way, I saw you this morning and my mind was made up." He placed his cool hand briefly over hers on the side of the pool. "I'll change the subject now so you have time to think. God, can you imagine how much oil was on that floor, for this crap to float? Decades of tourists eating those sandwiches, decades of waitresses plunking them down on tables, decades of country bands wailing sad songs about tears on their pillows."

Annabelle thought the lieutenant's face looked stern and lonely, a faraway melancholy behind the attempt at restoring the conversation to the neutral topics of relative strangers.

"Kiss me again," she said. "I can't think when you talk, which you seem to be doing a lot of. Where the hell are you shipping out to, you stupid brute?"

"Singapore. 'Stupid brute'? You and your monkey partner have called me a lot of names today," Ricou said, but he reclaimed her hands, holding them in a crushing, wet grip, and they kissed again, the freshening breezes from the Gulf tossing her dark hair around their faces. She was surprised, given the almost scientific detachment of his suggestion about blood tests, that Ricou took advantage of the isolation of their spot on the pool deck to move his hands over her body with slow thoroughness, to hold her breasts firmly over the halter top, the coolness of his palms invading her clothing and her warm skin like a long-forgotten balm. She put her hands on his shoulders, and the kiss came slowly to an end. He looked at her lingeringly—her eyes closed, her hair brushing across the smooth skin of her bare shoulders, her full breasts under the slow tracing of his fingers. He sighed. He put his hands under her arms and pulled her against him.

"That is so nice," she breathed, raising her head and gazing into the depths of his dark-blue eyes.

"Isn't it?" he said hoarsely. "I thought it would be."

She reached her arms around his neck and kissed him. He lowered his hands to her waist, pressing her toward him.

And suddenly his hands closed on her waist uncomfortably. He stopped, pulling his hands away. "I'm not behaving the way I meant to, the way I should. I want to make love to you the right way, not like that animal who touched you on the street. Maybe I'm only a half brute. I hope I'm capable of the weird and tortured new chastity, love American-style for the nineties."

" 'Chastity,' " she said as if she were savoring a new word, or an old word with a new meaning. " 'Torture' is right."

He smoothed his hands up her arms, tracing the straps of her halter, and took a breath, a deep, regretful frown in his eyes. He withdrew his hands slowly from her shoulders. He kissed her cheek.

He dipped his hands once again into the pool water and held them out to her imperatively. She stuck her feet toward him, and he scrubbed them, rubbing vigorously. The orange and black grit spread on the water. She gazed absently at the blue backdrop of the pool as the sticky dirt dissipated in ever-widening circles across the rippling water. She was collecting herself, retreating into the familiar safety of shallow commitments, having remembered, as though from a vast distance, to ask him what the navy found so interesting about Singapore, when she was struck by the appearance of the water.

"Wait a minute." She pulled her feet away, an alert look on her face. "That's what it was."

He stared at her, still bent over the pool, his hands dangling in the water.

"I have to go look at my shoes," she said, standing unsteadily but hastily.

He stood, shaking the water from his hands, and looked at her with mock concern.

"Shoes?" he echoed. "Do you often have these fits? Not that I mind visiting your shoes. I'm getting a little lonely for mine too. Annabelle, stop. Annabelle, do you realize what I asked you? You don't, do you?"

"Come on," she said.

He was cursing himself silently for being too sudden with her, for crowding her with his own inflexible life, for allowing her to see his need for a response from her to match his, but with a rueful, self-conscious smile he offered her his dripping hand.

They decided not to take the elevator, which seemed to be stuck on the fourth floor, and walked up the stairs. He stopped her on the third-floor landing, pulled her to him roughly, and kissed her urgently, greedily, his hands on her face. Another couple, on their way down the stairs, passed them circumspectly, and were ignored with comprehensive fervor.

When they resumed their progress up the stairs, their arms around each other, they were silent. She pushed open the door to 409 and led him to the bedroom. He stood in the doorway, watching her fling a couple of towels over the Jacuzzi as she searched for her shoes. She found one behind her suitcase and carried it to the Jacuzzi, flipping on the light switch that suddenly warmed the huge tub in the glow of scores of bulbs outlining the mirrored walls into which the Jacuzzi was built. She peered closely at the bottom of the shoe. The red pump was a sling-back, a Paul Merhige original, and the bottom of the rounded toe was covered with the distinctive silver grooved tap bearing the designer's initials. In the groove was a trace of blackish orange.

"Aha," she said.

"Do you think it will fit, Cinderella?"

"I think I'll send it to my lab in Miami to find out," she

said. "Along with a sample from the floor of Sloppy Joe's Bar. I have to go back."

"I hate to ask. Why are you so interested in the filthy floor of that overrated bar? Especially now that I have you all tidied up," he said, pointing emphatically at her feet.

"Because that overrated bar seems to have the same polish as the floor in the studio cottage of a certain overrated writer. It's what Sherlock Holmes would call elementary, my dear Roy."

ELEVEN

VERNON AVENUE WAS QUIET AND DARK, THE ONLY LIGHT A faint blue flickering from television sets inside the gingerbread houses, the background glow from reading lamps, the fluorescent haze from glazed bathroom windows. These were the small, antique Victorian homes of Key West's middle class, and, by neighborhood practice and agreement—as much as shared landscaping staffs—the bougainvillea carefully draped around the trunks of mahogany trees and the velvety lawns cushioned the night against intrusive noises here, just a couple of blocks from the public beaches on the Atlantic side of the island.

In a less acoustically tasteful neighborhood, Dave might have been noticed, for his dress shoes were elegantly soled for dancing, their slick bottoms just the type to make the most noise, but he passed unseen and unheard, the orchid trees perfuming his way as he stepped along, occasionally executing a pass or two from Fred and Ginger's "Continental," his favorite movie dance. Between these occasional lapses into graceful choreography, however, he moved with quiet, lynxlike stealth, using the shadows as he steered his course along the lawns of the wide street. His mood, never one to fall prey to lengthy spells of gloom, had returned to the lightly romantic, and he turned in at the gate of Number 18 and passed silently but with gay unconcern up the brick walk, mounted two steps to the gingerbread porch, and drew a small black case from the pocket of his tuxedo jacket.

He briefly flashed a penlight, attached by a rubber chain to his wrist, at the lock on the front door. It was a Schlage deadbolt. He felt the door and front window for signs of an alarm system, found no telltale wires or bumps, and chose a small pick from the assortment in the case. In less than twenty seconds he was inside the house, the door closed softly behind him.

He listened. From somewhere close by he could hear a clock ticking, and from across the room and beyond the doorway, a refrigerator motor, and from somewhere deep in the house, a steady fluid sound, probably a badly adjusted bulb in a toilet allowing a thin trickle of water to run into the bowl.

Feeling his way along the back of a sofa and toward the refrigerator sound, Dave pulled a pair of latex surgical gloves from his trousers pocket and put them on, longing for the days of proper white cotton evening gloves. He had touched nothing yet with his fingertips, not even the Schlage, and the kind of surfaces he would be interested in would take prints easily. And he expected that the home of N. S. Green, allergy sufferer, would be dust-free and just waiting for him to smudge a surface, leaving an infortuitous souvenir of Dave's unannounced visit.

He felt a wall protruding to his left and turned, his expensive dancing shoes soundless on the carpet, and he followed a short hall toward the toilet sound, groping the walls until he touched woodwork. The first room was a bedroom, which he searched quickly, his eyes now adjusted to the dim light, discovering nothing more interesting than an unopened jar of Vaseline in a table beside the bed and a copy of Hemingway's *To Have and Have Not* open on the floor, where it had apparently fallen. He made a mental note to cross the book off his vacation reading list, and moved on.

The bathroom at the end of the hall presented no opportunities for discovery beyond a collection of medicines in the mirrored cabinet. Dave was not surprised to find a package of L'Oréal hair dye, for the uniform and slightly brackish color of the attorney's hair had never been in doubt to Dave's sensitive eye, but he sneered at the box anyway, emitting a token sniff of disapproval because he believed in growing old gracefully, or at least getting a proper salon job. This, to Dave, like the morning's collect phone call, was damning evidence of Green's love of cheapness, a real grasp on the copper percentage of American legal tender.

There were pills and nasal sprays and salves and inhalers, and, below the cabinet on the floor, a humidifier, a rare appliance in sultry Key West. Dave was tempted to adjust the bulb in the toilet tank. He wavered, meaning to leave things the way he had found them, but finally decided to fix the toilet in order to eliminate one of the noises in the house, the better for him to navigate and concentrate should Green come home before he finished.

He peeled off his right glove, lifted the lid of the tank, flashed his small light, saw that the trouble was a misplaced rubber plug, rolled up his jacket sleeve, tugged the plug into alignment with the drain, and closed the tank. The noise quickly subsided and he left the bathroom, pulling his glove back on with a snap.

The other bedroom was Green's. Here Dave spent half an hour, sifting through drawers, flipping the pages of books, sliding his hands into pockets, lifting the mattress, shaking the shoes in the closet. He ran his hand over the closet shelves and over the floorboards. He found a gun inside a velvet case in the nightstand. With the penlight held steady in his left hand, he opened the case, noted that the gun was a .32-caliber Nambu, and sniffed the barrel. It had not been fired recently—or else it had been thoroughly cleaned—and he closed the velvet case squeamishly. Dave did not like Japanese guns. When it came to guns, he thought, it still paid to buy American.

Back in the hall he listened. Navigating now by the clock and the refrigerator, he made his way into the large, low-ceilinged modern kitchen. Here he was considerably slowed by the necessity to lift objects silently; searching a kitchen was a much noisier business than searching a bedroom, and he took his time, glancing only once at the green dial of his watch. When he had finished, it was nine-thirty.

Off the kitchen was a study, crammed with correspondence and books and files and stacks of newspapers and boxes tied with string. Dave estimated that to search this room would take at least two hours if he were to maintain his silence and thoroughness. He decided to leave it for last, even though it was the most likely place, against the chance that what he was looking for would turn up in a place more readily and quickly searched.

He returned to the kitchen and stopped to listen, arrested by an addition to the two noises he had isolated earlier for guidance. Just outside the kitchen door he heard a rough, scratchy sound, a low dragging sound he could not identify, coming from the pool area behind the house. That it was not Green, Dave was certain. It was too low and oddly rhythmic—sometimes missing the beat Dave expected—too close to the ground.

He opened the kitchen door, his nostrils assailed by an aroma of ammonia, acrid and pervasive. Green's house so far had manifested no overt cleaning odors, but the smell outside the kitchen was quite strong.

Dave left the door slightly ajar and flashed his penlight. He could make out the outlines of a small tiled pool and of a wet bar under a thatched Tiki roof. The entire area was screened, a precaution against mosquitoes. He headed for the bar at the other side of the enclosure, his dancing shoes making slight swishing noises on the rough chattahoochie, like a whisk broom drawn across a snare drum, as he skirted the pool.

The exterior noises were as muted as the rest of Vernon Avenue, with only an occasional sighing sound from the orchid trees whose thin shadows fell across the screens, except for that low rough scraping, like a heavy quiet machine in the distance, but close to the ground. Dave could not locate the source, for it seemed inconstant.

Hitching up his trouser legs with practiced panache, so that they broke just over the ankles of his black socks, he crouched beside a cupboard under the wet bar, opened it, and felt behind the bottles, exerting great care not to topple them. Noises he made out here would be heard by the neighbors, and he slowed his hands, moving the bottles one by one. Thoughtfully he removed his gloves and stuck them in a pocket of his jacket: He did not care to risk being seen wearing latex gloves if he had to make a quick exit through a neighbor's yard. He'd have to be careful about prints.

Behind a heavy gallon bottle of wine he touched his knuckle to a small wooden box with a simple latch holding it closed, about the size of a jewelry case, bracelet size. He lifted the latch with his knuckle and nudged the contents of the box, his right elbow resting on the bottles as he reached down to the little case behind them. He raised his eyebrows. He allowed the latch to fall, and suddenly held his breath, listening.

He cocked his head. That scratching sound was nearby, and he wondered if there were some motor under the sink in the wet bar to account for it.

He switched on the penlight with his thumb, casting the tiny beacon under the bar and then, swinging it to his left, into the cold yellow eyes of an animal, its massive, leathery head only a foot from his hand, the indistinct outlines of its huge body stretching at least ten feet toward the screened wall.

A cold film of sweat appeared instantly on Dave's body,

his hair prickling at the roots, the base of his spine almost numb from shock and immediate terror, and he froze, his thumb locked on the switch of the penlight, unable to move. The light shone steadily into the animal's right eye and on the tough dark skin surrounding it like an ancient piece of armor.

The only sound Dave could hear now was the thudding of his own blood pounding in his ears and along veins that felt strained to bursting, but the beacon in his left hand remained steady, from some miracle of arrested motion—some biochemical simulation of iron in his tendons—engineered by an adrenaline rush like nothing Dave had ever experienced.

And with startling clarity he realized why the latched box had been hidden out here by the screened pool.

His right hand was trembling where his knuckle touched the smooth wood and the cold metal latch, and this reminded him of what he had found. Slowly, hardly daring to think, he clutched the box and drew it over the wine bottle, his eyes never leaving the animal's.

The hand holding the penlight felt enormous and heavy, and Dave could feel it descending, centimeter by agonizing centimeter, over the broad, scaly snout. Along a path in the hairs standing up on his left hand, Dave could feel the animal's tepid breath.

He reached his trembling right hand up in the darkness, depositing the latched box on the wet bar with infinite patience and no noise. So attuned was he to the slow, trembling progress of the box that he imagined its atoms nestling gently among the atoms of the wet bar as it came to rest on the cold Formica surface.

As the muscles of his left arm continued to lose their ability to hold the penlight steadily up and, without his willing it, lowered the yellow beacon infinitesimally through the air— also atom by atom, he imagined—his right hand returned slowly to the cupboard. His fingers were now trembling more than ever and were covered with an icy lacquer of sweat. He did not know if the hand holding the penlight was also covered with sweat, for he could feel no sensation in that hand, not even the weight of his thumb on the switch that kept the light shining into the animal's eye.

His right hand slipped over the neck of the wine bottle and down the side, over the label, in a slimy, silent plunge, unable to maintain a grip on the cold smooth glass.

He willed that hand to rise.

This time he managed to close his fingers over the neck of the bottle, but his hold was precarious. He barely noticed that sweat dripped into his eyes, stinging them and falling in silent drops down his cheeks.

He tried to lift the bottle.

He couldn't do it.

The penlight in his other hand was falling farther, now illuminating only the lower half of that hideous yellow circle.

His hand slipped off the bottle, thumping lifelessly onto the shelf that held the liquor, and he noticed that his legs had turned to stone, their only sign of life needle-sharp pains in his crouched knees.

The fingers of his right hand tingled. In a reflexive movement he stretched them and came in contact with something soft.

It was a hand towel, something made of terry cloth.

He clutched it, squeezing it in his trembling hand. He could not lift the cloth nor open it with his stiff fingers, and he abandoned hope of wrapping it around the bottle.

But in the hyperawareness of his hand now processed in his brain, he realized that his palm was dry.

He slid his hand up the bottle and repeated the squeezing motion he had used on the cloth. The neck of the bottle felt like a piece of ice in his hand.

He closed his eyes, the drops of sweat clinging to his long lashes and brushing his cheeks.

He yanked the bottle and swung with all the strength of his tense shoulder muscles.

The bottle hit with a sickening clunk and rolled unbroken off the animal's head to the ground. In the fraction of a second that the light stayed on, Dave saw the eye close.

He sprang to his feet, grabbed the latched box from the wet bar, and almost teetered into the pool, his knees shaking. If the animal were still conscious, it could move much faster in water than Dave could. He backed with jerky strides and then ran frantically for the house, praying he would not lose his footing on the chattahoochie and fall into the pool. He leaped for the kitchen door and slid into the room, falling with a crash onto his left hip.

He lay there, stunned, for a few seconds, absurdly aware of the sound of the refrigerator motor and the clock.

He stood shakily, grabbed a towel from a rod over the sink, wiped his sweat off the floor with it and ran it over his dripping face, stuffed the towel into his black cummerbund, wiped both sides of the knob on the kitchen door, pulled it shut, and breathlessly headed for the front door.

Before he opened it, he took inventory, replaying in his mind his pathway across the pool area and the kitchen.

Green would find an unbroken wine bottle on the ground, and if Dave had left any marks, he hoped they would be smudged beyond the possibility of identification. Green would be missing one kitchen towel. And of course his toilet had been repaired.

And the animal. Dave shivered, and found he could not even conjecture about the condition of the animal.

He let himself out onto the gingerbread porch.

He locked the door behind him carefully and walked in the shadows to Vernon Avenue, checking his pockets stealthily.

The gloves, his picks—they were all there. His penlight dangled from his wrist. The latched box was still clutched in his right hand. He pulled the towel from his waist and stuffed it into his jacket pocket before emerging onto the sidewalk. Pausing at the corner of a green gabled house, he opened his right hand and saw that a long red dent had been gouged in the flesh, so tightly had he gripped the box.

He walked on, his breath coming more slowly. He silently congratulated himself for his decision to pass up the attorney's study.

If there were any secrets in that room, Green and his alligator were welcome to keep them.

WEDNESDAY

The cold was all through him, an aching cold that would not numb away, and he lay quietly now and felt it.

ERNEST HEMINGWAY
To Have and Have Not

TWELVE

AT TWENTY MINUTES PAST MIDNIGHT THE TWENTY-FIVE-foot *Reef Cowboy* slipped away from the Ocean Key House pier and snaked silently out of the marina, pushed through the still, black water under one immense, deep-blue canvas sail that was invisible against the night sky except as it occasionally appeared as a soft ghostly shadow towering against the thicket of bare masts swaying in the sluggish tidal water.

As it gained the entrance to the marina, the *Cowboy* tacked into the wind, crossing the harbor and main shipping channel without running lights, until it veered around the northern end of Christmas Tree Island. There, hidden by the scrubby contours of the evergreens, the boat's engine kicked in, and the *Cowboy* sailed south—emerging from behind Christmas Tree Island and running toward the low scrubby spine of Tank Island, cutting a straight line in the smooth, misty deep, its mast and sail only a suggestion of paler darkness on the curtain of night.

Ishmael Solas, his leathery face and elongated bald head darkened with mineral pitch, stood at the wheel, his large bony hands also darkened, his black jeans and sweater canceling his tall, rugged image against the sky. The only light on the boat was a green glow from the compass on the navigational panel. In the green spill from the compass light, Ishmael had anchored a small laminated set of coordinates with duct tape, but he did not consult them. He knew where he was going and figured to get there by dead reckoning alone. He could get anywhere, on any waters, if his price was met, and his price had been met handsomely tonight.

Once past Tank Island, he steered west-southwest, among tiny unclaimed, unnamed keys dappled on the shallow water, into the open sea, his keen eyes picking out the thin edge where the Gulf touched the vault of the sky, that crisp, barely visible line where one inky vastness met another. There was no moon, but Betelgeuse and Rigel pricked the sky like a sign-post. Ishmael knew the stars with an assurance most men reserve for the faces of kin, or the women they love.

He watched the sky for a time, correcting his course toward the west, the peripheral gaze of his gray eyes automatically registering both random and deliberate movements on the water, at this hour mere nuances of the dark—infrequently the dim running lights of some other lonely vessel, more often the sparkling steel-gray silhouette of a dolphin. Gradually the far lights disappeared, as the *Cowboy* increased its distance from land, and the dolphins assumed possession of the Gulf as Ishmael's sole companions in this secluded voyage through night. The only other call on his attention was a thermos of scalding coffee, which he slowly drained, sipping directly from the glass lip of the container because he did not want to drink from a cup that would be dirtied by the pitch on his hands.

About two hours out of Key West a shadowy figure climbed up the ladder from the cabin, to join him at the wheel. Butterfly Sue offered him a doughnut, but the pitch on her hands had intermingled with the soft powdered sugar, and Ishmael shook his long head disapprovingly, the skin of his weathered dome of a forehead wrinkling like crepe, in thou-sands of thin, parched lines. At his refusal she shrugged and bit into the doughnut, her white teeth gleaming against her blackened face, the roots of her blond hair dyed by the pitch, her head covered with a black baseball cap. They did not speak.

Butterfly squatted on the forward deck, licking her sticky fingers, squinting at the dolphins as they surfaced and cocking her head for the signature sound of the animals exhaling.

Ishmael suddenly cut the engine, and the boat slewed under its one blue sail, turning about awkwardly across its own wake. He reached to the panel and covered the compass with his huge blackened hand. Butterfly looked at him inquiringly, her blue eyes wide, but he pointed to the sail. Quickly she scrambled across the deck and under the boom, reefing the blue canvas and lashing it to the mast. The boat slowly came about to its original heading, silently wallowing in the heaving water. She lay curled on the deck, eyeing Ishmael's face, her small body crouched under the swinging boom. She reached up to stay it with her hand, her arm stiffened against its considerable weight. By the faint paleness from under the palm of Ishmael's hand, she saw him cup his ear, and she, too, listened.

The waves surged against the aluminum hull of the *Cowboy* with random slapping motions. A dolphin broke the water about fifteen yards from their bow, its gray mass gleaming dimly in the starlight, a variation on the satin fabric of the sea. And across the water, from perhaps a half mile's distance, came a deep, regular sound over the waves, the sound of a much larger engine.

She nodded to herself. Coast Guard. Maybe navy.

Ishmael stood motionless, at ease, giving the wheel some play, the fingers of his right hand edged with a faint green line about their black boundaries on the compass. His gaze swept the east and, squinting, found the dim green and yellow points of the cutter's running lights. Having located them, he closed his eyes briefly and turned his eyes to the west. Even such a nebulous disturbance in the regularity of the darkness as the cutter's lights half a mile away could interfere with the finely tuned night vision he had cultivated over the past couple of hours. Butterfly would stand lookout.

Even after she signaled all clear, Ishmael stood unmoving and patient, waiting another fifteen minutes to restart his engine. Butterfly put up the blue sail, and they resumed course, now faster, making better than twenty-five knots and running with smooth stillness.

Presently Ishmael spotted the low gray backs of the Marquesas Keys, and he turned the wheel, now heading due south under the cold track of Rigel. Dolphins no longer followed the *Cowboy*, but from time to time a small fish caught the cold distant fire of the stars as it leaped from the deep, always accompanied by the same shimmering series of watery notes along the arc of its path.

The engine stopped. Ishmael was certain that he was within a couple thousand yards of his destination. He locked the wheel and, from a wooden cupboard, lifted his magnetometer and side-scan sonar, along with the neat coils of their lines. He fastened them to their bolted rings on the deck and dropped them soundlessly over the gunwale into the black water, playing out the sixty-foot lines smoothly over his blackened hands.

Butterfly reefed the sail, Ishmael returned to the wheel, started the engine, and they began a slow, systematic sweep using only the power of the engine, radiating out in tight, ever-broadening concentric circles, dragging the magnetometer and the sonar.

The magnetometer struck first, with a set of *pings* that told Ishmael that his reckoning was sure and they had a hit. He shut off the engine, and Butterfly cast their anchor over the side.

They went to the stern, silent black wraiths on the two-dimensional backdrop of the blackest night, lifting a large aluminum elbow-shaped pipe into the water, covering the boat's powerful propellers. They worked with meticulous care and the swift, sure motions of long practice, bolting the pipe to the stern by feel and instinct, the bottom half of the elbow aimed directly at the floor of the sea.

Ishmael had been paid handsomely, but he had not been paid enough to squelch his curiosity, and it is possible that if he had been paid more, his curiosity would have been even hungrier.

He had been paid to turn his engine back on at this point, thereby driving a wall of water downward through the pipe—it was called a mailbox—and he was simply supposed to deliver the water in a steady burst, sailing in a wide circle, to blow up the sand on the bottom around whatever was down there.

Most people who hired his salvage boat wanted to use the mailbox to *uncover* what lay hidden under the sand, and would never instruct him to use the blowing pipe in a circle, which could only create a hill of sand on the bottom over the specified area. Ishmael knew he had been paid to cover up whatever lay here in the dark, on the floor of the sea, although those precise words had not been used. He had been told to blow the mailbox when the magnetometer and sonar agreed with the taped coordinates.

And Ishmael had decided, somewhere during the silent voyage out, to see for himself what was below in this particular room of the quiet, murky mansion of the Gulf of Mexico.

He signaled to Butterfly, a simple gesture indicating "down," and stripped off his black clothing. She obeyed his gesture by shedding her own clothing, the scores of tiny yellow and orange and red butterflies tattooed on her small, sinewy body seeming to leap into cold, silver fire in the starlight, glowing against her silken flesh, her blackened hands and face fading from sight as the rest of her body emerged as a sinuous, gaily decorated pennant against the thick, dull fabric of night.

The ink that had penetrated her skin had been mixed with a trace of phosphorus, and Ishmael scowled at the delicate, lacy wings of the sparkling butterflies responding to the faint, far-away radiance of the stars of Orion.

Butterfly and Ishmael took off their wristwatches, placing them in a shallow well next to the boat's compass, and donned tanks, regulators, masks, fins; with the water temperature at about seventy degrees, they would need no protective clothing if they kept the dive extremely short. But Ishmael had no plans to linger.

He took a heavy, old-style SDG-Sam wide-beam lamp from a hook, and they went over the side together amidships, taking giant strides off the low diving platform. And the black water closed over them.

Only when he reached a depth of ten feet did Ishmael switch on the powerful yellow Sam light. The nearly opaque wall of water before them took on a grayish-green tinge in the darkness, and Butterfly experienced a sensation of peering through an endless block of thick glass, as if she were seeing this watery world through a green paperweight in a darkened room, but to Ishmael the lamp turned the underwater cosmos into a living landscape, filled with pale gold butterflies that seemed to dart and flicker in the water with a strange independent life.

She followed Ishmael down, down slowly through the illusion of thickness, down to almost fifty feet.

Ishmael trained the lamp over the floor of the sea, and they saw a neat, partial gridwork of thin plastic pipes that looked as though it had been recently and incompletely laid—certainly it was not finished yet—and the sand below the grid bore the marks of a rake. He moved his hand tentatively through the sand under the grid, stirring gently. As Butterfly watched, he pulled a shimmering gold chain out of the sand with a sucking sound, and he glanced at her, his gray eyes narrow, his pupils enormous behind his mask. The chain bore a heavy cross studded with shiny green stones—emeralds, he guessed. He handed her the chain and swam purposefully and slowly over the grid with the lamp, poking his hand in the sand frequently, but careful to avoid the garden eels standing vertical in the water, the hard tips of their tails inserted into the sand. When they were startled, garden eels could deliver a nasty bite.

He plucked a red rosary from under the grid, an ordinary-looking set of coral beads that he tossed back onto the sandy bottom. What seemed to be buried here, under only a film of sand, consisted of a widely distributed miscellany of religious artifacts. He swam, Butterfly following and keeping well out of the sphere of light emanating from his outstretched hand.

He stopped, focusing the eerie yellow glow of the lamp on the bottom, under the southern edge of the grid.

A golden face, its dolorously smiling features partially buried in the sand, stared up at them, sapphire eyes twinkling blindly. Ishmael deposited the lamp on the sand, and Butterfly wrapped the heavy gold-and-emerald cross and chain around her wrist. They dug with their hands to free the golden countenance, but they soon realized that the face was attached to a golden neck, that the golden neck was attached to golden shoulders, that in fact a golden statue of titanic proportions lay here under the grid, a colossal ruby rosary around its neck, emeralds and sapphires spangled on its golden robe, its hands uplifted against its full breasts in deep reverence, a sunken Madonna of staggering value and beauty.

Ishmael passed a hand over the abundant skin of his long head, staring at the statue. It seemed to be frozen in motion, tilted out of the sand from its collar up, as if ready to emerge through the floor of the Gulf.

Suddenly he took Butterfly's hand, his visual acuity alerted by a slight shift in the darkness beyond their light.

Or maybe he smelled it.

Butterfly's digging ceased, the sand they had disturbed

began to settle again to the bottom, and the dim outline of a barracuda wallowed on the boundary of their vision, watching her.

Ishmael moved quickly in front of Butterfly, his hand extended toward the lamp. He wanted to shut off its yellow, distorted radiance. But he would have to wait to retrieve the light until the barracuda lost interest in Butterfly; he did not dare touch the Sam lamp with his hand—the great fish was attracted to shiny objects, and the old-fashioned lamp's brass fittings gleamed in the murky amber glow. Butterfly hastily scratched the gold chain off her wrist and tossed it into the surrounding darkness as she herself backed away from the sphere of light, the luminous tattoos disappearing into the gloom with her, as if she had stepped through a door in the water.

When the barracuda finally turned its cold vacant eyes and went on its way, its silent spectral visit to this graveyard of the Madonna at an end, Ishmael grabbed his light, shut it off, and groped for Butterfly's naked flesh, tapping her on the base of her spine; they swam slowly to the surface, this return journey in total darkness, kicking their fins in strong, rhythmic ease, following their anchor line up, ascending at twenty feet per minute, more slowly than their air bubbles, more slowly than the barracuda hunting on the bottom.

They emerged silently into the cool air.

The woman heaved herself up over the side of the boat, her heart still thudding under her breasts, and stood to extend a hand to Ishmael after she shed her tanks. She pulled him on board with an expert motion and removed her mask. She sat naked on the deck, pulling off her fins, and the cool night breeze raised gooseflesh on the wings of the silvery butterflies on the indistinct whiteness of her skin as the phosphorescent tattoos radiated the fire they had borrowed from the constellations wheeling overhead.

Without glancing at the woman, Ishmael stood in thought

beside the black circle of his clothing on the deck, his mask still covering his face, the green light of the ship's compass casting its glow over his mask and sliding down the tempered glass lens in salty emerald droplets.

He held up his long hand, palpating the air. The wind had begun to shift, promising bad weather by morning.

As Butterfly watched, the exotic fauna of her flesh glinting under the stars, he moved to the stern and turned on the propellers inside the mailbox.

THIRTEEN

ANNABELLE STRETCHED, BRUSHING HER FINGERTIPS against the quilted headboard, and glanced toward the open door to the balcony, startled to see menacing black clouds streaked across a leaden sky. With the ominous rumblings from across the gray harbor, the air seemed full of unusual portents to her, as though, whether she willed it or not, she stood on the cusp of a *vita nuova*, a disorder she could resist but not stop, an interior rebellion where she herself was the enemy. A crack had opened in her silent universe, and she imagined she could hear a well-remembered voice; but it was somehow different, subtly tricking her with a shade of sound, a texture of noise. Nikki, but not Nikki; Roy, but not Roy.

She frowned sleepily to herself and gave the cat a friendly pat on the head.

"What alarming calisthenics you're doing," she said. "I hope you don't have fleas."

Millie de Vargas's cat touched Annabelle's shoulder with an exploratory paw and opened its mouth, emitting an audible mew.

"I wonder if any noise came out of that leonine mouth," she said, rubbing the cat's chin. "Dave says you're afflicted with dumbness. I wonder if that's worse than being an unnatural, hollow, stupid block of wood like me. I'm slightly mad, you know, Cat: a deaf woman who thinks she's hearing things."

She glanced again toward the balcony door, and this time she was startled to see a pink sheet inching its uncertain way into her line of sight from above, like a brave pastel banner flapping in fitful winds against the threatening background of sky. Soon she saw shiny black flats, then a pair of thin legs wrapped around the sheet, anchoring it in the gusts from the harbor, then a pair of bright pink shorts, followed by a white shirt and sinewy tanned arms, and finally Dave's head, his brown hair whipped into a tangle by the rough winds blowing from the west.

He dropped lightly to his feet and peeked into the bedroom.

"I've been to your door five times already," he signed. "It's past ten o'clock. Get up. We're in for a storm, it looks like. Can I come in?"

"I'm naked. Go back upstairs and raid your servi-bar for anything the cat might eat while I put something on."

He crossed the bedroom and left the suite through the door.

Five minutes later he was back at the door, and this time she was waiting for him, wearing a pale yellow robe and holding the door open.

"Good morning," she said.

Dave could smell her toothpaste—Crest, he thought. He held out cans of anchovy paste and sardines marinara, eyeing her robe with distaste. "That's a really sickening shade of primrose," he announced. "Makes you look bilious."

She gave him a dirty look and reached for the cans. "He's going to get tired of this stuff," she said, moving into the kitchen. "Where's Marcel?"

Dave followed her, and, when she turned from the sink, he signed, "I left him upstairs. We had an argument."

She dumped the contents of the cans on a plate, using a spoon to spread the sauce, and the cat sprang to the counter, eating eagerly.

"The cat's manners leave something to be desired," she said. "He also forced himself into my bed last night."

Dave studiously avoided making a comment. He placed the latched box on the counter next to the cat.

"Guess where I found this."

She looked at the box, opened it, and snatched her hand away.

"It's okay," he said. "I've already dusted and photographed the prints."

She touched the wet ink pad inside, noting that her finger came away an alarming purple, and pushed the small printing blocks around in the box. "I hope these don't belong to Gabriel Perez?"

Dave shook his head. He held out his right hand for her inspection. He, too, bore the purple stain of the ink, on the knuckle of his index finger. "I can't get it off," he said. "It's permanent ink."

"Every time I see it, I'll think of those terrible letters poor Millie got," Annabelle said, holding up her finger and staring at the ink mark. "Dave, from the woman's point of view, they were almost unbearably invasive, a sort of verbal rape on cheap paper. Ugh." She closed the wooden box. "Tell me where you found this little engine of pornographic hatred."

"Attorney Green's castle, just past the moat and the dragon, in the dungeon. And let me tell you, Miss I-think-I-know-everything-about-women's-issues, from the man's point of view those letters are pretty hateful too."

"Sorry," she said. "That was stupid of me. I'm in a mood. What made you look at Green's?"

"Well, mostly the fact that I don't like him, but there actually was a bit of detective work involved. Wanna hear?"

"Of course."

"Sometime I'll have to tell you about Green's nice pet."

"He doesn't have a pet. He's allergic."

"Oh, yes he does. I'm thinking of becoming allergic too. But that's a different tale. You want to know what made me suspect that he was the mad purple-prose writer of Key West." Dave reached toward the fruit basket on the counter, but stopped his hand in mid-grab. "Popeye send you this?"

"The hotel management. Dave, what made you suspect Green?"

Dave selected a banana and peeled it slowly, concentrating on making neat, symmetrical divisions in the skin. "His glasses," he said, eyeing the pale fruit and taking a bite.

"His glasses?"

"Yeah, didn't you notice?"

"How could I help notice? He's always swinging them around."

"Exactly. He can't keep his hands off them. Annabelle, look at your hand. Look at mine."

She complied, wrinkling her nose at the small purple stains.

"So?" she asked.

"I actually touched Green's glasses. Icky things. I picked them up when he dropped them in the office. The plastic covers on the earpieces of the glasses are three distinct colors: yellow, which I take to be the original color, but faded; brown, which I take to be stain from the dye he uses on his hair, which is Preference, by L'Oréal"—Annabelle's eyes widened at Dave's revelation—"and pinkish lavender, which I take to be what this ink will look like when it's had time to wear a little. Same color family. Same as the ink on the letters. It took me a while to realize, but you'll have to admit, Annabelle, no one can top my eye for color. You'll really have to do something about that robe."

She regarded Dave with candid approval. "You don't miss much with your X-ray vision, Superman." She opened a drawer, extracted a steak knife, and began to pare the soft, fuzzy skin of a kiwi. "My, my. What a nasty trick to play on his partner. I wonder why he did it."

"It can't have been for the literary exercise. He's no Hemingway."

"He isn't even Norman Mailer. I take it you were not an invited guest chez Green?"

"Well, since I should have been, I took the liberty of supplying the deficiency in his manners by letting myself in. Of course Green's little toys prove nothing, beyond the fact that he was harassing his partner and threatening to kill her a little, both harmless little hobbies for an officer of the court to dabble in. Via the United States mail. That's a couple of felonies. But since we're not the cops, or even the correspondence-etiquette squad, do we care? We're looking for a murderer."

"I never thought he was a very likely candidate anyway."

Dave looked skeptically at her as she rinsed the knife. "Why not?" he signed when she placed the knife in the drainer. "He's *my* favorite."

"Dave, think about his allergies. The Hemingway estate is crawling with those six-toed cats. Green would be incapacitated before he got anywhere near the studio. The whole place is practically swimming in cat enzymes."

Dave pushed his lips with a finger, casting his glance thoughtfully at the cat on the counter. "Damn." He absently reached to scratch the cat's back. "What's the deal on these enzymes? I've never heard about them."

"People who are allergic to cats aren't really allergic to the hair, as many think. What they're allergic to is the enzymes loaded in cat saliva. Since they're always licking themselves, they're always covered with those enzymes, and they leave them around wherever they go."

"That's disgusting," Dave said with feeling, withdrawing his hand from the cat.

"Be that as it may, and despite Green's printing press, I

don't feel like we've made any real progress. You snagged Noah Green, all right, but that won't get Gabriel Perez out of jail. I keep coming back to him. Animals and people do leave characteristic marks behind them. And Hardy Security and Electronics guard Gabriel Perez left something better than enzymes in the studio—his fingerprints." She gazed thoughtfully across the counter into the dining room. "It always comes back to Perez," she murmured. "Our eyewitness."

"Yeah. The dope. Speaking of whom, by the way, the lawyer Arantxa found says he is holding off on posting bail for Perez. Says he thinks Perez will be released soon, today, for lack of evidence. Arantxa called me this morning with the news update. She's on her way here, by the way. Which leaves your father in unsupervised control of the Pink Building. Do you think he can be trusted not to make off with the erasers and so on?"

Annabelle smiled. "Probably not." She picked up the banana skin and tossed it into the disposal. "You may think I'm contrary, but I'm starting to think the evidence is looking pretty bad for Perez, motive or no motive, especially since we're getting nowhere trying to come up with a replacement for him." She dried her hands on a towel and used it to wipe the counter when the cat jumped to the floor. "Is Joel Schockett coming with Arantxa?" Dave nodded. "Millie's will is still under my pillow, and I won't feel really comfortable until I deliver that document into the hands of our legal department. However, contrary to my expectations, I slept like Rip Van Winkle's doxy last night."

"They'll be here around noon." A vein in Dave's temple twitched. "Annabelle, about last night."

"Yes. I have things to tell you too. Big, shocking things about the way insider Key West works."

"That's not what I mean. What got into you? You were supposed to meet me for dinner, and instead I found you carousing with Captain Hook down on the dock."

"Carousing? And what makes you think I was supposed to meet you for dinner? He asked me first."

Dave threw her a goaded look and walked around the counter into the dining area. He took Ricou's typewritten note from the table and waved it over the counter between them. "What do you call this?"

She looked puzzled. "Oh, there it is," she said. "I looked for that last night in my handbag and couldn't find it. I wonder how it got on the table."

"You didn't see my note?"

"What note?"

He tossed the note onto the counter, where it skidded across to her.

She read Dave's scribbled invitation to dinner and suddenly understood his reaction on the sunset dock. She raised her eyes to his. "I never saw it, Dave." She hesitated, seeing the chagrin in his eyes. "You did look stupendous, Jorge Enamorado, even if you were slightly *encolerizo* at the time. I've never seen you that mad."

Suddenly a wary light shone in Dave's brown eyes. "Where's my mask?" he demanded.

"The Hemingway mask? Where'd you leave it?"

"Don't play games with me. I left it right here on the table. My note was in the mouth."

Annabelle gazed distractedly at the dining table. "It must be there, if that's where you left it. I didn't touch the ugly thing."

"Well, it ain't here, fathead."

Annabelle placed her hands on the counter and peered over onto the floor. "See if it's down there," she said.

"Annabelle, it's gone."

They looked at each other across the counter.

Dave abruptly turned and swept his eyes around the large room. He stalked out to the balcony and disappeared from her view. He reentered from the bedroom, having completed a rough circle through the suite.

"Anybody here with you last night?" he asked, his signs businesslike and crisp.

"Just Roy, for a few minutes." Annabelle's eyes grew large. "If you're thinking he took it, think again. He didn't."

"How do you know? Was he wearing his halo?"

"No! But he wasn't wearing that dumb mask." She glared at him. "Why are you making such a big deal about this anyway?"

Dave eyed her pointedly. "Because, my dear fathead, if the killer wants to make an encore appearance in the role of the Literary Strangler of Key West, he'll be needing to freshen up his facial wear. The police have his first mask. And I don't imagine he'll just walk into a shop on Duval and buy a new mask the way I did. Might leave a fresh trail. Might make people wonder if someone close to the late Millie de Vargas— Green, for example—were to go up to the shopkeeper and say, 'Pardon me, can you help me find a Hemingway mask? I left mine behind at the scene of my last murder. Please don't tell the police I was in here. Have a nice day.'"

"The police," she said weakly. "Oh, dear."

"Yeah—oh, dear. Well said. That's beautiful. Oh, dear."

"Dave, I meant: Oh, dear, I saw Detective Ruggierrio last night. She practically offered to sit on some evidence for Noah Green. I wonder what her price was."

"Come again?"

"I was going to tell you, but you blew me away with the missing mask and those printing blocks of Green's. God, he seems to be everywhere we turn."

"I'm just glad he wasn't in his house when I turned there."

"He was busy buying drinks and who knows what else for the local powers. Let's take this chronologically." She ran her hands through her untidy hair. "Where to start? I feel suddenly sick. Are you sure about the mask? Maybe you took it upstairs when you were getting dressed for dinner." He shook his head with certainty. "As long as we're on that subject, where'd you ever get the tux on such short notice?"

"At the Margaret Truman Costume, Tuxedo, and Piano Shop, right here on Duval. They close at five, so I just squeaked in before closing and helped myself from the rack. I've got my eye on an exquisite pink tux—but you'd have to have just the perfect occasion for such an extravagance." Dave halted himself, his dreams of sartorial splendor suspended by the reality of the missing mask. He hurried on. "I checked the doors and windows while I was there. Whoever stole that Dracula cape and left it on Ernest Hemingway's doorstep needed to know nothing special about locks. And I've ruled out the shop's owner as our wandering vampire—he's totally nearsighted and could not possibly have found Millie's neck, even with the help of radar. He works alone there, renting party clothes and tinkling the ivories. Now tell me about Ruggierrio, the salescop. You did say she offered to sell some evidence?"

"I think so. So you were snooping at that costume shop."

"Ever so casually, while I did my shopping. Speaking of shopping, Ricou's too young for you. Don't give me dirty looks like that." Dave cast his eyes over the fruit basket, selecting an orange deliberately while Annabelle frowned at him. "You just need to watch your step, that's all." He touched her hand fleetingly. "Anyway, we've learned everything about the Dracula cape from that costume shop that we're going to learn. Although I may decide to get that pink tux. Unless you want to buy a piano?" A thoughtful look crossed his face. "I wonder if they sell any that are easy to play."

He seemed to muse on the possibility, and Annabelle considered him with a deeper frown, a sudden thought crossing her mind.

"Did you wear that beautiful tux to burgle Green's house?"

"After I calmed down, had a bite to eat, and realized I had nothing better to do than embark on a crime wave in the attorney's neighborhood, committing my full quota of breaking and entering for the month of January. Please, let's not talk about that anymore. I've forgiven you. Tell me the blasted cop news."

"You've forgiven me? It was all my fault?" She snorted inelegantly when he put up his hand in defeat. "That's better. Okay. I saw Green in deep conversation with Ruggierrio in Sloppy Joe's, where she probably acquired that beer belly. I expect they were the only natives—or should I say conchs?—in the bar."

Dave arched an eyebrow. "I would have thought fat female cops were too utterly contemptible for the likes of Green. What was he doing? Pumping her, paying her off, or trying to date her?"

"My guess is pumping her. And maybe paying her off. Maybe Green's more frightened by Millie's murder than he wanted to admit to us. Anyway, she told him that there was something typed on the fatal ribbon. This is consumingly interesting. It said, quote, 'There will be no Hemingway Resort.' Just like that. And then Ruggierrio offered to sit on the discovery. I couldn't tell what Green's response was. His back was sort of to me. Ruggierrio also had interesting things to say about the autopsy, but I can't stand here anymore talking about her sins. That missing mask is freaky. Somebody was here. While I was out last night."

"Or while you slept so soundly," Dave said gently.

She shivered. "Let's get out of here. I'll tell you everything else on our way to the playhouse—which I hope is open—to converse with the grieving brother."

She hurried into the living room and knelt by the coffee table, where she reached inside a sardine carton. Nestled in the box, which she and Ricou had found in a Dumpster behind the hotel, were her shoe and a small square of linoleum, cut with Ricou's knife from the floor at Sloppy Joe's. "While I get dressed, will you see about messengering this stuff to the lab in Miami? I'll tell you about that too. And will you call my dad to alert him that this junk is on the way? I want an analysis of the sticky orange stuff." She bent to look under the couch. "It's not under there either."

When she reentered the living room, eight minutes later, wearing red shorts and a red T-shirt, a white silk scarf tied around her waist, her hair brushed until it shone, Dave had already delivered the box into the hands of a bellhop, along with a twenty-dollar bill. Dave had printed the address of the Pink Building for the bellhop, who had promised to see the shoe and linoleum off to Miami immediately.

"Our first stop had better be a shoe store," Annabelle said. "I forgot to bring any."

"Are you ready?"

"Yep." She patted her handbag. "I've got the will in here."

"Annabelle, don't you think Millie de Vargas was taking a big risk entrusting that letter about the new will to Green to give to you?"

"He looked me in the eye and said I must be expecting to receive the letter. She probably told him that I knew all about it. He didn't dare not give it to me. Anyway, I think she had a backup plan. Remember Aunt Ashleen's reaction when we went to collect the will? She wasn't at all surprised to see us or to hear about a secret compartment. She only asked one question, remember?"

"She wanted to know whose instructions about the secret compartment we were following."

"Right. That was all. I'll bet she knew about it all along. She just wanted to make sure Millie's wishes were being carried out. Let's go." She hesitated. "Do you think that mask could have disappeared innocently?"

"No."

"Do you think we should tell the cops?"

Dave lowered his brows ominously. "Maybe they already know."

FOURTEEN

ANNABELLE AND DAVE LEFT THE SUITE AND WALKED together down the stairs and out to Duval Street, where they hurried along until they came to a sign pointing to a Mallory Square sandal factory. There they purchased a pair of red Kino sandals for the unheard of sum of seven dollars and then crossed the square to the Waterfront Playhouse, a cool misting rain falling with more steadiness than force.

The theater was even more dismal in the rain, a small, forlorn white-stucco building backing on the harbor. The front entrance and foyer were now unlocked but deserted, posters on the walls hung with peeling tape, the doors into the theater closed, their small glass windows covered with grit. Annabelle and Dave decided to look for signs of life at the back of the building and walked out into the mist and around to the stage door, which was open and from which a series of screams was issuing that caused Dave's hands to spring into motion in order to translate them into words for Annabelle.

"No, no, no, no, no! You block, you stone, you worse than useless thing! Shut up, shut up, shut up! Caliban is supposed to be savagely drunk, reeling with alcohol. But you trudge around the stage with all the emotional authority of chalk. God! How can we open this abortion in three nights?"

Annabelle and Dave climbed a small set of concrete stairs leading into the theater from the stage door. They found themselves in the wings, eavesdropping on an apparent madman, who was flailing his arms and berating a tall man with a curiously shaped bald head, a long and stretched-appearing skull. The man was clutching a prop bottle and looked crestfallen, the skin covering his long head creased in a thousand tiny folds as he raised his forehead to look at the other man from under his eyebrows, evidently thoroughly cowed. Three other actors on the stage shifted uncomfortably, uncomfortably witnessing both the outburst and the humiliation. Annabelle recognized one of the embarrassed onlookers as the large-boned waitress who had served her and the lieutenant sandwiches at Sloppy Joe's Bar. The waitress had shed her white leather attire for jeans and a wrinkled shirt, her spike heels for canvas loafers, her tough demeanor for red-faced mortification.

The shouting man jumped from the stage to the theater floor, flinging himself loosely into a seat and clutching his head in his hands as though to prevent it from flying apart.

"Why me? Why?" he wailed. "Why must I always be saddled with these fucking amateurs? I could drag more feeling out of tofu."

"I'm sorry, Fran," the man with the long wrinkled head said, his voice shaking. "You want I should try again?"

" 'I'm sorry, Fran,' " the wailing man mimicked, the fine skin on the bridge of his nose creasing as he imitated the other man's voice. " 'I'm sorry, Fran. You want I should try again, Fran?' God Almighty, Ishmael! This is supposed to be Shakespeare, not Norman Lear. And all you can do is whine 'You want I should try again?' What the hell made you think you could act anyway?"

Dave had been signing the scene for Annabelle, and she gazed with fascination at the players and the lively slice of theater life they had stumbled into.

"*You* did, Fran. When I played the coach driver in *Cinder-*

ella last month. And you said I'd be perfect for Caliban." The bald man sat down heavily on a log placed on its side center stage. "At least I know all my lines."

A transformation crept over the features of the director. His face assumed a cunning aspect, his eyes blinking rapidly.

"So you do, Ishmael. You know all your lines. Which is more than I can say for the rest of this misbegotten cast." He glared at the other actors standing behind Ishmael's log. "And I don't know how we're going to make this work, unless I reverse all your lobotomies. You don't need a director; you need some ability."

Dave stepped gracefully onto the stage from the wings.

"Excuse me. Sorry to interrupt your rehearsal. Are you Francisco de Vargas?" Dave's strong and melodic tenor voice filled the 186-seat theater from mahogany rafter to mahogany rafter.

The director stood slowly, his hands planted on the arms of the seat for support, a reverent, hungry gleam in his eyes. He approached the stage, the long, full sleeves of his blue-satin shirt billowing as he seemed to wrench words from his jaded soul:

"Ariel. As I live and breathe. You've been sent to me by a just God to grace this production with your enchanted voice and make this old theater sing in triumph." He leaped onto the stage, his blazing eyes never leaving Dave's face. "Say something else. Let me hear the elfin perfection of your voice again, crying out your molten desire to be free of the fetters we mortals would place on you."

Dave was signing for Annabelle with prodigious speed. She was watching with amused detachment from the wings, her forward movement suspended by the look of dawning ambition on Dave's face.

The director did not pause in his overtures. "And look, look at the purity of those gestures, harnessing the forces of wind and rain and sun, the very cosmos at your fingertips. You are my Ariel to the life."

Annabelle had known from the word *Caliban* that this director was in the midst of staging Shakespeare's last play, *The Tempest,* with the long-headed man as its monster and some as-yet-unseen actor as its sprite, but she doubted that Dave had recognized the references, and she studied his radiant face as he gazed dumbly at the director with something approaching real respect.

She judged it was time to interrupt Dave's new vision of himself bathed in the glow of footlights, so she stepped around a metal table containing audio equipment and cassette tapes and moved forward onto the stage, saying in her clear, carrying, but soft voice, "Oh, brave new world, that has such people in't."

The director seemed to hold his breath.

When he did breathe, it was to utter "Miranda" in fadeaway tones, and he glided toward Annabelle—like a sprite himself, she thought.

"Actually I'm Annabelle Hardy-Maratos. That's Dave. Can we speak with you for a few moments?"

"Tell me, only tell me, you're here to audition," he begged, taking her hand and leading her to the apron of the stage.

"I'm sorry to say we're here to speak with you about your sister's death."

A veil of grief descended over his features. "Ah. 'We are such stuff as dreams are made on, and our little life is rounded with a sleep.' Millie was a good sister."

Annabelle saw that Dave was coming out of his stupor, a sort of partial suspended animation in which his signs to her had all but ceased, but she kept her attention on de Vargas. "You have Prospero's lines. Are you playing the magician as well as directing?" she asked.

"The show, as they say, must go on. I shall dedicate Friday's performance to Millie." He threw his arm in a sweeping blue-satin curve toward the primitive lighting booth jutting out over the last seats, as though his sister were present there as a spirit to watch over the theater. He shrugged, dismissing whatever phantom he had conjured in his mind. "Would you like to sit down, Miranda?"

De Vargas led them down narrow steps and onto the floor of the theater. He chose some front-row seats and bowed them with consummate grace into their chairs.

Dave attempted to regain the rhythm of his signing while keeping a fascinated eye on de Vargas.

Placing his hand casually on Dave's bony knee, the blue-satin folds of his sleeve brushing Dave's leg, de Vargas sat gracefully back at a leisurely angle in his seat, beside Dave, whose expressive face now froze as he stared at the stage before him. Annabelle, who sat on Dave's other side, thought she could see a train of thought passing at lightning speed behind her friend's sudden tension. His feet were twitching, and she thought he was considering making a break for it, his dreams of theater stardom chased by the unwelcome touch of Francisco de Vargas's hand.

De Vargas, ignoring Dave's tension and apparently never at a loss, continued, speaking to them as if they were old and very dear friends of his, and he tightened his grip on Dave's knee while addressing Annabelle. "Do you know what the worst part of community theater is?"

Annabelle shook her head.

"The community!" de Vargas declared in a rush, barely allowing her time to react. Dave began to sign with great speed. "You can't imagine what I've gone through to mount this production, at a staggeringly dirt-cheap cost, just to bring Shakespeare to this philistine town. Every other half-wit in Key West thinks of himself as an artist and then hangs out a shingle, supporting himself on the gullibility of tourists who got their ideas about taste from watching pseudointellectual freaks like Oprah Winfrey. Can you imagine? Just yesterday, right on Duval Street, I saw the archetypical Key West oil painting. It was a black-and-white study of the sunset! God! I can't stand it!"

De Vargas flung himself out of his seat and took an energetic turn about the stone floor. Dave rubbed his knee in relief.

Annabelle stood and inserted herself in the director's path.

"Why are you staging *The Tempest* at all, if you feel that way about your audience?" she asked.

"So they'll all feel bad—those underqualified lisping mock-intellectual John Simon wannabes," he snarled, clipping each word off with uncannily crisp enunciation. He saw the look of shock on her face but continued on wildly without check. "They're going to be force-fed this play. Key West is going to have Shakespeare if I have to ram it down their throats using the deadwood up there on the stage!"

"Mr. de Vargas, please," Annabelle coaxed, attempting to take his hand. "Let's sit down again."

They sat as before, de Vargas jerking his fingers through his hair.

"Mr. de Vargas . . ." Annabelle began.

"Oh, please. Call me Fran. What did you say your name is?"

"Annabelle."

"And your little friend? The one who's been interpreting for you so divinely, just like a gymnast with those wonderful hands."

Annabelle's little friend squirmed as de Vargas curled his arm comfortably about Dave's frozen shoulder, and Annabelle marveled at the lightning mood swings of the flamboyant director.

"He's Dave the Monkeyman."

"What a darling name," de Vargas said, pinching Dave's cheek. "You'll have to tell me what it means sometime. Something ultraspecial, I imagine." He turned to Annabelle. "And you want to talk to me about Millie."

"Yes."

"Why?"

Annabelle was momentarily taken aback.

"Because I run the security company whose guard, a man named Gabriel Perez, has been arrested on suspicion of your sister's murder," she explained.

"Oh. Him. Perez." De Vargas shook his head, his black hair swinging across his temples. "No, he didn't do it, my darling Annabelle. But I don't know who did. Probably somebody out to get her for that resort, although what the big deal is about that, I couldn't say. It's not as if anyone in Key West is capable of appreciating the aesthetics of a simple sunset anyway, not without a gallon of rum to make it all clear to them. Let 'em build their eyesore, I say. Who the fuck cares?" He pinched Dave's cheek again and then patted it vigorously, punctuating his words. "Who the fuck cares, Monkeyman? Only, they were too late, if you know what I mean."

"I don't know what you mean," Annabelle said.

Dave massaged his flaming cheek.

"Millie sold her shares in the resort almost two months ago and got out."

Annabelle gasped.

Dave was sitting forward in his seat. "What?" he squeaked. He cleared his throat, glancing over his shoulder as if trying to locate the source of that squeak. "What?" he repeated, in a deeper tone.

"Yeah. She sold. I wish I had money. I'd show Key West what stagecraft really is." He gestured expansively toward the stage. "I'd have ethereal blue curtains, made from the finest silk, and garlands of pink gauze, and—"

"Mr. de Vargas. Fran. Do you know whom she sold those shares to?" Annabelle asked urgently.

"That pompous ass Green."

"Who?" Dave asked, but this time his question came out as a deep, reverberating boom. He cleared his throat again.

"Green, Noah S. Just what he needs, more big-money income property. Green's such a cheap bastard, he made her sell really low. When that hotel goes up, it's going to make a fortune. Can you imagine? Unrestricted views, deep drainage, whatever they call it. It can't miss. I wish I owned stock. Since Green has it all now, I'll probably inherit diddly. Maybe some really putrid mahogany Madonnas—now, there's an example of Key West art for you—and the proud name of de Vargas will be mine alone. Goody."

"Why did she sell out, Fran?" Annabelle asked, her eyes wide. "I thought the resort was almost ready for groundbreaking."

"She told me she had received some horrible threatening letters and wanted to shake the dirt off her skirts. Some melodramatic Catholic twaddle about 'suffer the children,' or 'love thy neighbor,' or 'play bingo.' I'm really sick of the fucking hypocrisy about that fucking resort. There's a lot of people here in Key West just waiting to soak in all the dough from the new hotel. But will I get any? Oh, no. Not me. I'll be sitting here in the shadow of the new hotel, Little Fran de Vargas and his chickenshit theater of the absurd."

Annabelle considered the deep chagrin on his almost-handsome face. There was something about his face—some permanent discontent, some slight twist to his features, some lurking distress in the eyes—that prevented the attractive individual components from adding up to a total of beauty. Perhaps it was unhappiness, Annabelle thought.

"Mr. de Vargas," she began. "Fran . . ."

He smiled wistfully at her gentle tone.

"Fran, where were you at sundown Monday?"

He laughed, a truly spontaneous, delighted, full-hearted laugh. "That's good. Not even the cops have dared to ask me that—I am the chief mourner, you know, which gives me a sort of above-it-all status, at least among the local gentry, a sort of license for disdain. Well, I'll tell you, Miranda. I was here.

Yes, yes, very here. Working on the antiquated lighting system." The unhappy, skewed look descended on his features again, and the moment of physical beauty that had accompanied the laugh was gone. "I've spent hours, what you might seriously call the best years of my so-far-fucking life, on this hulk of a shell of a disaster of a would-be theater. Just to put on a few decent plays that nobody appreciates."

"Surely you underestimate your audience?" Annabelle suggested, with an understanding smile.

"If I only had a little more time, a little more money, some real actors . . ."

The tall man with the long head appeared on the apron of the stage.

"Can we take a break, Fran?"

De Vargas leaped to his feet.

"A *break*? To take a break implies you are taking a break *from* something." His tones were ominously silken. "We will break when you accomplish a miracle and get the granite out of your veins."

He bounced on the balls of his feet and smacked his palms on the floor of the apron, lifting his agile hips onto the stage and standing up, all in one fluid motion.

"Places everyone. If you can find them without a divining rod."

Dave pulled on the sleeve of Annabelle's shirt.

"Noah Green's a really bad man," he signed. "And a frightful liar."

"The Planning and Zoning office sure didn't have a record of the sale, unless we missed it. I wonder if Fran's the only one who knows about the stock transfer?"

"That would be my guess. I'll bet Green is *lying* in wait, biding his time before he records the bill of sale. And I'll bet Green does not know that Millie talked to her brother. Let's go find little Noah S. and dunk his head in the harbor to teach him a lesson about lying to his betters. He certainly led us to believe Millie still owned a big piece of the resort. In fact he said so. And he said Fran would inherit it, along with her other real estate—not possible if the shares are Green's." Dave made a fist and considered it curiously, muttering to himself: "*Cristo en la cuchara. Pendejo. Eso es pura paja.*"

Annabelle, too, was thoughtful, but she turned to watch the action unfold on the stage as the tall man began to moan his lines and move stiffly about. Now she could see that he was wearing a straggling, long brown tail, attached to his jeans with a large safety pin. She smiled to herself, shaking her head.

Although she could not hear the lines, she knew them well, and she thought the tall man's unusual face showed promise of bringing the role of Caliban to life. De Vargas was wrong about this actor's potential. He was just missing something, some insight.

Dave tugged on her sleeve again and pointed to Caliban. "Odd head. Looks like a newborn."

"No. He looks like a timber wolf. All big ears and round blue eyes."

Annabelle stood and reproduced the fluid motions that had taken de Vargas onto the stage.

"May I make a suggestion?" she asked.

"Oh, anything, darling Miranda. We're obviously getting nowhere." De Vargas stepped to the edge of the stage and dropped angrily to the floor of the theater.

Annabelle approached Caliban as he sat on the log, the bottle clasped lightly in his long fingers. She squatted before him and spoke in low tones. "You're playing Caliban as if he were a wicked human, aren't you?"

The actor nodded glumly at Annabelle.

She put her hand encouragingly on the actor's long arm. "You know, I think Caliban would think of himself as an animal, an animal that has been badly treated by the rotten humans he's come in contact with. If you tried that, tried to hate the people on the stage, tried to think of yourself as better than them, wounded by them, sick of them—well, it might work better. Use your props the way an animal would. Can you try that?"

A spark of recognition shone in the man's eyes, which, Annabelle could see now that she was closer to him, were a silvery gray. He nodded shyly. She patted his hand, which had streaks of black makeup—which she thought a nice touch for the character—stood, and signaled to Dave.

He took a more circuitous route to the stage, giving de Vargas a wide berth, climbing the narrow flight of stairs at stage left, and together they returned to the wings.

As they were leaving, Dave turned back, drawn by a series of movements from the stage.

The tall man had bent himself over the log, using his arms and hands as if they were paws. He was giving Trinculo and Stephano instructions on how to murder Prospero, the magician, who, in this production, was also Francisco de Vargas.

"There thou mayst brain him," Caliban said, a drop of drool hitting the log. "Having first seized his books, or with a log batter his skull." Caliban caressed the log lovingly in illustration. "Or paunch him with a stake, or cut his wezand with thy knife." Caliban pounded on the log and howled, a blood-curdling noise of despair and gladness together, and he reached down and curled his tail, cradling it in his arms like an infant.

Dave felt a chill along his spine. Annabelle's shoulder touched his as she watched, spellbound, from the wings.

From the cold and dark theater floor came the sound of applause. Francisco de Vargas stood there, having risen slowly to his feet, his eyes huge, clapping, if sardonically, for Caliban.

And behind him, standing in the aisle at the back of the theater, was a man dressed all in black, a stocky man with a red face above the collar of a priest of the Roman Catholic church.

FIFTEEN

"LET'S GO AROUND TO THE FRONT AND TRY TO CATCH THE padre on his way out of the theater," Annabelle whispered. "He looks like he wants to talk with Francisco."

"You think that's our archdiocesan heir apparent?"

"Yes, and I think he's carrying around a large piece of the Millie de Vargas puzzle." She frowned, remembering the directorial moods of the murdered woman's brother. "I hope Key West's answer to Joseph Papp is minding his language."

"His fucking language," Dave corrected her.

She led the way from the wings, back to the stage door and outside. The rain had stopped, but the sky was much grayer, darker, especially in the west, where a thin black bank of low clouds seemed to hover on the far horizon, spitting jagged flakes of lightning into the turgid Gulf.

They sat on the damp front steps of the Waterfront Playhouse, watching the tourists who were hurriedly dodging in and out of the Sponge Market and other small shops on Mallory Square, many of them looking for games to play in their hotel rooms when the inevitable heavy rain broke over the city and their outdoor plans.

"Francisco de Vargas is quite a *hand*ful," Dave said.

"He's an exaggerated self-portrait, I think, constantly being created and revised. He suspects he's a failure, and is full of thwarted passions and self-dramatization and great misdirected disappointment."

"He's full of something." Dave leaned his elbow on the stairs. "Francisco can't single-handedly save the world from what he sees as Key West's ghastly artistic affectations."

Annabelle picked a blade of Bermuda grass and contemplated it.

"I don't know, Dave. D. H. Lawrence said that the two great American specialties are saving the world and plumbing." She watched as the gusting wind from the west bent the blade of grass over her hand. "Maybe Francisco can't save Shakespeare in this city. Maybe no one can save the world. But it would be nice if we could just make this little corner of it cleaner by doing something about that snake Noah Green. Something to neutralize him if we could, before the new will is read and he makes more trouble."

"Tell me—do you regard the little attorney more in the light of a clogged toilet or a threat to world peace?"

"He's a threat to my peace, my sense of the decent limits of self-expression."

Dave put his chin in his hands, leaning on his knees. "What can we do about him? It seems to me that Millie's already fixed his wagon, with the new will."

"Maybe. This new will may not deflect him all that much." She smoothed the blade of grass between her fingers. "In a way, I pity Francisco de Vargas, although he didn't seem to have high expectations. It didn't seem that Francisco even knew the terms of the first will." She sighed. "And, to a lesser extent, I feel sorry for Ashleen Ricou and the Hemingway Museum. I hate to see a giant lobbying group like the Catholic church get its hands on a fortune." She smiled grimly. "But that's not our problem. Our problem, as soon as Hardy's legal department gets here, is going to be how they all take that new will. Including Green."

She glanced at Dave, who was nodding his head violently in agreement.

"We'd better start notifying the heirs and would-be heirs," she said. "I just hope we gain some new insight into the financial background of the murder. What do you think?"

"I think I'd like to see Green swing his glasses when he hears the bad news he's going to be out two million smackeroos. He could buy a lot of stamps and stationery with that kind of pesetas."

Annabelle's green eyes began to smolder with an idea. "Stamps and stationery," she repeated. "Maybe there is something we can do about him." She tossed away the blade of grass. "Dave, the King of the Liars sits on his royal throne only two blocks from where we're sitting. Why don't you go invite him to join us here on the steps for a few minutes, so we can hold his feet to the fire? We can think of this damp spot as a sort of temporary Star Chamber, a Spanish-Inquisition-By-The-Sea."

"He's a bad man. Why do I have to go?"

"Because I'm the president, and you're the chief financial officer," she explained with exaggerated patience. "That's why my toys are bigger and shinier than yours."

He grinned and took off across the square at a trot, as always when he moved without some effect in mind, a picture of athletic grace and strength. She thought about the many movie characters he had befriended as a child, wondering how he would have fared if he had hung out in gyms instead.

Out in the harbor a steely gray Coast Guard cutter plowed its steady way toward the Trumbo Street docks, a dark, looming presence against the smoky gray of the sky. A white navy Sikorsky SH-60B helicopter churned the mists low over Tank Island, heading east, toward the city, and she wondered where Lieutenant Roy Ricou was, where his classified assignment took him during the daylight hours. She felt an unaccustomed, wild mood descend over her at the thought of him; she felt chafed by the unraveling threads of the almost flawless widow-hood that had followed her deliberately ideal marriage to Nikki, chafed by the neat designs of an anesthetic, practical celibacy that had set her apart as insensibly as her hearing loss.

To shake off the mood, she rose and entered the theater foyer, gazing at curling posters for *Cinderella* and other chil-dren's plays directed by Francisco de Vargas. No doubt those were popular fare, but she imagined his disdain for his audi-ence as he struggled to keep the theater alive by staging works he undoubtedly considered unworthy.

She wondered what the priest was saying to de Vargas, what consoling words he had brought all the way from the cold January of New York to the end of this warm southern archipelago catering to dreams and ego and artistic tempers. She tried to see through the tiny windows in the doors separat-ing the foyer from the descending rows of seats, but the grit on the glass was thick and old. She opened the door a crack. De Vargas was sitting with the priest in the front row, his head bent over his linked hands. She closed the door softly and retreated outside to her perch on the steps.

She was startled a moment later when the frayed knees of a pair of blue jeans entered her peripheral vision, just inches from her shoulder as she sat on the steps. The waitress from Sloppy Joe's Bar was leaving the theater, carrying some cloth-ing in a net bag. She waved uncertainly at Annabelle, a little toss of her big hand, and walked off toward Duval Street.

Annabelle considered the varieties of people, the long, the short, the dark, the light, the wide, the thin. This blond wait-ress was big, without being fat, and, since she was the only female Annabelle had seen in the theater, she wondered if this were Francisco de Vargas's Miranda, the beautiful, virginal her-oine of Shakespeare's play.

Soon Caliban emerged from the theater. He, too, de-scended the steps, but he stopped.

"Thanks," he said, "that felt really good. It's the first time Fran ever applauded any of us."

"It must be very difficult for him now, with his sister's death."

"I guess." The man seemed to hesitate, thinking. "But he's always like this. Well, good-bye, miss." He seemed to hesitate again, the overabundance of skin on his curious forehead wrinkled in what appeared to be profound thought. "Fran's an okay guy. Really. He's just got a tough job."

He jogged off into the gloom, his long strides taking him in a direction opposite to the one taken by the waitress, toward the charter boats in the marina. Annabelle watched him until he disappeared around the wall separating Mallory Square from Ocean Key House and the pier.

Across the square she saw Dave walking rapidly, eating a bright-green Popsicle and leading the attorney, who, in a natty three-piece suit, was lagging behind and swinging his glasses. Dave looked like a native, a conch; Noah Green, like an import from New York City, from the canyons of the Wall Street district, their respective airs of breezy unconcern and heavy fretting giving them those labels in her mind more than the clothing they wore.

Dave plopped down beside her on the steps, his gold bow tie looped over his wrist. "It wasn't easy prying Noah away from the helm of the Hemingway Resort Ark." Dave held out his wrist to her. "Will you take this off my arm? I don't want to get Popsicle sludge all over it."

She unfastened the contraption and took it from him, eyeing it speculatively. "What do you want me to do with this thing?"

"Oh, just stick it in your purse with your gun," he said airily, putting out his tongue to lick the Popsicle. "The tie has served its purpose. My tongue is so numb. Can you understand me when I talk, my dear?"

"How do you know I've got my gun?"

"Detective work, pure and simple. I looked."

Green stepped across the moist grass of the theater's small yard and approached their outpost on the stairs of the Waterfront Playhouse.

"I'm hardly accustomed to doing business this way," he said angrily. "Your man says you have something urgent to discuss with me and that you're allergic to mahogany."

Annabelle's half smile curved her mouth, and she glanced at Dave, whose tongue, licking the Popsicle, had taken on the color of strained peas.

"Mr. Green, I've got some disturbing news for you about your peculiar way of practicing law," she said, her voice matter-of-fact.

Dave squirmed in anticipation, his eyes glued to the attorney's face, which had paled under its pink skin.

"What are you talking about?" Green demanded, scowling, his head turned to one side. "What kind of a game are you playing?"

"It's called 'Annabelle Says,'" Dave explained. "Wanna play?"

"Are you insane, getting me out in this weather for a stupid game?"

Dave resumed his signing duties here, having deposited his Popsicle stick in a flowerpot on the bottom step. He started from "insane," placing his hand at the side of his forehead, giving the hand a quick twist in and out several times, a gesture even Green understood.

"What an intriguing question, coming from you," Annabelle said.

"I don't have to stand here and listen to this." Green turned on his heel and started to walk away.

"That's true," Annabelle said, watching Dave's rapid gestures. "Mr. Green, if we were keeping score, you'd be way ahead on insults. That's an arrogant and rude way to treat a deaf person."

Green stopped dead in his tracks.

"Oh, let him go, Annabelle. He's a bad man." Dave accompanied his signs with words in his strong tenor voice, but not so strong that Francisco de Vargas might hear him from inside the theater. Dave was taking no unnecessary chances with the invasive cast-recruitment policy of the eager director, despite that brief, golden vision of stardom on the boards.

Green turned slowly, and Annabelle saw that a dull flush had suffused his pale face.

"What do you want?" he asked. "Why did you insist on getting me over here? I'm busy, and it's going to rain. I'm very susceptible to changes in barometric pressure."

Annabelle put her head back and gazed at the sky. It was indeed heavy-looking, pregnant, seeming to hover just above their heads, pushing toward the earth.

She shifted her regard to Green.

"I'll be brief."

He looked at her speculatively, something in her soft tone disarming his wariness.

"I'll give you a few minutes," he said, looking first at the sky, then at his watch.

Dave snorted.

"That's all I'll need," Annabelle said, still in her soft voice. "I'll tell you what we know and what we want."

Green stuck his left hand in his pocket and continued to twirl his glasses with his right.

"First, I know that Barbara Ruggierrio made you an improper offer last night," Annabelle said.

"You're out of your mind."

"No, just an excellent reader of lips, Mr. Green."

"You can't prove a stupid charge like that."

"Maybe not. How about this one? We know you sent anonymous letters to Millie de Vargas, threatening her with unspeakable harm, in unspeakable language, if she did not cease her efforts on behalf of the Hemingway Resort. I can quote them if you like." Green opened his mouth, but snapped it shut again immediately. "We also know she sold you her stock in the resort, almost certainly as a result of those letters. So you lied to us, which is nothing on the cosmic scale of things. Many people have lied to us. But you bullied Millie, manipulated her illegally for your own profit, demonstrated a demented psyche by the dirty and cruel means of that manipulation. This all adds up to criminal behavior, counselor." Annabelle took a deep breath. "Do you want to say anything yet?"

"I don't know why you're doing this, or what the hell you're talking about. In fact, my original impression of you was right. I think you're being extremely irresponsible, young woman." Green twirled his glasses with rapid fury, the gold frames whirring in the misty air.

"We have proof." She held up her finger, showing him the purple ink staining her skin.

Green stared and swallowed. "I don't know what you're talking about." He was suddenly perspiring freely, his forehead shiny. He slipped his glasses into the breast pocket of his jacket, after experiencing some difficulty holding on to them.

"What I'm talking about is the printing set you used and the letters you sent. Complete with fingerprints."

The hand inserting the glasses into the pocket seemed to freeze.

"So it was you. You burglarized my house. I can have you arrested. The police in this town listen to me." Green lowered his hand self-consciously and attempted to force a worldly smile, but it soured on the way to his lips, becoming instead a half smirk tinged with fear. "We're really two of a kind, we two. We can work out some accommodation. That's why we're here, correct?"

"Not at all," Annabelle said, shaking her head. "You see, you're not going to get anything in the deal we're about to make. You're going to tell me about those shares Millie sold to you, and you're going to undertake a little writing assignment."

"I didn't buy those shares. I didn't." Green hesitated, licking his lips. "Not right off. She insisted."

Annabelle sat up.

"What's the difference? They're your shares now, and it's your controversy out in the harbor."

"Okay. So I lied about that. But that doesn't make me a murderer, if that's what you're trying to insinuate. I was just trying to save myself a little bad publicity and the same kind of trouble that got Millie killed. Do you know about the message the police found on the typewriter ribbon?"

Annabelle nodded. "But you didn't know about the ribbon when you lied about the shares."

"Everybody lies in real estate. If I had to pay a nickel for every time I've lied or been lied to, I'd be ruined." He put his head down and watched his shoe stroking the grass.

While Dave produced the words in rapid gestures, he and Annabelle exchanged looks, hers sour, his blatantly disgusted.

"You *are* ruined, Mr. Green," Annabelle said.

"Are you going to tell anyone about the letters?" Green bleated. "What good will that do your man Perez? Why are you sticking your nose in my affairs? They have nothing to do with Perez."

Annabelle stood and walked in a circle around Green.

"Apparently all you can understand is pure self-interest, Mr. Green. Pure, unadulterated debits and credits in the ledger of the personal condition of N. S. Green, attorney-at-law."

Annabelle stood facing the attorney, her hands in the pockets of her shorts. Dave had risen to stand beside her, signing.

"Well, counselor, here's a little piece of information for your file on Noah S. Green's welfare. Millie left a new will, a holographic will superseding the one you've been gloating over. I leave it to you to imagine the legal position of the new will, given that it was executed by an attorney. By the terms of the new will, you're not going to get that little two-million-dollar bonus. How does that rub your self-interest?"

"I don't believe you." Green passed his tongue over his lips. "You're making this all up in some outrageous attempt to get a hold on me. And even if it were true, you're trying to blackmail me. You've got that printing set so that I won't contest this so-called new will." A small glimmer shone in Green's eyes. "You entered my house illegally. You *are* blackmailing me."

"No, Mr. Green, I'm not offering you even the hope that a blackmailer customarily offers her victim. You're finished as a lawyer. You'll be lucky to stay out of jail."

The rain had begun to fall in large, slow drops, darkening Green's shoulders and running down his face.

"What do you want?" he breathed. His hands were shaking; he reached for his glasses, shaking the earpieces loose from their folded position against the lenses. Dave noticed that the glasses trembled, the rain running in greasy rivulets on the lenses.

"I want it in writing, Green. All of it. Mr. Enamorado will escort you to your office, where you will record, in your own handwriting, the fact that you bought Millie's shares, having coerced her by sending threatening letters via the United States mail. That's a felony. Two felonies."

Green stared at her, speechless.

"And Dave," Annabelle added in sign language, "get those letters from the windowsill before this rain makes me a liar."

Green plucked at Annabelle's arm, and she stared at his hand in surprise, as if she were shocked to learn that he had hands.

"Don't touch me," she said quietly.

He withdrew his hand with a sharp jerking motion, as if he had been stung. More than any of her other words, this simple request, delivered without emotion, in wholly disinterested tones, convinced him that this unnatural, cold woman was not toying with him, that he would never get the printing set back, never see the letters again unless they were an exhibit in a trial, and convinced him that there was indeed a new will. No woman had ever spoken to him like that, not even the formidable Millie de Vargas.

"Just tell me who inherits in the new will," he whined. "I have to know."

"I don't owe you any consideration, counselor. My attorney will read the new will in my hotel room this afternoon. If you want to come, you'll be allowed to listen then."

"But—"

"One more thing, Mr. Green. What was Ruggierrio's asking price for sitting on the typewriter ribbon's message?"

Green was not prepared for this fresh attack, and he stumbled as he took a step back, away from Annabelle.

"You see, Mr. Green, I do read lips well, don't I?"

"She wants a share in the resort," he whispered hoarsely.

"That's what I thought."

"Let's go, Green," Dave said. "You've been dismissed."

"Just a minute, Dave," Annabelle said. She walked with him under a tree, out of earshot of Green. "Just for laughs, take a look and see if he's got your mask." She stood between him and the attorney. "Stick out your tongue."

He did, showing her a coating of shocking green that looked like something out of a swamp movie.

"What flavor was that Popsicle?"

"Industrial-strength floor wax," he said. "I'd better go before those letters turn to Popsicles. I'll act like you were telling me to put lighted matches under his fingernails. Quick, he's looking; hand me a matchbook."

"Get out of here, you clown."

She watched Dave and the attorney silently cross deserted and glistening Mallory Square in the rain, and she stood under the shelter of the tree, waiting for the priest.

Few people came and went in the square. Traffic on the harbor was one-way and thin, into docks and marinas, out of the weather. She wondered again if the lieutenant were out on the water, then wondered if his secret work were conducted in some ill-lit bunker filled with fantastic and deadly devices, deep beneath the surface of the coral island, or if his work would turn out to be some prosaic paperwork labyrinth.

The door of the Waterfront Playhouse opened, and the priest stepped onto the porch, holding his open palm out to test the rain. Annabelle left the shelter of the tree and ran up the stairs, under the canvas awning partially shielding the porch.

"Hi. Are you Monsignor Cullen?"

"Yes, I am. Who are you?"

Annabelle was struck by the mournful appearance of the priest, his dull blue eyes large and downcast, his red cheeks hollow, and she put aside her earlier concern about Millie's carte-blanche endowment of the man's church with a fortune. Only Millie's wishes counted now.

"I'm Annabelle Hardy-Maratos, and I've come to invite you to a party this afternoon, Father, as the guest of honor. Shall we go inside, out of the rain?"

SIXTEEN

JOEL SCHOCKETT, THE YOUNG HEAD OF HARDY SECURITY'S large legal department, sat at the glass dining table, the holographic will spread open before him, a scholarly crease in his smooth, tanned forehead, a can of diet Coke in his hand. His expensive but conservative blue suit showed no wrinkles and merely the correct amount of white cuff at the sleeves, but his dark-brown hair was gathered by a gold band and hung over his collar in a thick ponytail. Annabelle had asked Schockett, after the interview when she had hired him to run the legal wing of her company, about the ponytail. "It throws people off," he had replied. "It's a contradiction. Besides, I like it."

His Rolex watch thumped the table metallically when he put down his empty soda can.

"So, is this a legal will?" Annabelle asked.

"From a linguistic and evidentiary point of view, it's quite legal, in fact, admirably executed as an enforceable instrument, very clear, very concise, free of precious ambiguities," Schockett said. "It's blessed by brevity. We'll have to let the handwriting people determine whether there's any indication of forgery. But that seems only a formality, since the document is properly witnessed and notarized. Milady de Vargas knew what she was doing."

Annabelle looked up at the man seated beside Schockett, Albert Hernandez, the handwriting expert who had already examined the will and compared it to Millie de Vargas's writing on the security contract she had signed with Hardy Security on behalf of the Hemingway Museum, as well as with a long, detailed note provided by Ashleen Ricou concerning loose carpeting on the Hemingway mansion's stairs. Hernandez sported a dense blond beard which seemed designed as cover for the pitted souvenirs of acne. His hands rested on the glass table comfortably, his air the detached poise of a professional witness.

While preliminary discussion took place at the glass table, Annabelle's other guests had taken up positions around the suite, waiting to hear the new will, having—with the exception of Ashleen Ricou—expressed themselves uniformly as shocked and disbelieving, but curious. Ashleen Ricou had kept her thoughts to herself.

Her faded blue dress ruffling in the wind, Ashleen Ricou stood by the balcony door with Monsignor Tim Cullen, to whom she had unbent sufficiently to allow for tepid conversation about the rainy weather, which now, at one o'clock, seemed certain to cancel Key West's sunset party. Noah Green sat by himself in a chair in the corner of the living room, his face a careful blank, alternately crossing his elegantly clad legs and twirling his glasses and glancing at Schockett's ponytail, in a combination of semicircular actions that reminded Dave of a metronome. Francisco de Vargas wandered about the suite, restlessly adjusting his long blue sleeves and muttering to himself, lines that Annabelle recognized as belonging to Prospero, *The Tempest*'s sorcerer and island king. Detective Lieutenant Barbara Ruggierrio and her partner Frank Ho were seated on the couch in the living room; they said they had come to deliver the news that Perez had been released from jail but that he was still on call as a material witness.

When Ruggierrio, standing at the door of the suite, had insisted on staying to hear the will, Dave, who saw in the detective's timely arrival N. S. Green's pipeline at work, had said, "This is the Annabelle Hardy-Maratos suite. It is not open to the public. Get out."

But he had been overruled by Annabelle. "If we don't let them stay, they'll just slow us down by making us repeat everything down at the police station. Let's not get bogged down in duplication of effort."

He had squelched an itching temptation to offer a crisp fifty-dollar bill to Ruggierrio for her current views on the strangling, or to start a pool with her regarding the outcome of the will.

He now sat on the counter between the dining area and the kitchen, swinging his legs unconsciously in time to Green's motions across the big room. Millie's Cat was in the stainless-steel sink behind Dave, watching the scene with alert interest. Dave had been disgusted when Green had reacted to seeing the cat by saying "Hello, Ignatius," and the cat had smirked and rubbed the lawyer's elbow. Green had flinched and had taken a seat as far away from the kitchen as possible, but there appeared to be no overt animosity on either side of the exchange.

Arantxa, who had arrived with Schockett—"Dr. Annabelle, I knew you'd need me with all these people; is Mr. Dave behaving?"—sat beside Annabelle at the table, setting up her equipment.

Annabelle's secretary had mastered a system called "real time" stenography, using a twenty-three-key computerized stenotype machine and her own system of shorthand. Arantxa could capture up to 260 spoken words per minute, with a 98 percent accuracy rate. The words would be printed on the screen of a laptop computer for Annabelle only seconds after they had been uttered. The technology had been pioneered in courtrooms so that deaf people could participate fully in their trials, but Arantxa had adapted her own symbol system to the technology, and she often worked with Annabelle in situations where many speakers, speaking from many directions, would be contributing. The stenotype machine and laptop were on the table, and Arantxa was plugging them both in to current adaptors.

The handwriting expert cleared his throat importantly and aimed his red face directly at Annabelle, mouthing his words with exaggerated emphasis for what he imagined to be her benefit. He had never worked with her before or indeed with any deaf person.

"The handwriting is the same. I could give you particulars, and I would in a courtroom, but Schockett and I have agreed that for now it's enough to say that I've satisfied myself as to the handwriting on the holographic will. It is the same as the handwriting on the other samples. I have no doubt whatsoever." He plunged a finger into his beard, massaging his face, no doubt, Annabelle thought, a vestigial gesture, going back to the days of his adolescence. She looked away from him, toward Schockett.

"I guess we can begin, Joel," she said.

Dave leaped off the counter and signaled to those who were expecting inheritances to gather around the table, but it was Francisco de Vargas who actually herded them individually to the dining area, just the way a director would who was blocking out a scene that was giving him trouble.

Ashleen Ricou, Monsignor Cullen, de Vargas, and Noah Green took their seats; Dave remained standing, taking up a position behind Green's chair; and the two police officers stood in the living room, their faces stoic and impersonal, their posture an attempt at casual belonging.

Joel Schockett placed his hand on the wrinkled holographic will, and when he began speaking, Arantxa's plump hands flew over the keys of the stenographic machine with swift sureness. Annabelle concentrated on the screen of the laptop.

"This holographic will was found by Dr. Hardy-Maratos and Mr. Jorge Enamorado in a secret compartment at the bottom of the main staircase in the Ernest Hemingway mansion at Nine-oh-seven Whitehead Street here in Key West. Is that correct?"

Annabelle and Dave simultaneously said, "It is."

"And Miss Ashleen Ricou witnessed their discovery. Is that correct?"

"Let me see that paper." Ashleen Ricou's voice was a cold command.

Schockett held out the document without releasing the corner, and she inspected the writing on the back, where Annabelle had scrawled, *Found in the presence of Ashleen Ricou and Jorge Enamorado, January 21, 1994.* The initials *AH-M* followed the date.

"This is the paper they found," Ashleen Ricou said.

Schockett took another paper from the table.

"This is a letter to Annabelle Hardy-Maratos, from Milady de Vargas, dated November eighteenth of last year, and delivered to Dr. Hardy-Maratos by Noah Green yesterday in the offices he shared with de Vargas. Is that correct?"

Green hesitated. He glanced at Annabelle's face as she read the computer screen. *She's a doctor?* he thought, swinging his glasses tentatively over the table. Dave poked him in the back.

"That's correct," Green muttered.

"Would you mind speaking up?" Schockett prompted him.

"That's correct," Green said.

"What's this other writing on the back of the letter?" Schockett asked. Annabelle looked up from the screen, saw her own handwriting and Ricou's, the penciled conversation in

Sloppy Joe's Bar, and said, "Just some notes I made. Is it a problem, Joel?"

"Not if they're your notes. It's your letter." He resumed his speech for the group. "This letter directs Dr. Hardy-Maratos to retrieve the will from its hiding place in the Hemingway mansion and, further, it directs her to act as executor of the new will, if she is so willing. Are you so willing, Dr. Hardy-Maratos?"

"I am willing," Annabelle said, her eyes on the screen.

Francisco de Vargas interrupted, his index finger lightly tapping the surface of the table. "Why her, I wonder? Millie never told me anything about this."

"I believe your sister regarded Dr. Hardy-Maratos as a capable and disinterested outsider," Schockett said gently. "The choice was your sister's to make."

Schockett turned from de Vargas, scanning the faces around the table. "As you all know by now, the date of this will found in the Hemingway mansion is later than the date of the only other will known to have been executed by Milady de Vargas and in the possession of her law partner, Noah Green. I will read the new will now, on the civilized presumption that we can all remember that the possessions given by this instrument were Milady de Vargas's to dispose of according to her own lights."

Schockett paused and again ran his eyes over the faces around the table. Francisco de Vargas shifted in his chair, a look of open curiosity on his face. Ashleen Ricou preserved a rigid, disapproving countenance. Monsignor Cullen looked uncomfortable, his face a warm red. Noah Green kept his eyes on the table, his glasses remarkably still in his hand.

Schockett read in his warm, deep voice:

"I, Milady Maria de Vargas, being of sound mind and body, hereby leave all the worldly goods of which I die possessed, with the exception of my share of the law firm of de Vargas and Green, to the use of Monsignor Timothy Cullen,

Archdiocese of New York, on the hopeful assumption that his good judgment will tell him how to use any part of those goods in support of the Hemingway Museum or the Waterfront Playhouse, both in Key West, Florida. My share in the law firm of de Vargas and Green I leave to my partner, Noah S. Green, and I hope that he will continue its proud tradition of making Key West grow."

A profound silence filled the room when Schockett's deep voice ceased. Annabelle looked up from the screen of the laptop. Monsignor Cullen seemed to be experiencing difficulty swallowing.

Francisco de Vargas was the first to speak.

"That's nice," he said, his face flushed an ugly red. "Are you a patron of the theater, Monsignor?"

Cullen blinked his eyes rapidly and shook his head, patently distressed.

"Son, you should be patient. I'll try to do what's just. I'm as surprised as you are. Naturally I'll talk with the Cardinal."

"Is *he* a patron of the theater?" de Vargas asked nastily.

Cullen's face and voice now took on a gently dazed tone: "Historically the Church has been opposed to the drama, all enactments being, essentially, mockeries of the only enactment the Church recognizes—the Mass. I'll have to ask the Cardinal. Really, I never expected this."

"Goddammit. Can't something be done?" de Vargas said, on the edge of hysteria. "This is totally unfair!"

"You should keep a civil tongue in your head, Francisco," Ashleen Ricou snapped. "The museum had as much right as anybody to expect an outright gift, and you won't see me complaining. It was Millie's money."

"What about you, Noah?" de Vargas asked, his voice suddenly a silken stream of sound, replacing the brittle quality of his previous words. "Are you taking this like a little man? Surely you expected more? The law firm is worth nothing without Millie. Everyone knows my sister shriveled up your little balls years ago."

Green opened his mouth and then promptly closed it. The law firm would indeed be worth nothing if he could not practice law. He looked at Annabelle and put his glasses quietly on the table. "Millie had the right to leave her possessions to whomever she wished," he said, his voice steady. "I'm very proud to receive full ownership of the firm, the way we always planned. Go to hell, Fran."

"Well, really," Cullen tittered. He encountered a bland look from Dave, and looked down at his hands.

Schockett's deep voice resumed control.

"Since, as I understand it, most of the property referred to in this will is real estate, it will take some time to sort everything out, a chore that will fall to Dr. Hardy-Maratos and her assigns. Until then, bickering is pointless, although you'll probably bicker anyway. This is a curious will, to say the least, and I don't think any of you will see any monies for some time."

"Well, I'm not sure what to say," Cullen said softly, a wavering question on his thin lips. "Nobody here seems to know but me. I really don't know what to say."

All eyes but Annabelle's traveled to his red face.

"Doesn't that document say anything more?" Cullen asked, his thin lips trembling.

Schockett looked at him from under raised eyebrows. "What are you getting at, Father? I read the entire will."

"Well, I don't know how this can be," Cullen said, "but there should be something about the treasure."

"Oh, God. That old legend!" De Vargas scraped his chair on the floor as he flung himself back from the table. "Don't make me sick."

"I have it on the best authority that Millie had at last found the sunken treasure," Cullen insisted. "In the Gulf of Mexico. She told me so herself."

"What's this?" Ruggierrio said, crossing to the table.

"There's no such thing," Francisco said with acidly emphatic bitterness. "Just a hopeless and hoary old bedtime story that nobody ever believed. The curse of the de Vargases. You're just as likely to win the lottery. Likelier."

"But Francisco, it's the de Vargas treasure," Cullen said. "Millie really found it."

The room erupted in confused sound, even Ashleen Ricou raising her voice, but Schockett's firm tones finally prevailed.

"What are you talking about, Monsignor Cullen?" he asked.

"Well, I don't know the whole story, how it began and all, but it's really quite a yarn, what Millie told me." He cleared his throat. "It's an old, old story. Francisco knows it, don't you Francisco?"

De Vargas rolled his eyes.

"I know the story," Ashleen Ricou said, "and so does every conch raised on rum and romance. But it was never more than an adventure story. Key West is full of that kind of romantic nonsense. We all know better than to put any stock in it." She gazed coldly at the others. "Or we should know better."

"But Millie wrote to me," Cullen insisted. "I have her letter with me somewhere." He patted his pockets. "She said she found the treasure herself. That's why I'm here; that's why I flew down here"—Cullen paused, lowering his eyes—"only to learn of the tragic death of Millie de Vargas, when I thought my trip was going to be such a happy occasion of joy and celebration." He paused again, again lowering his eyes, but, to Dave's alert eye, covertly surveying the gathering. "Anyway, she said that her family has some old map—I think it's been in the family for years and years—indicating the location of the Madonna de Monte de Plata. That's a huge statue of the Blessed Virgin made out of gold, covered with jewels and lavish inscriptions, all sorts of fabulous stuff like that. It came from Peru about four hundred years ago and was on its way to

Spain when a hurricane wrecked a large portion of the fleet of galleons escorting it, along with a bunch of other treasures. What was the name of the ship, Francisco? The one carrying the Madonna?"

"I don't remember," de Vargas mumbled.

"I'll think of it in a minute," Cullen went on. "I wish I could find that letter. Millie wrote to me just last week that she had found it. And she wrote the name of the ship."

"It was called the *Nuestra Señora de Antorcha*," Ashleen Ricou said firmly, over the noise of Francisco grumbling and swearing in Spanish, and Barbara Ruggierrio demanding in English to be told what was going on.

"That's it!" Cullen agreed brightly. "And it's been lost for centuries, and the de Vargas family has some historic claim to it, although it's supposed to be very unlucky, and Millie said the Madonna was extremely beautiful and real gold. She saw it."

"If there is such a Madonna," Annabelle asked, her eyes on the screen, catching up with Cullen's words, "did she indicate how much it would be worth? What kind of treasure are we talking about here?"

"Well, Millie wrote that much of the rest of the treasure was also intact, the silver and gold ingots, and religious artifacts, and the statue is truly gigantic and solid gold and covered with thousands of precious gems—" Cullen was interrupted by a loud snort from de Vargas, which he ignored, continuing in his excited tone. "That's what she said, Francisco. And, the whole thing is worth about four hundred million dollars."

In the stunned silence that filled the room the mournful cry of seagulls on the waterfront strained the air. Annabelle looked up from the computer; the characters had ceased to flow across the screen.

It was Dave who broke the silence.

"Holy . . . Jumping . . . Christ-on-Caffeine . . . Jesus.

Talk about a motive for murder. Four hundred million dollars? Annabelle, you were right."

"What?" Green turned in his chair to stare at Dave.

"Annabelle said that Millie was killed because of something she found, not because of the new resort. It's the sunken-Madonna thing. It's gotta be." Dave paused. "Annabelle, I take back everything I said about your brains when I was wearing that Hemingway mask"—he blatantly studied the faces around the table—"which is missing."

Dave got no response to this venture.

Ruggierrio stepped to the group at the table. "Now, wait a minute. You're talking about this treasure like it was real. Like it was just given away in that new will to the priest here. Like you all believe it. What is this?"

Green frowned at Ruggierrio, but said nothing.

"What is this?" Ruggierrio repeated.

"A crock," de Vargas announced. "A simple crock of starry-eyed, pie-in-the-sky, fairy-tale, visionary, Cinderella shit." He spat the final word. "The epic saga of the fucking de Vargas family." He stood with fluid grace, bowed punctiliously to the assembled audience, and walked out of the suite.

Dave viewed his performance with a critical eye. "De Vargas certainly knows how to make an exit," he declared. "I hope you were paying attention, Arantxa."

Everyone started now to talk at once again, except Green, Annabelle, and Arantxa, who was frantically trying to sort it all out on her machine. Annabelle read the confused words coming over the screen for a moment, then abandoned the attempt, holding up her hand and waving it. Quiet slowly descended.

"Joel," she asked in her soft voice, "assuming there is a treasure, and assuming that Millie found it, as Monsignor Cullen says, who owns it? The Monsignor?"

Schockett smiled down at the table, a hovering, whimsical

tilt to his lips. When he looked up at Annabelle, she could see the smile reflected in his eyes.

"You want my guess?" he asked, his smile broadening.

"Yes," she responded, an echoing smile lurking on her lips.

"According to the will, Milady de Vargas left all the goods *of which she died possessed* to Monsignor Cullen's use. If that treasure is still lying on the floor of the Gulf of Mexico . . . I'd say it was not in her possession."

Dave's jaw dropped as this sank in.

"Christ on the crapper, Joseph on the john, Our Lady on the loo," he exclaimed. "Saint Peter on the potty," he added for good measure, whistling, his eyes huge. He caught sight of Cullen's red face. "Pardon my free speech." But Cullen was not looking at Dave; his eyes were focused on Schockett.

"What does that mean, Joel?" Annabelle asked, her smile now fading into a look of worried speculation.

"Yes, just what are you getting at?" Cullen sputtered.

"Well," Schockett said, his blue eyes lit with enjoyment, "there was a landmark ruling in 1978, by a Judge Walter P. Gewin of the U.S. Court of Appeals. Basically the treasure belongs to whoever salvages it. I'd say we've got a four-hundred-million-dollar horse race."

"And I'd say," Noah Green announced, closing his fist and snapping his glasses in half with a loud pop, "that Francisco de Vargas has gone to look for the map."

SEVENTEEN

"THIS IS PREPOSTEROUS," MONSIGNOR CULLEN BLUSTERED, gulping on his own breath. "The will makes it absolutely clear that Millie de Vargas expressly wanted the Church to have that treasure. What's the point of reading a will you just throw away into the wind? Why, what you're talking about is no better than downright stealing. I'm calling the legal department of the Archdiocese of New York, and we'll get our own lawyers down here."

"Are they bigger than our lawyers?" Dave asked sweetly.

Cullen actually cast a stricken glance around the dining area, evidently looking for a telephone, but Ashleen Ricou stopped him by rising slowly from her chair—a stiff, regal presence in a faded blue floral-print cotton dress, soft and thin from repeated washings, faded from long days in the sun. She did not raise her cold voice, but her tones washed over Cullen in an icy flow that checked his volition.

"I have never taken what does not belong to me, and I am not going to start now. But I think that lawyer makes sense." She gestured autocratically to Schockett. "The treasure belongs to the person who finds it, and I know my duty to the Hemingway mansion. I am going to look for the map."

She stalked out of the room toward the outer door, her

back ramrod straight, and Dave heard her knees crack as she pulled open the heavy door.

"Almost as good as Francisco's exit," he said, leaning an elbow against the kitchen counter. "What about you, Monsignor?"

Cullen rose from the table, a slow and building fury burning his cheeks.

"I wouldn't know where to begin to look," he snapped. "Not like these people who have lived here all their lives and grew up on the treasure stories."

"Millie didn't even give you a tiny hint?" Dave asked skeptically.

Cullen attempted to brush past Dave and lurched toward the counter. With breathtaking suddenness, Ignatius hissed and spat—a terrible throaty noise that sent a sharp chill through Dave—arched his back, and took a step backward in the sink.

All eyes were now focused on the cat. Even Annabelle had looked up from the screen, her attention caught by the animal's dramatic posture, its back curved at the ceiling, its tail bushed out to three times its normal size.

"What the hell is the matter with you?" Dave demanded.

He tried to soothe the animal, but it sidestepped away from his hand, its glowing yellow eyes on the priest, the fur on its back standing at an angle to its spine in ragged patches so dense and dark they appeared to have turned brown.

Dave cast a look of surprise at Cullen, who was watching the cat nervously.

"He doesn't seem to care for you, Monsignor. He doesn't seem to care for you at all. In fact I think you're at the top of his list of things to do today. What unexpected prejudice is this? He likes me. He flirts with Annabelle. He even tolerates Noah Green. He developed a perfectly spontaneous rapport this morning with the bellhop, and *he* was wearing two tacky pink-flamingo earrings and Old Spice aftershave. This indiscriminate cat seems to like everybody." Dave continued to regard Cullen. "But he doesn't like you. I wonder why not?"

The priest shrugged his shoulders but did not take his eyes away from the cat, which appeared to have gathered itself onto its haunches in preparation for a spring, its teeth bared.

Dave managed to lift the cat out of the sink, carrying him closer to Cullen, who backed away toward the wall. The cat emitted another hiss—this one high-pitched and piercing—as well as a startling series of growls deep in his throat.

"This cat's enthusiasm for his emotions is really quite admirable," Dave said wonderingly, pinning the cat's struggling hind legs against his own chest. "He really doesn't like you, Monsignor. Have you two met before? But how can that be? The cat's been staying with Annabelle, and you just got into town."

"I've never seen that cat before," Cullen muttered. "Get him away from me."

Stroking the cat's head with his free hand, Dave turned with deliberate caution and slowness away from the priest to Noah Green, where he still sat at the glass table, the snapped halves of his glasses under his hand. "Did you lock this cat out on Millie's office window?" Dave asked.

The attorney glanced at Dave contemptuously. "Me? What good would that do? His hairs are all over the office anyway. I'm not allergic to the *cat*; I'm allergic to his hair."

Annabelle stood, her eyes still on the screen.

"Monsignor, it's hard to believe you have never encountered this animal before." Annabelle stifled a smile at the priest's expression of frozen bug-eyed horror. "When did you arrive in Key West? You clearly implied you arrived after Millie de Vargas died."

Cullen was against the wall, the cat producing deep rolling noises in its throat, Dave once again holding the animal within a foot of the priest. Suddenly the cat lashed out with its claws extended, swiping the air in front of Cullen's red face.

"Get him away from me," Cullen squeaked, jerking his hands in front of his face. "He doesn't like me. I accidentally stepped on him once."

"That's interesting," Annabelle said. "And when was that? I've had him since early yesterday afternoon, when, I presume, you were in New York. It's easy enough to check the airlines."

Cullen muttered something, his head going down behind his hands, breaking the stare between himself and the cat. Dave saw that a long and recent scratch crossed the top of Cullen's right wrist like a bolt of red lightning.

"Father," Dave said. "You have an appalling scratch on your hand. Did you know that modern science is a wonderful thing? They can do enzyme tests now to determine which cat did that to you, should you wish to prosecute."

Behind Dave, and despite himself, a thin smile punctured the rigidity of Noah Green's face.

Cullen whispered, his hands still covering his face: "Monday night. It was Monday night."

Annabelle raised her eyebrows as she saw the words appear on the screen of the laptop. "What were you doing in Millie's office, which is where I assume you met the cat?" she asked.

He lowered his hands, warily eyeing the cat, which perversely, Dave thought, was now distractedly chewing a spot on its foot.

"I was looking for Millie," Cullen said. "I got in a day or so early. I went to the Hemingway Museum, but it was already closed." Here he encountered a hard look from Ruggierrio. "I looked Millie up in the phone book, but her home number was unlisted. So I went to her office."

"How'd you get in?" Dave asked.

"The door wasn't locked. Why are you making this like an inquisition? It was perfectly innocent."

"The cat doesn't think so," Dave said.

Annabelle looked up from the screen, across the table toward the lawyers. "Mr. Green?"

"He could be telling the truth. I was working late that night, after the sunset, the night of Millie's death, but I left the office to have dinner across the street. Sometimes I leave it open—the bouncer at the bar downstairs tries to keep an eye on things. I don't remember if I locked it that night."

"What were you doing to the cat?" Dave asked Cullen, holding the animal closer to the priest, but the cat's passion seemed to have burned itself out—either that or it had sensed a formidable protector in Dave and had come to dismiss the priest from the security of Dave's encircling arms.

"I stepped on him going into Millie's office," Cullen said. "I didn't mean to, and I tried to make nice to him, but he kept howling at me like that. That's when he scratched me. I tried to make him stop that awful noise, and he went out the window. As soon as I saw that, I closed the window. Get him away from me."

Annabelle now looked at Ruggierrio. The detective was staring at the priest.

"Father, I've got a few questions," Ruggierrio said. "Including where you were at sundown on Monday."

"What do you mean by that? Do you mean questions about Millie? I don't know anything about her death. You heard what I said."

"I hope you don't mind telling it to me again," Ruggierrio said dryly. "And maybe you can also tell me when you first learned about the change in the will."

A dull flush bloomed over the priest's neck above his collar.

"By the way," Dave suggested companionably, hoping to speed Ruggierrio on her way by interfering, "don't neglect to ask Monsignor Cullen what he really did to the cat. I don't think the animal would be this bent on vengeance merely for the common mistake of doormatting him. Tell him confession's good for his soul."

Ruggierrio hunched a shoulder, motioned for Dave to move away from Cullen, and she left the room with the priest, followed by her partner, whose silence, Dave noted, had been preserved inviolate.

When they were gone, Schockett and Hernandez were also standing, ready to leave.

"Interesting—the principal heir apparently in town at the time of the murder and keeping silent about it," Schockett said. "I think I'll go downstairs and register, in case you need me." He tugged gently at his sleeve. "Annabelle, have dinner with me?"

"I can't tonight, Joel."

Schockett hid his spiking disappointment behind a hasty smile. "I'd love to join the treasure hunt, but the Gulf's a big haystack. Are you going to look for the needle too?"

Annabelle reached to grasp Schockett's hand warmly, a worried expression on her thoughtful countenance. "I don't know. Thanks for the dinner offer. Some other time?"

He smiled, shook hands with Dave and Arantxa, and left the suite with Hernandez.

"Dr. Annabelle, do you want me to stay?"

Annabelle put her arm around her secretary's shoulders and hugged her. "Please," she said. "Tell them downstairs that I said to give you Room Three-oh-nine if it's available."

"Won't that make you feel like a bloodsucking capitalist?" Dave signed. "Just asking. Nothing against Arantxa."

Annabelle ignored Dave elaborately, her attention on the secretary. "You'll like Three-oh-nine. You can just leave your machines here."

While Arantxa packed her equipment into their cases, Noah Green sat quietly at the table, watching her efficient motions and absently toying with the broken frames of his gold glasses. Soon, however, he, too, stood.

"I'll be going now. Vastly informative afternoon." He moved toward the door.

"Just a minute, counselor," Annabelle said, stepping around the table.

Green halted disjointedly, as if he were a marionette whose strings were in need of repair.

"Don't get any ideas about looking for that Madonna," she said coolly. "Or if you already have ideas, don't start thinking about salvage. Do you understand me?"

Green stood in the hallway, not moving, not showing by any sign that he had heard her.

"Mr. Green. Do you understand me?"

Slowly Green's head bobbed, up and down, up and down, and he continued his interrupted walk to the door, pulling it open and closing it softly behind him, his head bobbing the entire way.

His broken spectacles lay on the table, a sad gold-and-glass metaphor, Annabelle thought, for the attorney's self-destructive blindness to the colliding desires and whims of other people, other egos.

Annabelle stretched, crossed the living room, and stepped out onto the balcony. The sky was showing an ugly yellow tinge under the distant bank of black clouds. A lone pelican skimmed the surface of the harbor, leaving a faint trail on the swollen gray water. Gulls on the sunset deck over at the Pier House perched in tidy, crowded rows on the railings, shoulder to shoulder, their tiny heads tucked away from the wind.

Dave came out to stand beside her, the cat curling itself into a comfortable, shapeless blob on his black flats.

The harbor was strangely barren, deserted and impersonal, the choppy gray water filled with milky crests and ugly brown patches of seaweed tossed up from the bottom. The air hung damply, dankly, over the water, the clouds low and pressing.

Dave wiggled his feet out from under the cat and left the

balcony, returning from the bedroom with a white sweater, which he put around Annabelle's shoulders.

She shivered.

"It's getting cold out," he said. He then switched to sign language, thinking she might be tired from using the computer screen. Sign language was always easier for her. "Francisco may or may not have the inside track on the Madonna," he signed, "if that map has been in the family. Cullen is going to be slightly delayed, assuming he means to join the hunt, and assuming he has a clue where to look. Maybe he picked one up in her office when he was introducing himself to the cat, or maybe Millie gave him one personally. I expect we both know where Ashleen Ricou will start—the Hemingway mansion, where we know Millie made a habit of hiding important things. Let's assume Green is going to mind you and stay home writing his memoirs. Perez—if we're counting him—is probably showering, watching the souvenirs of a night in the Key West Pokey go down the drain. Maybe he killed Millie for a copy of the treasure map. So"—he stretched his arms over his head, yawning extravagantly—"where do *we* begin?"

"The morgue," she said. "We're hunting a murderer."

EIGHTEEN

THE LOWER FLORIDA KEYS HEALTH SYSTEM WAS LOCATED on Stock Island, the next key up in the archipelago from Key West, and the twenty-five-minute taxi ride seemed long, dismal, and dangerous. The rain was falling in thick, opalescent sheets, and cars hydroplaned on the water collecting on the slick roads. Annabelle was absorbed in her thoughts. Dave was hungry.

Annabelle hated morgues, had hated them since Nikki's accident, and thought they were best left to police reports, but since Barbara Ruggierrio's offer of last night to Noah Green to tailor evidence to his liking or needs, Annabelle wanted to see the body of Millie de Vargas for herself.

The pink cab pulled into the facility off Junior College Road and stopped under the emergency-room canopy. Dave handed the driver a ten-dollar bill and told him to wait for them.

They were admitted to the morgue's office and file room by a cheerful, pink-garbed technician whose name tag identified him as Paulo P. Tercero. He did not offer any curiosity or resistance when Annabelle said that she was executor of the Milady de Vargas estate and had come to see the body.

He showed them into a cold room, one wall lined with

square stainless-steel drawers, and pulled out the drawer holding the remains of Millie de Vargas.

The face was puffy, discolored, and distorted, the eyes bulging, the gargoyle expression of death by strangulation. The short black hair was silky, clean, almost healthy in appearance. Tercero pulled back the sheet to uncover the body to the waist, revealing the cruel line left by the typewriter ribbon, as well as a small, perfectly round bruise on the side of her neck, about the size of a pea. The clean lines of surgical incision formed a sideways letter *H* on her chest.

"I don't get down to Key West much." Tercero put his head to one side, considering the corpse. "Hear she was killed in the Mark Twain house."

"Yeah," Dave said seriously. "No place is safe anymore. What about stomach contents?"

"The stomach was empty. She didn't have no dinner. Do you want to see her foot? Huh?" Tercero asked.

"Huh?" Dave echoed.

Tercerco pulled the sheet away from the other end and pointed to the right foot.

"It looks fine to me," Dave said, swallowing.

"You mean because of the bead found in her shoe, don't you?" Annabelle asked.

"Yeah. How she could have walked on that thing without getting a bruise, that's the question, huh? She sure has good-looking feet. Huh?" Tercero seemed proud of the corpse, and Dave looked at him uneasily, not sure of the etiquette obtaining in morgues, but certain that he found Tercero's matter-of-fact pleasure in the corpse's feet distinctly distasteful. Dave looked at Tercero more closely.

"Haven't I seen you somewhere before?" Dave asked, his head to one side, considering the man's face.

"Yeah, man, you go to the Comedy Club in Miami? Huh?" Dave nodded.

"That's where it must have been. I'm Paul Hummingbird. Funny guy, huh?"

"Yeah. Huh." Dave glanced at Tercero's name tag again.

"Stage name, man," Tercero said.

"Do you have the clothing?" Annabelle asked, bringing the exchange to an end.

"Sure. Come over here."

Tercero crossed the room and opened another, smaller drawer. Annabelle looked inside. There was a neatly folded pile of white clothing, a pair of almost new white spike heels, no jewelry.

"Wasn't there any jewelry on the body?" Annabelle asked.

"Not a single piece," Tercero said ruefully. "You'd think with nice clothes like this she'd at least have a gold watch or something. Not much stuff for a bigshot lawyer to die in, huh?"

Annabelle lifted out the top garment, saw that it was a silk blouse, and took the next piece in her hands. It was an expensive white linen suit jacket. The pockets were empty. Beneath it lay red-silk panties but no nylons, no bra. There was, finally, a linen skirt, its hem marred by a gray streak.

Annabelle replaced the garments, examined the shoes, put them back in the drawer, and turned away. She thanked Tercero and prepared to leave. The technician pressed a couple of business cards into Dave's hand. "Come see me. I do all the clubs in Miami," he said.

"You oughta get down to Key West, man," Dave said. "The Mark Twain house is full of great gags."

"Twain's a funny guy, huh?"

On the way back to Key West, the rain unabated, Annabelle was once again lost in thought. Dave studied her profile, the lights of oncoming cars causing shadows of raindrops to slide down her smooth, high-boned cheeks. She turned to him, seeming to sense his regard.

"Dave, if this murder has truly been about that sunken

Madonna, not the resort as the typewriter ribbon indicated, and the motive was instead a whopping four-hundred-million-dollar statue, then the murderer may just be realizing that eliminating Millie did not leave the treasure safe. Or maybe he—or she—is counting on its being impossible for any of us to find the treasure without Millie's help. It may get pretty crowded out there in the Gulf, now that Monsignor Cullen has opened his big mouth—let the cat out of the bag, so to speak."

"He certainly seems to have shot himself in the foot about the treasure." Dave grinned. "Oh, well. Maybe he'll use his big mouth to call the Cardinal, and he'll get a little lesson in discretion. Annabelle, if he'd kept his mouth shut, he could be sitting alone on top of the Madonna right now."

"If he knows where it is. And he might have some company down there," she said. "The killer."

"What makes you think Cullen isn't the killer?"

The taxi's driver scrutinized Dave in the rearview mirror and then swerved to avoid a moped, its rider cursing and thoroughly soaked under his yellow slicker.

"If Cullen is the killer," Annabelle signed, "he sure supplied himself publicly with a giant motive by prattling about the treasure Madonna. Somehow I don't think this killer is that stupid."

"Maybe he's diabolically clever and he's trying to divert our attention . . . no, not Cullen."

The pink taxi pulled up beside the empty sidewalk in front of Sloppy Joe's Bar. Dave paid the driver, and they ran across the sidewalk, the rain splashing around their feet. Dave almost slipped on the wet linoleum inside the bar, but he regained his footing with quick grace, and they stood inside the open doorway wiping rainwater from their arms.

"I want you to see this floor, Dave," Annabelle said. "The sticky orange patina is just like that spot next to the cigarmaker's chair in Hemingway's studio. And Millie was killed in that chair. I keep thinking about this. Maybe you'll think I'm batty."

Dave walked slowly, gazing down over the dirty yellow-and-brown tiles, a frown on his face.

"I'm hungry," he said at last. "Let's get a sandwich. If you're not so batty that you've gone on a hunger strike."

They went to the deserted bar and sat on wooden stools, Dave reading the drink menu with fierce disapproval. "If they have to give a drink a fancy name, they're hiding a bad drink under a worse alias. Like that stupid collage in Señor Frog's. Long name, no worth."

The bartender approached them, a friendly grin on his bearded face. "What'll it be, folks? Something hot to keep the rain out?"

"Do you have anything simple? Like a hamburger and fries?" Dave was determined not to be taken in by menu polylogoism, artful or not, and he refused to consider the menu board on the floor beside him.

"Sure. For both of you?"

Dave nodded.

"Anything to drink?"

"Club soda," Dave said. "The house brand will be just fine. Hold the twist of lemon."

The bartender, impervious to sly insults, kept smiling and walked away into the kitchen.

"I don't know, Dave," Annabelle said. "Your theory of art. One of my favorite paintings is *The Anatomy Lesson of Doctor Tulp*. That's a fairly long title, isn't it?"

"Six words. That's nothing."

"I guess I'm thinking of that painting because it's a portrait of an autopsy." Annabelle rubbed her cold arms. "By Rembrandt. Know what I think?"

"What?"

"I think the reason there's no mark or bruise on Millie's foot is that she never walked anywhere in those spike heels with a bead in them. The bead got into her shoe, where they found it, after she was dead." The bartender reappeared from the kitchen, and Annabelle switched to sign. "And I think the same bead was what made that round mark on her neck, the kind of mark it should have made on her foot if she had walked with it in her shoe. I think that when the killer loosened his—or her—hold on the typewriter ribbon, the bead rolled down Millie's body and into her shoe. The question is, where did the bead come from?"

"That's easy," Dave said, taking his glass of club soda from the bartender. "The cops probably have this much figured out. Ruggierrio's probably peddling the news on the street to the highest bidder. It was part of a necklace. Why else would it be around her neck?"

"Then where's the rest of it?"

They sat in silence for a few minutes, Dave from time to time putting his hand to his throat and staring into the middle distance.

"Annabelle?" Dave's hand was around his own throat. "Don't you think the map must be in the Hemingway mansion?"

"It must be—that's why Millie hired the guards; I'll bet you any amount you care to name. But if you think Ashleen Ricou is going to allow us to root around that mansion, you're as batty as I am."

A huge black tray loaded with plastic baskets of food, a bowl of large pickles, and a ketchup bottle, approached them on the sturdy arm of a large blond waitress dressed in white leather.

"Hi," she greeted Annabelle. "This is on the house."

"Oh, no," Annabelle started to say.

The waitress began to unload the food on the bar. "Please. You were really nice to Ishmael this morning at the playhouse. He needs that, not what Fran does to him. Ishmael's a really good actor, and Fran knows it, but he's mean to Ishmael. He's mean to all of us, but he's especially mean to Ishmael. I think he's jealous. Ishmael actually had parts off-off-Broadway in New York before he came down here. Do you mind if I sit down?"

Annabelle smiled and pulled out the stool next to her.

"Thanks. That's a load off. My feet really kill me after I've been working a few hours, especially lately with our tough rehearsal schedule. Thank God I don't work weekends or Mondays, when the crowds are really pushy. We get a lot of bikers then. We're opening this weekend, you know. Ishmael loves the part of Caliban, and he wants to do a good job, and now he will, now that you've helped him. I was wondering if you could tell me anything about my part. Fran says I have to play my role like a babbling country dope, all wide-eyed and milk-maidy to offset Caliban, and I think that's all wrong. Too one-dimensional. But try telling Fran."

"You're playing Miranda, aren't you?" Annabelle smiled encouragingly at the waitress and took a steaming hamburger from one of the plastic baskets. "What's your name, your real name, I mean?"

"Beth. Beth Summers. That's both my real name and my stage name," she said, grinning. "Pretty rare in Key West. I love doing *The Tempest*. Shakespeare's the best, isn't he? I just have to say, and I hope you don't mind, it's pretty neat the way you seem to know more about Shakespeare than Fran, I mean, with being deaf and all. I mean, the theater's all about spoken words and all that."

Annabelle smiled. "But Shakespeare's all about the mysteries of the human heart. We all have hearts." Impulsively Annabelle leaned over and squeezed the waitress's big hand. "I'll be happy to talk to you about Miranda in a general way, although I have no intention of undermining Fran's vision of the play. Do you have time tomorrow? I really couldn't give you anything sensible now, because we're in kind of a hurry. We're going to leave as soon as we gulp down these burgers."

"Tomorrow morning, then? At the theater?" When Annabelle nodded, Summers stood. "Well, I better get going. Even with practically no customers, I'm not supposed to sit down. That's the hard part about waitressing. But an actress has to earn a living. See you tomorrow. By the way, the hamburgers here are actually pretty decent. Not like the sloppy joes." Summers smiled. "I gotta say, you always come in with the best-looking guys."

She leered at Dave, took the empty tray from the bar, and returned to the kitchen, walking slowly.

"Nice girl," Dave said. "Seems to have good taste."

"She does if she likes Shakespeare."

Dave suddenly gave Annabelle a piercing look. "I've never gotten the whole picture on Shakespeare. What I mean is, all those tights and doublets and codpieces. Why, even hot-blooded Romeo always looks like Barry Manilow's valet."

Annabelle stared at him.

"Well, I just have my own costume ideas, that's all," Dave said. "Do you like Shakespeare? Tell the truth."

"Enough to do my dissertation on him. You're not serious, are you, you cretin?"

"You did your dissertation on Shakespeare? I thought you did it on that woman stuff."

"Shows what you know. The 'woman stuff,' as you so delicately name it, would not have been an appropriate dissertation topic at Yale. Very few women authors have the canonical status for a dissertation. If I had even suggested such a topic, the graduate faculty would have turned over in their mass grave, squeaking and gibbering like the sheeted dead of Rome."

"Shows what they know, the cretins. I see your royalty checks every month."

They finished their hamburgers in silence, watching Jake Balls and the Hell Raisers setting up their equipment for the evening, the lank-haired drummer beating out a desultory solo on the cymbals.

The rain had slowed to a fine but increasingly chilly mist when they once again stood on Duval Street. People were slowly returning to the street, braving the mist in search of amusement. A taxi splashed toward them, and Dave held up his hand.

The pink car pulled up, Dave opened the door, and then realized he did not know where they were going.

"Where to, lady?" Dave smirked.

"The first pay phone you see and the public library."

Dave got in the cab and poked the driver's shoulder. "Can you turn the heat on, sonny?"

When the cab stopped again, beside a pay phone a block up Duval, Dave stepped out with a piece of paper in his hand. The numbers on the paper had been neatly typed. He reached into the deep pocket of his pink shorts, extracted four quarters, and started dialing the numbers Lieutenant Ricou had provided for Annabelle. While he held the receiver to his ear, Dave noticed his own invitation to dinner, scribbled on the back of the note. He shook his head, replaying in his mind last night's scene on the dock, this time taking Andy Garcia's role in *The Untouchables* and plugging Ricou with a .45. Unsuccessful in his attempts to speak with the lieutenant, Dave left messages at each number.

He hopped back into the cab. "Couldn't reach him. I guess he's busy. You know how it is when your whole life is just one peripatetic whirl."

Their next short ride took them to the Key West Public Library, on Fleming Street, several blocks over from Duval.

The library was small, the card catalog merely a set of narrow mahogany boxes standing on top of each other on a desk. Two elderly men were reading by a large open window, the edges of their newspapers curling over in the chilled, moist air. And an obviously tired woman was reading *In the Night*

Kitchen to a squirming boy; they were both sitting in child-size chairs at a low table on the opposite side of the room.

"What are we looking for exactly?" Dave asked.

Annabelle glanced toward the table. "I'll take 'de Vargas.' You look for '*Antorcha*, treasure of.' Anything like that."

"Think that's our letter *A*? The *Antorcha*?"

"Could be. Hurry."

Annabelle wrote a couple of numbers on a slip of paper from a small pad provided next to the card catalog and walked to the shelves, looking for the corresponding numbers posted on the wooden frames of the stacks.

She found both books, took them to a table by a window, and opened the first one, a coffee-table-size book called *Key West: The Wreckers and Their Dreams.* Shadows of the high window's rainy streaks fell onto the slick, shiny pages. After checking the index, she flipped pages quickly, finally turning to a page that faced a drawing of men climbing a mountain of silver.

Lured by tales of a precious gems and silver, she read, *Spanish adventurers flocked to the western shores of Peru, and although the legendary Monte de Plata was never found, these men did find gold and other mineral wealth to satisfy the craving of the Royal Treasury for replenishment of the monies depleted by the almost constant funding of wars.*

Annabelle read another long paragraph and then came to the passage she was seeking:

> When the fleet was wrecked in the hurricane of August 1614, the Spanish governor of Cuba ordered an immediate salvage attempt for the Nuestra Señora de Antorcha, *which was carrying the Madonna de Monte de Plata, as well as the bulk of the gold and silver ingots from the Royal Mint in Mexico City and bound for the Spanish Treasury in Madrid. Gaspar de Vargas sailed for the waters off Florida with five ships, salvage tackle, and divers, but his salvage operation was met with only dismal*

and tantalizing partial success. His divers, without any breath-
ing aids, were not able to salvage the forty- to fifty-foot depths,
de Vargas reported, and they returned with only a disappointing
handful of coral rosaries and tales of man-eating fish.

Annabelle returned to the index, searching for another
page reference.

She flipped pages again until she found the book's other
reference to Gaspar de Vargas:

He died of dysentery in March of 1620, leaving his plantation to
his son, Juan, and his dreams of salvaging the treasure galleons
to posterity.

She felt Dave's hand on her shoulder and looked up from
the book.

"See what I found," he signed, balancing a small open
book against his upper arm to make the signs.

He deposited the book on top of the one she had been
reading. There was a neatly clipped square hole in the page on
the right. She put a finger through the neat hole and glanced
up at Dave, her eyebrows lifted.

"Read that," he said, indicating the facing page.

Humberto Ruiz's attempt to reproduce the map he said he had
seen in Juan de Vargas's desk briefly spurred a treasure rush in
the middle eighteenth century, but that, like all previous at-
tempts to locate the mysterious Madonna de Monte de Plata,
failed, the map being vague and drawn from memory by a man
with little knowledge of navigation.

Dave sat down across the table from Annabelle.

"They should have had you around back then," she
signed. "You would have reproduced the map perfectly."

"Too bad, huh?" he said. "Well, it looks like someone got

here before us. Even Humberto's bullshit map has been cut out of the book."

She opened the book to the front cover, saw that the volume was numbered—a small 23 stamped on the first page—and signed by the author. It was a limited edition and, she thought, probably very rare.

Dave took the book from Annabelle and opened it to another page, one he had dog-eared.

"Dave, you're not supposed to do that. It hurts the books," Annabelle whispered.

"I was taught by the nuns that dog-earing is better than marking your place with ink," he said piously. "Read this." He returned the book to her, and she read the title, *The Richest Little City in America*, before reading the passage he had indicated:

> In addition to the many failures of the de Vargas family to locate the fabulous Madonna, other misfortunes seemed to haunt them whenever they attempted to pursue the dream of untold riches under the sea. The death of Gaspar from dysentery, when he was only thirty-five, was said to have begun what was to become known later in Key West as "the curse of the de Vargases." Gaspar's son, Juan, lost his left leg to a shark on a salvage expedition to what he claimed was the treasure site, and in 1701 Maria Angelica was delivered prematurely of a strangely deformed male child aboard a de Vargas salvage vessel. The child, Emmanuel Francisco, was said to bear a purple mark in the likeness of the Monte de Plata Madonna on his crippled hip. Although eyewitnesses varied in their accounts of other and subsequent misfortunes, colorful and grotesque by turns, there seems to be universal agreement that Alberto Phillip, who inherited the de Vargas Cuban estate in 1784, was accidentally strangled by a tow line when he attempted to follow the Ruiz map to the treasure. When the de Vargas family followed the tide of wreckers to Key West in the early 1800s, the Madonna salvage attempts ceased, and so did the incidence of eerie misfortunes

occurring among the descendants of the man who claimed to have failed in the original attempt at the treasure. Tales of the de Vargas treasure map, however, gained in detail over the years, and some Key Westers have even suggested that the storied original map was made quite accurately by de Vargas so that he could return to the site later, on his own, having lied to the Spanish authorities.

Annabelle closed the book.

"I wish there were a representation of the legendary Madonna," she signed. "The statue must be something to see, if it hasn't been exaggerated over the years. I don't believe this mumbo jumbo about a curse for one minute, but Millie's strangling does fit right in with this macabre collection of blighted treasure stories."

"I was going to add that in the margin, but thought you'd hurt me if I did. So, Francisco was not just gassing when he mentioned the family curse. My question is, since we're already way behind in the treasure hunt, where does this leave us?"

"It leaves us with a murderer who is probably doing something to safeguard his—or her—hold on the Madonna. And it leaves us with the secretive Lieutenant Roy Ricou," she said. "Which is right where we came in."

NINETEEN

LIEUTENANT RICOU WAS WAITING FOR THEM IN THE windy and damp open-air lobby of Ocean Key House, sitting back in a cushioned rattan chair, wearing a pair of silver aviator-style glasses and reading *The Joy of Signing,* by Lottie L. Riekehof, his long legs propped up on a low rattan table. In his lap rested a copy of *The Gender Contract,* Annabelle's book; several pages near the beginning were already dog-eared. He stood, tucking the books under his arm, when he saw her hurrying toward him through the mist on Duval Street. His uniform showed signs of having done service out in the rain, but he looked as though he had taken the time to shave.

"Lieutenant Ricou, we have to talk," she said immediately, taking his hand and dragging him out to the street, under the canopy of the hotel entrance, away from the listening desk clerk.

Dave, his arms crossed over his chest, lounged against the boards covering the window of a ticket booth next to the canopied hotel entrance; the booth, whose boards were papered over with black-and-white posters of former Key West mayor Captain Tony, was usually surrounded by people, tourists seeking information and tickets for sunset cruises, but the rainy weather and the massing clouds had driven would-be excursion sailors indoors and the ticket "captain" home early to watch soap operas and silk-screen a few shirts.

"What's the matter?" Ricou asked, taking Annabelle gently by the arm. "I hardly slept last night. You too?"

"I slept like a baby." She grinned. "You wear glasses." She noticed the titles of the books under his arm. "Oh, my God."

"These are all just props to impress you," he said in his lazy drawl, removing the glasses with one hand. "I can't actually read."

"You look positively erudite in glasses, not that I mean to feed your vanity."

"Why not? Don't you like me?"

"Too much. I should ask Dave to go upstairs for a minute. I feel terribly self-conscious standing here with him watching us. You know, after the scene last night."

"You must be having wonderfully indecent thoughts, to feel that way. Why don't you and I go upstairs instead?"

"We don't have time."

Ricou winced.

"I don't mean because you're shipping out—which I've decided is a really shabby military ploy designed so that you can sneak off just when things are getting interesting—I mean because I need to know something fast, and I think you have the piece of information I need. At least I hope you do."

"Ah, so you admit things are getting interesting between us?"

"How like a man!" she exclaimed. "Listening to only part of what I say."

"How like a woman," he retorted. "Dodging a direct question."

Annabelle stamped her foot, causing Dave, who was at least trying to eavesdrop discreetly, to start in surprise. She never stamped her foot.

"You're fencing with me," she said accusingly. "And it's

getting us nowhere. And your stupid aftershave is distracting me. What are you doing in Key West, Lieutenant Ricou?"

Ricou shifted his weight and regarded her sleepily through his lowered eyelashes. "I thought you understood that my assignment is classified."

"Don't give me that If-only-you-knew-what-I-know look."

"Is that what I did?" he asked, laughing.

"Yes. I don't really want to know what you're doing in Key West—well, actually I do—what I really want to know is this: Does what you're doing in Key West involve knowing what's going on in the Gulf?"

He laughed again. "Of course it does."

"Then can you tell me if there is a new salvage site within, say, ninety miles of this island? It would have to be a fairly big area, and, I think, deep." She thought back to the library books. "Forty to fifty feet deep. Not just shallow wrecks and junk metal."

"Ninety miles, huh? You do stop short of wanting to know what the navy knows about Cuba. That's good. So you won't be requiring our full intelligence on the submarine port at Cienfuegos?"

"Either you know or you don't know, and you're going to tell me or you're not. Don't play with me, Roy."

Ricou relented, turning her toward the marina and walking beside her as he spoke.

"There are three salvage sites that the navy has noted. I have to know about civilian underwater activity for what I'm doing here." He looked down at her, saw that she was about to ask a question, and anticipated her. "No questions about that, if you don't mind. But the salvage locations, you'll be happy to know, are not classified, as they are not navy business."

"Three? Oh, God. Three?"

"Sorry. Can you narrow it down?"

"How did you find them?"

"Magnetometry. A weapons project has to locate potentially dangerous obstructions and potentially endangered civilians, and locate them to a nicety."

"Magnets?" A flicker of hope came and went in Annabelle's eyes. "Does one of those sites register differently from the others? With more iron? Or iron scattered around?"

"Yeah." Ricou considered her. "One of them shows a scattering of hundreds of iron pieces."

"Muskets," she breathed. "Spanish muskets. It has to be that one."

"Muskets?"

"Can you tell me where it is? Can you take me there? To the exact location?"

"The navy's magnetometry is extremely precise, but you may have noticed that the weather is a mess."

Annabelle gazed out at the harbor, where thick, dark clouds were pressing in from the west. "I believe it's clearing up," she said, a hint of stubbornness in her green eyes.

"Why so urgent? Something to do with the murder?"

"Yes. This is something I only learned about a couple of hours ago. And so did several other people, including your aunt. I think—I'm worried—that the murderer may be desperate enough to do something mad to protect what he's already killed for once. People are now in active pursuit of what they believe is a treasure beyond—God, Roy, I'll explain all this later! I've got to get out there."

"Surely you can wait? Nobody will be out in this soup—it's going to rain like hell."

"I'd love to wait. But I don't think the murderer will."

Her grim tone startled him, and he studied the firm line of her jaw, the set look in her eyes.

"I'll take you," he said.

Spontaneously, and forgetting that a disapproving Dave was within sight, she kissed the lieutenant fervently on the lips.

"That's nice," Ricou said softly, placing his palm on her

cheek in what was becoming a familiar touch to her. "Very nice."

"You must have just shaved," she said softly, her lashes lowered, her hand stealing up to the collar of his shirt. She raised her eyes to his. "Dave says you're too young for me."

"Dave's a poop," Ricou said gently. "Just how ancient are you?"

"Thirty-four. How old are you?"

"Twenty-nine. What were you doing when you were five years old?"

She looked at him in surprise.

"When I was five? I don't remember that far back. Why in the world would you ask that?"

"To show you that the age difference is practically nonexistent. The first five years of your life are a complete loss. You don't even remember them. We're actually the same age."

"And I suppose you remember every second of your life from birth on?"

"Perfectly. I may even have prenatal memories from the womb, which would make me older than you. You'll have to change your clothing if you're going sailing with me. I'm not taking you out in this weather clad in your skivvies."

"I am not!" she said indignantly.

"Go get changed. By the way, do you have a boat?"

She stared at him.

"Don't you?"

In the end it was Dave who provided the boat.

He walked up and down the pier, inspecting vessels and assessing crews. He chose the *Wolf,* the flamboyantly decorated excursion pirate ship that was usually booked for sunset cruises for up to thirty people. Dave selected the *Wolf* partly for its size—easily sixty feet—which he considered vital with seas running to four or five feet and with small-craft advisories posted, and for its powerful engine, cleverly disguised to preserve the illusion of a nineteenth-century marauding vessel.

And he chose its crew, partly for their size, which was impressive, and partly because he judged them to be more nearly sober than other sailors he had seen sitting idle on their boats, waiting out the rolling clouds and light rain, losing money to a January weather front and rough seas and tourist nerves, waiting without much hope, he knew, for suckers like him.

He did not settle on the *Wolf* instantly. In the interest of comparison shopping he even questioned the crew of a sizable junk salvage boat called the *Reef Cowboy*. She was crewed by a small, pretty woman, wiry, with a couple of bright butterfly tattoos showing above the torn neckline of her hooded gray sweatshirt. Her eyes were suspiciously bright, and Dave thought she was probably wired on cocaine. He inquired about the price of the *Cowboy*, his hand loosely around the roll of bills in the pocket of his jeans. Dave watched her covertly; her eyes, he thought, gave her away. They were unsteady, dilated, and evasive. Cocaine eyes. Cocaine in the kind of doses that made users think they could fly.

"I'm already booked, man," the woman said, glancing significantly across the deck toward the cabin and tossing loose cushions into the hold. "You can probably get one of the glass-bottoms to take you out if you're not going past the reef."

She straightened and looked Dave over skeptically, as if amused by his desire to sail on such a gloomy afternoon, a sucker if ever she saw one. She could sail him three times around Stock Island and tell him they'd been to Cuba. "You ever been wet before? You don't look like you're much of a sailor. You'd blow away if you got out past the reef anyway. Why don't you go to the Key West Aquarium and look at the sharks?"

Dave struck a limp pose, his left arm gesturing daintily toward the west. "Don't you think this little shower is going to clear up?"

"Ishmael says it's not clearing up until a couple hours past sundown. You won't see any pretty colors in the sky tonight."

"Ishmael. Isn't he the guy playing the monster, you know, at the Waterfront Playhouse? Tall guy with the head?"

She laughed. "That's him. He doesn't look like much, but he's a really great sailor; there's nobody in Key West like Ishmael. He's tough."

Dave sneered, his hand on his hip. "Then how come he lets the theater owner beat up on him so much?"

"Oh, Fran de Vargas." She lowered her voice in friendly mock conspiracy. "Real men don't talk about little Fran de Vargas out here on the docks, not if they don't want fruit trouble. Only Ishmael gets away with buddying around with Pansy Fransy, but Ishmael's a tough guy, you know? Maybe you don't, come to think of it." She started untying the boat's lines, talking to Dave over her shoulder. "See, you have to understand about artists. Ishmael says Fran has a big dream, a vision with a capital *V*. You know: dinner shows, Burt Reynolds doing a weekend, an occasional royal performance by Wayne Newton, that sort of thing. And then there's a lighting booth, new sound stuff, maybe even a bar in the foyer, shit like that. Ishmael's into all that show-business stuff too. He likes Fran and he likes the dream. He's into it, you know?"

"What about you? What are you into?"

"It'll cost you a thousand to find out, man, some other time, some other weather, with or without the *Cowboy*—although what I'm into is only legal out in the open water. Like I said, you better go look at the sharks."

Since Dave might be paying four times a thousand for the more substantial *Wolf*, he did not react to her personal and frankly off-market price, nor did he react to her slow smile, nor to the taunting fact that she, too, was sailing in this wet, gray weather. But he did attempt to satisfy his curiosity about her unusual tattoos. "Where'd you get the drawings?" he asked.

"Bourbon Street, man. Best ink on the planet Mother Earth."

Dave cocked his head critically to one side while she unzipped her sweatshirt and exposed the butterflies on her small breasts.

"Ah," he mused aloud. "But is it art?"

Her hands on the zipper, she stared at him in disbelief.

He walked away down the pier, evidently pondering aesthetic questions, and struck a deal with the captain of the *Wolf*.

They sailed south, the squalling rain in their faces until Ricou convinced them to go below to get warm and dry. He stayed on deck, sharing the navigational duties with the *Wolf's* burly captain, working from precise mathematics supplied, unofficially, by the navy. For two hours Annabelle and Dave sat in the small, dreary cabin, playing checkers on a magnetized board and drinking hot chocolate from spill-proof mugs, both provided by the captain of the vessel, a quiet man whose thoughtfulness, Dave silently acknowledged with a curling lip, was directly proportional to the huge bribe he had given the man before sailing.

Ricou spent a brief twenty minutes below in the cabin, relieving Annabelle on the losing end of numerous games of checkers. It did not take much concentration to sit passively while Dave, who played a loud game, smacked the pieces together to make kings and chased the lieutenant's men around the board into rapid surrender, so Ricou began to learn the fingerspelling alphabet under Annabelle's amused tutelage. Her amusement grew as Dave's irritation increased. Dave clearly did not appreciate the lieutenant's imperturbable disposition—which Dave labeled in sign as "that smug bovine attitude," adding, "I wonder what it would take to make Ricou really mad. Maybe I'll try setting his knees on fire. You don't happen to have a blowtorch, do you?"

As Annabelle watched the games, she demonstrated the fingerspelling alphabet and told the lieutenant what she knew about the fabled statue of the Madonna de Monte de Plata.

"If it really exists," she said, "I'd love to see it and photograph it. It's got to be one of the most telling examples of Maryolatry the world has ever known."

"Maryolatry? The idealization of women?" Ricou drawled.

"Worse. The adoration of women. That's the toughest prison to get out of."

Dave bounced a king several times across the board, another game to his credit.

"I don't pretend to understand what makes him such a great dinner partner," Dave said when Ricou had returned to the deck to navigate the last leg of the rough journey. "He's worse at checkers than you are, Annabelle, and that's saying a great deal."

Annabelle had tucked herself into a worn plaid blanket on a bunk, tired of Dave's raucous brand of checkers, when Ricou came below wearing a wetsuit. She smiled cozily at him.

"Captain and crew think we're crazy *turistas*," Ricou said. "It's nasty out here past the reef. But I'm ready if you are."

He retreated up the narrow companionway, followed by Dave, who had raided the small refrigerator in the cabin and was stuffing cold Oreo cookies into his mouth.

Annabelle shed the blanket and took off her jeans and sweatshirt. Under them she was wearing an orange bikini. She stepped into a gray wetsuit, zipped it, and climbed the stairs.

The wind whipped her hair as she came on deck, and the rain lashed against her skin, but she was shocked when she saw that the sky had disappeared.

The earlier patchy gloom had deepened into a uniform and low hovering gray, the clouds almost resting on the water. She grabbed Dave's wrist and peered at the luminous green numbers on his watch. It was 5:20. The hidden sun would be down soon.

The water was coming toward the pirate vessel as heaving troughs of wet grayness topped with milky-thick mist, shimmering within the limited range of the ship's lights, and, beyond the lights, occasionally blocking out the pale grayness of the mists beyond them. Ricou stood on the deck, already wearing air tank, fins, mask, and regulator. Dave, too, was ready, and he helped Annabelle with her gear.

"Any sign of another vessel?" Annabelle signed to Dave.

He shook his head. "But we wouldn't be likely to spot one in this fog, not unless it was running under mega-heavy lights."

Ricou laced a long blue nylon line through their weight belts, and the three went over the side together in spread-eagle jumps, holding on to their face masks and their already lighted UK-400 wide-beam underwater safety lamps, borrowed from the crew of the *Wolf*.

Just under the surface they checked each other's gear, and Annabelle gave the sign for "descend." They went down one behind the other, Annabelle leading the way slowly, waving her powerful light before her in a steady motion of her right arm, her other arm held loosely against her side, her legs scissoring back and forth. Dave and Ricou followed with their similarly swinging lights. The three lights penetrated the grayness well, within a comfortable radius of almost twenty feet.

At first Dave kept a judicious eye on Ricou, but he soon satisfied himself that the lieutenant was a strong swimmer and an experienced diver, completely at home even at the relatively difficult depths they were diving.

When they reached the floor of the ocean, Ricou checked his compass and pointed south, and they swam together along the bottom. His navigation had been sound, for soon they saw a low but spreading hill of gluey sand. It did not look like any natural formation Annabelle had ever seen.

Dave signed, "Man-made. Can't be anything this regular down here."

They swam the periphery of the hill, occasionally touching the sand, poking it with their gloved hands, alert for signs of movement, signs that the strangler had come to watch over their efforts. At the southernmost end of the mound of sand, a glint of something metallic reflected back from Ricou's light, and he tugged on the nylon rope linking them together. All three stopped and gazed at the yellow spot protruding from the huge, low hill of sand. Ricou rubbed the spot, sending more sand sliding off the metal, which he now perceived to be a bright gold. He thumped it with his fist, and a dull, solid noise traveled out in waves from his hand. He pushed the sand, driving it down, away from the exposed golden patch. Dave joined him, and together they exposed a curving shoulder of enormous size, sparkling with emeralds and rubies and deep-blue gems that Dave thought were sapphires.

"The unlucky Madonna," he signed, unnecessarily, for Annabelle. She was stunned. She saw that Dave, too, was stunned, his eyes large and liquid behind the tempered glass of his mask.

Annabelle put her mask close to the side of Ricou's, to see his eyes reacting to the magnitude and grandeur of even this first glimpse of the statue's titanic curves. He stared at the great shoulder, his blue eyes reflecting the splash of gold before him.

"Let's try to see the face," Annabelle signed, the sign for "face" being readily apparent to Ricou.

They worked to remove the sand, but as they wiped it away, more sand fell to replace it. Presently Annabelle swung her light across the ocean bottom, catching sight of something red. She looked at it closely to make certain that she was not disturbing something alive and then, swimming the distance allowed by the play in the blue nylon line, plucked a rosary from the sand.

She returned and tapped Ricou on the shoulder and, when he turned, held the rosary under his light. He nodded. She was sure she had understood his nod. That was the deep-red color of the bead Ruggierrio had shown to Noah Green in Sloppy Joe's Bar. It must be.

The bead, she thought. The bead. It was a rosary bead. A

red rosary bead. A rosary had been around the throat of Millie de Vargas when she had been killed. A piece of the cursed de Vargas treasure. One of the library books had mentioned "a handful of coral rosaries." She wound the rosary around her wrist. She was excited, feeling a sense of history here on the bottom of the Gulf, as though a small door had been opened between her and Spanish adventurers from across the vast, empty lacuna of time.

After working together for fifteen minutes it became clear that they would make no progress uncovering the Madonna. Annabelle held up her hands and signaled defeat, the golden cross on the rosary dangling over her gloved knuckles. Consulting each other with their eyes, they agreed to give up the excavation and return to the ship, having seen for themselves the reality of the treasure and reassured that the strangler was not hovering over the vast wealth of the *Antorcha*, or over them.

Annabelle once again led the way, followed by Ricou, who was followed by Dave, and when they were within fifteen feet of the surface, she directed her light steadily upward.

As they neared the surface and they all began to signal with the beams of their lights toward the waiting crew of the *Wolf*, the water grew rougher, tossing them about in the twilight like buoys, even against their powerful, expert kicking, and Dave did not notice the great silver knife that sliced from below through the line linking him to Ricou. He continued to rise, until he felt something hot and biting on his right leg, and he looked down sharply, astonished to find that the heat was his own blood, welling out around the blade of a long knife attached to a gloved hand.

Dave rolled forward in the water in a powerful lunge, using his arms to somersault down sharply and away from the hand and the knife. He could feel the heat on his leg only intermittently and as though it were at a great distance. He clung to the handle of his powerful light and swung it up and around, and this time he saw his attacker.

The other diver was wearing a pink dive skin and a rubber Halloween mask stuffed tightly under the diving mask and the regulator. The lifeless, soulful, mustached rubber features of Ernest Hemingway leered at Dave through the tempered glass filter of the attacker's diving mask, the features dented and distorted by the silicone skirt of the diving mask, a regulator stuffed through the mouth hole, air bubbles streaming in gusts out the sides of the high cheeks and wide temples. Dave barely had time to register this bizarre arrangement before his attacker struck again.

This time Dave saw the knife coming. It slashed through his air hose. He dropped his lantern and forced himself not to gasp, for that instinctive motion would have filled his lungs instantly with water. The other diver wound an arm around Dave's throat and yanked. Dave struggled, kicking with his left leg, making sharp contact with his attacker's knee, and his throat was released explosively.

Dave grabbed his own damaged regulator, tore it from his mouth, and flung it aside into the rolling darkness. Then he swam with all his strength toward the surface, kicking awkwardly with his left leg only. He was glad that dropping his light had almost certainly rendered him invisible to his attacker, but at the same time he was terrified and disoriented as to his own location and how far the surface might still be above him. His lungs were bursting.

He felt, rather than saw, when he broke the surface, gasping and swallowing salt water, his lungs expelling the last bit of air he had held and only starting to refill with fresh air. He was immediately swamped by a wave, and went under.

When he again broke the surface, he took greater care to control his pounding chest, and this time he stayed above the crest of the wave long enough to get a ragged breath. He looked frantically around, praying for a glimpse of the *Wolf,* with its tall masts bearing the yellow running lights, but another almost unseen wave sent him down again.

This time the surface seemed farther to reach, and when he did reach it finally, with increasingly sluggish strokes, Dave realized that he was light-headed, and that the wound on his leg must be bleeding copiously, although he could no longer feel its heat.

Struggling in the waves, he tore himself out of the straps of his tank and shed all of his diving equipment except for his knife, which he clenched between his teeth. He unzipped his wetsuit and, taking a deep breath, submerged, peeling down the arms of the suit quickly and fighting free of the suit's left leg. He burst through the surface of the dark water again, gasping around the steel blade of his knife, air whistling into his lungs, the wet suit dragging from his injured right leg. He took several deep breaths, not fighting the waves, but rolling with them on his back, his right leg dangling beneath him, the suit dragging him wildly in drunken circles like a broken rudder.

He did not have the strength or the breath to call out. He floated for what seemed to him an eternity, rising on the backs of the waves, realizing dreamily that the knife was still in his teeth, which were chattering. It was the chattering that jerked him back to his predicament, out of the weakness and languor that threatened to overcome him. He took a breath and bent over double in the water, rocked on the waves, and, dragging the knife from his teeth, cut the heavy wetsuit from his wounded leg. At last free of the clinging suit and its drag on his body, keeping his head above the water as well as he could, he used the knife to slice and rip his swimming trunks. For long moments he rose and fell on the waves, unable to think why he had cut the trunks, and why he was clutching the rippled handle of the knife and the rags of his trunks, and why the world had grown so black. And then it seemed to him that a dream Dave, some phantom version of himself, managed to tie the shredded trunks around his bleeding leg, fashioning a tourniquet out of the handle of the knife.

He floated again, exhausted, dizzy, nauseated, on the rolling black waves, yielding to the fog of cold, welcoming sleep enveloping him, the roaring universe wheeling over his head.

TWENTY

RICOU BROKE THROUGH THE THUNDERING SURFACE AND immediately pushed his mask up on his forehead and removed his regulator. He tugged on the nylon line, and Annabelle surfaced beside him. The other end of the rope floated beside him, weightlessly.

"Where's Dave?" he shouted, forgetting she could not hear him.

She shoved her mask up, treading water with difficulty in the heaving waves, and looked around. A wave tore her away from Ricou, and she went under, but she still had her regulator in place and merely closed her eyes against the onslaught of the salt water. She grabbed the nylon line and pulled herself along it, back to Ricou. She surfaced beside him.

He held up the end of the slack and empty blue line. Annabelle replaced her mask and executed a shallow surface dive, swimming a powerful but slow circle around Ricou, swinging her light systematically. There was no sign of Dave. She surfaced again, tugging on her end of the blue line. Ricou grabbed her hand across a wave and pulled her to his side.

"Any sign?"

She shook her head.

Ricou pulled down his mask, inserted his regulator, and

they dived together, increasing Annabelle's circle of search, their powerful lights showing them only grayish-green emptiness. They ascended again after several minutes, removing their mouthpieces and calling out, looking around wildly in the darkness.

Ricou waved his light over his head toward the nearby lights of the *Wolf* and blew the whistle attached by a chain to the zipper of his wetsuit. When he saw sailors appear at the rail, he shouted, "Get the lifeboats into the water! Get anything that will float into the water." He blew his whistle again.

They swam to the ship, struggling through the waves, and he almost pushed Annabelle up the rope ladder swinging from the side of the *Wolf*. Strong hands reached down over the side to pull them into the ship. Ricou shed his diving gear and directed a nearby sailor to put up more lights. His own light he swung in widening arcs across the black water. The captain of the *Wolf* took charge of sending more light up into the rigging and sending the lifeboats over the side.

Annabelle was momentarily dazed and sat on the wet and rolling deck while the crew of the *Wolf* ran and skidded about tossing life preservers and barrels over the side and lowering lifeboats into the water. She saw two sailors hurrying into diving gear. She shrugged herself out of her gear and stood shakily, sitting down again abruptly when the boat yawed sickeningly into the side of a towering wave, tossing her ten feet across the deck and slamming her against the gunwale. A couple of sailors crashed into her, and she was stunned, gasping for breath while a sharp pain ran up her left arm.

When the boat righted itself, she saw that one of the lights mounted in the rigging had worked itself loose and was poised to plummet to the deck.

"Roy!" she called out wildly, and he turned. The light missed him by six feet and its plastic plates shattered on the deck. She felt ridiculous, and helpless. He slid across the deck and helped her to her feet, giving a hand to the other sailors as well.

"We'll find Dave," he said to her, facing her squarely. "Get below."

"I'm not in the navy," she returned. "You can't order me around."

He nodded, took her hand firmly in his, and pulled himself along the side of the boat, holding on to ropes and rings and any handhold he could find, toward the boat's stationary searchlight, which was bolted to the rail with heavy hardware.

"We ought to see his light," Ricou said, squinting into the darkness. "We ought to see his light."

"Do you think we should go back in?" Annabelle asked.

"We can't do shit from the water," Ricou answered harshly. "Our only chance is from up here."

"Why can't we see his light?" Annabelle fought down her rising panic and forced herself not to cry. "Why can't we see his light?"

Dave lay on the great heaving breast of the Gulf, feebly wondering how he could survive slipping one more time under the thin watery skin of that immense, cold bosom into the night below. He was confused; once, a deep, sucking fear that the black sky above was actually the water below threw him into a panic, and he forced himself to turn over and swallow what he had thought would be sky.

Several times he thought he saw the lights of the *Wolf*, a fairyland display of twinkling and swerving points of blurred yellow light in the distance, much farther away than he would have guessed. But since they looked like Christmas lights, he concluded that they were hallucinations, and he closed his eyes.

Several times he longed for his lost lantern, almost dredging up enough emotional strength to feel anger at himself for having dropped it in the struggle with the masked diver. Had that, too, been a hallucination, like the fantastic Christmas lights? He thought sleepily of a gold bow tie that sprang into dazzling light at the touch of a rubber switch. He wished he had such a tie now, to wear in the darkness. Perhaps all of his memories were hallucinations. That lovely face framed in midnight hair. A tiny green bird. A pink building, shimmering in golden sunlight.

Perhaps the only reality had always been this cold, black, wet, heaving world, where the only decision seemed to involve knowing the subtle difference between the sky and the water, the other memories only mirages, floating visitors from the imagination.

He could feel no pain in his leg. Perhaps that, too, had been the stuff of dreams. But the pain in his right shoulder was sharp, and solid. Something seemed to be hitting him. Where had that come from?

He turned his head and slipped under something rough, grazing his cheek with such raw force that his sleepiness vanished as he went down, down under the perilously slim tissue separating life from death, sky from water.

When he emerged once again, his head above the water, the rough thing touched his hand. It was an aluminum screw sticking out from an aluminum panel.

He tried to grab it, but his hand fell away, unable to gain a purchase. He grabbed again and banged his knuckles painfully against a sharp edge. He lunged desperately with both hands out before him, and he connected with the low, rolling side of a small boat.

His heart seemed to burst into flame within his cold chest, and he nearly cried out, but his attempt at jubilant expression turned into a cough that brought water rushing out of his lungs. He felt the boat slipping away, but the fire in his chest encouraged him, and he clung to the aluminum side like an angry cat on a window screen receiving a spray bath from a garden hose, very much against its will.

But the fire in his chest was short-lived. Every attempt he made to lift his cold body into the boat failed, ending in bruises and the reappearance of his sleepiness. Clinging to the boat with his limp right arm crooked over the side, shivering, he began to drift again, again into that world where the sky and the water were somehow one, somehow interchangeable in their blackness.

Something brushed his outflung left hand, his hand rocking aimlessly on the water. He turned, struck by the tiny green numbers on his wristwatch, the bright little shining numbers, sparkling prettily on the black water. The thing that had brushed him was a gray mass, its long back sliding along the waves.

A barracuda.

Dave flung his left hand over the edge of the boat, rocked it frantically toward him, sending in a wave of salt water, which he followed, sliding his nose along the bottom of the dinghy. He swallowed water from the bottom of the boat and spat it back out wildly.

He felt his heart racing, and he lay in a heap, getting his breath, restoring his respiration to something approaching regularity, restoring his spirit to something approaching hope.

Turning to look at his watch again, seeing in it a connection to that world that had colors other than black—that lovely face, that pink building, that little green bird—he thought that he had given himself a concussion getting into the boat, for the green numbers were now coming back at him double.

Curious, Dave studied the phenomenon, attempted to use it as a barometer of his own condition, a measure of the damage done to his head. The numbers were double, yes, tiny green reflections on the background of the silken wings of a beautiful butterfly.

A light and illusory creature of the air, the butterfly, a fragile miracle of aerodynamics, really, and evidence that nature could paint from the palette of sensitive genius, a splendor floating among the flowers of the night in the water. A butterfly on the Gulf. A cold butterfly.

Suddenly Dave was fully awake, his head pounding but alert. The butterfly was cold. He lifted his head and wrist from the cold body of the tattooed woman.

He found her throat, searching for a pulse. There was something around her neck, and he could find no pulse. He put his head between her tattooed breasts. There was no new sound, only the relentless droning thunder of the black waves against and beyond the aluminum hull. She was dead.

He could not grieve for her, had no room in his shrinking emotional reserve. Perhaps he would later. For now he could only wonder what made the butterfly reflect the luminous numbers of his watch.

What reflected the lighted dial of his watch, he reasoned, would reflect other light. Lights searching for him. Annabelle would search for him with lights. If she had not been harmed.

The thought galvanized him into action. He knelt on the bottom of the dinghy, rocking the boat from side to side against the countermotion of the water, sparks of black pain shooting up his right leg, drops of heat welling slowly from the wound, and he knew he was going to be sick.

He leaned over the side weakly and retched. He hung there, spent, shivering uncontrollably, hopeless for a moment, wishing he could distinguish the sky from the water, again uncertain in this spinning world of how to climb back to awareness, which direction to go, whether awareness lay below him or above.

He slid from the side on his belly, and groped and clawed the metal floor, searching for anything, a tool, a rope, an oar. He found two oars. He dragged them from under the aluminum seat and sat up, frowning in pain, his legs spread out before him.

He pulled the knife from the ragged trunks tied around

his right thigh and dropped it blade-first on the floor of the boat. The solid clatter of the knife against the metal cheered him—*I did that,* he thought—and he worked the knot in the trunks, peeling them away from the wound.

Working with a strength and singleness of purpose that he did not pause to consider, he lashed the oars together with the ragged strips of trunks, forming a loose **X**. He crawled and slid to the prow, dragging the contraption behind him, banging it awkwardly over the seats. He lodged the flat ends of the oars under the front seat, and his **X** leaned against the prow, at an angle of about sixty degrees from the horizontal. He crawled back to the body, dragging his bleeding right leg.

She was lying on her back and wearing only a string bikini, so he could not get a good hold, as he would have had she been more thoroughly dressed. He sighed and, with a silent apology, slipped his right hand under the front of the bra, grasping the strap. He wrenched and yanked her slowly forward, bumping her on the seats.

At last he propped her against the oars. She slipped sideways at once, and for the first time since he had made it into the dinghy, hope completely deserted him. It wasn't going to work.

He slipped his hand away from her cold body as he faced her in the boat. He lay against the cold aluminum side of the boat, gasping and coughing weakly, his shoulders banging the side as he shivered. He lay back with his eyes closed, his breath growing calmer, slowing, he thought, from his diminishing interest in it.

He opened his eyes. There was her face. She had had a pretty face, a young face, he remembered, but it was bloated now by the tight black thing around her neck, the pupils of the bulging eyes still dilated from cocaine, the black circles flooding out the blue of her irises. He raised himself on his elbow and stared at her neck. He poked a finger into the bulging flesh. She had been strangled with a length of videotape. He was shaking, and nausea seemed to drag at his belly from deep inside his cold body.

The videotape. He lifted her shoulders and propped her head tenderly against his chest, working patiently at the videotape with his fingers, untying the twisted knot, unraveling the snarl under her drenched blond hair. The tape was free, and, her head resting on his chest, he stretched out the piece of tape between his hands.

He pushed her away from his chest and shoved her again into position against the oars, winding the tape under her arms; his trembling fingers numb with the exertion, he tied her roughly to the oars with the length of videotape.

She slipped sideways, but not nearly so much as before. He crawled under her arm, braced his knees against the side of the dinghy, and propped her cold frame up on his shoulder.

The blackness roared now around his ears, and he felt his head drooping on her tattooed arm.

He fainted.

Annabelle and Ricou stood together at the rail, the powerful searchlight mounted on the rail shining out onto the blackness, reflecting nothing but the widening and dissipating circle of empty, meaningless debris surrounding them—the boats, tubes, and junk they had themselves flung overboard. The rain had stopped.

The *Wolf*'s men were gathered around the railing on all sides of the ship, but half an hour was a long time for a man to be missing at sea, a man who, apparently, could not call out for help or signal them in any other way; and the blasts on their whistles were coming less frequently, less heartily. The crew used their lights to sweep the surface of the sea, which was relinquishing its fury, the punishing waves rolling into wider furrows, the wind shifting and carrying a fresher smell. The cold front that the squalling storm had ushered in was bringing with it a crisp breeze from the west and the promise of clearing skies.

Two diving teams were now in the water. Their lights glowed eerily just under the surface.

Annabelle was hardly aware that Ricou's arm was around her. Her knees were stiff, she realized, from holding them steady to keep her balance on the rolling deck. Her hands, where they clutched the rail, were cold.

Someone, in the past ten minutes, had brought her a flannel shirt, which she wore over her wetsuit. Her hair hung in a wet stream against her neck. She reached up with one hand to wring it out, the gesture designed to hide the despair she was certain was all too apparent on her face.

"Where the hell is the Coast Guard?" she demanded through clenched teeth.

"We only radioed twenty-four minutes ago," Ricou said, bringing his arm up around her shoulders and looking at his watch. He glanced down at her, his face drawn, his eyes dark, and showed her the watch.

"I can't imagine what happened to him," she said. She knew that she had said the same thing, or something almost identical to it, at least five times. "Dave's a strong, reliable diver. I don't know anyone more resourceful. He's in excellent shape. He doesn't do stupid things. He should be here."

They had not spoken of the fear that Dave's absence, Dave's apparent inability to do anything to help himself, was connected to someone, some unknown someone, who had made it impossible for Dave to respond to their search.

Ricou had hesitated to show her the severed end of the blue nylon line. He did not know how she was sustaining hope, but perhaps he had been wrong to withhold the only information he had about Dave. He counted to ten internally, closed his tired eyes, tired from the salt water, the strain of squinting into the blackness. He decided.

He tipped the handle of the searchlight into her cold hand

and crossed to where his diving gear had lodged under a bench bolted to the deck. He extricated the nylon line, coiled it in his hand, and returned to her side.

He handed her the line, silently pointed to the smoothly sliced end, and moved her hand away from the searchlight.

She stood staring at the blue cord in her hand, her mind feeling numb.

"He was cut loose," she breathed. "He was cut loose. It wasn't an accident."

She turned to gaze up at Ricou. He was looking out to sea, but the grim line of his jaw told her that he had reached the same conclusion.

"It had to be somebody from this boat," she said. "There was nobody out there but us."

"Maybe." He said no more, and she was too stunned, too hopeless, to continue to speculate over something that seemed, for now, remote and irrelevant beside the one fact that filled her thoughts: Dave was gone.

For one wild moment that thought was displaced, as she wondered if Lieutenant Roy Ricou, who had been next to Dave, had cut his rope. But she dismissed the thought as quickly as it had arrived. It had not been Roy. She knew.

She felt his hand encircle hers. She held it firmly, the coral rosary she had found on the floor of the Gulf crushed between their palms.

"No," he said, turning to face her, his eyes gentle and warm. "It wasn't me."

Suddenly he stiffened beside her, wrenching his hand from hers, as a sailor called out from above, from the rigging.

"Over there!" the sailor shouted. "To the east. Shit, I think it's the east."

Ricou pivoted the big light to the east. Something low on the water was indeed twinkling oddly in his light, the strong beam of the searchlight annihilating the weaker beam coming from the rigging.

He turned to yell over his shoulder to the crew in general. "Does anyone have binoculars? A telescope?"

From the rigging came the same voice. "I've got one. I can see it now. Jesus Christ!"

"What is it?" Ricou shouted.

"Holy shit."

"What do you see, for God's sake?" Ricou bellowed.

"It's a woman. You gotta see this. It's a naked woman. Looks like a fucking mermaid. That's what it is. It's a fucking mermaid."

Annabelle grabbed Ricou's arm and jumped in annoynance.

"Tell me what's going on!" she demanded. "Is it Dave?"

Ricou looked down at her, a puzzled and sad expression on his drawn features.

"I don't know," he said. "They're saying it's a woman. A mermaid, of all things."

A dazzling smile lit Annabelle's face. She spun around, her arms out as if to embrace the sky. Ricou stared at her.

"It's Dave," she exulted, spinning. "I know it's Dave. Only Dave the Monkeyman would come back from the dead as a mermaid."

TWENTY-ONE

STARS BEGAN TO WINK INTO BEING IN THE WEST WITH rapid silver brilliance, as though they had been hidden behind a sheet that was speedily being pulled into the eastern sea by an unseen, giant hand. The *Wolf* put about to the east, its soaked rigging creaking as sailors put up canvas in the steady, freshening wind, cheering themselves with frequent glances toward the distant sparkling image they had found floating on the sea like a misty vision of seed pearls sewn onto a background of black velvet.

As the ship turned to its new course, Ricou adjusted the searchlight, attempting to keep its beacon trained steadily on the faint luminescent spectacle in the water about a quarter of a mile off the *Wolf's* bowsprit. Above the main mast the silvery white canvas billowed out under the snapping black-and-white skull and crossbones of the flying ensign; the huge Jolly Roger was also spread toward the east, and the mermaid.

Annabelle stood tensely beside Ricou, her cold hands clutching the rail, her initial exuberance gone, replaced by doubts, rationality; skepticism and hope were thrown together in an uncomfortable, fitful, warring combination, like strange cats and dogs tossed together into a bag and expected to fight it out until a victor emerged. And the doubts were winning.

Whatever was ahead of them in the sea was nothing like Dave's diving lantern. Whatever was ahead of them did not seem man-made at all, but rather fairylike, ethereal, perhaps even otherworldly. Not even Dave, with his powerful and eccentric imagination, could turn a prosaic diving beam, no matter how strong, into what seemed to be a cloth of fireflies, bobbing on the water.

The fireflies grew as the *Wolf* approached the drifting spectacle of lights. Ricou handed her the binoculars he had been given by the *Wolf*'s captain, and Annabelle was soon able to discern a pattern to the fireflies, now growing into bumblebee-size golden apparitions in the glow of the searchlight, now into hummingbirds of silver when the searchlight's beam dipped with the motion of the *Wolf*, the searchlight's influence on the distant pattern of lights then momentarily replaced by the increasing numbers of stars visible overhead.

She frowned into the binoculars, adjusting the focus.

Butterflies. They were butterflies, distinct and beautifully delineated. On the body of a woman.

The disappointment almost sickened Annabelle, but her doubts had conditioned her for this blow, and she moved the binoculars a fraction to the left to postpone sharing the discovery with Ricou. They must of course respond to the presence of anyone alone on this sea, despite the search for Dave. Annabelle turned the focus wheel distractedly.

And there, emerging in the glasses, apparently pinned under the arm of the woman, was Dave. She thought it was Dave.

A tiny flame of excitement rekindling the fires of her damped emotions, Annabelle handed the binoculars to Ricou, a question on her face. He took them from her, gazed into her eyes, where he could see the hope redawning, and held the glasses up to his eyes, finding his range and focusing.

Soon he grabbed her hand and gave it a quick squeeze. But he continued to hold the binoculars steady in one hand, turning the focusing wheel with his index finger. He also held the searchlight as they approached what was now clearly a boat, perhaps one of the lifeboats they had themselves cast into the water. Ricou frowned at the thought that, even in the rough seas they had experienced, the boat could have drifted that far from the mother ship.

Annabelle refused to allow herself to speculate on Dave's condition. Nor did she attempt to take the binoculars back from Ricou. Rather, she seemed content to wait while he watched, using only her unaided vision to gaze into the decreasing distance between the *Wolf* and the other boat.

When they were within a hundred yards of the boat, she suddenly yanked off the flannel shirt and began to unzip her wetsuit. Ricou grabbed her arm.

"What are you doing?" he demanded.

"He's my friend, Roy," she said simply.

"You don't know if he's . . . you don't know that he's okay."

"I have to be the one, Roy. I have to be the one who goes to him." Annabelle's unadorned statement moved him, but he carefully suppressed expression of his emotions, nodding to her.

She stripped off the wetsuit.

Ricou was momentarily furious with himself for the subtle shocks to his imagination rendered by the sight of the statuesque woman who stood on the dark deck wearing an exceedingly abbreviated orange bikini that, he realized in a powerful series of irrelevant images thrust into his mind, was the most daring bikini he had ever seen—ever imagined seeing. So he busied himself by handing the binoculars to a sailor, who received a daunting and frosty look from Ricou for the kind of frank, open-eyed, and detailed scrutiny of Annabelle that Ricou himself longed to indulge in, and began to take off his own wetsuit, to be ready to go over the side with her when they reached the other boat, which was now about fifty yards ahead of them to the east.

As it was, she was over the side before he finished divesting himself of the wetsuit, swimming with long, athletic strokes toward the strange couple in the boat, wrapped about each other in a surreal approximation of drunken, hearty affection.

Grabbing one of the diving lights, Ricou dropped over the side of the boat and followed Annabelle, overtaking her about ten feet from the boat. They closed the rest of the distance together.

Reaching the aluminum hull, Annabelle grasped the side, going hand over hand toward the prow. She stretched her arm over the side of the boat and touched Dave's shoulder. It was cold. For a swollen, stunted throb of time that seemed glutted, held in abeyance permanently between the past and the future, she responded to a stab of fear, but it passed quickly as she felt the buoyant life in that thin shoulder. "He's alive," she declared happily.

Ricou was beside her. "I'll boost you in. Get ready." He deposited his light in the boat.

She nodded, gripping the side of the boat with both hands. Ricou's hands went around her waist from behind, and they went under together, pulling the boat toward them. When they rose, Ricou tossed her up and over the side. She landed softly, her hands on one of the aluminum seats spanning the boat, one knee on the floor, perfectly positioned by Ricou's powerful and expert toss. She picked up the diving light and moved to Dave and the woman, the beam in her hand shining on the couple.

That the woman was dead she knew immediately. The face was like Millie's—distorted, bulging, horribly deformed into a mask of grotesque emotion, like a screaming curiosity, the tongue protruding, the eyes cruelly pushed from their sockets—but even so, there remained a recognizable beauty frozen behind the mask of death, a regularity and perfection of features. The angry circle around the woman's tattooed neck told eloquently its abrupt, conclusive story of passionate human interference with the workings of the dispassionate universe.

But Dave's chest rose and fell regularly.

She put the light down on the swaying floor, aimed generally at the prow. Gently, Annabelle removed the dead woman's arm from Dave's shoulder. She needed all of her strength to shift the body, attached as it was to the strange contrivance of the linked oars, so that she could work her way in beside Dave and attempt to ascertain the extent of his injuries.

An ugly gash showed red and black on his right thigh; the wound was deep and must have bled horribly, but something had knit the sides of the wound together enough to slow the seeping blood to a slight, pumping, trickle. Ricou watched, holding the side of the boat, as she bent to examine the wound, her shoulders held tensely.

She could find no other damage to Dave's body, except for some long scrapes on his cheek, his nose, his shoulder, and there were several other small bruises, but the loss of blood and the hypothermia would account for his condition, she thought. She said his name. Nothing, no reaction. She touched his cheek and said his name again. Perhaps she was imagining that his eyelashes had fluttered?—almost imperceptibly, but surely there had been some movement, some sign of returning consciousness.

She rubbed his arms with her hands. She rubbed his cold legs. She glanced around helplessly, wishing she had a blanket; Dave was so cold. "We have to get him to the *Wolf*," she said.

Annabelle turned in the boat, still rubbing Dave's legs, and gave Ricou a stricken look.

"Can you see her? How horrible it is? The woman's dead. Can you get the *Wolf* to lower a sling or something?"

She turned back to Dave, and once again she thought his eyelids moved. "I think he's coming around."

Her hands on Dave's legs, she looked over her shoulder at the approaching pirate ship, which seemed to be bearing down on them dangerously. Dave stirred in her hands, and she turned back to him.

His eyes were open.

She smiled at him, relieved, and he mumbled.

"What?" she asked.

He mumbled again, turning his head toward the side of the boat and coughing weakly. He coughed, his right shoulder scraping the boat. He winced and mumbled again.

"What are you trying to say?" she said, putting her hand on his chin.

She felt Ricou's hand on her hip and looked over her shoulder at him in the water.

"What?" she demanded impatiently.

Ricou bit his lip and reached for her hand over the side of the boat. "He says he wants me."

"That's ridiculous." Her eyes flashed, and she yanked her hand away. "Why would he want you?"

She bent over Dave again, trying to lift him. She could tell he was trying to talk to her. His mouth moved feebly, but he was no longer coughing.

Ricou grabbed her arm painfully.

"What?" she demanded, her attention unwillingly torn from Dave.

"Get out, Annabelle. Dave wants me."

Ricou's expression seemed odd to her, oddly closed. She could feel Dave moving and as she turned back to him, she was shocked to see that he was weeping, not, she thought, as though he were in pain, but as though he were deeply, deeply sad, as though he were mourning a loved one. But he faced her through his tears and moved his lips clearly. "I want Popeye's help."

She opened her mouth, ready to argue with him, unable

to comprehend the distance in his eyes, when Ricou's hand closed powerfully over her wrist.

"You're coming out," he said.

"Why?" she demanded, an obstinate set to her jaw. "Is this some macho thing? Dave knows better than that. Is it because he's naked? He's not such a fool."

"It's not because you're a woman, Annabelle," Ricou said, hating himself, his grip steady on her arm. "It's because you can't hear him."

She felt a sickening lurch in her chest.

Dave's hand seemed to crawl from his side, dragged to his eyes, wiping them weakly. His face was ravaged with sadness, but he said, "Please, Annabelle."

Ricou, rapidly assessing the emotionally devastating situation as one unlikely to yield a solution there and then, decided to act and he did not waste time. He released Annabelle's wrist, reached up quickly, grabbed her under the arms, and yanked her out of the boat toward him.

She went over the side with a splash, slapping out against both the water and him. He pinioned her flailing arms against him and held her until she ceased her struggles and glared at him, her green eyes a fair map to the new territory of her exposed emotions.

"Get back to the *Wolf*," he said. "I'll take care of him."

She went limp, and he released her.

She swam away, never glancing back, plunging her arms into the waves with vicious, powerful strokes. She was helped up the ladder by willing hands from the *Wolf*, the image before her of Dave, his face unfamiliar to her with its ghastly pallor and its air of refusal, saying, "Please, Annabelle."

Ricou hauled himself over the side of the boat and clambered to Dave's side, glancing at the serious wound on his slim thigh before asking, "Can you make it if I carry you? I don't believe the *Wolf* can fashion a winch as tidy as this homemade lighthouse you devised."

Dave's throat felt thready, but he answered, forcing a hoarse whisper. "Thank you, Popeye. I've broken her heart, you know." He tried to rise on an elbow but fell back limply. "I'm as weak as a kiwi skin. You'd better look over your shoulder."

Ricou turned, quickly assimilated what Dave had indicated, and fluently and flashily cursed the *Wolf.* The pirate ship was now towering dangerously close to Dave's dinghy, a piece of overeager and clumsy seamanship that brought a fierce, violent scowl to Ricou's face. "Stop your goddamn engines," he shouted.

When the *Wolf* had veered away, missing the dinghy by several feet and rocking it with bouncing waves, he shouted again to the deck. "Secure this boat. There's a dead body aboard. And stand by the ladder. Injured man."

"Didn't know you had such a temper, Popeye," Dave mumbled.

"Toss down a blanket," Ricou shouted. He turned to Dave, smiling lazily, and drawled, "Just miffed." He caught the woolen blanket in one hand and spread it softly over Butterfly Sue.

He squatted beside Dave and looked him over knowledgeably. "Are you going to throw up?"

"Yes. Hold my head. Can't do it myself."

Ricou moved him onto his side, his strong hands supporting Dave's jaw, his mind considering options. Dave was clearly out of resources, collapsing bonelessly back against Ricou's arm.

Deciding that the least potentially harmful route for Dave was eliminating any more contact with the hard surfaces of the dinghy, Ricou knelt carefully and picked Dave up in his arms like a child, surprised at how little he weighed. Ricou's assessment of Dave had not failed to take into account the athletic wiriness of his frame, and the smaller man had won his respect with the daring and resourceful use of the corpse, as grisly as that must have been for a man weakened by such a serious wound and by the terrors of the storm. It was in fact not just an achievement of pure grit, an emotional sturdiness that Ricou admired, but also a physical achievement against great odds.

"It was Hemingway again," Dave murmured. And he quietly fainted.

Ricou stood and went over the side, back into the water, cradling the smaller man against him gently, grateful that Dave was unconscious for the dunking. He quickly got Dave's head above water and swam with his inert body to the ladder, which he climbed slowly, having slung Dave's naked form over his shoulder in a fireman's carry. He handed Dave into the waiting hands of the crew, glad to see that Annabelle had wisely gone below, hoping she had found an outlet in tears, as Dave had in the boat.

Blankets were quickly supplied for both men, lights were carried to the little scene on the deck, and the captain, who also attended to any medical emergencies on board, wound gauze around Dave's wound after treating it with an orange disinfectant that Ricou privately thought absurd. Soap and water would have been more to the point, he thought, but he did not think Dave was in immediate danger any greater than had already been supplied by shock and serious loss of blood, neither of which would be affected in any way by the acrid orange substance now that the wound had been stanched.

Dave was removed a few feet across the main deck to the captain's cabin, still unconscious. The boat carrying the body of Butterfly Sue was taken in tow. And their course set for Key West.

Mugs of hot coffee made their appearance among the quiet crew. Some of the men gathered at the stern to stare at their grim, trailing cargo, and Ricou sipped from his steaming mug gratefully. He wondered if a mug had been taken down to Annabelle. He drained his, refilled it from a large urn near the wheelhouse, and carried it carefully down the ladder toward the aft cabins.

He peeked inside the cabin she had shared earlier with Dave. She was curled up on the bunk on her side, wearing jeans and a sweatshirt, her dark hair combed back into a smooth chignon at the nape of her neck, her head resting on a neatly folded plaid blanket. Her green eyes were open, and she was staring at the checkerboard lying spilled on the deck, the white and black plastic men still stuck to it by their magnets, in random disarray.

He did not think she had seen him, but she said, without moving her head from the blanket, "Is he all right?"

Ducking under the low bulkhead, Ricou stepped into the cabin, which was dimly lit from a small red battery lantern hanging on the wall. He wrapped his blanket around him closely so as not to trip on it and sat down beside her on the bunk.

She turned over on her back and fixed him with a dark gaze. Her troubled green eyes now seemed to him, with such depth of exposed emotion, such profound and painful isolation, to open a new universe, a solitary cosmos that he was stunned to discover to be vast and restless and disturbing, like the oceans whose moods and depths and impossible allure had commanded and obeyed him from his youth.

Deafness was something absolute, he thought. It did isolate her, no matter how cleverly Dave interpreted, no matter how well she integrated her ability to read lips into the hearing world's ways, no matter how, he now realized, he himself had pretended that she was not really different from other women, merely using an exotically distinctive method for communicating. Deafness did set her apart. And she was lonely now, locked in an isolation that frightened him, lonely and scared and worried about someone she loved, someone whose needs she had been absolutely unable to supply. Ricou was bowled over by the shallowness of his original perceptions of Annabelle.

He put his palm lightly on her cheek, touched and finely awakened by her soft warmth. "Dave fainted, probably from shock and loss of blood," he said gently. "His wound has been attended to, in rough-and-ready but thorough fashion, the bleeding stopped. He's covered with blankets and snoring in the captain's cabin. He snores, Annabelle, worse than a basset hound, so you may get even with him when he's ready to be teased again." He rubbed his thumb along her cheekbone. "Dave's a brave man. I've never seen anything like what he did. He must want to live very badly."

Silent tears coursed down her cheeks onto the blanket, but she did not sob.

"Do you think it was my fault," she asked softly, "for insisting on this mad escapade?"

Ricou saw with surprise that one of the demons in that dark cosmos revealed to him in her deep green eyes was the specter of guilt.

"No," he said emphatically, the honesty in his eyes warming her. "I think we were almost in time to stop the second strangling."

Annabelle expelled a shuddering breath.

"Almost," Ricou went on, his hand on her wet hair. "In fact I think we were within minutes of the butterfly woman's death. I think that's why Dave was attacked—to buy time for the murderer to get away. By the way, Dave said it was Hemingway again."

Annabelle wiped a hand across her cheeks. "I want this killer, Roy."

He took her wet hand in his, turning it over to glance at the coral rosary she wore around her wrist.

"You must be cold," she said after a moment. "You should put something on."

"Share your blanket with me."

She sat up and unfolded the plaid blanket. He handed her the mug of coffee. They sat together on the bunk, wrapped in the blankets, the smooth motion of the ship rocking them gently. Ricou put his arm around her, and she leaned against his chest, sipping the coffee.

"Your chest is so smooth," she said after some minutes, sliding his dogtags, trailing her fingers lazily, and sighing sleepily. "I like it."

"Me too," he said.

"What?"

He bent to face her. "Me too."

"Why?"

"Because *you* do," he whispered, the low tone of his reply springing from a sense of intimacy, a tone he needed to express even though she could never hear it. "I want you to like me."

She attempted a weak smile.

They sat together silently, Annabelle drifting in and out of a troubled sleep, Ricou unthinkingly logging in his mind the long return course of the *Wolf* as he heard the slight sounds of other boats, newer depths, in these waters he had become so familiar with so quickly. At last he knew they were near the island city when he heard the slap of water against the old pilings near the Truman Annex, at the southern entrance to Key West's harbor.

He was moving his arm, gently adjusting his position, when the sound of the explosion came, followed almost immediately by a lurching of the *Wolf* and a white flash that lit the cabin like midday. He dropped the blanket, jumped off the bunk, and ran for the companionway, Annabelle following closely. She had felt that lurch and had seen that flash and had caught the painful glare through the porthole of red and yellow flames lighting the sky, jetting hundreds of feet above the harbor.

When they arrived on deck, the flames were falling back

to the sea, around an epicenter two hundred yards ahead of the *Wolf* and only ten yards off Tank Island, along with slowly drifting pieces of debris from a boat, raining over the harbor like depleted fireworks. Bushes on the little island were burning.

Buildings along Key West's waterfront were lit with the falling fire, in a bizarre echo of fabulous sunsets.

Dave swayed and limped onto the deck, clad in a long white shirt with the flowing, gathered sleeves of a movie pirate and leaning heavily on the hilt of a bejeweled wooden sword, his face appallingly white.

"Hell and damnation!" he roared hoarsely, a dangerous light in his eyes, his lean, pale face flickering in reflection of the red fury of the explosion. "Can't a guy get any sleep in this psychotic town?"

THURSDAY

Why, who could prove anything?

ERNEST HEMINGWAY
To Have and Have Not

TWENTY-TWO

"I NEVER THOUGHT THE ANGEL OF DEATH WOULD COME to pluck me into the beyond wearing the face of Ernest Hemingway, my dear."

They were in Dave's suite, and he was propped up against what seemed to be about thirty pillows, the extras provided by the worried management of Ocean Key House when Dave had pettishly complained that he "rather thought a pea was protruding through the mattress," crabby but never dreaming that anyone would take him seriously.

Dave had been treated and had received eleven stitches and a whole-blood transfusion at the Lower Florida Keys Health System, and after refusing to stay another minute in "this blasted house of morgue comedians who can't tell Mark Twain from Mark My Words," he had been taken by ambulance back to Ocean Key House. The hotel's doctor had pronounced Dave in no danger, to which Dave had replied, with a fair amount of acid in his hoarse voice, "That's easy for him to say *now*." The wound had been washed and dressed for what Dave called "the millionth time—now leave it alone, you leering quack," Dave had been instructed to stay in bed and drink plenty of fluids—"Which would be just dandy if I hadn't already swallowed half the Gulf," Dave had said waspishly—and an offer of painkillers had been refused. The doctor had written out a prescription anyway, leaving it on the bedside table with a significant frown in Annabelle's direction.

"But even given the mask, could you tell nothing about your attacker?" Annabelle persisted, sitting beside him on the bed and still feeling miserable about failing him out at sea and ill at ease over some hidden or coming change in their relationship, some new footing where they'd have to examine the limits of her participation in that relationship, somehow scale back Dave's high expectations of her, or simply absorb into their conversations a new and distressing topic. She was nervous.

"It all happened so fast, like they say in the movies, that I barely knew what was happening. Just the sight of that hideous, rubber Ernest Hemingway mask, the knife, my regulator slashed, the coldness, not breathing. I wish I knew something." Dave's brown eyes were fierce. "Believe me. I wish I knew something. I suspect that Hemingway mask was mine, Annabelle."

Sunlight streamed obliquely into the room, slanting across the carpet from the south. The sky was a perfect, soft blue; the harbor once again alive with the gaily colored traffic of small boats traveling back and forth to the coral reef; the excitement concerning the overnight explosion of the *Reef Cowboy* transferred from the curious faces of sleepy mariners at the many docks and marinas into the capable hands of the Monroe County Sheriff's Department.

The boat had gone up in spectacular plumes of flame near the eastern shore of Tank Island, and the fire had scorched the island's small supply of scrubby bushes, yet had hardly made a dent in the desolation of that almost naked piece of earth standing between the city of Key West and her famous sunsets.

The sheriff, a man named Tomatohead Hockett, no doubt for the permanently sunburned scalp shining through his sparse blond hair, had also taken charge of the corpse of Butterfly Sue and the boat she and Dave had been found in, which, from the painted legend low on the aluminum side, had belonged to the *Cowboy*. Hockett had pointed out almost immediately, holding the frayed end of the dinghy's rope, that the small boat had probably been snapped loose from the *Cowboy* in the storm, perhaps without the knowledge of whoever had been piloting the salvage boat.

As for that pilot, Hockett had deputies canvassing the piers for possible reports of someone who had swum ashore while Tank Island burned.

Everyone knew that Ishmael Solas owned the *Cowboy*, but Ishmael had spent the evening at Sloppy Joe's Bar, filling in on the bass guitar with Jake Balls and the Hell Raisers, whose regular guitarist, a friend of Ishmael's, had been incapacitated in a fight early in the day on the docks.

Ishmael, in his grief for Butterfly, hardly seemed to mind that the *Cowboy* had been blown to smithereens in the lee of Tank Island. Speculation had always dictated that Butterfly and Ishmael were lovers, though Ishmael was steadfast in denying this to the sheriff, saying only that she was a good sailor and he would miss her. He had no idea who she had taken out on the *Cowboy* that afternoon. Butterfly hadn't told him. Some of Ishmael's neighbors at the marina told Tomatohead Hockett that they had seen Butterfly talking to a little Hispanic guy in jeans and a sweatshirt, but that he had left after only a brief exchange, headed for the *Wolf*.

Dave had confirmed the conversation for the sheriff, and he had repeated the conversation in its entirety for Annabelle.

"So she went on and on about Fran's and Caliban's stupid dream of making that theater worth something. Between you and me, I don't think Wayne Newton would be the way to go."

"Wayne Newton." Annabelle smiled, shaking her head. "Poor Francisco. What a delusion. He'd have much better luck even with Shakespeare. This town is pretty uptight about its artistic pretensions."

"Annabelle," Dave said, "do we know yet what was on that videotape around pitiful Butterfly's neck? It probably doesn't matter, was just whatever they had on board the *Cowboy,* but I can't help being struck, you know, by the oddity. It's like the typewriter ribbon, in a way. A vehicle of expression, a thing made to carry a message. You know?"

She nodded.

"The sheriff has it," she said. "He strikes me as much more substantial than Barbara Ruggierrio." Annabelle took a deep breath, feeling peculiarly out of sorts with herself, in addition to feeling uncomfortable with Dave. "Last night Ruggierrio suggested—had the gall to suggest—that the sheriff arrest you for the murder of the butterfly woman."

Dave considered this suggestion as though it were a delightful novelty, his head to one side. Marcel chose that moment to launch himself from the lampshade on the night table and landed on Dave's wounded leg. Dave put out his hand, the bird hopped onto the extended fingers, and Annabelle looked at Dave inquiringly. "It's all right," he said. "It doesn't hurt. He only weighs a feather."

Dave had been taken to the hospital, still draped in the pirate shirt, by Coast Guard paramedics who had augmented the thin shirt with fresh blankets. A cutter had followed the *Wolf* from the treasure site, having responded to the radio distress call from the pirate ship, arriving a mere thirty-seven minutes after the call. They reported to Sheriff Hockett, when asked, that they had sighted no other vessels in the area of the distress call.

Ricou had used the hospital's pay phone to call the Key West Naval Air Station and leave an urgent message for Commander Ivan Rzadkowolsky that an attempt had been made to blow up Tank Island. In her concern for Dave, it had not occurred to Annabelle that anyone could possibly care about lonely, forlorn Tank Island, but she had not said anything to the lieutenant.

"Somebody's at the door, Annabelle," Dave said, touching her knee awkwardly, wrenching her from the memory. "Before you go, I just want to say thanks."

"Dave." She looked down at her hands, spread open on her lap. "I talked to Roy. He said you saved your own life."

He reached out and lifted her chin with his fingers, gazing into her sad eyes.

"What saved my life," he said, "was knowing that you'd be looking for me if you had to drain the Gulf of Mexico to do it. It was your face that kept coming into my mind." He swallowed painfully. "You're the only human friend I've ever had."

Tears moistened her lashes.

"I'm sorry I hurt you, Annabelle."

She leaned toward him and kissed his cheek lightly, over a livid purple bruise showing behind the dark stubble of the beard on his cheek. Without premeditation Dave threw his arms around her and squeezed.

He was blushing hotly when she stood, but she pretended not to notice, and, feeling happier and relieved of a painful weight, she went out to the living room to peer down the hallway toward the outer door of the suite. She could see nothing through the frosted-glass panel, so she went to the door, put the chain on, and looked through the peephole, taking no more chances with Dave's life.

She saw the freshly shaved jawline of Lieutenant Ricou and smiled to herself. Taking the chain off, she pulled the heavy door open.

He stepped inside, carrying a basket of fruit and a large bouquet of white roses. "Don't get conceited." He grinned. "They're for Dave."

Considerably handicapped by his burdens, Ricou nonetheless responded with swift and encompassing efficiency to the deliberately sultry and teasingly slow kiss of welcome she bestowed on him, her relief at the resumption of normal rela-

tions with Dave partially transferred into this physical out-
pouring for the lieutenant.

"You took me off guard," he said. "I can do better. Let's try
again."

"Ah, a perfectionist. That augurs well for things to come."

"How are you?" he asked, casting his eyes over the brilliant pinks and reds and vivid purples on the black background of her calf-length sundress. "You look fresh, sunny,
and beautiful. As though you had had a full night's sleep, with
nothing more bothersome on your mind than which Caribbean island to honor with your presence. I like that dress."

She smiled.

Her hair fell in a dark cloud of soft fullness to her bare
shoulders, her cheeks showed a healthy color, and the smooth
expanse of bare skin when she turned, taking the basket from
his hand, revealed that the exotic dress was backless, dropping
slightly below her slim waist. She took his breath away, and he
reached his hand for her bare waist, pulling her back into the
shadows of the hall.

"Stay a moment," he said softly, his eyes alight and in-
tensely blue, his fingers tight on her waist. "This is for the
orange bikini."

He embraced her, and they kissed, the white roses in his
hand lying across her bare back.

"What the hell's going on out there?" Dave's querulous
voice was raised in hoarse demand.

Ricou laughed, and stood away from Annabelle, touching
her lips with a gentle finger. "You're being summoned," he
said, nodding toward the open door of the bedroom. "And it
sounds like the Hero of Latitude Twenty-four Degrees/Thirty-
seven Minutes is in a nasty mood."

She went quickly to Dave's bedroom door, still holding
the basket of fruit. "You have a visitor, Mr. Enamorado," she
said mildly.

"If that's *El Teniente,* tell him I'm asleep," he said in a loud voice.

Ricou walked to the door and looked into the room over Annabelle's shoulder, smiling lazily at Dave, and stepping around Annabelle to approach the bed.

Dave grinned shyly and put out his hand. "Nice to see you, Lieutenant. Thanks for dragging my bones out of the water."

"It was my pleasure," Ricou said, shaking Dave's hand.

Annabelle took the bouquet from Ricou's other hand and left the room. She returned with the flowers arranged in an ice bucket, which she put on the dresser. Ricou was seated in a chair he had pulled up to the bed. She sat on the opposite side of the bed, and he could now see a long purpling bruise on her left shoulder.

"You're out of uniform, Lieutenant," Dave said, eyeing the officer's black T-shirt, white shorts, and scuffed brown boat shoes. "Does this mean you're off duty? When do you ship out? It won't do to keep Uncle Sam waiting."

Annabelle clenched her hands and breathed. Singapore, which the navy hoped would make up in fresh strategic Pacific importance for their closing bases in Manila, was a long way from Miami.

"Not just yet," Ricou said. "Tomorrow night."

Dave glanced at Annabelle's face, which gave nothing away to him about her feelings on this matter. He was about to open his mouth, to ask Ricou about the new port of call, when there was another knock at the door.

"I'll get that for you," Ricou said, rising from the chair.

As the lieutenant left the room, Dave said, "Annabelle, it's not that I'm not grateful for this pirate shirt, but do you think you could find me something more my size? Don't get suckered into buying one of those stupid slogan shirts on Duval Street. I won't sit around in bed wearing 'My Parents Went to the Florida Keys and All They Brought Me Was This Stupid

Shirt.' And for God's sake, don't buy me one of those polyester neon sunsets that says, 'If You Support the Resort, Dial 1–800–EAT–SHIT.' "

"Why don't I just buy you a normal pair of pajamas?" she suggested. "How about some nice silk ones?"

"Waste of money. I don't wear bottoms."

Tomatohead Hockett stuck his head into the room.

"Glad to see you looking more fit," he said. "I'd like you to take a look at something if you're feeling up to it."

He stepped into the bedroom, glanced at the proportions of the Jacuzzi, and sent his eyes around the room. He was carrying a small gray machine under his arm, its short electric cord dangling loose against his side.

Ricou sat on the bed beside Annabelle, taking her hand without thinking, softly touching her bruised shoulder with his other hand. Dave, intent on the sheriff, did not seem to notice the lieutenant.

"Is that a video-eight machine?" Dave asked brightly, his interest immediately engaged. "It looks slightly different somehow."

"This is a little bigger than a video-eight," Hockett said, moving to the bedside table. "Do you mind?" he asked, gesturing at the lamp with his elbow.

When Dave shook his head, Hockett lifted the lamp onto the floor and deposited the machine in its place. He yanked the lamp's plug out of the wall and opened the machine, revealing a flat-screen monitor. "I borrowed this from a guy on Big Pine Key. He used to work for CBS News." Hockett knelt on the floor and plugged the cord into the socket behind the table. "What he did was he spliced that videotape you found around the butterfly girl's neck onto some leader tape. The wrinkles are pretty bad, and the tape's stretched, of course, but there's something there. He couldn't say what it was."

Dave watched Hockett's operations with fascination. The sheriff switched on the screen, took a tape from his jacket pocket, and held it up in his hand. "Your boss says you're an expert on the movies. I want to see what you make of this." The tape was in a small case, about three by four inches. "Ready?" Hockett angled the monitor toward the bed.

Dave linked his hands behind his head, absently shoving Marcel onto the pillows, and nodded. Hockett pushed the play button.

They all watched, Hockett standing by the player, as crackling snow and wavy lines appeared on the screen. The room was silent, except for the muted, distant cries of seagulls out on the dock.

"I don't know that much about the technology," Dave said, his eyes on the screen, "but couldn't computer enhancement reconstruct the tape?"

Hockett looked at Dave over the monitor screen. "The FBI can probably do that for us if we have to. But the tape does play back partially now. I want to see what you think. Stop it anywhere you like. Use the pause button to stop it or start it."

Dave nodded and concentrated on the screen. He raised his eyebrows at the snow and lines, at the occasional thick gray streaks showing behind the jangle of crossing lines. Annabelle and Ricou watched in silence. The electronic images separated into sporadic black-and-white splotches leaping on the snowy background.

Suddenly Dave reached for the pause button and stopped the tape.

"There," he said, touching the left corner of the screen. "That's Tyrone Power's hand."

Ricou looked at the screen and then looked at Dave with disgust. "You can't possibly know that. You're grandstanding."

"It does look like a hand," Annabelle said. "It is a hand."

"But Tyrone Power's?" Ricou glanced at her and back at Dave.

Dave returned Ricou's glance with bland unconcern. "Betcha a hundred bucks," he said simply.

"You're on."

"I'll be perfectly happy to throw in the name of the picture free of charge—but even I will need a little more than a wee flickering hand to tell you that."

Ricou and Hockett stared at Dave in open disbelief.

"A *little* more," Dave said. "Do we have any popcorn, Annabelle?"

TWENTY-THREE

DAVE STUDIED THE BUTTONS ON THE VIDEO PLAYER briefly and pushed the pause button again. A series of fuzzy images danced across the screen, a series that even Ricou thought were partially recognizable as containing human parts.

Once again Dave reached for the button. "There," he said, a note of triumph in his voice. "Ava Gardner's neck. I'd know it anywhere. See how thick and rhinolike it is?"

Hockett moved away from the machine and stood beside Ricou. They all looked at the screen. Hockett stood uncertainly, inclined to agree with the lieutenant about this little bedridden guru of film, uncertain if he was being had. But sending the tape to the FBI would take some time, and he didn't want to take time with this strangler. He'd sure like to know the name of the picture; maybe it would give him a lead. The town police had apparently drawn a blank, and Hockett wanted to move on this killer. Strangling was an ugly business, a nasty, intimate way to cut off a life.

Dave pushed the pause button and studied more of the distorted electronic signals, bending closer to the screen until he found an image that finally satisfied him, and he stabbed the button with his finger in a victory gesture.

"I've got it," he crowed. "That lousy dress. Ava Gardner at her worst. I'd like to have had a word with the costume department. Still, with that neck, there wasn't much hope."

Hockett watched wordlessly, content to let the little guy show off. He scratched his sunburned head as Dave started the tape again.

Now the images were splotched with occasional color, but the snow and lines moved through the pictures in chaotic, random patches of light.

Dave paused the picture again.

"That's the side of Errol Flynn's head," Dave said, melancholy fondness in his voice. "What a wonderful performance. He played the pitiful souse, and a very moving character study it was. It really makes the picture worth watching."

"Well, what film is it, if you're such an expert?" Ricou demanded, pure challenge in his voice.

Dave looked at him smugly. *The Sun Also Rises*. I'm not guessing, Popeye. It's the only film Ava Gardner ever made with both Tyrone Power and Errol Flynn." He seemed to consider a moment, a glow in his eyes. "Flynn was really something."

"Are you sure about this?" Hockett asked.

Dave's first response was a perfectly spontaneous but haughty widening of his brown eyes.

"Of course I'm sure. 1957. Directed by Henry King, a hamhanded has-been even then; God only knows how he got that immaculate performance out of Errol Flynn. It's a very sad picture to watch, because the actors are all pretty long in the tooth, especially Tyrone Power, who had become very queenly at that point. *The Sun Also Rises*. I haven't thought about that film in a while."

"A Hemingway book," Hockett mused aloud.

"Right," Dave said.

"Well, I'll be damned." Hockett went to the chair vacated

by Ricou and sat down. "You said the person who attacked you wore a Hemingway mask? You're sure about that too?"

"As sure as I am about that film—I saw them both." Dave pushed the power button and shut off the player. "The heads on this machine are probably ruined now," he said, ejecting the tape. He took the tape in his hand and held it up to the light coming in through the balcony door. "Pretty soon we'll be able to get these little guys on spools the size of audiotape. Can you imagine? Movies everywhere you go."

"*The Sun Also Rises,*" Annabelle murmured. "*The Sun Also Rises.*"

"Yeah, big help." Hockett stood and returned to the bed-side table. He unplugged the machine, closed the monitor screen over the control panel, and passed his hand over his head, which, despite the sunburn, was evidently not tender. "Not that I don't appreciate this," he said. "It's amazing what you did, son."

"Amazing?" Dave said. "Amazing? You call that amazing? That's the easiest hundred bucks I ever earned. It was noth-ing." He shot a keen glance at Ricou, who was studying Dave with narrowed eyes.

Hockett took the tape from Dave's still-extended hand. "Maybe I will send it to the FBI after all," he said, and when Dave turned reproachful eyes on him, he added, "just to be sure, you know."

Annabelle stood, extracting her hand from Ricou's, and walked with Hockett out of the room.

"So, Ricou," Dave asked sweetly, "was there something I can help you with? Perhaps a rabbit I can pull out of my hat? Or were you just in the neighborhood?"

When Annabelle returned, having seen Hockett from the suite, Dave was sitting up in the bed with his legs crossed awkwardly and Ricou had returned to the chair.

"Tank Island's taken a pretty good scorching," Ricou was saying. "I went out there this morning with Commander

Rzadkowolsky to survey the damage. The old fuel was removed years ago, but we were a little worried about some pipes in the ground. The navy is taking this explosion pretty seriously at both the tactical and the public relations levels. For all practical purposes Tank Island still belongs to the navy, and that explosion was too close for comfort."

"That island," Dave sniffed. "I wish it didn't exist. If it weren't for that island, maybe none of this would have happened. That stupid resort! Noah Green says the navy is going to cave in and cede the rights to the blasted Hemingway Resort. Don't mention the name Hemingway to me ever again. Or the word *navy*."

"Oh," Ricou said conversationally, "I don't think you have to worry too much about Tank Island, if it's the sunsets that are upsetting you."

Dave studied the lieutenant's face with a hard, suspicious glare, Annabelle with a suspended question in her eyes.

"What do you mean?" Dave asked warily.

"The navy has decided to retain its rights to the island, following my report on my assignment here," Ricou said, unaware that he had just succeeded in taking Annabelle's breath away, so still was she sitting on the side of the bed. "Actually the decision was made months ago, back in November or so. My report was only the last step in implementing the decision."

"Roy," Annabelle breathed, lacing her hands together in her lap. "What are you talking about? What is your assignment in Key West?"

"I can't tell you everything, but Rzadkowolsky gave me leave to tell you a certain portion of what is strictly naval business. No civilian has a right to any of this information, but in view of last night's murder and explosion, and in view of the attempt on Dave's life, and in view of a certain Jacob Hardy's long-standing acquaintance with one Ivan Rzadkowolsky, the Commander gave me leave to tell you two things, with your solemn promises not to leak the news to anyone, and I vouched for you both: A certain unpopular use of dolphins by the navy has now come to an end"—at the looks of heightened speculation he encountered on their faces, he nodded—"you'll remember I'm a weapons man. And to make up for the bad blood over the years, the navy is holding on to the Tank Island rights because the western side of that island is a dolphin playground, a breeding ground."

"The rights aren't going to the resort?" Annabelle said. "Because of the dolphins?"

"I've told you all I can," Ricou said. "You're the only ones on the island besides Millie de Vargas who have been let in on the secret, so I think it's safe to say that the navy's secret is safe. You see, the whole thing, the decision, is being sealed for thirty years, because if we admit we're ending the dolphin project, then we will also be admitting we *had* a dolphin project. The navy's not about to admit that. It never has. Not outright, not with full particulars."

"Millie knew?" Annabelle's face, unbeknownst to her, was now a fairly exact reflection of the thoughts racing through her mind. She went from shock to a dawning acceptance to questions. "How did Millie know?"

"She was negotiating on behalf of that resort with Rzadkowolsky; he finally told her to save her breath when she offered him shares in the resort in return for his cooperation. He told her to peddle her shares elsewhere; the navy wasn't yielding the Tank Island rights."

"And so she did," Dave squeaked. "She peddled her shares elsewhere—to Green. Ricou, we should have connected you to Tank Island." Dave pounded his pillows in glee. "Oh, this is lovely, lovely. This is great. Green owns shares in a dolphin habitat!"

Annabelle stood and took a turn about the room, Ricou covertly watching her under his lashes.

"I've been a fool," she said at last. "I've been a perfect fool, when the answer was actually presented to me—to all of us—on a plate. I've been refusing to see it, refusing even to look at it."

Dave threw his pillows aside and watched her pace back and forth on the carpet.

"I need to think," she announced. "But I can't think here. Dave, I'm going to the mansion."

He flung back the floral spread covering his legs. "Not without me, you're not."

"Oh, don't get up," she begged.

"Get out," he ordered. "I'm getting dressed. I know that tone of voice you're wearing, and I'm not going to miss all the fun. Besides, you'll need me to make pretty signs in the air. Get out, I said."

"Before I do," she said, ignoring Ricou's interruptions demanding to be told what she was so excited about, "promise me you'll get right back in bed if you feel dizzy or in pain." She turned to Ricou.

"Roy, can't you stop him?"

Dave flipped a hand in the air, sending Marcel squawking around the room.

"If you can't stop me," he signed, "what makes you think Jacques Cousteau here has a chance? Get out."

"Dave, you're going to open your wound," Annabelle fretted.

"Nuts," Dave growled impatiently. "The real problem is that I probably don't have anything decent to wear. Get out."

TWENTY-FOUR

USING HIS SILVER-TIPPED LAVENDER PARASOL AS AN impromptu cane, Dave climbed awkwardly into the cab, nattily attired in a yellow dress shirt with pleated front, yellow Bermuda shorts that bulged over his bandaged right thigh, a black cotton bow tie, black patent leather belt, and, as usual, black flats. His hair was combed over his pale forehead into a stylishly windswept set of bangs, and the smooth streaks that made paths around the bruises on his cheeks showed that he had made the effort to shave. That the entire operation, including a one-legged shower, had been completed in ten short minutes—from pirate shirt to parasol—testified to his orderly mind when personal fashion was at issue, and to Lieutenant Ricou's prompt exit from the bedroom of 509 when Dave had conceived the idea that the lieutenant could benefit from a few object lessons and a brief experience as valet to the oracle.

As Annabelle was about to step into the cab outside the hotel, the desk clerk ran out of the lobby, waving a piece of paper. Ricou intercepted the paper and handed it to Annabelle.

She read it and handed it into the cab to Dave.

"It's the report from my lab," she told Ricou. "The floor at

Sloppy Joe's Bar and the stuff I picked up in Ernest Hemingway's studio have the same chemical composition."

"Does that enlighten you?" Ricou drawled, leaning his forearm on the roof of the cab. "Annabelle, just what do you expect to find at the museum? The killer's long gone from there."

"I'm not sure." She studied his face. "Maybe just a fresh way of looking at things. Maybe I need to start thinking like an outsider, like a tourist. That's what Millie de Vargas found so wonderful about me, you know—I'm an outsider. And after last night in Dave's little boat, I learned I'm more of an outsider than I wished to believe."

"We're all outsiders, Annabelle. At one time or another."

Dave stuck his head out of the cab. "Would you rather be a six-toed cat? Think about it. Talk about insiders."

The cab took them down Duval Street, past Sloppy Joe's Bar; past the law offices of de Vargas and Green—now only Green, Annabelle thought—past the Margaret Truman Costume, Tuxedo, and Piano Shop; past Island Baubles and Bare Bodies; past Mahogany Maid; past Danny's Fish Market; past Dizzy Izzy's skateboard boutique; and around a corner to the west, onto Whitehead, pulling up beside the redbrick wall surrounding the Hemingway mansion.

They paid the six-dollar-per-adult admission charge at the open gate and proceeded up the cement walkway, around the small fountain, and onto the veranda, which, as usual, was tenanted by lounging cats, their celebrated feet the subject of much photography by the scores of tourists visiting the Hemingway Museum.

The mansion was hot; it even smelled hot, Annabelle thought. She led the way to the high-ceilinged and airy white kitchen, navigating past the flight of stairs that rose on the right, down a narrow hallway crowded with sightseers, and toward the left-rear corner of the old mansion. Annabelle stood beside the plush purple rope, gazing into the spacious kitchen.

"Look at the way the appliances and counters are all mounted on those wooden things," Dave signed and said, handing his parasol to Annabelle and remembering to include Ricou politely in the conversation. "I've never seen such a tall sink."

A cold voice spoke behind Dave. "They're raised like that because Hemingway was a tall man, and he liked to stand there and clean his own fish."

Dave automatically signed the words as he turned to face Ashleen Ricou's disapproving countenance.

"Was his wife tall?" Annabelle asked.

"Not at all. Hemingway would never have thought of that." Ashleen Ricou's tone seemed to indicate that there was no reason Hemingway should have thought of such a thing. "Hello, Roy. It's about time you remembered your duty to the family. You've been in Key West for quite some time." She presented her dry cheek for a kiss.

"Tante Ashleen," Ricou said, dutifully kissing her. "I'm sorry it's taken so long. You're looking well."

"Humph," she replied. "Keep your butter to yourself. What are you doing here with these people? I understand you were involved in that spectacle last night in the harbor."

"Involved against our will and inclination both, Tante Ashleen, and we're recent friends," he summarized, thinking rapidly. "Actually, recent friends in need. They need to look at the kitchen."

"Well, they've got eyes, haven't they?"

"I mean, they need to go into the kitchen," Ricou explained, and Annabelle was fascinated to see the play of his blue eyes as he met those similar blue eyes of Ashleen Ricou. He was smiling at the old woman in what Annabelle considered a shabbily unfair and hypnotic way, given that he had been ignoring his aunt for weeks. "You can arrange that, can't you, Tante Ashleen? You run this show."

"Humph. What do they need in the kitchen?"

Annabelle interposed. "Miss Ricou, I need to look at the floor, very carefully. I may find one of the last pieces of the puzzle that, when solved, will point the way to the person who killed Millie de Vargas on this property."

"The death of Millie de Vargas is no concern of the museum," Ashleen Ricou said tightly. "I've told that to the police."

But, Ashleen Ricou considered Annabelle. They were the same height, and Annabelle found it difficult to meet her gaze, but she did, presenting a serious expression but not one of supplication.

The older woman bent to release the rope.

"Only her," she said, blocking Dave with her thin arm, as strolling tourists gathered to watch this breach in the walls of the iron etiquette of the estate.

Annabelle handed Dave's parasol to the lieutenant and took off her red sandals, carrying them in her hand as she walked slowly across the worn gray indoor-outdoor carpeting, obviously installed by the museum since the days of Hemingway's occupancy. The sightseers behind the rope were a courteous group, not minding this favored treatment but curious as to its purpose. It seemed that they had all heard a great deal about "the Hemingway Murders" and were delighted to be witnessing what they assumed was detective work of the most elemental order. Their eyes and cameras followed Annabelle's feet as she walked back and forth across the carpet, her eyes lowered, her face a study in fierce concentration. She stopped by the low window at the left of the raised sink. She stooped, touching the carpet with her fingers, flicking the full skirt of her sundress away from the spot that had drawn her attention. She rubbed her fingertips together, frowning. She stood and crossed to the rope, which Ashleen Ricou released only enough to allow Annabelle to exit the kitchen.

The gathered crowd was full of questions, but the older woman shooed them away with a cold expression and a simple "Get away from that rope. Nobody's ever allowed in the kitchen, by museum policy."

Annabelle, Dave, Ricou, and his aunt left the stifling house by the back door, to stand in the relative coolness of the shaded veranda, facing the studio cottage across the small brick patio. Annabelle took Ashleen Ricou's surprisingly soft hand in hers and said, "I need to visit the studio. Will you come with us and let us in?"

Ashleen Ricou had indeed heard about the explosion in the harbor, and about the new strangling, and about the innocent role of these outsiders in that violence and destruction. It was one thing to dislike outsiders; it was another to treat an outsider with violence. Without a word the older woman led them across the patio and climbed the iron stairs. Two laughing teenage girls stood in the caged foyer of the studio, sticking their slim, tan arms in through the metal straps. Ashleen Ricou rattled her keys until the girls left self-consciously, departing quickly down the other set of iron steps.

"I thought the police said you didn't have a key to this studio," Dave said, gazing up the stairs and making up his mind to ascend them.

"If you think I'm in the habit of unburdening myself to the local police, young man, you have a very odd notion of my character." Ashleen Ricou opened the cage and disappeared from Dave's sight, into the studio.

Clutching the iron railing and leaning heavily on Annabelle up the narrow flight of stairs, Dave made the climb painfully, Ricou bringing up the rear and carrying Dave's parasol. Once inside, Dave took the parasol from Ricou, steered for the chaise longue, and sank down with relief, his face pale.

Annabelle sat sideways on the cigarmaker's chair, crossing her long legs and spreading out the folds of her skirt. Ricou remained standing in the open cage doorway, his hands in the pockets of his white shorts, while his aunt took a seat on a rattan chair across from Annabelle, but the older woman was up again almost immediately, pulling the cage shut behind the lieutenant and locking it.

"No one's allowed in here," she told a resourceful photographer who had been quick to spot the opportunity and had almost sneaked into the studio behind the lieutenant. She resumed her seat, and Annabelle turned to Dave.

"Dave, let's look at this problem coldly, as though we'd never been here before."

"That's gonna be hard," he said, gazing around uneasily. "It's hard to forget the graveyard of the Great White Hunter's helpless prey. What do you think he used, a howitzer?"

"He used a rifle," Ashleen Ricou said righteously. "Just like everyone else in Africa."

Annabelle smiled slightly. "Dave, let's start with the lab report that just came in from Miami. The orange substance on my shoe was the same as the substance on the Sloppy Joe's floor sample—food, a particular blend of grease and tomato sauce and chili peppers, the sloppy-joe sandwich's signature in fact. In the kitchen just now I found more of that sauce, I think." She glanced down at the floor of the studio, pulling her skirt away from the tiles. "This is where I found the first sample, beside the chair where Millie de Vargas was strangled."

"Annabelle," Ricou said, "if you're suggesting that the killer brought the stuff from Sloppy Joe's Bar onto this estate, then he must have been wearing shoes with a great deal of that substance on them. Otherwise, it would have worn off on the grass, or the sidewalk."

"I see what you're getting at," Dave signed. "You mean it must have been a regular at the bar."

"Or someone who works there," Annabelle said.

"That waitress?" Dave asked, alarmed. "That lovely girl who said I was better-looking than the lieutenant?"

Ricou looked curiously at Dave.

"Or someone who had access to her shoes," Annabelle said. "Her big white spike heels. The ones that hurt her feet."

"Why would anyone want to wear somebody else's shoes to commit a murder?" Ashleen Ricou demanded. "That's crazy."

"Especially when the murderer must have known there was going to be a witness," Annabelle said. "This is one of the things we've been looking at wrong. The murderer had to know there'd be witnesses. Remember, there are guards on the estate twenty-four hours a day. And we actually do have an eyewitness to the murder, almost. The murderer was seen. Gabriel Perez saw the murderer."

"Come on, Annabelle," Dave said impatiently. "Perez said he didn't see anybody. That's what started all this."

"Wrong. He said he saw nobody but Millie."

"So Millie killed herself, wearing a waitress's shoes?" Dave looked mulishly at Annabelle. "You'd better go lie down."

"No, I'll tell you what the guard saw. He said he saw Millie de Vargas. But he must have seen someone who appeared to be Millie that night. The guard saw somebody who was dressed like her—exactly like Millie, down to the white spike heels, like the heels we saw in the morgue. That's how the killer got around the estate without being seen, seen as the murderer, that is. He was seen as Millie de Vargas. And almost certainly wearing white clothing like the suit she died in. The only detail that would have varied, I suppose, was that red rosary Millie was wearing. I think the killer did not expect that detail, and that's why the rosary was removed from the studio—so the guard would not be reminded of any inconsistency in what he saw."

Dave seemed to chew on this. "Then why the elaborate stuff with the cape?"

"Because he couldn't let Millie see him, not dressed like her. She would have known immediately that something was wrong. The cape was designed to hide him from the only witness who would know he was not Millie de Vargas—herself. So he wore the cape before the murder, to hide himself from Millie; and he got rid of the cape after the murder, to hide himself from the guards, dressed as Millie."

"And Perez said he saw Millie in the kitchen, long after sundown, long after the time the medical examiner said she'd been killed." Dave attempted to cross his legs and winced. "That's why you were looking for that shoe-sauce stuff in the kitchen." Dave nodded. "So the murderer, biding his time in the mansion, still wearing heels and dressed like Millie, waiting for an opportunity to leave when the guards were not looking, maybe waiting all night—good God, that's why the orange stuff was over by the window; he was watching the guards—the murderer did not need the cape after she was dead. In fact, he wanted to be seen without it, as Millie. And that's exactly what Perez saw."

Annabelle nodded slowly as Dave went through this line of thought. She glanced at Ashleen Ricou. "That's why I wanted to come back to the mansion," Annabelle said. "I wanted to walk on the grounds, try to see what Perez saw. I wanted to sit in this chair, try to think what Millie thought, do what Millie did, without coloring my thoughts with the thoughts of Key West insiders, people like Barbara Ruggierrio. And people like you, Miss Ricou."

TWENTY-FIVE

"ME? WHY DO YOU SAY THAT?" ASHLEEN RICOU DE-
manded. "I never gave any opinion about this terrible mess."

"Yes, you did," Annabelle said quietly. "You've been insisting all along that the murder has nothing to do with the museum, that the museum is not involved."

"Well, it isn't."

"Of course it is," Annabelle said. "What a striking place to
commit a murder. What a striking place to die. Certainly the
place itself must suggest something. Perhaps that letter from
the typewriter . . ."

Annabelle shifted in the chair, facing the table, toward the
old Royal typewriter. She put her fingers on the keys.

"Let's see," she said, as if to herself. "Millie de Vargas was
sitting here, and the murderer, wearing that black cape and a
pair of women's shoes that have spent a great deal of time in
Sloppy Joe's Bar, but *not* wearing a red coral rosary like hers,
came up behind her and somehow forced her to type. He told
her to type, 'There will be no Hemingway Resort.'" Annabelle
turned back to the others, glancing at Ashleen Ricou again, her
eyes settling on Dave. "That's a very odd thing she typed.
You'd think if the murderer were someone furious about the

new resort, Millie would have been made to type something like 'Stop the resort,' or 'End the madness,' or something like that. But, no, the message she was made to type was a simple statement of what we now *know to be actual fact:* There will be no Hemingway Resort."

Annabelle glanced guiltily at Ricou, but he shook his head reassuringly. "My aunt won't blab," he said.

"Wait a minute," Dave signed, putting up his hands. "I thought that typed stuff was just a blind, to throw us off from the real motive—the Madonna."

"*Blind* is the perfect word for it," Annabelle said. "Because we have absolutely ignored the ribbon so far. The ribbon was typed on by the victim, presumably at the dictation of the murderer, in the act of the crime. We shouldn't have ignored it. Just as we cannot ignore the pictures on that videotape. Both murder weapons contain statements, Dave, just as you said; they carry messages. And both say something about the Hemingway Resort."

"What does the videotape say?" Ricou asked.

"It says that the sun also *rises*," Annabelle said. "That's not just a book or movie title; it's a complete sentence. It's almost sarcastic. Everyone has been so concerned about the sunsets, you see. But this murderer tells us that there are other things in life. It's a flamboyant, nasty thing to say, sort of like 'Well, Key West, this is what I think of your fixation with sunsets.' Then he blows up a boat before Tank Island. I find that explosion a sarcastic statement, too, and a very telling one."

"Well?" Dave was waiting. "What does it tell you?"

"It tells me that the murderer is bitter about the resort."

"Everyone's bitter about the resort they think is going up on Tank Island. We've known that from the beginning. And, anyway, that's what we were supposed to think. But this is about the treasure." Dave was looking pale, but he persisted.

"I just don't understand any of this," Ashleen Ricou said

with distress, but Annabelle was focused on Dave's remark about the treasure.

"Dave, the treasure was deliberately covered up. Who would do such a crazy thing? People want to *uncover* treasure. Why would anyone hide already sunken treasure?"

"To keep somebody else from finding it."

"By making it close to impossible to get at oneself?"

"Well, then, to protect it."

"Gold doesn't tarnish, and fish won't eat it."

"Well, then, oh, I don't know," Dave said, floundering in his reasoning and grasping at straws, swinging his parasol in an impatient arc, "because it was cursed."

Annabelle looked keenly at Dave. "Just so," she said.

"Francisco," Dave breathed. "The curse of the de Vargases." He frowned, considering the tip of the parasol. "Gee, I don't know, Annabelle. That's awfully gothic, even for Francisco. Do you think he'd believe that crap?"

"Maybe." She gave him a long look. "The curse certainly seems to have played itself out even in this generation. . . . Millie's dead." She nodded when a thoughtful look crossed Dave's face. "Played itself out, Dave—a little play. Francisco sets his stage; he has access to white spike heels, the kind Millie was wearing when she was murdered. Beth Summers, who works at Sloppy Joe's, is acting in *The Tempest* at the Waterfront Playhouse, and she wears spike heels with that white leather outfit. You and Roy have both seen her in it. And she brings her clothing with her to the theater. I saw her carrying her bag out of the theater."

Dave put the tip of his parasol quietly down on the tile floor. "And that large waitress's shoes would be big enough for a man."

Annabelle nodded. "She probably left them at the theater over the weekend—she doesn't work weekends, or Mondays," Annabelle continued. "That was probably the most difficult thing about putting the strangler costume together. The murderer had to have women's shoes that would fit a man's feet. And Francisco has black hair like Millie. And we've seen that he can be decidedly effeminate, and he is an experienced actor. He could have played his sister here at the estate." Annabelle pursed her lips. "It must have been quite a performance."

"Why'd he wear the rubber mask?"

"So she wouldn't recognize him at the fatal moment when he was close to her and use the typewriter in any way to identify him."

"Then you mean the letter *A* does not stand for the murderer?"

"I don't think so. I think, in contradistinction to what Miss Ricou has insisted, the museum is involved here." Annabelle looked around the room.

"Wait a minute." Dave also glanced around the room. "All this Hemingway stuff bothers me. What you say makes a certain amount of sense, I'll admit that, but you still don't have a motive for the killer if it is Francisco . . . if it was Francisco who stole my mask and attacked me."

"He could have seen you parading around in that thing the other day on Mallory Square. We stopped at the theater a couple of times."

"Okay. But. What did he have to do with the resort? He didn't even know what Ricou told us today. He had no way of knowing the resort had gone down the drain already."

"Are you sure? He seems to have known everything else Millie knew about the resort. She certainly told him about the shares she sold to Noah Green."

"But so what? He still had nothing to do with the resort. You're not suggesting he killed his sister because she was giving Green a well-deserved screw?"

"No. What I'm suggesting is that these murders were committed by someone who desperately wanted the resort to be built—not the other way around. Someone who wanted revenge because the resort was *not* going up as promised. Dave, in English literature revenge is the oldest, simplest motive there is for murder, and that's also the heritage of the English theater, especially Shakespeare. Francisco is steeped in that world, that world of blood for blood, great harm for great harm."

"So it's back to Francisco. Revenge for what? You can't ignore the typewriter ribbon's message. It's about the resort, the sunset. It clearly says . . . wait a minute."

"Exactly. It clearly says that there will be no resort: 'There will be no Hemingway Resort.' Not as a threat, but as a reason for killing. Almost as if the killer had said, "I am killing this woman because 'There will be no Hemingway Resort.' ' "

"But why would Francisco, or anyone, kill for that? I thought that was the consummation devoutly to be wished here in Key West. Everybody's against the resort."

"Not Francisco. Francisco never said he was against the resort. But you know what really should have told us? Your conversation with the Butterfly woman when you were looking for a boat. And I think it was that conversation that led to her death. She told you, Dave, in detail, about Fran's theater dreams. The theater's all he cares about."

"That still has nothing to do with the resort."

"Wayne Newton? Burt Reynolds? In a small community theater? I think not. They're the kind of entertainers who book themselves into big, showy, Las Vegas–style hotels."

A faint light dawned in Dave's eyes, and Annabelle gazed at him intently.

"Dave, I'm relying on your memory. Did the resort plans, the ones I showed you in Millie's office, did they call for a theater?"

Dave stared at her, then closed his eyes. "Left to right, and clockwise around the courtyard thing—barber shop, beauty salon, Uncle Wiggly's Cabbage Garden Restaurant, Matthew's Muscle Gym, access walk to indoor pool, Barnett Bank. Ah.

There it is! The Jake Barnes Cabaret Nightclub and Theater. Jesus, it's big."

"Jake Barnes was the emasculated hero of *The Sun Also Rises*," Annabelle said slowly. "I wonder whether that was Francisco's little irony or his sister's?"

Dave opened his eyes. "Francisco must have been counting on the theater for his very own. I wonder if Millie had promised him that? If so, he must have been a tad disappointed when he found out the deal had come undone. I wonder if she stuck it to her brother the way she stuck it to Green."

"Well, we know she did a fairly cruel thing to Noah Green, no matter how much you and I think he deserved it."

Suddenly Ashleen Ricou spoke up. "She was a cruel woman. That parade of Catholicism didn't fool me. She was mean and greedy, and I'll never forgive her for this . . . this horrible nightmare in Ernest's home." She burst into tears.

Dave looked at Ashleen Ricou in horror, as though she had just stripped off her cotton dress and gone dancing around the studio in her slip—probably her frequently mended slip, he thought.

Lieutenant Ricou went to his aunt and knelt beside her, taking her hand.

"Millie never had a thought in her head for a human being's feelings," Ashleen Ricou sobbed. "I hated her. She was mean to me, to all the volunteers, telling us all the time that she was going to put Ernest's cats to sleep because they were ruining the furniture and smelling up the place, or that she was going to install surveillance cameras over the cash register because she thought the volunteers were making mistakes, or that she had hired those guards because she thought we were stealing, or that we were all too old to work here anymore. And she said she was going to get college interns to run the museum when she had gotten rid of us old women." She looked up, her papery face streaked with tears. "But she never did those things. She just liked to *say* them. We were all so scared. It was just like the new will: She teased us, and then took away her promise." A canny light shone in the woman's blue eyes. "And she demanded my key to the studio, saying I wasn't to be allowed in Ernest's studio anymore."

"How come you've still got a key?" Dave asked curiously. "Not that it makes any difference to me," he added hurriedly when she shot him an iron look through her tears.

"I told her I lost my key, you sniggler."

Cowed by the return of Ashleen Ricou's belligerence, and perhaps buoyed by having induced it, Dave sat back on the chaise longue and swung his parasol lightly, apparently hiding behind the need to think, which he was doing aloud: "Nice, tidy, artful little murder. F.D.V., F.D.V.: Francisco de Vargas. No letter *A* there. So what about that, Annabelle?"

She turned in the cigarmaker's chair and spread her fingers on the keys. "She's sitting here, her life about to end, and what was she thinking? She didn't know her killer. He was caped and masked. What would she have been thinking in the last moment?" Annabelle put her head to one side, a sudden light in her eyes and a lift to her shoulders. "The Madonna!"

Dave stood, hobbled around the gateleg table, and faced Annabelle. "That begins with *M*, you fathead. Besides, you just said the Madonna wasn't the motive."

Annabelle continued despite this interruption. "We know she found the Madonna. Hmm. And she was wearing a coral rosary, as we surmised from that single bead. A rosary from the treasure site . . . a rosary around her neck when she was being strangled . . . she was thinking about the rosary, the Madonna, the treasure. And of course—I've got it—she wanted to leave a clue for the priest. In the last minute of her life she was still trying to buy and sell property, trying to buy her way into paradise by endowing the Church with the treasure. So she pulls off the key to indicate that the map to the treasure is hidden—where?"

Dave stood by the gateleg table, his face blank. Then he smiled beatifically, the pallor of his face flushed with crimson.

"*A. Aseo*—Spanish for 'toilet.' I said from the beginning it would be something in Spanish."

A halcyon expression on his face, Dave hobbled to the sunny bathroom beyond the chaise. He entered the small room, dropped his parasol on the windowsill, and opened the tank of the toilet. He craned to look inside. He closed the lid and returned to the room, his parasol dragging behind him. "Nothing there but water."

"*A.*" This time, Ashleen Ricou spoke. "For *A Farewell to Arms.* That's the only one of Ernest's really famous novels that begins with the letter *A.*" She stood, her knees creaking, and crossed to the bookshelf behind Annabelle. Her hand went almost automatically to a volume on the second shelf, as though she knew all the books intimately from decades of dusting them. She flipped the pages gently, then with increasing vigor. "There's nothing here," she said mournfully, holding the book open in her hands.

"It's got to be something in this room," Annabelle said, casting her eyes around. "Something that would point to the map unmistakably, or so Millie must have thought. What could it be?"

"Well, I don't know about you," Lieutenant Ricou drawled, his voice sleepy as he rose from beside his aunt's vacated chair and stretched his long limbs lazily, "but is anybody besides me hungry?" He looked at his watch. "For what it's worth, I can tell you what struck me when I entered this room for the first time today. You'll probably think it's too simple."

"Well?" Dave demanded. "Are you just trying to get even because I won the bet about the videotape? Acting like you're so smart."

"What is it, Roy?" Annabelle asked.

He pointed above her head, and she turned.

Dave glanced at the head mounted on the wall. "That animal-head thing? Animal?"

Ricou nodded. "The antlers."

TWENTY-SIX

"THE ANTLERS?" ASHLEEN RICOU SNIFFED AND TURNED TO consider the stuffed trophy above her on the wall.

"I suppose those animals really are the first thing you notice," Annabelle said, "if you haven't got your nose stuck in the typewriter or on the floor. My, my. I wonder. They're what a tourist—a real outsider—would notice."

All four came to stand together under the head, gazing up at its graceful curves and shadows.

"What is that thing exactly?" Dave asked.

"It's a gnu," Ashleen Ricou said.

"Gesundheit," Dave offered.

The lieutenant frowned at Dave. "Let me have that chair, Fidel, and I'll take a look."

Dave moved aside so that Ricou could drag one of the rattan chairs under the mounted head.

Quickly—in fact with surprising spryness in light of her creaking joints—Ashleen Ricou leaped to snatch the cushion from the chair before her nephew could put his foot on it.

"Don't you dare to put your great dirty foot on Ernest's cushion," she said, a martial light in her eye. "You have the big ugly feet of all the Ricous," she added with steely pride.

Ricou glanced sheepishly at his worn brown boat shoe,

turned to wink at Annabelle, and, balancing himself by placing his left hand on the wall, stepped onto the bare rattan base of the chair.

He reached his right hand up to the wide antlers, explored them lightly with his fingers, saying over his shoulder "freshly dusted, a tribute to somebody's housekeeping," and took a firm grip on the hard bony spray of elegantly spread branches on the right.

"There's a new weapon for you, Popeye," Dave said, watching the operation with a sapient eye. "I mean a gnu weapon."

Ricou turned the antlers, and they came off in his hand. He almost dropped them in surprise.

"Be careful up there," his aunt shrieked. "That belongs to Ernest."

Ricou handed down the antlers to Annabelle. "Gently now," he said. "They're heavier than they look."

She carried the antlers to the tall window behind Hemingway's leather trunk, branded with a large and simple "E H" in black letters, and pushed the trunk aside with her foot. She held the antlers pointing toward the floor and peered inside.

And there was the map.

Screwed into a neat twist of paper, there was the map.

She pulled it out and held it curiously up to the soft green light filtering in through the palm fronds over the mansard roof. The others joined her at the window, looking at the map over her shoulder. Ricou took his glasses from a pocket and put them on.

"Why, that's not any ancient map, like in the stories," Ashleen Ricou blurted. "It looks brand-new."

"Yes," her nephew said, putting his hand on her shoulder and leaning closer to Annabelle, narrowing his eyes at the map, at the sophisticated and delicately drawn blue lines and gray shaded areas. "It looks like a geologist's map, an underwater topographical survey based on sonar and magnetic fields. She must have paid a pretty penny for this chart. It covers quite a large area of the Gulf near the Marquesas."

"Can you tell, Roy? Is it accurate?" Annabelle asked, watching Dave's signs.

"Yes, very, I think," Ricou said. "But it won't help you find the Madonna unless you already know which stone to look under. Of course, Millie could have used the map to eliminate about ninety percent of the stones covered in the survey area, but the rest would be trial and error."

"But she knew where the treasure was," Annabelle said with an impatient snap. "She had one of those rosaries. At least she had one of the beads. And she told the Monsignor she'd found the treasure at last."

"Maybe there's something in the other side of that pair of horns," Dave suggested, although the disgusted look on his pale face did not indicate that he was nursing large hopes.

Ricou returned to the chair and once again manipulated the armor on the animal's head. The second set of antlers came down.

"God," Dave said with feeling. "That poor gnu. How would you like it if we twisted your horns off, *Teniente*?"

The lieutenant widened his eyes as he let Dave's remark settle, unanswered, in the air around them. Ricou shook his head quickly, held the antlers upside down, and pulled out a small, folded square of paper. He spread it out by flicking it open in one hand.

"That's from the library book," Dave said, interest in the search rekindling on his face. "I can see it so clearly. It's an exact fit."

Ricou looked at Dave with one eyebrow arched.

"Annabelle and I found this book that talked about an old map, and the facing page had a square cut out of it. Annabelle, that's the old Humberto Ruiz map, you know, the one he drew from memory. I'll betcha anything."

The four stood together under the denuded animal head,

and Annabelle handed Ricou the geological survey. He crossed to the gateleg writing table, where he deposited the antlers and spread both maps out. He stood studying them, his hands resting on the table beside the maps.

"If you use this very naive drawing, this very impression-istic drawing of peaks and valleys and so on," he said slowly, pointing to several places on the square map, "and put it to-gether with the modern survey map, you'd have a pretty exact idea of where the treasure is. That is, if the little drawing is accurate, and I'd say it is. Look at this."

They all gathered around the table, and Ricou pointed out the spot where the survey seemed to match the Ruiz drawing.

"Not one map," he said, "but two, neither one worth any-thing without the other, but together a treasure map indeed."

"I want those papers," Ashleen Ricou suddenly said, hold-ing out her hand peremptorily. "They belong to the museum."

An uncomfortable silence filled the studio.

Annabelle sat down in the cigarmaker's chair, and abruptly she started laughing.

"Give them to her, Roy," she said, her eyes sparkling. "She's right. They belong to the museum. They certainly don't belong to anyone else that I can think of."

Dave leaned against the wall, chewing the inside of his cheek. "She'll just use the treasure to refurbish these dead things," he signed.

Annabelle, still laughing, turned to sign language to have a private word with Dave. "At least she won't use them for anything selfish. And it is in the cause of literature."

"I thought you didn't like Hemingway."

"I don't. But a lot of people do, and they'll be reading *The Old Man and the Sea* by Ernest Hemingway a lot longer than they'll be reading *The Gender Contract* by yours truly."

Ricou picked up the two maps and handed them to his aunt. "I hope you have better luck with the golden Madonna than the de Vargases did," he said. "And I forbid you to start after the treasure until Francisco is in jail. When the time comes, I'll show you how to read the map. Or I'll take you out there myself."

Ashleen Ricou snorted, refolding the maps and cramming them into the capacious pocket of her dress. "What about these people? Don't they already know where the treasure is too?"

"I never want to see that hill of slimy gray sand again," Annabelle said with warmth. "I risked the lives of people I love in the graveyard of that hideous golden, ecclesiastically sanctioned monument to the sadistic enthrallment of women, that travesty of piety and greed. I hate it."

Dave saw what was coming and turned around to face the wall.

"People you love? Plural?" Ricou asked gently, and before the astonished gaze of his Aunt Ashleen, he gathered Annabelle into his arms with glad tenderness, his hands on her naked back.

"Roy Rameelieu Ricou," his aunt said ominously, "I will not stand by while you force yourself on a woman in Ernest Hemingway's own writing studio. I thought you had some self-control."

The lieutenant released Annabelle reluctantly, but his aunt had not finished.

"You were born with a handsome face, and I see that the navy has done nothing to temper your natural belief in your own impulses." The old woman's eyes glinted with apocalyptic fervor.

Dave turned around to face the scene of combat.

"That doesn't sound like a family testimonial," he said. "Rameelieu?"

"Tante Ashleen's tirade has nothing to do with me," the lieutenant said, grinning wickedly. "It's a comment on an entire species—the Impulsive Male Species."

Annabelle stooped to retrieve her red handbag from the

floor, a faint flush on her cheeks, regretting her unthinking words, and she said, "Miss Ricou, I thank you for your help, hope you'll keep your mouth shut about the business of this mansion as well as you have from the beginning of our acquaintance, and bid you good-bye. It's time to share our conclusions with Sheriff Hockett and let him deal with Francisco de Vargas. Dave, can you make it down the stairs?"

At his curt nod she headed for the studio cage, but Ashleen Ricou stepped in front of her with the key. As she unlocked the cage, the older woman turned and touched Annabelle's hand with her bony fingers.

"Thank you," she said simply.

Annabelle pressed the cold fingers. "Miss Ricou, I've got a debt to a cat that I need to repay. Can this estate support one more feline? A very friendly one?"

"What kind of cat? How many toes does it have?"

"The regular amount."

"You can bring it here whenever you like."

It occurred to Annabelle, as she went down the stairs, that the older woman might consider six toes per paw the regular amount for a cat, but she let the brief worry fade from her mind. A treasure map in exchange for cat boarding was a good deal in Annabelle's book, and soon the friendly Ignatius would ingratiate himself with the older woman. Annabelle did not pause to consider the potential for shattering changes in the cat population's famous toes, a potential that Dave would have seen immediately—the orange cat they had rescued from the law offices of de Vargas and Green had not been neutered.

At the top of the stairs Dave, who had missed the brief exchange between the women, swayed, his hand going out to the rail.

Ricou was beside Dave before he could topple over. "Need help?"

Dave shook his head stubbornly. "Just a little lightheaded. It'll pass."

"All the same, let me go first. If you fall, you'll have the satisfaction of mowing me down."

"After you, Rameelieu." Dave grinned, but it was a shaky effort, and there was a bleak paleness around his mouth.

They reached the front gate without incident, and Annabelle was surprised to see a pink taxi already waiting for them, the driver standing by its open door. She pivoted to look back at the mansion and caught a glimpse of Ashleen Ricou at one of the tall windows overlooking the veranda. Annabelle lifted her hand in salute and turned back to the street just in time to see Dave collapse on the pavement.

She hurried to his side, but Ricou had gotten there first and was lifting Dave to a sitting position. Dave opened his eyes briefly, seemed about to say something, and closed them again, his head resting against the lieutenant's shoulder.

Dave was conscious but obviously extremely weak.

"We'll have to get him back to bed," Ricou said.

Annabelle clutched her handbag and considered Dave's pallor. "I wish he'd stayed in the hospital," she said. She glanced up and down the street, at Dave, at Ricou. An idea was taking rapid shape in her mind. She seemed to come to a decision. "Roy, why don't you go have something to eat? I know you said that you're hungry, and the cab driver and I can manage Dave."

Ricou looked at her thoughtfully. Was this her way of atoning for her failure to be of help to Dave in the boat? Was this a nurturing instinct or was it some misguided attempt not to be a drag on one Lieutenant Roy Ricou? Did she think he was tired of playing attendant to a sick man and a deaf woman from Miami trying to catch a murderer in the closed society of Key West? Had she considered that the murders now involved him too? Did she think he would want to spend the short time remaining to him before sailing for the Orient doing something less restricted than nursemaiding Dave? Or perhaps she just didn't care for him as much as. . . . If only he knew her better. He studied her face, wondering if her obviously un-calculated remark in the studio cottage—and his own selfish quickness to capitalize on it—had anything to do with this withdrawal, but he was convinced somehow by the vibrancy of her eyes that, whatever her motives, at least she was all right.

He helped Dave, protesting lightly, to his feet, and Anna-belle got into the taxi. She slid over to the middle of the seat and put out her arms to help Ricou position Dave comfortably against her side.

Ricou leaned into the cab. "I can't phone you, obviously. Shall I come by? Would you rather be alone? Can I sit with the invalid? You know, Annabelle, none of this is burdensome to me, if that's what you're thinking."

She extended her hand to him, a distracted but grateful smile lighting her face. "You do favor the direct approach in your dealings, don't you, Lieutenant Ricou? You're a rare hu-man being. Come by the room later, please." She squeezed his hand.

He gripped her hand a long moment, searching her face, before shutting the door of the pink taxi.

"Ocean Key House," Ricou told the driver. He stood watching the taxi until it made the turn toward Duval Street. And then he strolled north, his hands in his pockets.

TWENTY-SEVEN

BY THE TIME THEY REACHED THE HOTEL, DAVE WAS fretting about what he called Annabelle's "cloying ministrations—who the hell do you imagine yourself to be? Albert Schweitzer?" But Annabelle insisted on summoning the desk staff to help get him upstairs.

"You might as well just put me on one of those luggage carts and roll me around like a useless Gucci garment bag," Dave complained. But he was woozy and gratefully put his arm across the shoulders of a bellhop who had come to help him to the elevator.

Annabelle sat on the side of Dave's bed until he fell into what seemed to be a restful sleep. She pulled the curtains over the open balcony door. The long folds of fabric moved gently in the warm, salty breezes coming off the harbor, and Annabelle quietly left the darkened suite.

She went quickly down the stairs, her long skirt billowing out behind her as she turned corners in her winding progress. At ground level she turned east, through the garage, headed for Mallory Square.

The Waterfront Playhouse looked deserted. She tried the front doors, but they were locked. She jumped down the small flight of stairs, a grim, reminiscent smile touching her lips involuntarily when she spotted Dave's green-stained Popsicle stick, and walked rapidly around to the side of the building. The stage door was closed, but she went up the short flight of steps and pushed gently down on the handle of the door. It opened, revealing a musty dimness inside, and she slipped into the quiet playhouse, pulling the door behind her, careful to leave it slightly ajar.

She felt her way through the gloom of the wings onto the stage, her outstretched hand trailing along a scenery flat that smelled of fresh paint. Stepping onto the stage, she could see that the dim light disturbing the otherwise throbbing darkness of the theater came from what was probably the prop room, across the stage and past the wings on the other side.

Through the open door she could see a man seated at a table, his back to her, his longish black hair falling just over the collar of his white dress shirt. She slipped off her sandals and went quietly toward the light. The man was Francisco de Vargas, she was sure, and she drew her Walther TPH from her handbag, stooping to lay the bag softly on the stage.

She approached the prop room, the gun held out before her in her right hand. Her tightly suppressed anger pinched at her heart now that she saw him. She must have made some noise, must have disturbed something that she could not discern from the blank well of her deafness, for the man seated at the table turned suddenly when she was still ten feet from the door. She stopped.

He was wearing a Hemingway mask. Dave's Hemingway mask. She knew, because there, on the chin, was the brown splotch where Dave had killed the fly.

"Don't move," she said. "I've got a gun, Francisco."

He stood, and she saw that he held a length of furry brown cloth wound around his hands and stretched taut between them across his chest. Caliban's tail.

The mask seemed to respirate, to vibrate, and he must

have said something to her. She raised her left hand to the gun, cradling her right hand, and started forward again.

He stretched his hands out toward her, the tail wound around them grotesquely, taking a step toward her. Then, with abrupt grace, he stepped to his right, into the shadows, and was gone. The light in the prop room went out.

Now Annabelle was not only deaf, she had been plunged into blindness as well. She backed up against the rear of the stage, the gun held out before her, trying to penetrate the darkness with her eyes, encountering a cool, rocky surface against her bare back. She dropped her left hand behind her and felt the wall. It was cochina, the coral rock that gave the little theater the resonating accoustics that were its only mark of distinction. The rock felt damp.

She strained her senses, trying to feel the air, anything, to tell her where Francisco was in this claustrophobic pit of darkness, pounding silence, and clammy fear.

The odds were all on his side. She had the gun, but could hardly fire wildly into the dark. He, who knew the theater, was also blind in the dark, but he could hear, hear her if she made a move. She did not even know where the light switches were. What did she have that he did not have? The gun. She thought of her handbag on the stage floor. A gun, a rosary, a bow tie, a pencil, a room key. What could she do to even the odds? She could hardly make Francisco deaf too.

Or could she? She closed her eyes and tried to picture the theater as she had seen it yesterday. She opened her eyes and slipped down against the wall to her knees, thrusting the gun into the front of her dress and tying her long skirt around her waist so that she could crawl silently across the stage; if Francisco were waiting, standing in the dark, his hands stretched out to drape the Caliban tail around her neck, she would not walk tamely into a noose of his devising.

So she crawled forward slowly, groping on the floor for her handbag. She inched her way along with agonizing deliberation so as to make absolutely no noise. When she felt the cool leather of her handbag, she almost gasped, thinking at first it was the tip of Francisco's shoe, but she swallowed her breath, praying that she could not be heard gulping. She stayed where she was, on all fours, breathing slowly through her nose.

When her breathing was once again steady, she picked up the bag and extracted the gold bow tie and the rosary, putting them in her pocket. She replaced the bag on the floor and continued her slow crawl, alert for changes in the air, changes in odor.

She wrinkled her nose and realized thankfully that she was near the freshly painted flat. She used it as a landmark and turned to her left, crawling toward the wings. She stopped.

Some current of air had been disturbed, but she could not reckon its source. She stayed still, not daring to move, breathing silently, she hoped. And then she realized that the stirring of the air had been the closing of the stage door she had left ajar. She was trapped.

The air did not stir again, and after long moments she once again crawled toward the wings, her right hand groping from time to time into the still darkness. Finally her fingertips brushed the smooth metal surface of a furniture leg. She stopped.

Gently, slowly, she pulled the rosary from her pocket and closed her hand over the beads. Judging by the smell of the fresh paint, she estimated the location of the stage apron, raised her arm, and hurled the rosary as far as she could, wondering if it would break when it hit the floor among the seats.

She quickly ran her fingers up the metal leg and along the smooth metal surface of the audio board she had remembered.

On her knees and with a random hope, she selected a tape from the top of the stack on the table and inserted it into the slot she could feel with her other hand, pushing the tape in slowly and gently, hoping the machine was well maintained. She moved her fingers over the controls, feeling for the raised letters and slash marks of the volume knob. When she found them, she rested her fingers over the knob and felt desperately for the On switch with her left hand. She couldn't find the switch.

She drew a deep breath, kept her right fingers over the volume knob, and grabbed Dave's tie from her left pocket. She positioned it carefully on the metal table, then squeezed and dropped the bulb. For only an instant the tie lit up, a wink of a green-and-raspberry splash. She was able to see the audio board's On switch and flipped it at the same time she frantically twirled the volume button clockwise as far as it would go. She leaped to her feet and ran across the blackness of the stage, toward the prop room, imagining the earlier journey over these boards, trying to repeat it.

She bumped the flats, knocking one over, she knew, because she felt the rush of air drawing the trailing folds of her skirt toward the back of the stage. She pulled the Walther from her dress and plunged ahead in the darkness, holding the gun in front of her.

The gun struck wood, and she almost pulled back on the trigger in a reflex motion. She touched the wood with her left hand, realized it was the doorframe, and stepped inside. If she had any chance of finding the lights, it would be here in the prop room, because Francisco must have shut them off from here.

She stepped to the left, toward where Francisco had disappeared. She felt the walls wildly, knocking something feathery and soft to the floor, ripping a poster, tearing her hand on a nail, and at last she found the bank of switches, at least twenty switches. She pushed them up rapidly, in groups of four or five, with the side of her hand, and lights went on all over the playhouse, including in the prop room where she stood.

Stepping quickly back onstage, the gun held firmly in her right hand, she cast her eyes around the theater.

Francisco was standing at the center of the stage, the mask pushed up on his forehead, the monster's tail still wrapped around one of his hands. He held her coral rosary in his other hand.

"I've been waiting for you, Miranda, waiting while you set your stage," he said, gleams of amusement dancing in his eyes as he covered his ears, the monster's tail rising in a dangling loop against his white shirt. "I'm quite unable to hear myself talk."

Keeping the gun and her eyes aimed at him, Annabelle sidestepped across the stage to the audio board and turned off the switch. From the corner of her eye she saw that the tape she had inserted in the machine was marked "Storm/Act One/Scene One."

She returned to center stage, facing Francisco as he lowered his hands once again to waist level, holding them both out to her.

"I've been checking the props for *The Tempest*," he said sweetly. "How do you like this excrescence of a tail?"

"Put it down, Francisco."

"No, I don't think I will, Miranda. I know I'm quite finished, you see, so I have nothing to lose. And I have Beth Summers, your charming waitress friend, stashed away in my little theater of horrors. She tells me she is awaiting an acting lesson from you this morning. I think you won't risk her—oh, the platitudinous sound of it—her neck, will you?"

"Where is she?"

"With all of my precious belongings, my pitiful worldly goods."

"Such as the rest of the rosary that was around your sister's neck?"

"Are you a souvenir collector, Miranda?" He tossed Annabelle's rosary to her in an underhand flip. She caught it with her left hand and dropped it over her neck. Francisco lowered his right hand to his trousers pocket and extracted a handful of beads, holding them out to her, against the background of the monster's tail wrapped around his hand. "Do you want these too? Do you imagine they have ink from a typewriter ribbon on them? I wonder if they do? You see, I have been quite unable to determine that myself, in my layman's ignorance. Perhaps you can tell me."

He took a step toward her, still holding out the red beads on the brown cloth that covered the palm of his hand.

"Stop or I'll shoot you, Francisco."

"I feel sure you won't, Miranda. Women are always promising things they don't deliver."

He took another step.

Annabelle fired.

A spreading red stain appeared on his right sleeve. The coral and garnet rosary beads spattered from his hand onto the stage, along with large drops of his own blood. A look of acute surprise washed over his features, his eyebrows raised, his eyes large, his lower lip pushed slightly forward.

"How could you, Miranda?" he asked wonderingly, pain pulling at his cheeks, forcing his lips back over his teeth. "How could you do such a thing?"

Annabelle looked at him as he lowered his eyes to stare in sincere horror at the redness soaking his white silk shirt.

And keeping the gun aimed at his arm, she said, softly, "It's not such a magnificent consummation when your victim can fight back, is it, Francisco?"

"My dear," he groaned, "a director never likes it when an actress writes her own lines into the play."

TWENTY-EIGHT

"YOU GOT RID OF ME—YOU DELIBERATELY DITCHED ME— so you could blow your way into this viper's den without interference."

The words were soft, lazily uttered, but the lieutenant's blue eyes were filled with a cold anger, and though his hands were stuffed in apparent casualness into the deep pockets of his white shorts, there was a certain rigidity about the muscles in his upper arms that belied his posture of ease.

"Francisco was mine," she said simply.

"No," he drawled, "Francisco de Vargas belongs to the state of Florida. He's not your personal trophy."

"Of course he's not. I don't collect trophies like animal heads on a wall. I meant that he was mine to confront, to see this nightmare end, to arrive at the end of the conundrum, if you will. What if I had been wrong? What if the murderer were not Francisco? I had to know." She brushed his arm accidentally, and she could see a vein throbbing under his tan skin. "Roy, I had to know for sure who had inflicted so much harm on Dave." Annabelle found herself on the verge of large explanations and gestures, and she hastily put her hands in her pockets, unconsciously mirroring the lieutenant's bearing.

"I wouldn't have killed him, Roy. In fact I wouldn't even

have fired on him if he had given me an alternative. But I won't apologize. Francisco de Vargas got no more than he insisted on."

Annabelle jerked at the long skirt of her dress, glancing down and pulling it impatiently away from the hinge of one of the wooden seats where it had caught when Ricou had entered the brilliantly lit theater and walked down the aisle toward her, to where she stood facing the stage. He had spun her around, gently but with steely firmness, his hands on her waist, and the hem of her voluminous skirt had snagged on a screw rotting out of its metal fastening. All of the seats, it was evident, were in some phase of succumbing to damp and disrepair in Francisco's crumbling theater.

Sheriff Hockett knelt now on the old stage beside Francisco de Vargas, exercising great care not to touch the coral and garnet rosary beads spilled in shallow red pools that had also been fed by the director's blood. Two deputies flanked Hockett, their hands on their holstered guns, and several technicians from the Monroe County Sheriff's Department were at work on the stage, efficiently and quietly photographing, cataloging, and dusting the elements of the story Annabelle had blocked out for Hockett. They stepped gingerly around the redness on the stage when the outer door opened to admit the paramedics from Pegasus Air Ambulance who had come to remove the wounded de Vargas to the emergency room on Stock Island.

Beth Summers had been found by one of the deputies on the cold prop-room floor, alive but petrified into a stony heap, dumped under plastic pumpkins and a cardboard chandelier, her hands and feet tied together to the legs of a desk, her blond head and large shoulders crammed under a set of skirt hoops, her mouth gagged with a feather boa. After being untied, given a drink of water, and allowed to fulminate against Francisco's cruel treatment of her and against the horrifying, deafening noises that had subsequently poured into the theater, she had walked by herself out into the bright sunshine to a waiting surface ambulance, her injuries small but sufficient to cause the sheriff to insist on her immediate removal to the Lower Florida Keys Health System. He would hear her story in full at the hospital, he said.

It had been a Popsicle vendor who had summoned the Monroe County Sheriff after hearing the single gunshot inside the theater. The vendor was a newcomer to Key West, working the ice-cream trade on the side while building a clientele for his crystal-and-straw sculptures of seagulls, and he had been unable to find a law-enforcement official indigenous to the gingerbread city in the ripped phone book attached to the pay phone he had used in Mallory Square. Since it was the sheriff's department that answered 911 calls in Key West, Barbara Ruggierrio had been bypassed without a hitch or, indeed, without an intention on the part of the Popsicle salesman, who had leaped at the chance to dial those three magic numbers for the first time in his life. The vendor now wheeled his Popsicle cart around the square, sharing his ideas on art as well as the little gossip he had concerning the arrest of Francisco de Vargas.

Annabelle had been glad to see the sheriff's reassuring red scalp, and she had relinquished her Walther and her lonely guardianship of Francisco with relief. She had stood over him in tense silence on the stage, never lowering her gun, unable to try the stage door and keep an eye on Francisco at the same time; and he had been unwilling to speak at all after delivering his pungent line to her about actresses who ruined his plays.

She had stayed with Hockett and de Vargas on the stage while the first paramedics on the scene treated the gunshot wound. They had peeled away the soaked sleeve of Francisco's shirt to reveal that Annabelle's .32-caliber bullet had ripped through the bone and flesh and had gone out the other side of his arm, leaving an oozing hole and an ugly jagged rip through a curious mark on the skin of his forearm. Powder burns encircled the hole and the rip.

"What is that?" Hockett had asked in an awed voice. They had stared as the paramedic cleaned the wound, slowly revealing the rough shape of the purplish head and shoulders of a woman, the head seemingly bowed in contemplation or prayer, the torso below the shoulders forever blasted away by the bullet.

"That's not a tattoo," Hockett had marveled. "It's a birthmark."

It was then that Francisco had uttered his only words in the sheriff's presence: "The curse of the de Vargases," he had said, in rasping low tones that traveled around the theater in a worthy testimonial to its fine accoustics. "The Madonna is real, you know."

Annabelle was sickened by the sight of that birthmark, or whatever it was, sickened by the blurred resemblance Francisco imagined it bore to the legendary Madonna, which, except for the one golden shoulder, she had never seen, not even as a picture in the library books. She wondered if Francisco believed that the congenital blemish on his arm, now destroyed, betokened the grip of that old curse, stretching out to him across the silent centuries, wondered if even Francisco were self-centered enough to believe that he had been singled out to be so marked for ill fortune.

Feeling slightly nauseated, she had walked down the stairs toward the seats ranged in curving rows before the stage, feeling that the melancholy history of that unhappy family had turned its final grisly page, spurred by the willingness of the de Vargases themselves to believe in their own central position in history.

And now there was Roy, Roy who was furious when he should be shaking her hand, furious when he would undoubtedly have said something coarse and congratulatory if she had been a man, furious when he had no right to butt into her affairs—well, that wasn't quite true, she thought, considering his instinctive use of kindness and common sense the night before, but, she thought, then he had been invited to share in her affairs, and this was different.

"It's the wiliness of it, Annabelle," he said, his blue eyes fierce. " 'Why don't you go eat something, Roy?' 'I know you're hungry, Roy,' " he mimicked her. A smile was on his lips, but anger lurked dangerously in his eyes. "Why didn't you just tell me the simple truth?"

"What? And I suppose I should have said, 'Stand aside, you big handsome galoot, this little woman is going after a killer.' " Annabelle looked at him scornfully. "You know what you would have done? You would have put your manly arms around me and you would have told me to stop spouting that nonsense and go take a tranquilizer, after patting me fondly on the behind."

In spite of himself, and in spite of his very real anger, Ricou could not prevent a twitch of a smile from showing in his eyes. But he said, "You don't know that, Annabelle. You never gave me a chance to react at all. You just assumed I was like every other man of your—I'm beginning to suspect—extremely limited acquaintance."

"How dare you? Are you suggesting—you *are* suggesting—that I don't know what I'm talking about. That's such a familiar paternalistic, homunculitic strategy—claim the poor woman doesn't know what she's talking about. Oh. This is just perfect. You *are* just like every other man of my limited acquaintance." Annabelle flung the words at him. "Except Dave," she added, throwing this promising fuel on the fire.

"How the hell did I get myself into such a tangled feminist dialectic?" he demanded, no longer smiling at all. "You're being completely unfair, and you just completely twisted what I said."

"Well, if you don't like the feminist tangle, go away!"

He glared at her in silence, the tension tightened to bare control. And then he seemed to force himself to relax, the taut muscles in his arms visibly easing. He took a breath.

"That's my cue, isn't it?" he asked, raising his voice without thinking of her inability to hear the change, raising it out of frustration and disappointment. "You want me to walk out of here dramatically, don't you? You're terrified that I actually care enough about you to demand some accountability from you—this has nothing to do with gender—and you're so pigheaded that you can't stand the threat. Well, you're not going to sacrifice me on the widow's pyre of your fear of involvement. I'm going to stay here with you if we have to argue all day." He glanced impatiently past her shoulder, responding to a wave from the sheriff.

"My fear of involvement?" she demanded, her color rising. "What the hell do you call a career in the navy?"

"If you two want to fight," Hockett said, "you'll have to take it outside. We're sealing up this place."

"What did he say?" Annabelle turned to see that the stage was now bare except for the sheriff.

Ricou took her arm, she faced him belligerently, and he said, "He's kicking us out. Let's go to your hotel and finish this."

They walked down the aisle side by side and left the theater by the stage door, silence and resentment on both sides. They crossed Mallory Square, the warm, early-afternoon sun having drawn crowds to the waterfront, and they passed among the throngs, still silent but hardly ignoring each other. Both were aware of tension between them like a magnetically charged field.

When they reached her suite and she pushed the door to open it, Ricou put out his hand and leaned against the heavy door, opening it with ease. She tossed him a defiant glance, threw her key on the dining table, and stalked out to the balcony.

She sat down in a metal rocking chair and glared at the harbor. He pulled an identical chair over to face hers and sat down. He took her hands from her lap and held them tightly.

"Annabelle," he began.

"Oh, why go on with this? You're just leaving anyway."

"I'm leaving, but I'm not leaving you. It's not like there's another woman, or like I'm crawling off to die somewhere, or like I just don't give a damn. What a brilliant new impasse: My carefully earned and ordered life now becomes the convenient villain. Stop thrusting me away before I have to go. I am not getting out of your life, and you're changing the subject."

"No, I'm not. This is the subject: making demands on each other." She curled her lip at him. "Well, if I can't, you can't."

"Who said you can't make demands on me?" He looked steadily at her. "Make one and see what happens."

She met his gaze. "Stay."

He slowly withdrew his hands from hers. He could hear the cry of the gulls from the sunset deck below and the low rumble of maritime engines plying the harbor, and his heart seemed suddenly wrong, suddenly out of sync, somehow too big, too full, and his mind seemed sluggish, stupid, vacant, and he looked down at his hands lying palms-up on his lap, and he remembered the feeling when he had been standing on Whitehead Street and her cab had pulled away from the curb.

"That's not fair," he said finally, leaning back in the chair.

Annabelle knew it wasn't fair, but she rocked her chair stubbornly, a strange satisfaction rising in her at the hurt in the lieutenant's blue eyes. At the same time a fugitive desire to apologize randomly and in toto for everything she had said also arose in her, and she felt the weight of seven years of avoiding intimacy, seven lonely but safe years. She did not know what to do.

"Of course it's not fair," Dave said, swinging down hand-over-hand on a pink sheet and sliding onto the balcony shakily. His brown hair was sticking out from his head in several pillow-induced directions, his yellow shorts and shirt were wrinkled and sweaty, and his feet were bare.

"Annabelle, does your refrigerator have any ginger ale?" he asked crabbily. "I have a powerful thirst. Have you fed the cat? Where is the cat? I wish you two would go argue somewhere else. I can't sleep. And Caliban's been pounding on my door, looking for you. I can't wait to get back to good old urban, crime-ridden, drug-wallowing Miami. Paradise is for the birds."

"Aha," Ricou said, laughter in his eyes, "that's right. You're going back to Miami, aren't you?"

"So?" Annabelle said.

"Well, I demand that you go to Singapore with me instead," Ricou said lightly.

"That's not fair," Annabelle said, smiling slowly.

"That's really not fair," Dave said decidedly. "Whoops. There's the door. I'll bet it's Caliban. I just told him to try down here. Let me answer it. He'll get a kick out of seeing me again so soon." He headed for the door, tucking in wisps of his shirttail.

Annabelle and Ricou looked at each other.

"If *Life with Dave* is what you are accustomed to, no wonder we're having this argument," Ricou said. "The demands he makes are so bizarre, you have only to congratulate yourself whenever he stops short of enrolling you both in a singing hopscotch tournament."

Annabelle bit her lip. "Roy, I'm sorry."

"I'm sorry too. God. I'm so sorry. What I meant to say, my love, back there in the de Vargas Thrill Palace, was that I was frightened for you, frightened by the vulnerability of your handicap. It scares me, Annabelle. And I was disappointed that you didn't trust me enough to share your decision to go after Francisco. Maybe when you know me better, you will trust me."

Annabelle heaved a deep sigh and blew her breath out through her lips. "And what I meant to say was that I misled you because I was afraid you'd waste time trying to talk me out of it—and there was no way I wanted to be talked out of it. I can't allow my deafness to shrivel me up, to cripple me, to allow others to be active for me. I wanted Francisco." She paused, smoothing her skirt over her knees, "And I also meant to say that I wish you didn't have to leave so soon. I want to know you better."

"Annabelle, let's go somewhere." He inserted his hands behind her knees and pulled himself closer to her rocking chair. "Alone. Let's not waste today hurting each other. We've got the rest of the afternoon, and the evening, and the night, and the morning, and another afternoon." He nodded down at his arm. "I had a blood test this morning at the base hospital. You see, I am serious about you."

She leaned forward and placed her hands on his knees. "It's going to be a long wait, Lieutenant." She shook her head slowly. "You're an idealist, you know. Very old-fashioned, with all your 1990s savvy." She smiled sadly. "I know something about idealism, Roy. I know it fades—like my doctoral career, like my perfect marriage, like many things that have mattered to me."

Dave popped his head and hands onto the balcony and produced a flurry of hasty signs: "Annabelle, get in here. Caliban says the play has smashed to pieces, and he wants you to glue everything back together before tomorrow night. I don't know where he got the idea that you were Miss Shakespeare Fix-it." He leveled a considering gaze at Annabelle. "He says the sheriff has de Vargas. I don't know why Caliban thinks that makes the play your problem."

Annabelle stood, gave Ricou a warning look, and gazed longingly at the pink sheet dangling from Dave's balcony. There seemed to be no other avenue of escape.

Ricou followed her into the suite, cold air pouring over him in icy blasts.

"I put the air-conditioning on, Annabelle," Dave said,

from his perch on the desktop. "It was like the inside of Linda Tripp's wig in here."

Ricou shook his head as if troubled by gnats.

Ishmael Solas was standing in the living room, his grief, Annabelle realized, held in check by this mission to her, by this attempt to preserve the opening performance of *The Tempest*. The autopsy of Butterfly Sue had produced the sad conclusion that she had died of strangulation, but that her death had occurred while she was loaded with cocaine. It was clear now that Francisco must have been aboard the *Reef Cowboy* and heard her talking to Dave on the pier about those dreams for a workable theater, the dreams of Las Vegas–style grandeur. Francisco, only a mediocre sailor himself, according to Hockett's deputies, had needed Butterfly to navigate the *Reef Cowboy*, to follow the *Wolf* until they reached the treasure site but, once there, had strangled her with the videotape to end her disturbing tendency to talk indiscriminately when under the influence of cocaine. Whether Francisco had been aboard the *Cowboy* waiting to see who went after the treasure, or whether he had been aboard the boat to share Butterfly's habit, the sheriff was not certain. He was sending his deputies around to discover what he could about the personal habits of Francisco de Vargas.

Ishmael had been absolutely silent regarding any dealings he might have had with de Vargas outside the theater, and Annabelle wondered if he, too, knew the location of the treasure site, had perhaps even seen the Madonna. Unlike Francisco, he was an excellent sailor. And the *Cowboy* had been a salvage vessel.

Now Ishmael stood beseechingly before her, his silvery eyes watching her as she stood silently regarding him in the cold room.

"I'm here to ask you, miss, if you'll talk to me about the play. I was wondering if you thought there was any way to save it? Fran's not the only one who put his heart and soul into this play."

Annabelle's own heart went out to him, but this was not her problem. It was time to let the curse of the de Vargases fade into decent oblivion.

She was about to speak, to tell Ishmael that what he was asking was impossible, when Dave put out his hand in an Olympian, sweeping curve.

"You'll need a new magician guy," he said airily, as though "magician guys" grew on palm trees. "Francisco can hardly play the part from his hospital bed in the clutch of the long arm of the law. And besides, you wouldn't want him to now that we know he can't be trusted to stand behind a person and keep his hands to himself."

Ishmael blinked. "Nobody could learn Fran's part in one day. But, I thought, seeing as how this lady seems to know the play already, maybe she could do it."

Annabelle stared at Ishmael.

"She'd be all wrong for the part," Dave said, apparently pleased by his own frankly negative appraisal of the casting department's latest blushing ingenue. "You want somebody with a little pizzazz for the lead role: a certain *je ne sais quoi,* a grand air of mystery"—Dave was warming to his topic—"a worldly presence, a sort of majestic aura of command, some good old-fashioned razzle-dazzle. A magician who knows how to dress the part." He looked at Ishmael. "I'll do it."

"Well, of all the conceited buffoons." Ricou burst out laughing. "Your arrogance is priceless. You couldn't learn the part in one day, you jackass."

"Wanna bet a hundred bucks?" Dave asked, his eyes glittering.

TWENTY-NINE

 "THE WHOLE PLAY?"

"Roy, Dave has a photographic memory. What he sees he remembers, without omission or distortion. It's in the same neuro-spectrum as a learning disability, but at the opposite end. He's a supervisual learner. That's partly why he's so good at Sign."

"I don't believe it. Nobody's memory is that good."

"Dave's is."

The small Navy Airframe AB-MK7 seaplane skimmed the water softly and came to rest on the calm, powder-blue surface of the Gulf of Mexico. The tranquil blue immensity stretched in all directions, undisturbed by landmass or coral structures. It seemed empty: a vacant, flat, pale-blue room, the blue sky its walls and its roof, the water its endless undulating carpet.

Ricou shut off the engine. He leaned back in the gray leather bucket seat, closed his eyes, and reached over to take Annabelle's hand. They sat together in the cockpit, the plane rocking them gently on the water.

Annabelle studied his profile, the hard, lean lines of his cheeks and jaw, the dark stubble on them giving depth and texture to what seemed to her an exercise in nature sculpting from the clean perfection of a geometry based on the mathematical harmonies of the right angle.

Sensing her scrutiny, he opened his eyes and turned his head to face her, his blue eyes content, dreamy, and somehow earthy, unlike the arctic crispness she had grown accustomed to seeing. She leaned her head against the leather upholstery and smiled at him.

Her eyes, he thought, considering her in the deep, reverberating silence peculiar to the open sea at rest, were the dusky green of late summer, of orchards and fields of indigo north of New Orleans. Her skin glowed with health; it was flawlessly smooth, except for the small smile lines that formed when she looked at him as she was now, her lips curving slightly, with that unspoken question that he always met in her eyes, always that question, that haunting, sweet, sad question under the delicately arched eyebrows and the thick lashes, in the depths of all that summer green.

"Let's go see how they're doing," he suggested.

He followed her from the small cockpit, which, now that the plane was idle on the water, was growing warm and close. He ducked through the small doorway and joined her in the cramped passenger cabin, where there were only three seats and space for light cargo. He released the latch on the door, pushed it outward, and propped it open with a metal bar built into the hinge, allowing in the welcome and salty breezes from the Gulf.

He sat on one of the seats, his elbows on his knees, his chin in his hands, as she stood in the aisle, preparing to disrobe.

He watched her hungrily as, meticulously and slowly, she undid the row of tiny pearls on her long white sleeveless blouse, finally dropping it at her feet and standing before him in the orange bikini top and white Bermuda shorts. He touched her stomach with his palms and fingers, and she stepped closer to him, her green eyes dark and inviting. He held her loosely for a moment, his cheek resting against her stomach, his eyes closed, the stubble on his face pricking her skin.

She slipped off the shorts, crossed to the door, put her left hand out to grab the triangular support of the port pontoon, and stepped down onto the gray, flat-bottomed float under the wing.

He quickly pulled his shirt over his head, unzipped his shorts, dropped them beside her clothing, and followed her out of the plane onto the pontoon. He slid his arm around her waist, and together they surveyed the water and the old wooden fishing boat anchored in the warm, pastel blueness about thirty yards to the east.

Ashleen Ricou, a yellow baseball cap covering her iron-gray hair, a faded pink cotton dress straining across her bony back, was leaning over the side of the old boat, her hands in gardening gloves around a thick rope that she was guiding while two other gray-haired women behind her cranked a rusty and reluctant winch hauling the rope and its load to the surface. Two other women hung over the side of the boat beside Ashleen Ricou, calling out encouragement as they peered into the water through thick, gold-rimmed spectacles covered with identical clip-on sunglasses.

For the most part, the women ignored the seaplane, intent on their work, and soon their diligence was rewarded when a big wooden basket—like the bins in the Mallory Square Sponge Market—made its appearance at the surface on the end of the rope. The two women operating the winch knotted the rope around the wheel and came to the side to help Ashleen Ricou, who was apparently in charge, raise the heavy basket into the boat. The rays of the late-afternoon sun, until now spread with soft equality over the pale-blue water, seemed to leap to the basket, throwing off bright gleams in all directions, coloring the faces of the women leaning over the boat and turning the water lapping against its sides into splashes of gold.

Annabelle glanced at Ricou and slipped off the pontoon into the water, exclaiming at the shock of its coldness. In that light, in the midst of all that sunshine and pale blueness, the water had appeared warm and inviting, soporific; she shook herself vigorously as Ricou joined her in the water, and they swam briskly toward the fishing boat together.

As they neared the boat, two divers surfaced. One was a lanky boy of perhaps thirteen years, who yanked out his regulator and shouted, "Here's a gold necklace that weighs a ton."

He brought his right arm out of the water, a fall of glistening drops cascading down his thin arm as he heaved a flash of gold into the boat. One of Ashleen Ricou's aides, a stocky woman with long gray braids, hurried to examine the object he had salvaged, and she held up the long gold necklace, its exquisite emeralds refracting and shattering the sunlight. Her eyes were large as she raised the necklace over her head and executed a creaky jig, but Ashleen Ricou frowned at her over her shoulder, and the woman in braids hastily crammed the necklace into the huge pocket of an ancient gray apron that had seen the cleaning of thousands of the more prosaic catches of these waters.

The other diver was a woman, her gray locks plastered against her head under a white bathing cap. Her left arm, its folds of rippling fat encased in a pink dive skin, was wrapped in coral rosaries; she had raised that arm in a fierce salute, after the manner of victorious basketball players, when she breasted the surface. The woman in the apron slapped the diver's open hand and punched the lid of a wicker picnic basket on the boat's floor.

The lieutenant grabbed the side of the boat.

"So, Tante Ashleen, no Madonna yet?"

"We're not going to bother with her," she grunted. "Nothing but bad luck will come of disturbing that godforsaken statue. It was God's will that she was lost in the hurricane all those years ago, and it's God's will that we leave her alone now, nasty golden idol. We only want the jewelry."

"God wants you to have the jewelry?" he asked, laughing.

"Well, the jewelry and the gold and the silver and whatever we can get into these baskets," she said, straightening her spine. Ricou could hear his aunt's joints protesting, but he smiled at her grim happiness as she went on. "This will keep Ernest's house open for a long time, and pay the vet bills, which are enormous, and keep the lawn mowed, and buy a new cash register, and . . ." She hesitated, looking shyly at Annabelle, who was holding on to the lieutenant's shoulder. "And we were thinking of keeping the guards too," she finished in a burst of swelling pride in the new economic prosperity of the Hemingway Museum. She smiled. "Miss, when all was said and done, and Fran de Vargas was playing his horrible game, your guard did what he was supposed to do—he kept his eyes open. You can't ask more than that."

Annabelle smiled broadly, the corners of her eyes crinkling in the sun. "From the looks of things," she said, "you'll be able to buy new carpeting for the kitchen too."

"Don't be silly," the older woman said sternly, an ingrained streak of parsimony causing her hands to curl tightly around the rope. "It won't do to waste money. We're just going to have the old one steam-cleaned. It'll do nicely for many years to come if we don't allow anyone in there." She peered at her nephew's face. "You need a shave, Roy. Fine officer you are, going around looking like a bayou rat."

"Has there been any sign of the Monsignor?" the lieutenant asked, wiping water from his face with his hand.

"Not a peep," his aunt replied. "Thank God."

"It will probably take the lumbering bureaucracy of the Catholic church months to mobilize anything like a salvage operation, assuming the Monsignor can even find this place, with no map, and no personal friends in the navy," Annabelle said, casting a smile at the lieutenant. She reached to pat the frail hand of his aunt. "And no unwieldy bureaucracy is going to be able to catch up with you. You may not have might and wealth and political clout, but I'm very impressed with what you've already accomplished with your spirit of community cooperation. This"—she gestured at the boat and the basket—"reminds me of the organizing principle behind a barn raising."

"Or a quilting bee," Ricou said, laughing.

"Which we won't have to have this year," the woman diver said loudly. "Thank the Good Lord for this gift of gold from the sea. This kind of work does not bring on my arthritis like a quilting bee."

The women on the boat invited Annabelle and the lieutenant to join them for a picnic tea of deviled eggs and ham sandwiches, but they declined with thanks, since their own picnic was waiting for them in the seaplane.

Annabelle shook hands with Ashleen Ricou from the water, saying, "If you're serious about the guards, just call my assistant Jorge Enamorado at the Miami number."

"Enamorado? Is he the eel man?"

"The Monkeyman," Annabelle corrected her with a laugh, and swam away toward the plane.

They ate conch salad and drank mugs of gazpacho before dressing and flying to Nassau in the Bahamas. They phoned Dave from Paradise Island Airport, but he was testy and curt, saying, "I'm busy. Ishmael's writing down the stage directions so that I can remember them. Ask Annabelle how to pronounce all those words where Shakespeare leaves off the consonants and sticks in the apostrophe. Never mind; Ishmael says he knows. I gotta go."

Annabelle and Ricou watched the sunset from the warm Bahamian beach, ate dinner at a small café on the water, and strolled around the quiet old city, which was mostly empty at night, now that after-dinner tourism was moving to the outskirts and the big casino hotels. They spent the night on the beach, the sand long retaining the warmth of that sunny day. They fell asleep together about three o'clock, wrapped in each other's arms, and awoke at sunrise.

"Sunrise," the lieutenant said. "I've always liked it better than sunset."

He brushed sand from her leg and gazed out into the pale morning light over the sea.

"Roy?"

He turned back to her and gripped her hand tightly. "Please don't believe we're just going to fade out, Annabelle."

"I'm trying, but what strength I have is only my own, *Teniente*."

They returned to Key West before that city was awake, landing on the still-sleepy harbor, their only company the serious deep-sea fishers heading out into the Gulf, and the gulls, always the hungry gulls. Ricou walked beside Annabelle along the bleached wooden pier to Ocean Key House. He stood with her in his arms before the hotel on deserted Duval Street, silent with her, for nearly ten minutes, and then he left her at the lobby and headed back to his quarters at the Key West Naval Air Station to pack his bags and turn over his duty logs.

When she reached her suite, there was a short note from Dave pinned to her pillowcase—like all of his notes, it was messy and badly punctuated, where it was punctuated at all:

I've taken the C-A-T since you are neglecting the animal and I am feeling much better if you care and been eating like a pregnant manatee Is Ricou going to miss his U-boat to Singapore, and does he need help packing? I can spare some time for the lieutenant now that Ive memorized the play, which is pretty good!

She took Dave's note, fell onto the bed, and slept for three hours.

FRIDAY

That was a very strange night.

ERNEST HEMINGWAY
A Farewell to Arms

THIRTY

 "STAND STILL AND STOP SWEATING," ANNABELLE HISSED. "Are you ready?"

Dave was shifting from side to side, flapping his arms and occasionally cracking his knuckles. "Do I get twenty seconds to think about my answer, or is this the lightning round?"

"This is the lightning round."

The curtain was about to rise, and Annabelle stood beside Dave in the wings. She could not tell if he was nervous, or excited, or simply full of excess energy after spending a day and a half in bed reading, and she had refrained from tactless comments about his eccentric costume for fear that his bouncing behavior arose from stage fright; she was unwilling to compound that horrid emotion for him, if indeed that was what had given him these monumental jitters. She could almost smell the adrenaline on his breath.

The pink-satin tuxedo, which she had gone to pick up at five o'clock, just as the Margaret Truman Costume, Tuxedo, and Piano Shop was closing, was certainly eye-catching, she thought. Its lapels spangled with orange-red sequins, the tux fit Dave's willowy form like paint on a lightbulb, and in fact there was something incandescent about him this night; on his

radiant person, even the pink tuxedo acquired a weirdly dignified distinction.

"It's spankingly original," he had said, his thumbs lifting
the lapels as he pivoted to show the suit's magnificence.

She did not think Dave's understanding of the play could
be profound, given his choice of apparel for Prospero, Shakespeare's Milanese magician, but he knew his lines. That much
was certain.

She had almost been late to pick up the tuxedo, for, as she
was going out the door of Dave's suite at a quarter to five, Beth
Summers came bustling toward her in the hall, stopping her
with a frantic appeal to help her figure out the character of
Miranda.

Annabelle, for one blazingly insightful instant—a sort of
de facto director's epiphany—understood and sympathized
with the attitude Francisco de Vargas had shown toward amateur actors.

"You've only got three hours until the curtain goes up,"
Annabelle had snapped, exasperated by this eleventh-hour
plea. "I've been here all afternoon."

"I know. That's what makes it so awful. Tell me what to
do."

Trying subconsciously to come to terms with how to play
her own coming farewell scene with Lieutenant Ricou, Annabelle had wanted to shove the woman into Dave's room and
shut the door on her, but she relented, the piteous appeal in
the woman's eyes appearing to be a prelude to tears, and Annabelle did not think Shakespeare's Miranda would be im-
proved by red eyes.

"It's very simple," Annabelle had said, getting ready to
dash down the hall. "Play her like a real woman. Act like she's
got some brains."

Summers had stood dumbly in the hall, her face burning,
as if Annabelle had struck her.

Dave had not discussed the play with Annabelle at all,

perhaps because she had spent the afternoon waiting nervously in his suite for the lieutenant to phone or to arrive. She had paced, and sat quietly staring at the harbor, and paced some more. Ricou had finally called at four, telling Dave that he'd been detained in three separate meetings by Commander Rzadkowolsky and would be back in downtown Key West as soon as possible. "Tell Annabelle I'm sorry I'm so late," he had said.

When Dave had hung up and relayed the message, he looked sharply at Annabelle's face as she sat expectantly by his side on the bed.

"Do you want to go back to Miami, my dear?" he had asked gently. "I'll take you if you want to go."

"No."

"Should I be asking you about *El Teniente*'s intentions toward you?"

"No."

"Are you all right?"

"No."

"Do you want my opinion?"

"No."

"Well, you're going to get it anyway. I don't know how you've gotten yourself all ripped along the seams over a guy from a right-wing organization like the United States Navy, but four days in such a wacky place as Key West is no basis for knowing your own mind." Dave had rubbed his chin thoughtfully. "Or even being in your right mind at all."

"Dave," she had whispered, leaning her forehead on her wrist, "I'm so scared."

He had sat up alertly. "What of?"

"I don't know. It's not just Singapore—that's only distance, and distance can be overcome. But he won't really be in Singapore. He'll be on a submarine—that's a special set of circumstances, and circumstances can't always be overcome."

"Is any of this unhappiness, this fear, coming because you

can't use the phone, because you can't communicate that way?"

"Maybe I'll never even *see* him again, Dave. Like Nikki."

Dave had swung his thin legs over the side of the bed and had thrown his arm across her shoulder, patting her helplessly.

At seven o'clock they left for the playhouse, Dave resplendent in pink satin, and at three minutes before eight o'clock the lieutenant had still not made an appearance.

Annabelle tiptoed to the curtain and pushed the dusty red-velvet folds aside an inch or so, enough to allow her a solid view of the packed house.

Key West had turned out in droves to see this strange production after the news of the sensational and last-minute cast change had swept among the shops and bars of Duval Street and along the waterfront on the coattails of the hot gossip regarding the arrest of Francisco de Vargas—"that flaming fairy," some said—for the murder of his sister, the acknowledged nemesis of Key West who had been behind that dreadful resort going up on Tank Island. The news of the cast change had been followed by the sizzling rumors of another impressive charge being added to Francisco's—"Manly Franly's," some said—list of crimes, the new charge being the deliberate destruction of the *Reef Cowboy* in that spectacular explosion out in the harbor. It was well known that Ishmael Solas, the rugged owner—"supposedly rugged," some said—of the *Cowboy,* also had a major role in the new Waterfront Playhouse production, and the news that Ishmael was still intending to appear in this play that had been Francisco's—"that dreadful twinkie," some said—pet project was followed by the even more marvelous whisperings that Ishmael's dead lover, that Butterfly Sue woman, was also among the victims of Francisco de Vargas—"that raging twit," some said. When Key West collectively disseminated the titillating reports that Sloppy Joe's Bar had contributed the female lead from its pool of stocky waitresses, and that this particular waitress had apparently been gagged, bound, and tortured by the erstwhile director—"Pansy Fransy," some said—the city had turned out in astonishing numbers and electric anticipation to witness the theatrical flop of the century.

Ishmael, responding to the rumors, had immediately raised the price of tickets, and it was going to cost the citizens of the Gingerbread City to come laugh at his expense. And, he thought, they might as well contribute handsomely to his down payment on another boat, for he fully intended, now that his eyes were open to the treacheries of the Key West theater scene, to go salvage that golden statue and move back to New York, where, at least, playgoers paid exorbitant prices in the hope of *not* seeing a flop.

The full volunteer staff of the Hemingway Museum was ensconced in front-row seats, looking peculiarly grim in their cotton dresses for some reason, and Annabelle, who, as a rank outsider, was not privy to any of the rumors, wondered why those old women continually turned in their seats to glare with such surprising ferocity at the bikers, the gentry, the artisans, the sailors, and the beach bums—all of them conchs—sitting behind them.

Annabelle, not at all attuned to the tide of sentiment among the homegrown Key West audience, thought that the crowd merely looked unusually avid, and she patted the curtain into place and turned to Dave, signing, "I'll be here in case you forget your lines."

She had offered to stand in the wings during the performance and sign his lines if he should need prompting. Dave had scoffed, refused the offer, and condemned her sense of fair play.

"I've got a bet on, fathead."

"Well, all the best," she had said, kissing him on his bruised cheek. "You can't miss when you've got great material."

Ishmael, at the audio board just off the wings, pushed in the first tape from the top of his stack of cassettes, and once again the sounds of a mighty storm filled the little theater. The house lights went down.

Annabelle fretted throughout the first scene, pacing in the wings. The audience was restless, given to odd squirming and pointing during what should have been the powerful opening of *The Tempest*'s disaster at sea.

But when Dave stepped onto the stage with his large Miranda in the second scene, the audience held its breath. They had been expecting a travesty, a washed-up farce, a weak and putrid attempt to pass off a howler of a two-bit and completely ignorant cast—"actually illiterate," some said—as a community theater bringing a little Shakespeare to the subtropics. They had not expected this debonair, eerily aristocratic son of David Niven who draped himself against a stage tree without once destroying the illusion of solid woody growth, and fixed the audience with a haughty gaze, icicles dripping from his posture.

But it was Dave's first line that mesmerized them.

He paced languidly to the proscenium arch with his daughter, Miranda, bowed regally to her, and started down the stairs, his tenor voice ringing throughout the playhouse: "Be collected," he commanded sternly. "No more amazement." He strolled along beside the cochina wall at the left of the theater. "Tell your piteous heart there's no harm done."

The audience did not know what to make of this, but they knew they were in the presence of an entertainer of no mean order, and they sat back in their seats, their eyes on Dave's urbanely sauntering progress through the playhouse.

Dave continued his leisurely promenade around the theater, rendering Prospero's lines with casual sophistication and occasional gentle flourishes of a lavender parasol.

He stopped beside a leather-bedecked biker and turned his pink back to the large man. "Lend thy hand," Dave said majestically, holding out his shining arms. "And pluck my magic garment from me."

Apparently hypnotized and with an absolute lack of self-consciousness, the big biker stood and helped Dave out of his tuxedo jacket. He handed it back to Dave, who folded it gracefully and dropped it on the floor.

"Lie there, my art," he said sadly, gazing with realistic grief at the jacket, and walked away without a backward glance.

What legions of movie actors had contributed to Dave's interpretation of Shakespeare's mighty sorcerer, Annabelle did not know; but she watched him, like the rest of his audience, wrapped around his dexterous fingers. He never dropped a line, missed no opportunity to treat his audience with a lofty disdain, and haunted the corners of the playhouse with his pink and debonair presence.

Annabelle was watching breathlessly from the wings, completely swept away on Dave's vision of the broad world of the theater, when she felt a cool hand on her arm.

She turned and saw the lazily smiling coutenance of Lieutenant Ricou.

"I have to go," he whispered.

She took his hand, her heart suddenly full, and they left the theater quietly by the stage door, stepping out into the cool night air, the soft, salty tang of the harbor lying on the thin mist collecting over Mallory Square and sparkling in its low gaslights.

They walked quickly to the waterfront, their hands clutched together almost cruelly. A small gray navy cutter was waiting at the end of the dock that seemed to stretch forever into the harbor.

"You're not going to Singapore on that stupid thing, are you?" Annabelle asked with a lump in her throat. "And why at this hour?"

"She's taking me out to the *Ohio*. Submarines don't park

in Key West Harbor, and they always sail under cover of darkness. I have two minutes. Don't talk."

He kissed her tenderly and quickly, then crushed her in his arms, burying his face against her hair. They stood together, the breeze whispering around them, caressing them with soft, silken touches.

Ricou released her, put his hands on her shoulders, and gazed down at her. "Write to me. Write me long letters. Tell me details. Tell me what you do, what you think. Tell me the arrogant, crazy things Dave does. Go look at your mirror and tell me what mood is in your beautiful summer-green eyes." He lifted a hand to touch her hair. "I have to go now."

He could hear scattered applause from the playhouse, carried out over the harbor on the mist.

He put his hand into his trousers pocket and extracted two hundred-dollar bills. He tucked them into her hand and closed her fingers over them. "Give these to Fidel, will you?"

"Lieutenant Ricou, I'm glad we met." Her eyes were moist. "You're not caving in, are you?"

She shook her head, staring at him, memorizing him.

He leaned down, kissed the hollow of her throat, and ran the length of the old wooden dock toward the waiting ship.

She walked slowly back to the Waterfront Playhouse, numb.

She tried to reanimate her absorption in Dave's inspired performance; she felt detached, surreally floating in the theater's wings, the lonely isolation of her deafness nothing now to the solitude cloying at her from Mallory Square's misty waterfront.

Slowly, however, as she began to notice little things about Dave—the sweat gluing his thin white dress shirt to his torso, the slight but stiff drag of his right leg, the pallor of his skin under the bruises and heavy makeup—she began to lose her preoccupation with her own condition.

Dave never let up, using even his mounting weakness to

depict the sorcerer's final disillusionment with the trap of magic, and when, in the last act, he threw away the ancient book of magic spells, tossing it into the third row, declaiming in wild, hoarse, exhausted tones, "This rough magic I here abjure," the audience was exhausted too.

At the end Dave stood alone on the apron of the stage, his face haggard and drenched with sweat, and he drew a cigar languidly from his shirt pocket, smoothed it with his fingers, and held it under his nostrils, sniffing the fine Cuban tobacco. He lit it with a caress of a silver lighter and considered his audience over the bright yellow flame. He closed the lighter with a snap, and great blue puffs of smoke rose into the playhouse, their wispy dissipation in the spotlight an ethereal farewell.

He delivered the epilogue with the cigar in his white teeth.

The audience was on its feet before he arrived at the final couplet:

As you from crimes would pardon'd be,
Let your indulgence set me free.

He bowed briefly from the waist with ironic punctilio, took two steps backward, and the worn velvet curtain closed in front of him and his cloud of smoke.

The rest of the cast surrounded him, and the curtain immediately parted again.

He almost dropped his cigar when he saw a huge bouquet of wild-orange bougainvillea passed up onto the stage by the Hemingway volunteers. He took the bouquet, smiled lopsidedly at Ashleen Ricou, bowed to the front row, and gestured expansively to the rest of the cast.

Though all of this was a silent tableau for Annabelle, when the life-size Katarina Witt doll was carried down the middle aisle by the woodcarver, the only artist in the city who had won Dave's approval, the startled tears in his eyes spoke volumes to her.

He bent over the proscenium and lifted the doll in his arms. He tried to see Annabelle in the wings, craning his neck and stepping back from the spotlight to thank her, but she was gone, and he was tugged and pushed again to the front of the stage.

Annabelle stood on the steps outside the stage door, her hands in the pockets of her slacks, gazing at the harbor.

Tank Island was only a black streak on the water, something that could have been the wake of a ship departing into the Gulf.

She went down the stairs slowly and walked back to the hotel.

THIRTY-ONE

AND OUT ON TANK ISLAND A SMALL ALUMINUM BOAT WAS being dragged up onto the rocky soil. The acrid smell from the explosion still filtered up into the air around the seared bushes and clung to the island like a damp sweater.

Noah Green wrinkled his nose fastidiously. He left the boat perched on the edge of the island and strolled around the charred grass, a smile lurking at the corners of his small mouth. He thoughtfully nudged some loose, sandy soil with the toe of his expensive loafer.

At the center of this dismal little slash of earth, he stood and faced west. The sky was dark but infinitely dotted with silver lights. The suns of other planets—he thought, idly twirling his new gold glasses—the sources of thousands, even millions, of other sunsets, but not one of those sunsets, he was sure, was capable of creating the excitement of the one he would own once the little formality of those navy prerogatives was behind him. He sat down carefully on the black remains of the always-pitiful vegetation of Tank Island and linked his small hands behind his head. Things weren't going to be so bad after all, no, not so bad at all.

He still had his resort shares, all of them, and he had been rapidly but quietly buying out the other shareholders over the course of the last day and a half.

There would be no imbecile treasure hunts for him. He was sitting on his gold mine.

That woman from Miami who had tried to ruin him would never know the full extent of his coming wealth.

It was an odd thing about her, he thought, crossing his ankles in their silk socks and twirling his glasses. Despite her smugly moralistic views, she had been right about one thing.

It was that thing she had said about debits and credits in a ledger, the sum of his personal condition. Well, she was right.

When it came to his personal condition, Noah S. Green would make certain that the ledger always balanced out in his favor.

Yes, when it came to Noah S. Green, he thought—lying back on scrubby, scorched Tank Island and gazing at all those suns in the night sky and listening to the soothing sounds of the dolphins breaking playfully through the placid water—yes, it would be Noah S. Green who saw to it that he got exactly what was coming to him, to the letter.